Hammer of the Gods

The Desolate Empire
Book Three

Christina Ochs

christinaochs.com

This is a work of fiction. Names, characters, places, and incidents are the products of the author's imagination or are used fictitiously. Any resemblance to actual events, locales, or persons, living or dead, is entirely coincidental.

First Edition

Cover design by Amygdaladesign.net

Lujin Press
Nashville, Tennessee

DEDICATION

To my siblings: Steve, Ron and Cindy

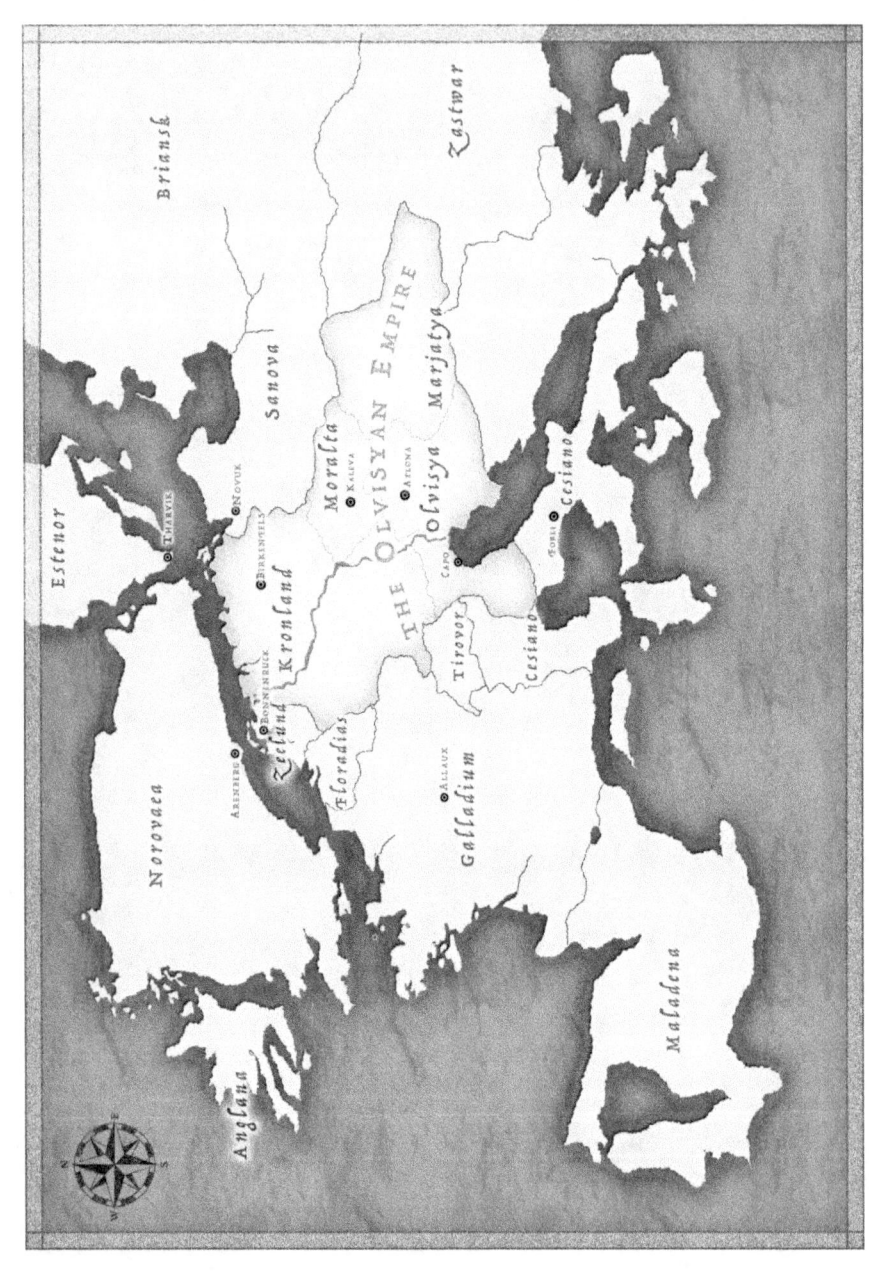

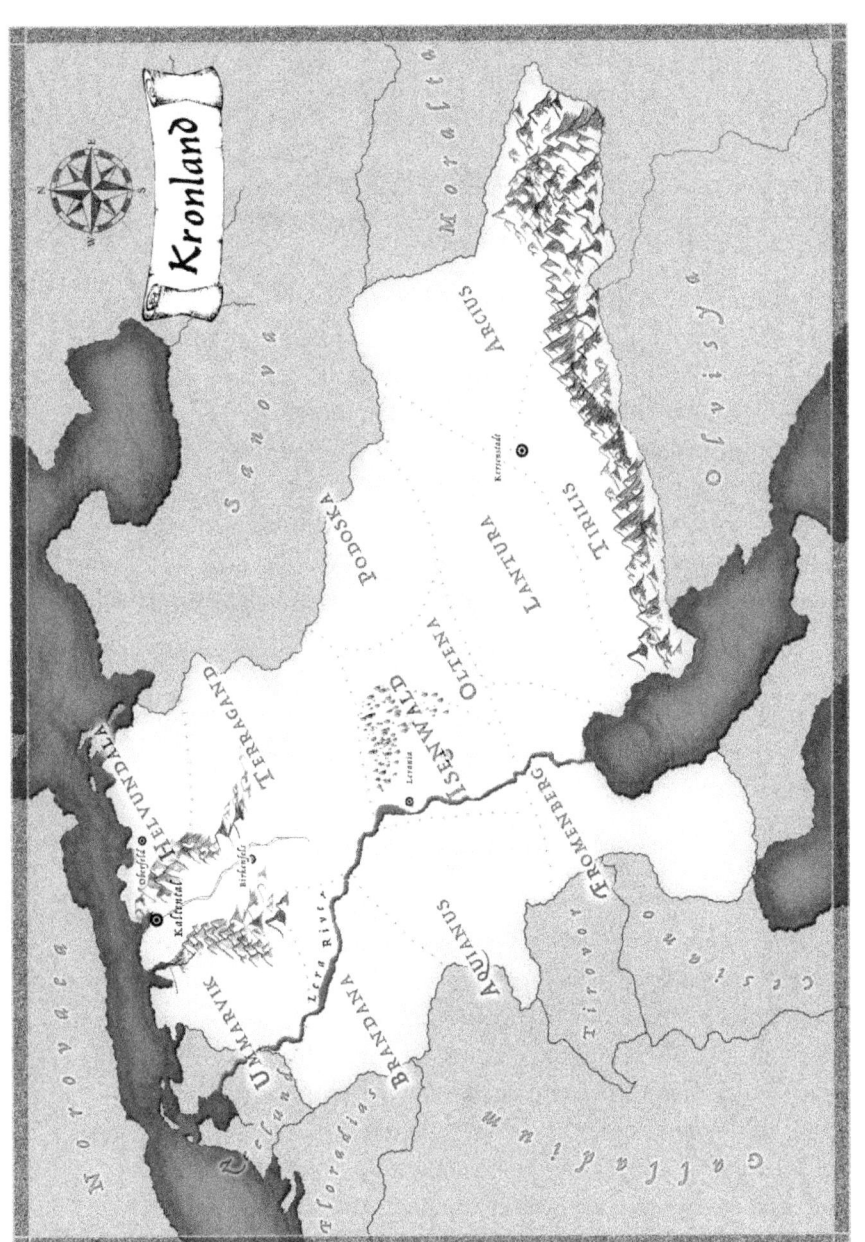

ACKNOWLEDGMENTS

Writing a book this length is always a monumental undertaking, and I couldn't do it alone. First of all, as always, I must thank my husband Ben, who makes sure my life is arranged so I can write as much as possible. Having that kind of support makes all the difference, and whenever I feel like slacking off, remembering what he's sacrificing to make this happen for me gets me back to work.

I also want to thank my family and friends, who've been so wonderfully supportive in buying and reading my books, as well as spreading the word. My heart is always especially warmed by support from people I haven't seen in many years.

As always, my beta readers are nothing short of heroic. Those who've made it this far have read three very long books not too many months apart, and provided invaluable feedback and suggestions. Clarissa N. Goenawan has an eagle eye for plot holes and was so committed, she read the last chapters just hours before going to the hospital to give birth to her third child! Cindy Borror is my fastest reader and also my little sister. I greatly appreciate her excellent sense of the characters and the emotional heft (or lack thereof) of the story. Cheryl Carter never fails to spot anachronisms or character inconsistencies and is especially useful as a model fantasy reader. Patricia Bailey's own book will come out next year, and her experience and skill as a writer is always useful to me in tightening things up and helping me keep to my mantra of "Don't be boring!"

With Hammer of the Gods, I started something new: an early reader team. It's a small list so far, but I'm so grateful to Amy Braun, Whitney McGruder, Andrew Western, Greg Mitchell, Marcia Kuma and JoLayne Skoglund for plowing through a somewhat error-ridden version so they can be among the first to review.

ELEKTRA

"Karil, bring me that sword."

Elektra realized Karil must be the boy by the fire, and understood an instant later what the sword was for. She worried she'd cry again, but was too frightened for tears. She breathed in great, ragged gasps, and tried to scramble to her feet, forgetting they were still tied together. She fell to the ground again, jagged rocks digging into her side.

"Better if you don't make such a fuss," the man said. "I promise to do it fast. The blade's nice and sharp so I doubt you'll feel a thing."

"Vica will strike you down before you can harm me," Elektra said, her voice quavering, not because she really believed it, but because she needed to hope for a miracle. She clenched her teeth, vowed not to cry, and reminded herself she was an archduchess, an acolyte of the League of Aeternos. She wouldn't go to her death like a sniveling peasant.

The man laughed. "Surely you don't hold to that nonsense. Ah well, if it gives you comfort I suppose there's little harm in it." He turned away. "Karil, bring it here."

The boy still stood at the fire. "I don't want to."

Elektra realized she'd been holding her breath. She exhaled, and scrutinized the boy more carefully. As she had noticed before, he appeared to be around her age, short, but powerfully built. He didn't look like a soldier, but held the sword as if he knew his business. She wondered if he might save her, but looked at the big man again. Impossible. Even with the armed boy on her side she could do nothing against such a brute, one of the Sanova Hussars, trained and experienced killers the lot of them.

The man sighed. "Don't be ridiculous Karil. We agreed to do this."

"But she's just a girl. A child, still."

Elektra bristled at that, but remembered the boy was trying to help, so she gave him her best pleading, helpless look. Then she offered a quick prayer to Vica to guide her thoughts and words to wisdom.

"I see that," the big man said. "So were my children. Do you know how old my little girl was, Karil? Not even three. And the boy lived no more than a few months before Teodora murdered them both." His voice grew rougher. "Janna too, and you loved her even before I did."

Elektra began to understand. "Did they live in Kersenstadt?" She asked, surprised at how clear and strong her voice sounded. That must be the work of the Goddess, and the realization gave her more strength.

The man turned back to her. "Yes, and they died there too, thanks to your mother setting the whole city aflame."

Everyone knew it was Quadrene fanatics who'd burned Kersenstadt to the ground, but Elektra could tell such facts meant little to this man. "I am very sorry," she said. "It was a terrible tragedy and entirely my mother's fault, I'm sure. But what do you hope to accomplish by sending her my head?" She was heartened to see the boy quietly slide the sword back into a scabbard.

"Revenge," the man said. "That's all. You needn't lecture me about how it won't help."

"I wasn't going to." Elektra felt an odd coursing in her veins. She was no longer afraid. Even if this man killed her, it would be while she received the highest blessing from the Goddess. It would be a martyr's death, and she would join Holy Vica in the halls of paradise. Still, she wasn't ready to die just yet. "Not only will it not help you feel better, it will not help you thwart my mother. I am in a far better position than you to do that."

"You should hear her out, Braeden." The boy knelt in front of Elektra and cut the ropes binding her ankles with a short knife. She whimpered as the sensation returned to her feet in a rush of prickling pain. "Give me your hands," the boy said and she looked into his eyes. They were large and dark, though not warm, but she saw he wouldn't hurt her. She let him cut the ropes around her wrists.

Elektra looked up at the man named Braeden until he met her eyes, then said, "I promise not to escape. Let's talk about how I can help you."

ANTON

Anton liked spending time with his friends, but sitting in school all day made him tired. He left the Maxima's schoolroom with Maryna one afternoon.

"I'm worried about the count," he said.

"Is he not recovering well?" She frowned. Maryna was just like her father, Prince Kendryk. Very nice, and always concerned about others.

"He's doing all right. He's even able to walk and he'll be riding soon. But he's always in a terrible mood, and drinking too much." Anton shifted the heavy stack of books to his other arm. He would be up late studying tonight. Natalya Maxima had insisted that both Maryna and he learn the Ancient Tongue, even though Anton didn't see any use for it.

"Perhaps a doctor should see him." Maryna stopped as they reached the gates to the Maxima's palace. From here, she would continue to her parents' home while Anton went back inside. He always walked Maryna this far until her guards took over.

"He hates doctors," Anton said. "He almost killed the last one when he told him he needed to cut back on the liquor."

"Oh dear," Maryna said, with a nod to her guards, both of whom greeted Anton with friendly grins. "What about Natalya Maxima? Surely he likes her."

Anton sighed. "Maybe." He didn't want to explain how seeing the Maxima made the count even more upset. Just the sight of a beautiful woman made him worry that none of them would ever like him again. Anton knew that wasn't true, but there was no telling that to the count in the state he was in. "I'll come up with something."

He watched Maryna walk down the street, still so tiny between the two tall guards. He hoped she would be all right. After his rescue from the empress's dungeon, Prince Kendryk hadn't been in Allaux more than a month before leaving again, taking Maryna's mother along. They had to go to Zeelund to arrange something Anton didn't quite understand.

3

Maryna had begged to go too, but they told her they could travel more quickly without children. Anton was happy she was here, but saw she was taking her father's absence hard. She'd always been close to him and was anxious to have him nearby as much as possible. Before turning the corner, Maryna turned back and waved at Anton. He waved back before returning to the Maxima's garden.

He dawdled along the path, watching water spring from the fountain and run back down over a marble statue portraying a woman from a story in the Holy Scrolls. But the statue made him blush, and Anton didn't remember a story that ever made him do that. Thanks to Natalya Maxima, he'd studied all the stories of the Scrolls much more thoroughly than he'd ever wanted to. Anton looked away from the statue and went inside. It was cool and dark in here; the floors and walls were of marble, hung with silk and rich tapestries.

By now, Anton was used to it all, so he didn't stop to gawk. He took the stairs two at a time, stopped in his room, and dumped his books on the bed before going to the count's chamber. The count had a suite inside the palace and Anton had a room of his own. It looked like something only a prince would live in, and Anton still couldn't believe it was all for him. There was even a rope he pulled if he needed anything, and one of several maids, each prettier than the last, would appear and bring him whatever he asked for. And yet, he missed being out in the field, riding Skandar all day and fighting in battles. He hoped before too long he could do that again.

It was dark in the count's room, the curtains drawn at the windows, and around the big bed. "I'm here," Anton shouted by way of warning, throwing open the curtains at the windows. He opened a window wide, since it was hot and didn't smell too good. Then he went to the bed and pulled those curtains open too.

"Go away," the count grumbled into his pillow.

"You know I won't." Anton tried to sound cheerful, though he was sick of doing this every day. "It's time for you to get up, have a wash, and walk around a little."

"I don't want to today," the count said, opening his one eye, then closing it against the bright light.

"Doesn't matter," Anton said, pouring water into a cup from a pitcher on the table. "You have to. Otherwise you'll be here forever and I would hate that."

The count pulled himself up and leaned against a pillow half-seated, still blinking against the light. He took the cup and drank. "Why do you stick

4

around?" he grumbled. "You should have gone to Maladena when you had the chance. You'd be working for a real general by now, not to mention having a pretty girl keeping you warm at night."

"Too late for that." Anton kept his tone brisk while he poured water into a basin, and tried to forget about Maladena and Lora. He hoped she was doing well there, but remembering her made him sad. He'd made the mistake of telling the count about his shipboard romance, and now he liked to needle Anton about it.

"Come sit in this chair," Anton said. The count needed a shave and wouldn't do it himself. Anton suspected he didn't like looking in a mirror with the one eye gone. Anton was used to it by now, but the count avoided mirrors, so he hadn't yet become accustomed to it.

"Don't want to." The count threw the cup at the wall. Water splashed the silk wallpaper, but the cup bounced off with a *thunk,* and rolled across the floor. That was why Anton had long ago asked the maids to bring only pewter and tin cups, so the count couldn't destroy any more of the Maxima's fine crystal.

"Don't care," Anton said, grabbing a dish of soap and the razor. "If you're difficult, I'll call the Maxima."

The count turned pale. "You wouldn't."

"I would."

"Fine." The count hauled himself out of bed and limped across the room.

Anton almost ran to help him, but made himself stand still. The count managed well enough on his own, and he'd build up his strength better that way. "We'll go to the stables today," he said, once he had the count in the chair. "Cid misses you."

That made the count sit up straighter. "Do you suppose I can get there?"

"Sure," Anton said, scraping the razor along the count's cheek. He wasn't at all sure, but they needed to try. "We'll go slow, and take the back way, so you can sit down as often as you need to." He didn't say that going through the servant's quarters meant the count wouldn't run into anyone he knew who'd feel sorry for him, and look at him in that way he hated.

The count was silent for a long time. Once Anton finished shaving him, and handed him a towel, he dried his face and said, "All right. I'll try it. I'm sick of being stuck here too. Even if no woman ever looks at me again, I can still fight, don't you think?"

"Women will look at you again." They already did, though Anton knew the count wasn't thinking about the maids who brought his food, cleaned his room,

5

and made eyes at him, same as always. "And the sooner you get back to riding Cid and practicing with your pistols, the sooner you can get back into the fight."

LENNART

Lennart threw down his quill, stood up from his desk, and walked to the window. Midsummer, the gardens in full, fragrant bloom. A perfect time to launch an invasion, with long days, the seas smooth as glass, and Brynhild Mattila muddling around northern Kronland. He wished he had more information about what was going on between her and Teodora, but his spies provided only theories.

He hated sitting at a desk all day. But he needed to handle this part before getting into the field. He expected his ruling council to give in to his requests, but he owed them an exact accounting of his plans and what he needed to implement them.

Lennart had also promised not to make a move on Kronland until he received financial guarantees from Galladium, and there had been no word on that front. Princess Gwynneth had sent a letter weeks before, saying she and Kendryk were headed for Zeelund to arrange funding. He reckoned between travel time and dealing with bankers, it might take a few months more.

But as the months dragged on, Lennart worried Mattila would bleed all of Kronland dry before he got there. He reminded himself that wasn't his concern; the rulers there needed to take responsibility for their own kingdoms. The way he saw it, the Kronlander's dithering had ultimately caused Arryk's defeat, but he wouldn't let it happen to him. Lennart would take a more forceful approach from the start.

The door opened after a soft knock. Ludvik Meldahl entered, bearing another sheaf of papers. "Not today," Lennart said. "I've had enough."

"There's always tomorrow." Meldahl dumped the papers onto Lennart's desk. "Why don't you go, Your Highness, and I'll sort through these. Maybe I can get the pile down to half by morning."

"I probably should," Lennart said, though he stayed at the window. He needed to spend more time with Raysa, with her still far too shy and frightened of him. He'd told Gwynneth he wanted a docile wife, but he didn't want a fearful one. Lennart didn't deny it; things between him and his bride were still awkward. He had expected no better at first, but hoped matters might change once she settled into her new home.

He'd barely so much as talked to her before the wedding, with all the affairs of state that needed attending to first. Queen Ottilya had insisted on monopolizing his time. Lennart wasn't sure if she was trying to keep him from frightening her daughter or if she wanted to make his life miserable. No question she wasn't his first choice as mother-in-law; he'd rather fight her than be family.

"You should go." Meldahl already sat at Lennart's desk, his blond head bent over the papers piled high on it. "The queen is in the garden, playing the lute. Every young man who walks by makes eyes at her. You must put a stop to that."

"You're right," Lennart said. "What is she playing?" He liked music, but of the brisk military sort, or merry drinking songs.

"Who knows?" Meldahl waved his hand. "Ask her."

"I think I will." Lennart opened the tall glass door leading to the garden. It was warm, so he left his doublet unbuttoned and paused beside a fountain, trailing his hand in the cool water. Then he stood up and listened. He heard the faint plucking of the strings well enough, so he followed the sound to its source.

The queen sat in a pavilion, surrounded by silk cushions and a bevy of Sanovan ladies. Lennart didn't approve of so many Sanovans gathered in his country, but he wouldn't deny Raysa her friends. This was hard enough for her.

He stopped in the pavilion doorway. Raysa's head was bent over the instrument, so she didn't see him standing there. It wasn't until a few of her ladies jumped to their feet and curtsied, that she looked up and stopped playing.

"Don't stop," Lennart said, with a nod to the ladies. He had been trying to make them understand that he didn't insist upon the same protocol they were accustomed to, but so far he'd had no luck. Perhaps he'd have to formally order them to be less formal.

He took a seat on a cushion across from Raysa and gave an encouraging nod. Raysa met his eyes briefly, then went back to playing. When she finished, Lennart said, "Very nice," though it had just been a lot of tinny, mournful plucking. Not the least bit merry. Then he turned to the ladies. "I'd like to speak to the queen alone."

They scurried out, exchanging meaningful glances. He wondered how he might get rid of them for good. Perhaps he could draft them into the military.

"I'm sorry," Raysa said, when the others were out of earshot, though they still stood far too close for his liking, staring and whispering. "They're dreadfully silly."

"I'll send 'em away if you like." He wanted to, but hoped she'd take it as a joke if she didn't agree.

"Would you?" She laid the lute on the bench next to her and folded her hands in her lap. "Mother insisted I bring them, but they aren't my friends, and none of them like it here."

"I'm happy to do it, though you can do it as well. You're the queen, you know." He grinned at her. He'd held an elaborate coronation for her a month past, but she still didn't seem used to the idea. The Estenorian people weren't either, regarding any Sanovan on their soil with suspicion. It didn't help that Raysa showed no inclination toward public appearances or any more socializing than was absolutely required.

"I suppose I could, but I'd feel bad and mother would be angry."

"So let her be angry. What's she going to do?" It had become clear to Lennart during his time in Novuk that Queen Ottilya was fond of her daughter. But she hid it well, mostly by shouting at her and bullying her relentlessly. It had angered Lennart, and the moment they were married, he made it clear to Ottilya he'd no longer tolerate that. Still, it would take time for his wife to realize her mother didn't have any power over her.

Raysa nearly smiled. "You're right. I'd still rather you did it, if you don't mind."

"I don't mind. You won't be lonely?"

"I'll need attendants, but one or two will be enough. And it seems the people here will accept me more quickly if my ladies are Estenorian; don't you agree?"

"You're right." Lennart said, surprised and pleased. "Do you have anyone in mind?" He doubted she'd become acquainted with much of the nobility here.

"No." She looked down again. "Someone kind and quiet. I can't abide all the chattering." She looked back up, her fair skin flushed. She really was lovely.

"I know someone then," Lennart said. "Meldahl's daughter Silvya is of an age with you and just like her father: smart, sensible and quiet. I'll arrange an introduction if you like."

"All right." Raysa's voice was so soft he could barely hear it. "I trust you."

He wished it were true. Hoped it was true.

ELEKTRA

Elektra held her breath until Braeden spoke.

"All right," he said. "We can talk. Karil, get biscuit and cheese out of that saddlebag, and bring the young lady some water."

"It's Your Grace," Elektra said, feeling the need to establish her proper authority without delay.

Braeden stared at her. "You've got to be joking."

Elektra stared back at him coolly. "Not at all. I may be your prisoner, but I'm still the Archduchess Elektra and everyone refers to me as Your Grace. Kindly do so from now on."

"You're a little too much like your mother," Braeden growled. "Maybe I should kill you after all. I swear, if I let you go, and you turn out to be like her, I'll kill you later."

"Please do." Elektra rubbed her wrists as the sensation returned more painfully than she might have liked. "I pray to Vica every day that I won't turn out like her. It would be a tragedy."

"That's more like it." Braeden looked less menacing now. "Fine then, I'll call you Your Grace if it makes you less stroppy."

"Thank you," Elektra said primly, both to Braeden and to the boy, Karil, who presented her with some weevily-looking biscuit and a hunk of cheese. She resisted wrinkling her nose at the food, remembering that she was a hardened veteran of a long military campaign. She bit off a large piece of biscuit and chewed, trying hard to imagine she noticed nothing wormy wriggling in it.

"Better wash that down fast." Karil handed her a tin cup.

"Mmph," she said and took a long drink of water, washing the horrid mouthful down before she spit it out. She hoped it stayed down.

Both Braeden and Karil seemed impressed. Good.

"Now," she said, laying the food in the grass after deciding she wasn't that hungry after all. "Let's talk about my mother. I doubt very much sending her

11

my head would bother her in the least. She doesn't care for me at all. In fact, I don't think she usually remembers she has children."

"I still think it would send a message," Braeden said.

"Just a message that you're unhinged." Elektra did her best to pretend they weren't talking about sending her own head to her mother in a bag. "Trust me, she wouldn't care. She might even put it on a spike alongside the Moraltan rebels to show how much she doesn't care. You have no idea what she's like."

"I know what she's like," Braeden said. "I've spent far too much time with that witch. But you might be right. In all the time I'd been with her, she never once mentioned her children. I didn't even realize she had 'em until someone else told me."

Elektra winced. For as long as she could remember, she knew her mother didn't love her, but it still hurt a little to hear it put like that. She schooled her face into impassivity. For this to work, she had to appear hard. "I'm not surprised in the least. So are we in agreement that sending her my head will accomplish nothing?"

"I agree," Karil said right away, and Elektra shot him a grateful look.

Braeden shook his head. "I can't believe I'm letting the two of you get away with this. But you're probably right. So what do we do now?"

"First, we determine what we want. Then we figure out how to do it."

"I want the empress dead," Braeden said. "And to have her suffer a bit on the way."

"Fair enough," Elektra said. "What about you?" she turned to Karil.

"I want her dead too. Oh, and I want independence for Marjatya."

"Hmm." So the boy was Marjatyan. Pig-headed fools, the lot of them, but that didn't mean they couldn't be useful to her. "You do realize that when I become empress I'll be able to grant Marjatya independence?"

"You'd do that?" Karil's eyes nearly started out of his head.

"I wouldn't like to. But with the proper incentive I might be persuaded to some kind of accommodation."

"Enough with the politicking," Braeden said. "It's your turn, girl—I mean, Your Grace. What do you want?"

"I want to be empress sooner rather than later." Elektra had always wanted that, even when the idea terrified her, as it no longer did. "And the best way for that to happen, is for my mother to die."

"Rather convenient for all of us then," Braeden said. "Between the three of us, I reckon we might find a way."

"But we must be careful," Elektra said. "It goes without saying I can't be implicated in any scheme."

"I suppose not," Braeden said. "Is there anyone you can rely on to help you? Anyone else who wants her dead, and you in her place?"

"*Everyone* wants her dead. But there is one person who wants it, and can do it. You must take me to Brynhild Mattila."

TEODORA

"She cannot do this." Teodora glared at Solteszy before he replied. She knew what he would say, because Teodora had uttered those words far too many times, and Solteszy always responded the same way. He would say it was already done; Brynhild Mattila had defied Teodora's orders yet again.

Solteszy opened his mouth, then closed it again.

"I won't tolerate any more," Teodora said. "I'm sure the aristocracy is already laughing at my inability to control my own general."

Solteszy put down his quill, and ordered the papers in front of him. They sat across from each other at her large desk, going over the morning's correspondence, which included an encrypted dispatch from a spy on Mattila's staff.

"They may laugh," he said. "But even as they do, they know full well no one has ever controlled Mattila. None would do any better in your position, and all of them realize it."

"That doesn't help." Teodora felt deflated, too tired to be angry. She stood, stretched, and walked to the window. Dew lay on the grass, and though the sun barely cleared the tops of the eastern hills, it promised to be a fine, warm day. Seeing it from the window was the closest Teodora would get to enjoying it.

Not that she enjoyed anything. Not anymore. Demario, the only man she'd ever loved, was gone, dead by her own hand. That he'd hated and betrayed her at the end made it no easier to face. In addition, summarily executing one of the Queen of Maladena's favorite generals led to diplomatic problems with Maladena, and no more loans from its treasury. Teodora needed the money, but found she didn't care.

She'd always had a passion for ruling, for the glory of the House of Inferrara, for the power of the Olvisyan Empire. But even that had faded. Teodora had faded. When she regarded herself in the mirror by the flattering candlelight, while her maids dressed her hair long before dawn, she saw a drawn, dried-up, middle-aged woman who no longer cared about anything.

Even rage at Mattila's insubordination flickered out all too quickly. It had been months since Teodora had the pleasure of reducing a lady-in-waiting to tears, or smashing priceless porcelain in a fit of temper. She'd tried to work herself up to it several times, but didn't enjoy it like before.

The sun rose higher, and light flooded the garden, in full summer flower. Livilla would be here any day now, with Elektra. Perhaps that would help. Livilla always offered comfort without pity. That was all she needed. That, and time.

Teodora turned back to Solteszy, his head bent over the pile of letters, and sat down across from him once more. "What should I do?" she asked. Solteszy wasn't a friend, exactly, but he was no weak toady, and always offered honest, practical advice.

He looked up. "Don't issue Mattila any more orders, for the time being. She will simply delight in defying you."

"That's true. But I can't allow her to become yet another renegade Kronland ruler."

Mattila had violently objected to Livilla making peace with King Arryk in Norovaea without her consent. She also objected to Livilla "kidnapping" Elektra from Arenberg. Teodora refused to reply to these messages, and responded with more emphatic orders that Mattila withdraw her armies from Norovaea and subdue Terragand.

Mattila hadn't replied to these orders, but Teodora's spies told her she'd withdrawn south to Brandana. Once there, she sent its ruler, Princess Floreta, into exile in neighboring Ummarvik, intending to declare herself *de facto* ruler of the kingdom.

"She hasn't done it yet," Solteszy said. "In fact, until she makes an official declaration, this is what you tell everyone: Mattila is in the lengthy process of pulling her army out of Norovaea. She is regrouping in Brandana to prepare for an offensive into Terragand. No one need realize what she is planning."

"So I pretend Mattila is following my orders. Perhaps I can hint we're planning something big for Terragand?"

"Certainly. Because you are, aren't you?"

"Yes, I am. And once I've done it, I'll be happy to issue Mattila an order she can openly defy, so I can declare her rebel." Ever since she'd been forced to work with Mattila again, Teodora vowed daily to destroy her if it took her last breath. Her only regret was that there was no punishment terrible enough to redress the wrongs she had suffered. But she would enjoy trying anyway.

GWYNNETH

Gwynneth was enjoying herself, although she found dealing with bankers tedious. But Bonnenruck during the summer was pleasant, and she enjoyed having Kendryk to herself. They'd traveled with only a small armed escort, Gwynneth's ladies, the indispensable Catrin, and Kendryk's manservant. To save money, they stayed in a small suite of rooms at an inn near Bonnenruck's banking quarter.

"It feels like we're playing at being commoners." Gwynneth smiled at Kendryk as they got ready for dinner. Even though they'd traveled without fanfare, word of their arrival had spread, and now they received frequent dinner invitations from the Bonnenruck quality.

"Just a little." Kendryk smiled back at her. "Though I have to say I got enough of that during my stay in Atlona."

"I imagine most commoners are treated better than that." Gwynneth still couldn't keep from getting angry whenever she imagined Kendryk in a dungeon, although he spoke about his time there without rancor.

"I imagine most commoners don't have servants," Kendryk said.

"I suppose you're right. How dreadful. Though it's true I've made do with only Catrin before."

"I hope you'll never have to endure such hardship again." Kendryk's eyes twinkled, so she could tell he was teasing her.

Gwyneth waited for Catrin to finish her hair, and turned toward Kendryk, smiling. "I'm really very happy, you know. I don't want you to think I'm discontented in the least. Of course I want to go home again, but right now, being with you is enough."

"I agree," Kendryk said. "You can go, Catrin." He took Gwynneth by the hand, pulled her out of the dressing table chair, and looked her up and down. "Beautiful. I'm sure all of the Bonnenruck ladies will be jealous."

"Some, perhaps." There wasn't any point in false modesty. Gwynneth had sometimes worried in the past few years she was losing her looks, but now that Kendryk was back, she felt younger and prettier than she had in a long time.

She didn't have money to spend on clothes and jewelry, but Catrin was clever with the needle, keeping her gowns in good repair, and adding bits of ribbon and lace to update them. Her pregnancy didn't show yet, though she'd have to tell Kendryk soon. Just not tonight.

She leaned forward and kissed Kendryk on the lips, careful not to crush her lace collar or muss her hair. "You're looking rather fine yourself."

Even though Kendryk affected a far more somber look since his return, he still looked handsome and dignified. On Gwynneth's insistence, he'd left his hair long, and now it fell far past his shoulders. The gray streaks made him appear distinguished, and they matched his grave manner. He was even more serious than he had been before, and while she missed his easy laughter and the sparkle in his eyes, his demeanor fit their uncertain situation.

He took her by the hand. "We must go. We're the guests of honor, but it's still rude to be more than a few minutes late."

She had become less punctual after spending so much time in Galladium, where no one seemed to care when you turned up as long as you looked good and had something witty to say.

A boat waited for them, bobbing in the canal's waters at the inn's front door. This was a wonderful way to travel, with the sky so blue overhead and the evening sun slanting across the brightly painted buildings. Their hostess had sent the boat, and two finely liveried oarsmen rowed them to the mansion in short order.

"Isn't this nice?" Gwynneth squeezed Kendryk's hand.

"If you have canals and good weather." Kendryk squeezed it back.

The boat bumped into a dock in front of a magnificent house, and one man leapt out to tie it off. He and the other man lifted Gwynneth onto the dock, all without the least harm coming to her dress.

"Marvelous." She smiled at each of them in turn, and the younger of the two blushed. Kendryk was right behind her and she took his arm as a bewigged footman held the front door open for them.

Their hostess stood inside, already sunken in a curtsy. "What a beautiful home you have." Gwynneth smiled at her.

"Thank you, Your Grace." Kamyla Melchor straightened up. "I apologize for the lateness of this invitation, but I've been on my honeymoon and just heard you were in town when I returned."

"No need to apologize." Kendryk smiled at her. "It seems congratulations are in order."

"Thank you," Kamyla said, though she didn't appear particularly happy for a newlywed. Gwynneth would have thought a woman of her age and station could marry whoever she chose without pressure from anyone. Perhaps the husband wasn't turning out as well as she'd hoped.

Kamyla led them inside, and the next half hour passed in a whirl of names and faces. Gwynneth and Kendryk already knew many people, but Vrouw Melchor had assembled a larger crowd than usual. Once Gwynneth met the new husband, she understood the bride's less than giddy behavior. Devries Geerts was short, fat, and bald. While Gwynneth had known other men of the type to be merry, likable sorts, Geerts was not one of them, with a perpetually down-turned mouth, and beady, unfriendly eyes.

"What does Vrouw Melchor see in him?" Gwynneth whispered to her dinner companion, a jolly young woman who looked like she enjoyed gossip.

"Money," the woman whispered back. "A few years ago, her husband was kidnapped by pirates and disappeared. She lost a few ships along with the husband, and fell on hard times. None of her schemes succeeded, and everyone's certain she had to marry Geerts in exchange for him bailing out her business."

"How dreadful," Gwynneth said. But as she looked around the ornate dining room and identified the exquisite china and crystal as Sanovan, she told herself she'd probably do the same, rather than give up something this fine. But when she looked at Geerts again, she wasn't so sure.

After dinner, the talk in the drawing room was all business. No one knew precisely why Gwynneth and Kendryk were here, but everyone correctly guessed it had to do with money.

"You ought to go see the brothers Van Arnam," an old man with enormous whiskers told Gwynneth. "Their rates aren't the lowest, but they're more reliable than anyone."

"I heard all Bonnenruck bankers were reliable." Gwynneth smiled before taking another sip of her wine.

"It's true, they are," the man huffed. "But the Van Arnams more so than any others. Especially if you need foreign transactions of any kind, which I assume you do." It seemed the old fellow was cannier than he looked.

"Hmm," Gwynneth said, hoping none of Teodora's agents were in the room, though she wouldn't put it past her. "Thank you for the advice."

BRAEDEN

Braeden wondered if he had eaten bad cheese, fallen asleep, and was having a strange dream. But it seemed he really was making plans to assassinate Teodora with her own daughter. He sat around the fire with Karil and Elektra, discussing the best way to broach the subject with Brynhild Mattila.

They have a history," Elektra said. "I don't know exactly what it is, but it seems long ago Mattila did something terrible to Mother and perhaps to her dreadful friend, that Daciana Tomescu." She shuddered.

Braeden at least approved of that view of Tomescu. In fact, he was looking at the little archduchess in a different light. Now she no longer cowered in Mattila's shadow, she seemed far more confident and energetic. She also seemed a religious fanatic, but Braeden didn't mind that too much, as long as it didn't get in the way of his plans. "Daciana Tomescu is dead," he said.

"She is? How do you know?"

"My stepson shot her in the head during Prince Kendryk's rescue. And then he blew up the rest of her." Braeden felt a swell of pride, talking about Anton and what he'd done. Then he wished Janna were alive to know what a hero he was.

"That's marvelous news." The archduchess beamed. "I always hated her and imagined I'd have to kill her before I could get to mother. I confess I found her terribly frightening."

"She was," Braeden said. "But she's gone now, and hopefully that's upset your mother at least a little."

"I hope so too."

Braeden found the girl remarkably hard-hearted, but didn't mind if she directed it toward Teodora.

"You say that Brynhild Mattila wants Teodora dead as well?" he asked.

"She hasn't said it outright, but I'm sure she'd love to get Mother out of the way. She imagines she'll become regent until I turn seventeen. I don't intend to allow that, but we can let her believe it as long as we need her."

Braeden frowned, remembering something Barela had told him. "I have it from a reliable source that Livilla will be regent, should something happen to your mother."

"Yes, that's been my understanding as well. I wouldn't mind, since Livilla is one of the few people in the world I can trust. But if Mattila hopes to eliminate Livilla, she's in for a surprise."

"Interesting." Braeden had never paid much attention to the politics of succession. "Who else can you trust, besides Livilla? Anyone?"

Elektra frowned. "Mother Luca perhaps. She's always kept my secrets, and even tried to shield me from Mattila when she was in a rage."

"She your personal priestess?" If the girl had some affection for this woman, it could explain the strong religious feelings.

Elektra nodded. "She's also close to Livilla."

Braeden stared into the fire. "As far as I can tell, Livilla is fond of your mother. So we can't rely on her to help us. Or your priestess."

"No, I suppose not. But it doesn't matter. The fewer in on the plan, the better. Now, this is what we should do."

It annoyed Braeden that Elektra acted like she was in charge, but he supposed she was accustomed to it because of her rank. "What should we do, Your Grace?" He hoped his tone made it clear he wasn't too impressed.

"You will take me to Mattila straight away. She's probably still in Brandana, and shouldn't be hard to find. I can get a personal audience with her, and then I'll ask if she'll see you too."

"That's dangerous," Braeden said. "By now word should be out that I rescued Prince Kendryk. I suppose everyone on the imperial side will try to kill me."

"You were with General Barela then?" Elektra's face fell. "I'm so sad Mother killed him. He always kissed me so nicely, and brought me the loveliest presents." Elektra's lip curled. "Typical of her to kill anyone good. It's a shame Prince Kendryk got away after all the trouble he's caused, but I'm sure Mattila won't care. If anything, she'll be glad you thwarted Mother."

"The question is, what will she do when she sees me?" Braeden asked. The hopelessness of his situation was becoming clearer with every step he took. For all he knew, there was a price on his head, and he wasn't safe anywhere outside Galladium.

"Hard to say," Elektra said. "But if you can no longer show your face at court, Mattila is the only person who can get close to Mother with a weapon. I'd do it myself, but I'm sure I can't get away with it. I'd even considered poison, but I need Livilla's help for that, and she wouldn't do it."

"I could create a diversion I suppose," Braeden said, and then remembered something. "We have to be careful with Karil, too. He escaped with Kendryk, and I'm sure the empress would like him back in the Arnfels."

"You were a prisoner of my mother's?" Elektra looked at Karil with renewed interest.

"Hostage," Karil said. "Held to make my father, Count Andarosz, behave himself."

"I've heard of your father," Elektra said. "A dreadful troublemaker, like all Marjatyans."

Karil, looking pleased to be considered a troublemaker because of his nationality, asked, "So my father is still alive?"

"He was a year ago. I saw his name on a petition of complaint lodged by the Marjatyan nobility against the empire."

Karil grinned. "That's wonderful news." He turned to Braeden. "If he's alive, I needn't be in such a hurry to return to my family. I can help you with this first."

Braeden didn't want Karil involved, but, he had an unusual opportunity right now with the archduchess still in his clutches. "We'll see," he said. "Let's talk to Mattila and find out how soon she can act."

TEODORA

"I trust you can subdue Terragand before winter," Teodora said.

It was a statement, not a question, and Niklas van Ensden agreed. "I don't see why not," he said. "The opposition is weak. That they have Birkenfels is insignificant if we hold the rest of it."

They walked together through the dusky gardens of the Palais Arden. The air was cool and fragrant, and the Arnfels stood silhouetted against a sky streaked with pink and purple. Teodora was less keen on enjoying the view and more interested in not being overheard. She didn't want her plans for Terragand common knowledge just yet.

"What about Kaltental?" she asked. Duke Aidan Orland holding that crucial port was another fly in her ointment.

"We can take it. Orland can't have more than a few thousand troops, and Kaltental's fortifications are weak."

"Do that first then." Kaltental possessed important strategic value as a defense against invasion from Estenor, should Lennart be fool enough to try it. "If needed, you can besiege Birkenfels through the winter. I doubt they can survive it this time."

Ensden grimaced. That castle had been his undoing once before.

"Oh come," Teodora took his arm. "Won't it be satisfying to finally overcome that place?"

"I'll be satisfied once it's done, Your Highness."

"So will I." They strolled the pathways in silence for a moment. As dull as Teodora felt these days, any talk of Terragand or Birkenfels reminded her of Kendryk, and the rage welled up, stronger than ever. Unlike the joyous anger which energized her while plotting the downfall of her enemies, this was an unpleasant combination of fury, terror and helplessness. It was a humiliating reminder of what she'd felt upon first hearing of Kendryk's escape and Daciana's death. It was said he hadn't done the deed himself, but Teodora didn't care. He still bore ultimate responsibility.

That he was out of her reach right now was intolerable. If she hadn't feared Galladium's vast armies, she would have invaded straight away and laid waste to the land until she killed Kendryk, or captured him again. But this time, he wouldn't escape. She would put him to death at once, unless she caught his family too, and then he could watch them die first. That thought made her smile.

"I don't suppose Mattila will aid me," Ensden ventured cautiously, disturbing her reverie. Teodora had not yet told him about the general's latest outrage.

Teodora shook her head, deferring dreams of vengeance for later. "I doubt she will." She gnawed on her lip, wondering how much to tell Ensden, then decided he needed all the facts if he was to succeed. She took a deep breath. "To be honest, the general is nearly engaged in treason. She lagged in withdrawing from Norovaea, refuses to move on Terragand and worst of all, seems inclined to install herself in Brandana permanently."

"She wouldn't dare!" Ensden was shocked, which likely meant he knew nothing about it.

"I have it from unofficial sources, you understand," Teodora said, pleased that the information wasn't yet common knowledge. "She has declared nothing formally, but if she does, I need you to be in a strong position to oppose her. That's why we can't waste any time in getting to Terragand."

"I would have liked to go sooner," Ensden said.

"I wish I could have sent you." Teodora left it at that. He knew well enough of the problems with Maladena, and how difficult it was, getting the remnants of Barela's staff to conform to her direction. Queen Beatryz had demanded the return of her troops, while Teodora ignored her messages. Naturally, some officers had received direct correspondence from the queen and caused trouble, but it took only two public executions to bring the others into line. All of them now served under Ensden.

Ensden turned to her with a rare, frosty smile. "I'm grateful for your trust, Your Highness. If the gods will it, I will make Terragand yours by winter, and Brandana will follow in the spring."

Teodora was expecting Livilla herself, not a messenger. She forced her hands not to shake, since this couldn't be good news. Elyse brought it to Teodora in her dressing room, but now disappeared quietly into the shadows.

There were only a few lines, unencrypted. Teodora sank back into her chair. "Unbelievable," she said. "Who would do such a thing?"

Elyse stepped forward. "What's happened, Your Highness?"

"The Archduchess Elektra has been abducted." Teodora found her mouth unexpectedly dry.

Elyse made a noise. "Has there been a demand for ransom?"

"Not yet." It was a relief to realize that perhaps it was nothing more than that; brigands taking advantage of the situation to grab a wealthy hostage. For all of her dismissive thoughts about her oldest daughter, Teodora found herself far more upset than she expected to be. She wondered if some of this was injured pride; her first impulse was to rail against those who failed to respect her authority. And yet, something unfamiliar niggled at her. Worry for her daughter, since she must surely be frightened and uncomfortable, perhaps even hurt. What if the brigands didn't know who she was, and treated her roughly?

Teodora slumped back in her chair. "You can leave," she said to Elyse.

When the door fell shut behind the lady-in-waiting, Teodora let her face fall into her hands. She had been so certain she'd provided enough guards, and she knew Livilla would be careful. What had gone wrong?

Livilla arrived ahead of the rest of her convoy, riding a post horse. For an older woman, she had surprising stamina. Still in her riding clothes, she burst into Teodora's bedchamber, late at night.

"I came as quickly as I could," she said. "You received my message?"

"Yes," Teodora said. "Come, let's sit." She had just crawled into bed, but wanted to hear exactly what had happened. "Are you hungry?"

"Never mind that," Livilla said. "You have received no further word about Elektra? No demands for ransom or anything else?"

"Nothing." Teodora pulled on a dressing gown. The day had been warm, but a cool breeze came in through an open window. She told her maid to shut it, then sent her out of the room.

Livilla sighed. "I am so sorry, my dear. It was entirely my fault. I ought to have doubled her guard while we passed through such a lawless area."

"I should have thought her usual guards were enough." Elektra had left her original contingent behind in Arenberg, but Livilla brought just as many to escort her from there. "Were the brigands many?"

"I'm not sure," Livilla said. She sagged into the chair, looking tired, small, and older than even Teodora felt these days. "They killed only one guard and wounded another. There was a great deal of shooting and chaos. Mother Luca was riding by her side and said she left the road when the shooting started. Luca tried to follow, but by the time she could, Elektra had disappeared."

Teodora sat up suddenly. "Do you suppose Elektra or Luca planned it? Perhaps she wanted to get back to Mattila."

Livilla frowned. "I doubt that very much. Elektra complained that Mattila treated her abominably and she hated her. And Luca is reliable. I am certain she is not in Mattila's pay. But now I wonder if Mattila planned it. She was surely angry that I snatched Elektra out from under her nose."

"Oh, she was," Teodora said. "Very angry, and about the Norovaean treaty as well. I suppose it's entirely possible she did this. But if she did, why haven't I heard from her? I'd expect her to crow about it, or demand something for Elektra's freedom."

"So would I," Livilla said. "She'd dearly love for you to declare her ruler of Brandana, and Elektra would be the perfect leverage. And surely, she's had time to deliver a message to you by now. Still, let's wait another day or two. Perhaps you'll hear from her."

"I must do something in the meantime," Teodora said. "I'll send out as many search parties as I can. We'll start from where she was caught and cover all of Kronland until she's found."

KENDRYK

The days spent with the bankers were long and tedious, but it wasn't like Gwynneth to be bothered about those things. So Kendryk worried when he saw how pale and tired she looked at the end of each day. "You're sure you're not ill?" He asked her one evening at bedtime.

She sat in bed already, her book on her lap. She had put it down after only a few minutes of reading, which was unlike her. "No, I'm not ill." She paused for moment. "Come here. I must tell you something."

Kendryk slid into bed next to her, picked up the book and put it on a shelf in the headboard. "What is it?" He could guess, since he wasn't stupid, but knew she'd want to tell him herself. He tried not to let his face betray his excitement until she'd told him.

"I'm pregnant again." She looked unsure, though he didn't understand why.

"That's wonderful news," he said, with an encouraging smile. He was a little concerned about enlarging the family while they were so strapped for cash and everything else remained uncertain, but it was bound to happen sooner or later.

"You're sure? I was so worried because we have no home and ..."

"Stop it," Kendryk said. "I'm happy, all right? And yes, I'm a little worried about the future, but it won't be long before Lennart comes and sets everything right. Perhaps by the time this baby is born, Terragand will be ours again." That was excessively optimistic, but he loved the idea.

That brought a smile. "I doubt he'll manage it that quickly. This one will be here by spring."

"So soon? That means—" He counted months in his head. "That means you've been pregnant for a while. You might have told me earlier. When have I ever been unhappy about that news?"

"You're right. I've known since before we left. But I didn't want you to leave me behind, or send me home. I'm having an easy time of it."

Kendryk sighed. "I wouldn't have left you behind. I wish you'd told me, though. We might have traveled more slowly, so I could keep you comfortable."

"It wasn't necessary. And like I said, I'm fine. A bit tired the past few days, but that's probably because these bankers are so dull."

"They are, aren't they?" Kendryk settled into bed, and pulled Gwynneth into his arms. "I wish we had one of our own to advise us. I try to be certain I understand everything before agreeing to it, but I'm never completely sure."

Gwynneth snuggled closer. "I'm not sure either. It doesn't help we're trying to do it in two languages. I understand the Galladian side well enough, but the Zeelund tongue can be hard to follow when they talk fast."

Kendryk laughed. "I'm glad you're admitting to that. I thought I was the only idiot in the room. It doesn't help when we keep hearing about the horrible things Mattila is doing in Brandana. I want to hurry, so Lennart can get here before winter."

"He can't; I'm almost certain of it. But bad weather won't stop him. He'll come as soon as he has the money."

"I hope so." Kendryk wanted Lennart to invade soon, but he also didn't want to bind him or Gauvain to terms they would regret later. "But in the meantime, are you sure about continuing to meet with the bankers? Now you've admitted you understand no more than I do, I feel better about going by myself."

She poked him in the ribs. "Very funny. No, I'll come and just leave early if I get too tired. This will be our fifth child, Kendryk. I expect it to be as easy as the others."

LENNART

"Thank Ercos," Lennart said, throwing the letter onto his desk. It had come from Prince Kendryk in Zeelund by fast courier.

"Good new?" Meldahl asked, sitting in a chair nearby.

"Yes. The Zeelund bankers have approved a loan on behalf of Prince Kendryk. Naturally there's no mention of Galladium providing the collateral, but that's as it should be. No need to get Gauvain into hot water with the empress before it's time."

"He's having trouble enough over the Dallmaring Provinces," Meldahl said.

"Indeed. I don't wish him more problems, but I don't mind them providing a distraction from me."

"I doubt it's much of a distraction. Teodora must expect you to do something."

"I'm sure she does. But it looks like she's not having any luck getting Mattila to behave herself. The last reports say she's still in southern Brandana, moving slowly, picking the place clean. I wish I knew what she was up to."

"Just as long as she doesn't move into Terragand. Give us time to round up allies before we face her. I'm worried about Count Ensden. I've heard he marched out from Atlona with ten thousand troops, and there's almost no question he was heading for Terragand."

Lennart frowned. "I've been making overtures to Prince Stepan Falk in Helvundala, and can't say I'm impressed. By all accounts the old prince was difficult to deal with, but the youngster seems a slippery fellow. Won't commit to anything, though he buries it well enough in flowery words."

"He'll come around once we're camped on his territory." Meldahl was as relaxed as always.

"He'd better," Lennart said and stood, handing the letter to Meldahl. "We can safely plan a winter or early spring invasion. Let's be ready to go by the end of the year, while keeping an eye on Mattila's movements. We must mop up Ensden in any case. I'll go tell the queen."

"Still no sign of—?" Meldahl was too discreet a fellow to ask outright, but Lennart knew exactly what he was talking about. Everyone's concern was that Lennart have an heir on the horizon before he put himself in harm's way again.

"No." Lennart sighed. "It hasn't been that long, though I can't help but worry. It would be a weight off my mind." Lennart hoped a few more months would do it. He hated putting that kind of pressure on Raysa, but any consort to a ruler understood that the first order of business was getting an heir.

He took his time wandering the palace's corridors. Outside, the trees were turning, and winter would soon be here. Even if he started preparing today, he couldn't launch an invasion before the weather turned.

This time of the afternoon, the queen was always in her suite, practicing music or working on embroidery. Lennart had often invited her to hunt and ride with him, and while she had gone a few times, he saw she hadn't enjoyed herself, so he let her be.

The palace's ornate decor transformed once he entered the queen's apartments. One of the first things he did when Raysa arrived in Tharvik was instruct her to decorate her rooms exactly as she chose. They hadn't changed since Lennart's mother had been a bride. Within weeks, the musty, dark rooms turned into airy chambers with light walls and delicate furniture, everything upholstered in pale pink and purple silk.

It was the most feminine space Lennart had ever seen, and he couldn't deny it made him uncomfortable. He was too big for the spindly chairs, and altogether too loud and rough. It might be he frightened his wife, but she had her own way of putting him off balance. At least that helped even the score a bit. He grinned to himself before entering her sitting room.

"Good afternoon, Your Highness." Raysa sat at the harpsichord, picking out yet another mournful melody, but she rose immediately. "Is everything all right?" It was unusual for him to pay her a visit in the middle of the day.

"It is. I have news from Zeelund. Would you excuse us, ladies?" He nodded at Silvya Meldahl and the other attendant, a Countess Something-or-Other recently arrived from the provinces. Older than either Raysa or Silvya, she seemed even more sober and serious. Lennart wondered if the three of them ever had any fun.

Once they were gone, the door shut behind them, Lennart found a seat on the sturdiest-looking bench in the room and patted the spot next to him. "Come here, sweetheart."

Raysa sat down, and he noticed with some pleasure that she leaned against him a little. Perhaps they really were becoming friends.

He put an arm around her, but lightly, and said, "The money from Zeelund will arrive soon. I'd like to be ready to leave for Kronland by the end of the year."

"I see." She looked up at him, her brow furrowed. "I'm afraid I still don't understand why you are doing this. Now you're at peace with Sanova, why put yourself at risk in Kronland?"

Lennart smiled down at her. It was true, he'd done little to explain the situation to anyone but his ruling council, since Galladium's money would be more convincing than any argument. "It's a complicated situation, but it comes down to someone stopping Teodora before she overruns all of Kronland. If I don't stop her, she'll turn all twelve kingdoms into her personal domain."

Raysa frowned. "I suppose that's bad, but I still don't see why it matters to Estenor. If Teodora gets her way, she'll be your new southern neighbor instead of the princes there now."

"And that's the problem exactly. Teodora won't leave our trade routes alone if she has a chance to control them. Right now, we have treaties with all of the coastal countries guaranteeing the right of our ships to pass. We've already watched her nullify treaties as a matter of course. She can cut off our access to the west and the ocean. It's a risk I can't take." There was also the religious aspect, but he didn't want to bring that up yet.

"I suppose I understand, though I wish you and Teodora would negotiate first."

Lennart chuckled. "No one who's talked to Teodora has come away with an acceptable deal. No, we'll negotiate when I stand at the gates of Atlona, and not before."

She stared up at him, her eyes wide and anxious. "It all seems so uncertain and dangerous." She sighed and looked down. "I feel so bad I haven't done my part. I understand the importance of having the succession assured before you go."

"Please, don't feel bad," he said, squeezing her shoulder. Her bones seemed so fragile under his hand. "We haven't been married that long. It took my parents nearly two years before they had me."

"We don't have two years," she said, turning to look straight at him. "Why don't I come with you?"

Lennart was both surprised and gratified that she'd thought of it. He'd been rather worried that she'd wish for him to leave instead. He smiled. "That's sweet of you, but I'm afraid it's impossible, at least at first. The situation will be precarious, and until I've achieved a major victory, I doubt any of Kronland will be safe for you. Besides, a military camp is no place for a fine lady like you."

"I don't mind." She swallowed hard, and he saw she made an effort to seem brave. "I know you'll take care of me. It's just—" She twisted her hands in her lap. "What if something happens to you? Silvya told me you always lead your armies into battle. How can I be sure you won't be killed?" Her voice wobbled.

Lennart wondered if she cared, or if she didn't relish the thought of being a widow. "I doubt I'll be killed," he said. "I've always been lucky, and I trust the gods will protect me. And if something happens, I'll fix it so you're free to return to Sanova if you like."

"I don't want to go back," she burst out, then paused and sighed. "I realize that perhaps we're not as comfortable together as we should be. But I'd still rather be with you, either here or anywhere in Kronland."

Lennart was taken aback, and for a moment, struggled with what to say. Then he cupped her face in his hands, kissing her softly on the lips. "I like being with you too. Tell you what. As soon as I have a safe situation in Kronland, I'll send for you. Is that all right?" He kissed her again before she nodded her agreement.

ELEKTRA

Elektra fancied herself a toughened veteran after spending so much time in military camps, but traveling cross country with Braeden and Karil was harder than she'd ever imagined. At least it was summer, so the nights were warm and it didn't rain too much, but she often thought of her beautifully appointed little tent with longing. She didn't even have a change of clothes, and had to sleep on the ground, wrapped up in a dreadful-smelling horse blanket.

She had been very near Olvisya when Braeden and Karil kidnapped her, and now they had to get all the way back up to Brandana without being detected. At first, Braeden made them travel only at night, which was even more difficult. "There'll be imperial guards everywhere, looking for you, Your Grace."

She still hated the tone he used whenever he said the words "Your Grace," but didn't want to argue with him every time he opened his mouth. And besides, she was still rather frightened of him, though she'd never show it. Even though he'd made no further move to harm her, Braeden still had a wild, haunted look in his eyes she recognized as desperation. And she understood well enough how dangerous the desperate could be. Elektra just hoped he could keep from losing his mind long enough to carry out her plan.

"Exactly what is your plan?" Karil asked her one night, speaking softly while Braeden slept. Karil took the first watch, and Elektra had given up trying to sleep on a forest floor which seemed to consist only of a vast network of roots.

"I haven't worked it all out yet," Elektra admitted, and decided this was at least half the truth. These two were best kept in the dark about the other half. "I hope Mattila has an idea. To be honest, I'm afraid of her too, and I hate her almost as much as I hate Mother. I suppose I must find a way to kill her next."

"That must be a bad way to live." Karil was staring into the flames of the little fire quickly turning to coals.

"It's awful," Elektra said, realizing for the first time how much she hated her life. Perhaps that explained the constant fear and anger she felt. "I sometimes wish I had been born a peasant rather than an archduchess. I'm not well-suited to this role."

"Are you sure?" Karil grinned at her. "You're a natural at acting haughty and bossy."

"Really? Thank you." She decided to take it as a compliment. "I try, since I don't have much choice in the matter. And I'm certain it's far better to be empress than archduchess."

"Archduchess seems a good life," Karil said. "With not too many responsibilities and lots of servants."

"Oh yes, plenty of servants. I only realize now how comfortable I was, and how uncomfortable I am now. And it's true I had few responsibilities. But the other side of that is, I had no control over my life. I was always told where to go and what to do, with no choice about any of it."

"Sounds a lot like being a prisoner."

Elektra laughed. "That's exactly what it sounds like. So you understand what I'm talking about. That's why I must become empress before I lose my mind. I see all the mistakes my mother makes and know I can do better. I even think I know how to end this war."

"You do?" Karil looked astonished.

"Yes. If I were empress it would be over in a few months. Lennart would stay in Estenor or pick a fight with someone else, while I'd send Mattila to enjoy her retirement in Moralta."

"You'd give up Kronland to make peace?"

"Oh heavens, no. I'd keep Kronland. It ought to be easy enough once the heretics are destroyed."

Karil laughed. "Then you have no idea what you're doing. Most Quadrenes will die rather than convert back to your way."

That made her angry. "It's not *my* way; it's the only way. And that's why it will be easy. Once Holy Vica sees I am doing her will, she will strike down the Quadrene heresy in the blink of an eye."

"Your Grace, you are an idiot," Karil said.

"How dare you!" Elektra wanted to slap him, but reminded herself he was just an ignorant boy who hadn't been educated by a Maxima and a League priestess. She decided to take the mature path. "I'm ordering you to remember your place and be more respectful."

"Or what?" Karil's face now bore a challenging smirk.

"Or I'll refuse to grant Marjatya its independence when I become empress."

"Oh that," he said. "I doubt you'll do it in any case. Inferraras are well-known liars."

"Insolent brat!" Elektra shouted and lunged for Karil, losing her temper and her dignity in the same instant.

Karil laughed and jumped out of her way while she stumbled over a rock and landed back on the ground. The commotion awakened Braeden.

"Hey, what's going on?" He sprang to his feet, a pistol in each hand. "Are we under attack?"

"Only by Her Imperial Stupidity," Karil said.

"You must punish him," Elektra said, turning to Braeden. "I will not be spoken to that way."

"I'm not punishing anyone," Braeden said wearily. "And whatever you two were fighting about, stop it. You don't have to like each other, but you do have to get along until we complete this mission. After that, you can duel with pistols for all I care. Go to bed, Karil, I'll take the next watch."

"Good night, Karil," Elektra said loudly, then added under her breath, "Pig-headed Marjatyan."

Braeden heard. "Shut up and go to sleep, Your Grace," he said.

Elektra opened her mouth to protest, then met his eyes, shadowed by the dying embers. She closed her mouth, and lay back down on the hard ground.

ANTON

"I feel bad taking you out of school," the count said to Anton.

"Don't," Anton said. "I hate school. I have to learn the Ancient Tongue, and it's horrible." He didn't mention that Father Bertrand, the schoolmaster, also rapped him across the knuckles when he fidgeted. At first, Anton's hands were unbearably sore, but he'd developed calluses by now.

"Why?" the count asked. "Haven't the Scrolls been translated into all kinds of languages by now?"

"They have. But the Maxima reckons that a true scholar ought to read them in the original."

"That woman." The count shook his head. "She's attractive, but rather intense for my liking. And being in debt to her makes me uncomfortable."

They would be ready to go as soon as the count finished rounding up those of his troops still in Allaux. Natalya Maxima had kept paying them while he recovered, so he only had to retrieve them from the various taverns and inns they'd scattered to. Some had sold or gambled away their equipment, but Natalya advanced the count enough funds to buy everything new. It seemed the Galladian king had unbelievable wealth, and let Natalya spend as much of it as she wanted.

Anton piled all of his books on a table in his room and resolved never to open them again. With only a day of school left, what could Father Bertrand do if he hadn't learned his lessons? Besides, he needed to get Skandar and his equipment ready to go.

The count had decided to leave Galladium and strike out across Kronland, hoping to join King Lennart of Estenor when he invaded. "I'm sure he'll land in the north somewhere, secure Helvundala and Terragand, then work his way west to take on Mattila," he told Anton. "Everyone says King Lennart is a far more serious character than Arryk ever was."

Anton pulled a face. King Arryk had impressed everyone when he first invaded too, and that had ended in disaster. But Anton did wonder about this Estenorian king. Maybe he was the fellow all the priests hoped for. Though Anton didn't care about that, he would enjoy being on the winning side for once.

As excited as he was to leave, Anton still hated saying goodbye. He started with Natalya Maxima, much as she intimidated him. She visited his class every day on her way to the garden, and this time he ran after her. A priest and her secretary accompanied her, but she turned to Anton when she saw him following her. "Walk with me for a moment, Anton," she said in her soft, husky voice, with a smile both warm and mysterious.

A flush spread across Anton's face, while he forgot what he wanted to say. "I, uh—" he began.

"Come," Natalya said, taking a seat on a stone bench in the garden, and patting the spot next to her. "I'll catch up to the two of you in a moment," she told the others.

Anton sat, not feeling much better, especially now he was alone with her.

Natalya turned to him, her smile more gentle this time. "Now," she said. "What is it?"

"I'm leaving," Anton finally choked out. "But I just, I just wanted. Um."

"I thought you might go with Count Orland," she said, her green eyes serious.

Anton had never been alone with her, or so close. She smelled like a heavenly mixture of flowers and spices. It was hard to think. "Um, yes. I." He took a deep breath and looked away, trying to gather himself. "Yes. I'm going with the count." He turned back to her, and now it was better. "I wanted to thank you for everything. For taking such good care of the count, and keeping his army together, and letting me go to school, even though you forced me to learn the Ancient Tongue, and made me study with Father Bertrand. Everything." By now he saw Natalya was trying not to laugh, so he stopped talking.

She took both of Anton's hands in hers. He felt shaky.

"You are most welcome," she said. "You and Count Orland have done our cause a great service, so of course, we took care of you. I will be sorry to lose you, though I won't miss the count." She frowned slightly, and continued. "If ever a man belonged on the battlefield and nowhere else, it is he." She sighed and let go Anton's hands. "I had hoped to have more time with you, because my greatest fear for you is that you turn out like him."

Anton bristled. He wanted to say the count was a good person, but realized that wasn't exactly true.

"I'm sorry." Natalya's voice was still soft. "I understand he is like family to you, and you have been so loyal to him. That doesn't mean he is someone you should strive to be like. I realize you like fighting, but there is so much more to life. I hope you come to enjoy other things as well. Please know you are always welcome in Allaux, should you need a safe place."

"Thank you," Anton said, and meant it. When Natalya rose, he stood, and watched her until she joined her companions. He wasn't in love with her exactly, but there was no question his insides felt very strange. He stood there a moment longer, then remembered he needed to say goodbye to Maryna and Devyn, so went back to the schoolroom as they were letting out.

"Father Bertrand was angry that you walked out, but I told him he should be kind, since you were leaving," Maryna said.

"And then he said you were—" Devyn began, rather loudly.

"Hush, Devyn," Maryna said. "The father's words were rude and shouldn't be repeated. All the same," she turned to Anton, "you should say goodbye to him."

Anton didn't want to, but he hated saying no to Maryna, so he delivered a brief, formal farewell to his teacher and other classmates before rejoining Maryna and Devyn.

"You'll have supper with us tonight," Maryna said. "I've already told my governess and she's arranged it."

Anton knew the governess would hate the idea, since she didn't hold with young duchesses and dukes associating with commoners like himself. But he also knew Maryna could be forceful, and looked forward to seeing the look on the governess's face when he showed up. "That's very kind," he said.

"Not at all." Maryna turned to him. "I want to do more, but I can't think what. We'll miss you terribly."

"I'll miss you too," Anton said, thinking he was always saying goodbye to these two. He wanted to add that they'd see each other again soon, but had a hunch that might be a lie.

TEODORA

In spite of feeling like a great weight pressed down on her without ceasing, Teodora pushed herself hard daily. She was up well before dawn, even though it took two sturdy maids to pull her out of bed when her mind and limbs protested being awakened too early. She breakfasted while being dressed, then met Count Solteszy in her private study for a good three hours of work before it was time to see petitioners. Most days, they were joined by the Countess Biaram, who'd proven herself an industrious gatherer of intelligence.

The autumn mornings were cool now, so the heavy drapes remained drawn, and a fire crackled in the hearth while Teodora and her advisers sipped coffee brewed in the Zastwar style. It was far too strong to taste good, but there was nothing better to shock mind and body into wakefulness.

Teodora shuffled through the correspondence on the table. No new messages, though more might trickle in throughout the day. She had heard nothing further from Mattila, and no one could say exactly what Lennart was up to either.

A thorough search encompassing southern Kronland had turned up no sign of Elektra. Teodora couldn't imagine what might have happened to her, but ordered her troops to keep looking.

Ensden had marched across Lantura and Oltena without meeting opposition, and another month would find him deep inside Terragand.

But unease plagued Teodora as long as Mattila lurked like a spider, just over the border in Brandana. The usual lack of money didn't help. Ensden's army would live off the land, but only until winter. Teodora needed to raise funds for him to buy food, fodder, and supplies once the weather turned cold. She also had an idea for getting rid of Mattila, but that would require even greater amounts of coin.

"Any response to your letter to Natalya?" Biaram asked. They had sent a message a month before, asking for a loan in exchange for ceding the contested provinces.

"Nothing definitive," Teodora said, though the thought angered her. "She says they have little cash to spare right now. Something about a peasant revolt and trouble on the Maladene border. I'm sure that's just an excuse." Teodora drummed her fingers on the table. "I need a more reliable source of funds. I must get rid of Mattila, and the only way I can is to remove her from command, while bringing her army under my authority."

"You have the legal right to do so," Solteszy said, rubbing his eyes. He'd probably had no more sleep than Teodora. "But if you do it, you must be prepared to provide those officers with a firm incentive. Some are personally loyal to Mattila, but most work for pay. If you take over and offer them real coin instead of the promise of plunder, it can be done."

"I must do it soon," Teodora said. "Where will I get the money?"

"Can you make friends with Queen Beatryz again?" Countess Biaram asked hesitantly, as though she expected Teodora to overrule her.

"How?" Teodora glared at the countess. "She's angry with me over Barela, and I can hardly bring him back to life." She hated so much as mentioning his name, but there was no question his memory now stood between her and what she needed. Teodora clenched her skirts in her fists. She would not let him get the better of her, even in death. "There must be another way."

There was silence for a moment, interrupted only by the shuffling of Solteszy's papers. Teodora ground her teeth. "Well?" It was Solteszy's job to come up with good ideas. She stared at him, waiting.

He leaned back in his chair, looking thoughtful. "You can ask for an early payment of reparations from Norovaea."

The first payment wasn't due for almost a year. "What if Arryk says no?" Teodora hated asking for anything, especially from rulers who somehow thought they were equal to her.

Solteszy shrugged. "He likely will. Perhaps you can offer an incentive. A reduction in the total amount or a lower rate of interest, perhaps?"

"I shouldn't have to make concessions to get my money." Teodora pondered for a moment, then smiled. "That's what a hostage is for, isn't it?"

Solteszy raised his eyebrows. "You'll kill Prince Aksel if Arryk doesn't send the money?"

"Why not? Isn't that part of the agreement?"

"Not quite. Prince Aksel is being held to ensure Arryk no longer interferes in imperial affairs. The money is a separate matter."

"I disagree." Teodora didn't care about technicalities in treaties. "Arryk owes me money, and I want it sooner rather than later. If he refuses, I'll kill his little brother." She settled back into her chair and waved her hand. "Write the letter and send it by fast messenger. I'm sure you know how to be diplomatic but firm." She stood. "I'll deal with the little prince."

BRAEDEN

It was bad enough Braeden had to avoid soldiers from both sides, while covering hundreds of leagues back to Brandana. He was sure imperial troops were after him, but he also couldn't risk running into Martinek or Faris on the other side, and have them capture the archduchess. Though it was true, he'd consider turning her over because she and Karil would not stop squabbling, and he was sick of them both. They argued about politics and religion without ceasing. Elektra had taken it into her head that Karil was both a heretic and Marjatyan rebel, and set out to make him change his mind. Being a stubborn sort, Karil was not about to have his mind changed, least of all by a hated Inferrara.

"I don't see why you can't simply submit to your rightful rulers," Elektra complained as they rode along a quiet forest path. "The gods have set them above you to impose order and protect you. Why don't you let them do it?"

"Because they're wicked," Karil said. "And everyone knows the Inferraras are mad. You're the perfect example."

"Braeden, Karil is being dreadful again," Elektra whined.

"I don't care, Your Grace." Braeden longed for cotton to put in his ears. "Karil, don't let her provoke you."

"I'm not provoking him. If we're to negotiate when I'm empress, he must learn to behave properly."

Braeden sighed heavily. "I'm sure everything will come right once you're empress." He was having his doubts on that score, but kept them to himself. "No need to discuss it now. Please do shut up, Your Grace."

They were all miserable at this point. They had run out of food, and though they still had coin, Braeden was wary of buying any at town markets. Fortunately, it was harvest time, and they managed to live off what they stole out of the fields they passed, but what they found was often neither filling nor appealing. Less than half the fields in this area were under cultivation, since so many farmers had been run off by armies marching back and forth.

Elektra's fancy riding clothes had fallen apart, and now she wore Karil's spare shirt and breeches, which were too big, and not at all pretty, as she complained. Braeden sometimes wished he'd killed her that first day. He would have carried on to Marjatya with Karil, and by now the two of them might well be relaxing in the Andarosz castle.

He looked at her sideways, and she scowled, spurring her horse forward. Maybe he should just get rid of her anyway. At this point, Karil might not object either. He could do it while both of them slept; she'd never even notice until she woke up in the presence of her goddess, or whatever it was she hoped for. Besides, would she be able to convince Mattila of anything? How did he know she wouldn't betray him?

He turned that risk over in his head, and decided it was worth taking. The young lady seemed to take her oaths seriously, so after they'd crossed into Brandana, he pulled her aside one evening while Karil slept. He didn't need him adding any snide remarks.

"Your Grace," he said, trying to sound as deferential as possible. "I must ask something of you."

She inclined her head. Braeden recognized the gesture as one of Teodora's.

"I must ask you to formally swear upon your goddess that you won't betray me to Mattila."

Elektra laughed. "Gracious, you are a suspicious sort. It never occurred to me to betray you."

The falseness of her laughter made it clear it had in fact occurred to her, and not just because he'd brought it up. "I know," Braeden said. "And I'm sorry. But I must be sure before I let you go."

"Of course," she said. "I suppose you are taking a big risk, sending me to Mattila by myself."

"I am. So here's what we'll do. You'll take out your little icon of Vica and swear on it you'll not betray me or Karil, and that you will hold to our agreement until the empress is dead." He'd seen the tiny icon she carried, and noticed that she prayed over it.

She frowned. "You aren't devout and Karil is a heretic, so why would you trust in Vica to hold me to my word?"

"I don't," Braeden said, thinking again that killing her would be so much easier. "But you do, and that's all I need."

"Very well then." She pulled the icon out of her pocket and placed it on her knee, putting one hand on top of it. "I swear by Holy Vica that I will not betray you, Karil, or our cause to Mattila. May the goddess strike me down if I break this vow."

"Good." Braeden nodded his approval. He wished he had another way to be sure, but this would have to do.

ANTON

The count led his force northeast, hoping to reach Helvundala before King Lennart invaded. "We must be careful," he told his officers before crossing the border into Brandana. "We don't know where Brynhild Mattila is. We've only heard that she's left Norovaea and that she might be anywhere in Kronland. I'd rather not tangle with her until we're part of a larger force."

All the officers agreed, and so did Anton. He'd had two experiences with the army of Brynhild Mattila and didn't care to have another. He didn't even want to see her again with all the armies of King Lennart behind him.

Later when he was alone with the count, Anton asked, "Isn't it late in the year for an invasion?" He remembered King Arryk's landing several years before in the middle of a winter storm. The king himself had been shipwrecked and lost a big part of his army.

"It might be late," the count said. "But Lennart is used to fighting in the winter. He's been at war with Sanova for years, and they never slowed down for anything, least of all bad weather."

"Why did they stop fighting now?" Anton wondered. He knew Lennart was coming to Kronland because Estenor was finally at peace with Sanova.

"He got married. His new wife is the daughter of the Sanovan queen. Now they're family, they won't fight each other, at least not for a while."

"So he had to marry some princess he'd never met to get peace?" Anton didn't like the sound of that. Most princesses weren't as beautiful as the Princess Gwynneth or as nice as the Duchess Maryna, who would be a princess too, someday.

The count shrugged. "Kings do it all the time. It's a good way to make alliances, though it doesn't always work. I suppose we'll find out if the treaty holds. Hopefully it lasts long enough for Lennart to finish off Teodora."

"I really hope he can," Anton said, though he still didn't believe anyone could.

Anton enjoyed being on the move again. The wine harvest was in full swing in eastern Galladium and western Brandana, and the count wanted to sample all the different varieties of the regions they crossed. Even though everyone in Allaux drank wine all the time, Anton never liked it very much. It was too sour. But he changed his mind after trying some of the Brandana wine; white instead of red, and rather sweet. It went down almost like water.

The count laughed at Anton while he drank his fourth mug, sitting outside an inn during a merry village festival along the Lera river. "You're going to regret drinking like that."

Anton scoffed. "I can hold my liquor as well as you can."

"Maybe, but I'm only on my second. Trust me, you should slow down."

Anton had never seen the count drink white wine before, so he doubted he knew what he was talking about. He let the pretty blond serving girl refill his mug a few more times, but before he could finish the last one, his head swam and felt very heavy. He laid it on the table, the count's laughter sounding far away.

When he woke up much later, no one was around, and his head pounded. The village was dark and silent. Anton remembered where the count was staying, but his head hurt too badly to move. He looked around until he spotted a well and staggered over to it, relieved to find the bucket mostly full. After dunking his head into it, the shock of the cold water made him forget about the ache.

Anton stumbled down the dark, quiet street and found the inn they were staying at, but it was too much work to go upstairs and find the count's room. So he laid down on the floor in the dining room, and slept soundly until the kitchen maid kicked him, shrieked, then fell right on top of him. There was a commotion until Anton woke up enough to reassure her he was a guest and not some kind of bandit. That didn't help his head, and the count laughed for a long time when someone told him what happened with the kitchen maid.

"I'll get a barrel of the sweetest stuff just for you. There's room in my wagons." The count thought it was the funniest thing, though Anton didn't agree.

His head didn't clear up until much later in the day, by which time he'd had to ride fifteen leagues. Every step Skandar took felt like a hammer to his head. "I'll never drink wine again," he muttered.

"Don't be silly," the count said. "Just don't drink so much at once. I tried to warn you."

"Hmph," Anton said, and resolved to stick to ale from now on.

Crossing the Lera River reminded Anton of the battle at Lerania. If he closed his eyes, he still saw people, horses and wagons falling into the water as the bridge collapsed, so he kept them open. They were farther north, and crossing a much sturdier bridge, but Anton felt nervous all the same. If Mattila had appeared right then, their position would have been just as bad as before. But they crossed with no incident and continued on into eastern Brandana. Anton relaxed a little. With any luck, they would find King Lennart with no problems after all.

LENNART

Lennart was pleased that he and Raysa had eased into affectionate companionship. He'd even made her laugh a time or two. But there was still no sign of a pregnancy even though they spent nearly every night together. He hoped there was nothing wrong with her, and resolved to ask the doctor to check carefully at her next visit. He knew it wasn't his fault, because he had two youngsters running around Tharvik already, products of a few youthful indiscretions.

And there was one more thing. He came to bed a little early one evening so they could talk. Raysa was still in her dressing room, running a brush through her heavy blond hair. Lennart paused in the doorway, enjoying the way it rippled to her waist. He wished she'd wear it long, but ever since their marriage she kept it up in elaborate, severe braids.

She smiled up at him. "You're early."

He came in, shutting the door behind him, then pulled up a chair so he sat across from her. "I wanted to talk to you."

"Have I done something wrong?" She put her brush down and placed her hands on her cheeks, where a slight flush was growing. "I realize I'm still not familiar with all of your customs."

Lennart leaned forward and took both her hands in his. "You've done nothing wrong, nothing at all. We get so little time to talk alone, and I wanted to discuss something that's important to me."

"Certainly." Her flush faded, but she left her hands in his, more relaxed now.

"We haven't talked about religion at all," he said, "but it's a big part of why I'm going to Kronland and I wanted you to understand."

"I see." She cast a glance at the little icon of Vica, sitting in front of a candle on a small altar next to her dressing table. "I'd heard rumors in Sanova that you were a heretic, but I refused to believe it."

Since their marriage, which had been conducted according to the Sanovan rites, they'd never attended temple services together. Raysa visited the palace chapel every day with her own priestess in tow, while Lennart went to the main temple in Tharvik.

He took a deep breath. "I might be a heretic in your eyes. It's true I follow the Quadrene creed."

She made a small noise of dismay.

He squeezed her hands a little more tightly, and looked into her eyes, even though he saw the hurt and confusion there. They had to get through this if things were to go forward. "The teachings of Edric Maximus and the words of the Holy Scrolls are very important to me, and I do my best to live by them. But I would never force you to give up your own faith."

He spotted the relief in her eyes and felt a pang. Maybe she still worried he was some kind of monster. He went on. "I don't expect you to understand, but please at least try. Not to the point of converting yourself, though I'd be thrilled if you did. But just so you see why I believe what I do."

He looked straight at her, holding her gaze, as if by doing so he might make her agree. She looked back, though her dark blue eyes filled with tears. He steeled himself for them to spill over at any moment.

Her lower lip trembled and then she spoke. "I'd like to understand, truly. But Mother Kassya says that the teachings of the heretic Landrus are poisonous and should be avoided by all true believers."

"I disagree, but I understand why she'd say that. And I won't ask you to defy her in this. You needn't read any of Edric's sermons, though you'd probably like them. All I ask is that you read the Holy Scrolls yourself. Surely Mother Kassya won't object to that?"

"I hope not." Raysa looked anxious. "But I'll do it anyway if that's what you want me to. I do wish to learn more."

Lennart smiled, trying to hide his relief, and pulled the little book out of his pocket. "You realize that the clerics of the empress's own League of Aeternos read the Scrolls, don't you?"

"I didn't know that." She took the book and looked it over. "It seems so small, after all of the fuss."

"But the ideas inside are big. That's the Olvisyan translation. We have one in Estenorian, but I find Edric's language more compelling."

"What if I don't understand?"

"The language is simple, but if you come across unfamiliar words or concepts, just ask me. Or ask Mother Kassya. I'm sure she'll have her own thoughts about it. Perhaps she'll even enjoy reading them herself."

Lennart didn't worry about the priestess too much. A kind, quiet older woman, she struck him as anything but fanatical. Any objections she might have would likely be voiced gently. Ottilya had tried sending along a harsh, unpleasant priest who reduced Raysa to tears constantly on the journey from Sanova, but Lennart sent him back as soon as they reached Estenor. Raysa had never asked about him once.

"I'll read them." She placed the little book on a table beside her. "But I hope I don't offend you if I keep praying to Vica that she might show you the true path." She bit her lip and blushed, then looked down. When she spoke, it was so soft that Lennart barely heard her. "I've become quite fond of you." She looked up at him, her gaze clear and earnest. "So I fear for your soul. I would be surprised if reading the Scrolls changes my mind about anything."

Lennart reckoned when she looked at him like that, she could worship fairies living in a teapot for all he cared. "Pray as much as you like," he said. "And I'll pray for you as well. I doubt we'll go wrong with that."

TEODORA

Teodora was glad when the Norovaean ambassador finally saw reason and contented herself with firing angry letters off to Arryk, instead of haunting Teodora's audience chamber daily. The woman was stubborn and tedious, but the time spent with her had paid off. Arryk might disregard Teodora's messages, but he couldn't ignore his own ambassador's pleas. With those as proof of Aksel's jeopardy, he would send Teodora her money, and do it quickly.

Teodora returned to her chambers late one evening, annoyed to find her youngest daughter waiting for her.

"Whatever do you want, Zofya?" she asked, sinking into a chair. She was too tired to be angry. She looked her daughter over. Zofya now wore the plain white dress of the temple acolyte, which suited her. She had even grown taller and prettier. Perhaps the move to the temple school had been good for her.

Zofya fidgeted, a flush blooming on her cheeks. She took a deep breath, then said, "I want you to let Aksel Roussay out of the Arnfels right now."

Teodora shook her head, amazed the girl was even aware of the prince's existence. "Why do you care?"

Zofya swallowed hard, but looked Teodora straight in the eye. "I'm in love with him, and can't bear the thought of him in that dungeon. In fact, I'd like to marry him someday."

"What? The last time we spoke you were in love with Gauvain Brevard and terribly upset at the prospect of breaking the engagement."

"Oh, that was ages ago," Zofya said, with a wave of her hand. "I was so young and had no idea what I was doing. You were right; it's impossible to fall in love with someone you've never met."

"When have you met Aksel Roussay? Have you ever so much as talked to him?" Teodora knew he had been staying in Livilla's palace, but the temple school, though nearby, was an isolated world unto itself.

"All the time," Zofya said. "Mother Hela, my scientific instructor, says I'm particularly good at experimentation. And Aksel is of course a brilliant scientist. I've spent hours in the school laboratory with him. We've invented a—"

"You've what?" Teodora nearly came out of her chair. "You've been spending time alone with Aksel Roussay?"

Zofya had the good sense to look mildly alarmed. "Not completely alone. Mother Hela is always there, and so are the other students. But Aksel and I have become good friends; he says I'm nearly as clever as his sister, and everyone knows she's—"

"Stop that," Teodora snapped. "He would say those things. He's a Roussay, and they're forever trying to take advantage of any situation. You cannot trust him, and you will never see him again. I'll keep him in the Arnfels for the rest of his life if that's what it takes."

Zofya's lip trembled. "But you must let him go, Mother. We've nearly finished a device which could—"

"I don't care about your stupid device," Teodora screamed, unwilling to believe this was happening.

Zofya jumped, but quickly composed herself.

Teodora took a deep breath, but kept her tone sharp. "You will never see Prince Aksel again, is that clear? You can't marry him, since you are engaged to Gauvain Brevard, and you will marry Gauvain unless the treaty is broken."

Zofya's eyes lit up. "What might break the treaty?"

"Not you." Teodora fixed her sternest gaze on her daughter. She was pleased that Zofya wasn't easily intimidated, but it was an unhelpful trait right now. "You will do nothing to jeopardize it, or you will be punished. Severely."

"I don't care about that. I don't care what you do to me. I will marry Aksel and you can't stop me." Even though tears glittered in Zofya's eyes, her lip had a petulant thrust to it.

"You can't marry him if he's dead." Teodora let a smile spread over her face as Zofya's eyes widened in alarm. "He is a prisoner after all, and if his brother doesn't cooperate with me, I'll be forced to kill him." This wasn't quite true, but Zofya didn't know that.

Zofya leapt out of her chair. "You wouldn't dare!"

"I would. I'm the empress and can do whatever I want."

"You're horrible." The tears finally spilled over. "I hate you."

"I don't care." Teodora shrugged. "I must do what's right for the empire. You'll understand all of this once you're Queen of Galladium."

"I don't want to be a queen anymore." Zofya wiped her eyes with her sleeve. "I want to marry Aksel, and I'm sure he wants to marry me too."

"Has he proposed?" Teodora frowned. That would be a severe breach in hostage etiquette, though she wouldn't put it past a Roussay overstepping his bounds just as his older siblings liked to.

"No." Zofya sniffled, though she was clearly attempting to stop crying. "But he looks at me in that way. Oh, you wouldn't understand, Mother. I'm sure no man has ever loved you, or ever looked at you as if he—"

"Shut up!" Teodora shrieked, leaping out of her chair and striding toward Zofya, who quickly jumped up and ran to the other side of the room. Teodora advanced on her. "Shut up, you stupid, stupid girl." She bulled forward until Zofya was backed up against a wall. She slapped her hard.

Zofya gasped, but didn't cry out. A bright red mark bloomed on her pale cheek, though she never stopped staring at Teodora with furious dark eyes.

Teodora backed up. "Get out," she said, pointing to the door.

Zofya edged toward it, her eyes still fixed on Teodora's face.

"Get out and go back to the temple. You are confined to your room until I give the order."

Zofya had reached the doorway and turned to face Teodora. "I'll go. But I'm telling you, Mother. If you hurt Aksel in any way, I'll kill you. I swear it on Holy Vica." Her eyes blazed over the welt forming on her cheek, then she turned on her heel and was gone.

Teodora slumped into a nearby chair, needing time to pull herself together. It had been a while since anyone had defied her to her face, and that it should be her own daughter was galling. Even worse, it was as though the girl had known exactly how to hurt her, to make her want to protest that no, someone once really had looked at her that way and meant it.

A pain pierced Teodora's chest and she slumped back in her chair, breathing hard. She wondered if she needed to send for her doctor. If her work didn't kill her, her difficult children might.

But the pain went away after a time, and her breath came easier. A maid appeared and asked her if she needed anything before retiring, and Teodora sent her for a cup of tea made from herbs Livilla had given her. Finally left alone with the steaming, foul-smelling mug, Teodora sat in front of the fire. She was so tired, but knew she would get no sleep without this drink; it had been years since she'd fallen asleep on her own, no matter how exhausted she was.

She decided she'd talk to Aksel herself soon. If he had tender feelings for her daughter, perhaps she could find a way to use that to her advantage.

ANTON

Even though everyone relaxed a little after crossing the river, Anton was still uneasy. This part of Brandana was recently devastated by war, and the sight of burned farms and dead bodies reminded him of Daciana Tomescu's work. He was almost positive he'd killed her, but she was impossible to forget. He wished he could be certain she was dead, though everyone else seemed to think she was.

This was supposed to be friendly territory, since Brandana's Princess Floreta was one of the rebellious Kronlanders, but no one knew where she was, or who really ruled here. Maybe no one did. And everyone seemed very frightened of Brynhild Mattila's army. It had come through here earlier in the year while pursuing King Arryk, and had left destruction wherever it passed. Every now and then, Anton spotted farmers in the distance, harvesting the little food that had grown this year, but they always disappeared as soon as the count's forces drew closer. Anton didn't blame them.

The count was sure they would be safer once they crossed into Terragand. Mattila will want to work her way south, rather than east," he told Anton. "She'll take her time and make sure the area is subdued. Technically, Terragand belongs to Duke Evard Bernotas, but it's hard to say where he is. Even if he's rebuilt his castle, I doubt he'll be a threat."

Anton agreed. They'd burned Evard's castle at Emberg years ago, and had easily beaten the duke in battle. They could do it again without too much trouble.

"Otherwise though, Terragand is friendly." The count continued. "Friends of Prince Kendryk's hold Birkenfels castle, my father is in Kaltental, and the towns follow Edric Maximus."

"Why doesn't Mattila try to conquer Terragand with Duke Evard?" Anton asked.

The count smirked. "Because the empress wants her to, and Mattila hates doing anything the empress wants."

"That ought to make her mad," Anton said, glad about anything that made life difficult for Teodora.

"I'm sure she is," the count said. "Right now I imagine she's mad about a lot of things. But it's good for us that she and Mattila don't get along. We can get across Kronland and meet Lennart without being stopped."

But the count was wrong about that. When they passed the last crossroads before Terragand, they found their way blocked. "It's Mattila," the scout said. "Imperial and Moraltan standard flying everywhere; I'd stake my life on it."

The count swore. "What's she doing this far north? All the news we heard said she was going south."

"No idea," the scout said, and got out of the way. That was always smart when the count got angry.

"What'll we do?" Anton asked.

"Run," the count said. "We're not strong enough to face several thousand infantry supported by artillery. I can't get through or around that. We must head north, sail around to Kaltental if we have to." He gave the order to change direction, and they returned to the crossroads, heading north from there.

Just north of the crossroads, an even larger force blocked their path. The count fumed. "I'd head south, but I'll bet she's got troops there too. She's got a big enough army, she can put them everywhere."

"We'll have to break through," one officer said.

"We can't." The count slammed his hand down on the little table they all sat around. They'd been poring over a map for the past quarter hour, hoping to find a path they'd overlooked. "I only have two thousand and she's posted guns at every position. They'll make mincemeat of our horses and I won't have it. We must retreat west."

That meant heading back to the river. Anton's stomach roiled, but he got Skandar ready to go anyway.

The count sent scouts to make sure no one blocked the western road, and they went quickly. The baggage train fell far behind, but Anton already knew the count would sacrifice it if he had to. This time he put most of his money in Cid and Skandar's saddlebags. "If we don't make it," he told Anton, "get back across the river and head for Galladium. Natalya Maxima will take care of you."

Anton shook his head. He didn't want to think about crossing that river in a fight, even over a real bridge. "We'll make it," he muttered, mostly to himself, as if saying it would make him believe it.

They reached the river by the following midday, but Mattila's troops waited for them there too. They were surrounded. The count looked grim, but determined as always. "The force protecting the bridge is smaller, so we ought to be able to break through."

"They have guns guarding the approach," an officer said, looking pale.

"We'll have to ride into them." The count laughed, same as always. "If we're fast, we'll overrun their position before they can get off a second volley. What else can we do?"

ELEKTRA

As they neared Mattila's headquarters, Elektra became increasingly nervous. The general had always been dismissive of her and anything she said, so she worried about not being taken seriously this time. Still, it had to be done, and was the only way she'd finally be free of these crazed rebels.

"You're sure she'll grant you an audience?" Braeden asked as he readied her horse.

"She will, as soon as she recognizes me." She looked like a half-starved ragamuffin, but was certain others around the general would recognize her. That was one reason she'd insisted on riding into camp; she'd make a better impression.

Braeden helped her onto the horse. "We'll be here until nightfall. If there's no sign of you or a message, we'll disappear, and you'll never hear from us again."

Elektra looked down at him. "I'll send someone to signal you with a red flag." Braeden stared at her with that look he had. "Oh come now, I swore on the Goddess I wouldn't betray you, and I won't."

"Good girl," Braeden said. "Now off with you," and he swatted her horse's rump without so much as a "Your Grace."

Elektra was glad to be rid of him. For good, if all went as she hoped.

Mattila's camp, covering a large plain on the west side of the River Lera, was vast, but Elektra knew how to get in. She showed the sentries she was alone and unarmed, saying she had an important message for the general. "I was robbed on the way," she said by way of explaining her appearance. "But the message is safe."

After that, it was a matter of asking her way through to the general's tent. Once she came near, a clerk on the general's staff recognized her. He ran off and disappeared, but a few minutes later, an officer she knew approached her.

She dismounted, and Major Bonacci swept his hat off into a bow. "Your Grace, it is good to see you. Are you well? Unhurt?"

"Yes." It was all she could do to keep from dissolving into relieved, hysterical laughter. "I'm well enough, though—" She paused, looking down at her atrocious clothing, and the major understood right away.

"Come," he said. "You must be hungry and anxious to make yourself presentable for the general." He offered his arm, and escorted her to a nearby tent quickly being rearranged for her. "I have ordered food and a bath," the major said, "and will send for some appropriate clothing. Ah, here is a maid to help you."

"Thank you," Elektra said, relieved to be amongst civilized folk again.

Two hours later, she'd had three helpings of a delicious meal, some excellent wine to clear her head, a bath, and wore the uniform of a lieutenant of the guard. Major Bonacci waited for her outside the tent. "The general is anxious to see you," he said. "We were all worried that you'd been lost for good when so many months went by without word."

"I've had quite an adventure," Elektra said with a smile. She'd forgotten how attractive Bonacci was. So nice to look at after seeing no one but Braeden with his enormous beard—grown back after a few weeks on the road—and Karil's coarse peasant features for so long.

Major Bonacci showed her into the tent, and stepped back outside. The general was alone, scribbling something at a small table. She stood when she saw Elektra, crossed the tent in two steps and swept her into a rib-crushing hug. Elektra gasped, from both surprise at the unexpected affection and the wind suddenly forced out of her.

"Thank the gods, you're alive, Your Grace," Mattila said, after letting her go. "I found out soon enough that Livilla had nabbed you in Norovaea, but some months ago she sent word you'd been captured by brigands. And on top of that, the imperial guards could not find you, the incompetent louts."

"It's a long story," Elektra said, as the general led her to a camp chair, poured wine into a cup and put it into her hand. "But first, I've brought along someone you might find interesting."

"Your rescuer?"

"Not precisely." She decided to skip the story for now, and get to the important part. "Not more than a league from here, hidden in the woods, is Braeden Terris of the Sanova Hussars, and a boy who escaped from the Arnfels with Prince Kendryk."

"Extraordinary," Mattila said, regarding Elektra with approval. It was as though the dour general had turned into another person. "I always knew you'd do great things, Your Grace. How did you manage this?"

"By promising to help them with a pointless scheme they'd hatched. I assured them you'd want to help, but that was just so they'd bring me to you."

"Marvelous." Mattila rose, ducked her head out of the tent, and shouted at someone. Then she returned. "Braeden Terris has a price on his head; a big one. I'm sure your mother will be more than pleased to pay it out to you, though I'd advise sharing a little with those I send to bring him in. Ah, here she is."

The tent-flap burst open once again and a young red-haired woman strode in, then stopped and saluted the general.

"Captain Dura," the general said. "This is the Archduchess Elektra. She has delivered the traitor Braeden Terris to us."

The captain bowed to Elektra, but not quickly enough to hide the shock on her face. "Are you certain, Your Grace?" she asked.

"Absolutely," Elektra said. "And I can tell you where he is, and how to get him."

"I thought you'd want to do it, Captain," Mattila said, "After everything he put you through."

Captain Dura's green eyes flashed, then she swallowed hard and said, "You're right. Just tell me where he is and I'll bring him in, dead or alive."

BRAEDEN

As soon as Elektra disappeared, Braeden found a thicket to hide in, and tried not to worry. Time crept by, but after a few hours, there was a crashing noise that sounded like horses coming down the forest path.

He pulled out a pistol and told Karil, "Wait behind that tree, and don't come out until I give the signal. If you hear anything strange at all, run east and get across the border into Terragand. Make your way to Birkenfels and tell the commander there you're a friend to Prince Kendryk. He'll help you."

"I'm not running away," Karil whispered. "Especially not if that idiot Elektra has betrayed us. I would never give her the satisfaction."

"She'll be plenty satisfied with your head on the block." Braeden had no more time to argue. He saw the glint of metal and heard the snort of a horse. He waited until he spotted a waving red flag, then stepped into a small clearing.

His knees nearly buckled from the shock of seeing Franca Dura jump off her horse, stride into the clearing, and fling the red flag at his feet. Something in the way she did that told him she didn't come in peace.

Braeden raised his pistol, but knew he wouldn't fire. If he didn't have the stomach to kill Elektra Inferrara, there was no way he'd kill Franca.

"So it really is you," she said, her tone hard and angry. "You can put down the pistol. I'm here to bring you back to Mattila."

Braeden lowered the pistol. "To negotiate with her?"

Franca barked a harsh laugh. "To go to your death. The empress put a large price on your head, and Mattila is all too happy to award it to the archduchess, the sniveling little wretch."

"I knew I couldn't trust her." Braeden shook his head. "So that's it, then." He found he was glad it was Franca, of all people. He hoped that Karil stayed hidden. "I'd rather you finished me off now. I have no desire to meet Mattila as her prisoner."

"You don't even know, do you?" Franca shouted. The sudden noise sent a flock of birds fluttering out of a nearby bush. "What you did to us. You destroyed the Sanova Hussars."

"I don't understand,"Braeden said. Franca still wore the usual hussar armor, and even had a captain's sash wrapped around her waist.

"I don't suppose you would, with that thick head you have." Her eyes flashed angrily and Braeden stepped back. "You compromised the honor of the whole unit. When Teodora discovered you were part of the conspiracy to free Prince Kendryk, she assumed all of us were involved, from Novitny on down."

Braeden stared at her. It had never occurred to him that anyone would think he wasn't working on his own.

"She threw Novitny into the Arnfels and disbanded the unit in disgrace."

"Oh gods," Braeden said, sinking to his knees. "Please kill me right now. I never wanted anything like that to happen."

Franca took a step in his direction, then stood over him, staring down her nose forbiddingly. "Novitny is fine. Queen Ottilya made a fuss, and Teodora let him out on the condition he no longer work in her territory. He's gone to Sanova with several officers. Queen Ottilya sent them to mind the border with Briansk."

"What about Reno, and the rest?" Braeden could scarcely force the words out.

"Reno's been promoted to colonel, and heads a re-formed, somewhat smaller regiment under Mattila's direct authority. Lucky for us she didn't mind thumbing her nose at the empress."

"Looks like you've been promoted as well." Braeden staggered to his feet, dizzy with relief that he hadn't hurt his friends with his recklessness.

"Mm-hm," Franca said. "Mattila sent me to bring you in personally. She reckoned I'd be happy to do it."

"I don't blame you," Braeden said. "But I never thought I'd survive the rescue attempt, and never dreamed Teodora would blame the lot of you. I thought I'd go to Atlona, and that would be the end of it. I wanted to be sure none of you knew what I was up to, so you wouldn't be implicated."

"Hmph," Franca said. "Things didn't work out as you'd planned, did they? And now you're in a real fix."

"I agree," Braeden said. "But I'm glad it's you bringing me in. Feels like justice, eh?"

Franca pursed her lips and frowned. "I'm not bringing you in. I wanted to at first, but now that I see you, I can't do it."

So he wasn't prepared when she tackled him. He hit the ground with a thud, and then she was on him, landing a heavy punch to his jaw. His head exploded with pain, but he laid back and didn't struggle. He'd taught her how to punch like that. He was ready for another blow, but it never came.

"I hate that I can't do it," she whispered through clenched teeth, still straddling him. "But you're the closest thing I ever had to a father, and mostly, you were a good one. And after what happened to Janna and the little ones, I don't blame you for trying something crazy. I half wanted to myself."

In that instant, someone ran into her, throwing her off of Braeden, so he struggled back to his feet. It was Karil, bursting out of the bushes to rescue him. He and Franca wrestled on the dry leaves of the forest floor, throwing ineffective blows at each other until Braeden pulled them apart. "Stop it Karil," he said while the two of them scowled at each other. "She won't hurt us."

"I don't understand," Karil said. "It sounded like you were friends and then she hit you."

"Never mind that now," Franca said, knocking dirt and leaves off her clothes. "We have to be quick about this. I had to bring a few others with me so Mattila wouldn't suspect anything. I left them back on the road, but they'll be wondering what's going on if I take too long. Miro and Trisa are with them and should keep them a bit longer, but I don't want to take a chance. You need a head start and you won't get a long one.

"I'll make my way back to camp as slowly as I can, but then I must report that I wasn't able to find you. Since Elektra knows exactly where she left you, people will be on your trail. You must head straight for Terragand. Mattila's scouts range across the border, and they've reported a small army headed by Trystan Martinek just east of it. I'm sure he'll be happy to take you on if you can run into him."

"I need to get to Marjatya," Braeden said.

"You can't leave Terragand for a while. Ensden holds a great deal of it and you'll never get past him with everyone looking for you. Martinek is less than two days' march away, and with luck you'll reach him before getting caught. Expect Mattila to send a large force after you within a few hours."

Braeden found his mouth was dry. "We'll go east right away then. You'll be all right? Mattila won't be angry with you?"

Franca shrugged. "She might, but the others will back me up. You've got to go now."

"Thank you," Braeden said. "I mean it. I owe you a great deal for this. Oh, and I'm proud of you, Captain Dura."

"Stop that," she snapped. "You'll make me cry. Now off with you."

ANTON

Anton had been in a lot of fights, but never anything like this. He'd never ridden right into cannon-fire aimed straight at him. He worried he might be sick, but swallowed down his fear. There was no use in worrying when he needed to concentrate on getting through those cannon and onto the bridge.

"This'll be saber-work," the count said. "Have your pistols loaded, but draw your saber, and on my command we'll rush the infantry. They have no pike, and once their big guns have done their worst, we can overrun the rest."

He made it sound so easy. Anton checked his weapons, and Skandar followed Cid without Anton doing anything. The count's troops scattered across the road, and into the woods on both sides. He'd ordered them spread out so the guns wouldn't hit a large cluster. Once they'd fired, everyone would charge the bridge. The count rode down the middle, with Anton behind. Anton saw the mouths of the big guns at the bridge, their crews standing at the ready. His stomach roiled and his tongue stuck to the roof of his mouth. Even though he wore all of his armor, it felt useless.

The count looked back before clapping down his visor. "Come on," he said, "Let's get this over with." He urged Cid forward and Anton followed, hoping to somehow keep from being sick. He decided not to look at the guns, and stared up at the sky instead. If he survived that first barrage, he might get through to the bridge.

Anton was unprepared for the blast when it came. He'd never been so close to a cannon when it fired. A deafening boom was instantly followed by a shriek overhead. Skandar reared up and Anton hung on, unsure of what just happened. He stared at the the spot the count had been just seconds ago. A ribbon of smoke blew across the road, and disappeared. Anton knew he needed to leave, since the gun crews wouldn't take long to reload. But couldn't move, and it seemed Skandar didn't want to either.

The two of them stood there, staring at what remained of the count and of Cid. If Anton hadn't known the count had been right beside him, he wouldn't have known this mess of blood and bone was him. It might have been anyone—anyone and their horse.

Anton choked down the sick that filled his mouth. He had to keep going. The cannon fired again, and Anton flinched. Dust and screams filled the air.

Maybe it was someone else. Troopers galloped past, yelling and shooting. Anton would join them. Surely the count and Cid were already at the bridge, in the thick of things.

Skandar walked down the road, refusing to move faster. Anton applied his spurs, but Skandar still wouldn't hurry. Was he hurt? Anton looked down and saw blood on Skandar's leg, but couldn't tell how serious the wound was. At that moment, Anton realized blood covered him too. It drenched his armor, his clothes, and the rest of Skandar. He stopped. He didn't think he was hurt, but needed to check on his horse.

Anton dismounted clumsily, even while something in his brain clanged at him, shouting that he needed to keep moving and not stop here. But he wouldn't move until he knew Skandar was all right. All the same, he was unprepared for the blow when it came, and slumped to the ground as his vision turned to black.

BRAEDEN

After Franca left them, Braeden and Karil headed east as quickly as they could. But Karil's horse went lame, so they left it behind after they'd gone less than a league.

"Kazmir can carry both of us, at least for a while," Braeden said. They'd both lost weight in the past few months, and had few supplies to carry. "They'll be looking for two horses. Might be we'll throw them off." Even as he said it, he knew it was unlikely. Franca couldn't buy him more than a few hours' time, and their pursuers would have fresh horses, maybe even dogs.

The dense woods kept them hidden, but also made for slow going, since Kazmir had to pick his way across the uneven ground. A warhorse was not built for this kind of terrain.

They'd traveled only a few leagues before sounds of pursuit drifted their way. The road was a half-league away, and Braeden heard a large party pass, and even spotted the occasional glint of torchlight as the afternoon quickly turned to evening. He knew nothing about the area except that they would reach the river Lera soon, and that the road led to a bridge, which would now be watched. Braeden and Karil both carried many weapons, but he knew they had little chance in a direct confrontation with Mattila's troops.

"We have to find a ford," Braeden said. "None of the bridges are safe." To reach Terragand and safety, they had no choice but to cross the river.

"Is there a ford?"

"I have no idea." If they asked locals, they'd risk being recognized. But if they did it soon, there was a chance Mattila's troops hadn't yet spread the word. Braeden pulled Kazmir to the left. It would take longer to reach the river, but at least no one was behind them yet.

The path flattened and Kazmir moved a little more quickly. The trees thinned out as well, and the rising moon lit their path. Braeden stayed alert to every sound around them, though he heard nothing but the rustle of forest creatures and the occasional cry of a bird. Karil fell asleep against his back. Braeden cursed himself for ever getting the boy into this adventure. He should have taken him straight home instead of giving in to the temptation of the archduchess's lightly guarded convoy.

Braeden was hungry and thirsty, but didn't much care. He paused a few times to let Kazmir drink from forest streams, but didn't bother dismounting. They would make Terragand long before starving to death, or dying of thirst. Their odds of dying by other means were far greater.

Before dawn, they rode through a silent village. Braeden held his breath when a dog barked, but someone shouted at it, the dog stopped barking, and all went quiet again. Once they left the village behind, he hoped to find a remote farm where folk hadn't received news in some time.

The sun peeked over the tops of the trees when he came upon a girl driving a herd of cows into a meadow. She looked up at Braeden with wide, frightened eyes.

"Good morning, young lady," he said in as friendly a tone as he could manage through his fatigue. "I'm looking for a ford across the Lera."

"There's a bridge not five leagues up the road," she said pointing, while looking more curious than frightened.

"I need a ford." Braeden hoped she wouldn't expect an explanation.

"There's no fording the Lera," the girl said. "Too fast and deep. But if you don't want the bridge, you can try the ferry at Erzenbach. It's two leagues to the north and small, but should do for just the two of you and the horse."

"Thank you," Braeden said, then paused and handed her his last silver coin. He doubted he'd need it between here and Terragand. "If you'd be so kind, tell no one you've seen us."

The girl nodded, hopefully in agreement, staring at the coin in her hand while cows wandered off in all directions. Perhaps she'd never seen silver before.

From here he had no choice but to take the road if he wanted to find the ferry. Kazmir was tired, and Braeden couldn't hurry him. Once they got across the river, he'd find a safe place, and take a few hours' rest.

It took another hour to reach the ferry, but the road remained quiet. Every now and then, they'd spot peasants working the farms in the distance, but it wasn't a market day, so the road itself remained deserted.

Braeden breathed a sigh of relief when he spotted the path leading down the riverbank to the ferry. Before going farther, he dismounted and crept into the trees lining the riverbank. "See anyone Karil? Your young eyes are better than mine."

Karil looked intently, then shook his head. "Nothing."

"Doesn't mean they're not hidden somewhere, but we've got to get across this river. Let's go."

He led Kazmir down the sandy trail to the ferry tied at the water's edge. A man sat on the shore, throwing rocks into the current. Not a busy crossing then.

"Good morning," Braeden said, trying to look friendly and nonthreatening. "How much to cross?"

The man looked the two of them over. "Two coppers apiece, and three for the horse."

Braeden pulled the money from his nearly empty purse, and led Kazmir onto the tiny raft. It was attached to a thick rope stretching all the way across the river, and the ferryman cranked a large handle, working a wheel that propelled the raft across.

"Clever, isn't it?" Braeden winked at Karil, who looked rather green. The water was fast and the little raft pitched terrifyingly. Kazmir stomped, snorted and rolled his eyes, while Braeden held onto him tight.

It was a relief to reach the eastern shore. Braeden had kept a close eye on it while fingering his pistol, but saw no movement. Some trees were losing their leaves, but those along the river were bushy firs blocking much of the view. They got off the ferry, led Kazmir up the bank, and Braeden allowed himself to hope they might have a chance. Only a few leagues now to the Terragand border.

"Braeden," Karil said in a small voice. "I see soldiers ahead."

KENDRYK

Kendryk had barely set foot inside the house in Allaux before children swarmed around him. Just as happy to see them, he sat down on the floor of the main hall and let them climb on him. He'd hated leaving them again so soon after their reunion in the spring, but no one else could do what he had just done in Zeelund.

All three of the older ones piled on his lap, while Gwynneth held onto a wriggling Stella. "Did you know Mama is going to give you another little brother or sister?" he asked the others.

"That's wonderful," Marya said as expected, then got up to put her arms around Gwynneth. Kendryk stood, with Devyn hanging on his arm and Andres clinging to a leg.

"It won't be until spring," Gwynneth said, handing Stella to Kendryk. He nuzzled her soft cheek, her black curls tickling his face, until she nearly squirmed out of his arms. He put her down and she ran off into another room, the nurse on her heels.

"If a baby is coming why isn't your tummy fat?" Devyn asked, peering at Gwynneth's midriff, at eye level.

"Devyn, it's rude to comment on a lady's figure unless you're paying a compliment," Kendryk said.

"But she's not a lady. She's Mama, and why isn't she fat?"

Gwynneth shook her head, but smiled down at him. "It's too soon, darling. The baby is still tiny. I'm sure I'll be fat before long."

"But then you shouldn't say anything, Devyn," Maryna put in. "It's very rude. You must listen to Papa."

"You can't tell me what to do." Devyn had a belligerent thrust to his chin, and Kendryk saw he was ready to start a fight. He'd have to talk to Maryna about being less bossy.

He decided to give Devyn something to do. "Devyn, can you get Stella and meet us in the drawing room? I'm sure you want to unwrap the presents we've brought you from Zeelund."

Once the presents were brought out—an embroidered cap for Maryna, beautifully carved wooden practice swords for Devyn and Stella, little wooden shoes for Andres, and a small mountain of brightly painted toys for everyone—Kendryk said to Gwynneth, "I must visit the Maxima at once. You can stay with the children and I'll return in time for supper."

"I should go too," she said, but he could see how tired she was.

"It only takes one of us to give her any news we haven't sent in letters. We'll meet with the king tomorrow, and the four of us can discuss everything more thoroughly. Why don't you send the children to the nursery with their new things and rest before supper?" He stood and kissed the top of her head. "I must go speak with Natalya," he told the children. "I'll be back in time to tuck you   in."

Natalya greeted him with a smile. "I got your letter only yesterday. You made excellent time."

"We did, although I tried to go slower for Gwynneth's sake. She was as eager to get back here as I was."

Natalya sighed. "It might be our time together will end soon. Lennart ought to receive his first subsidy within the month, and he's already begun preparations for a full-scale invasion. I know Terragand will be yours within the year."

"I hope you're right," Kendryk said. "As soon as we receive word that Lennart has landed in Kronland and where, I'll ride to meet him. Gwynneth and the children must stay here." It occurred to him that the pregnancy had come at an opportune time; otherwise Gwynneth would insist on coming along. Brave as she was, he badly wanted to keep her out of harm's way.

"I agree," Natalya said. "It's best if you're with him from the beginning. He seems confident of gaining Kronland allies, but it won't be as easy as he thinks. Princes like Falk and Dahlby will be more inclined to follow you than a foreign king."

"I'm not sure anyone will want to follow me, after everything that's happened."

Natalya shook her head. "Kendryk, you must stop seeing yourself as a failure. No one else does. You might have lost a battle long ago, and been the empress's prisoner, but everyone sees your rescue as a miracle. Many still

71

believe you are the chosen ruler, and that the gods made your escape possible for that reason."

"That seems a strange way of looking at it." Kendryk wished no one would ever talk to him about the prophecy again. "It's obvious that Lennart is the chosen prince."

Natalya gave a dismissive shrug. "I don't agree, and neither does Edric. But you can take that up with the Maximus when you see him again. It would be wise if you collected him before meeting with Lennart. I last heard he was in eastern Terragand, so I'll write to him and let him know to expect you. He will be very helpful in swaying the rulers who still view Lennart with suspicion. I doubt anyone will say no to you and Edric combined."

"I hope you're right," Kendryk said.

"I usually am." Natalya said it in a joking tone, but Kendryk knew she was serious, and he agreed.

TEODORA

Teodora waited a few weeks before visiting Aksel, hoping an extended residence in the Arnfels might soften him up a little. When she was ready, she sent an order ahead to have the prisoner cleaned up, and put in a better room for her visit. One step inside Kendryk's squalid cell had been enough to put her off for life.

"Is he restrained?" she asked the guard before entering the cell.

"He is, Your Highness."

"Then you can stay out." Teodora swept into the cell, the door banging shut behind her.

An attractive, bespectacled young man sat in a chair, manacles binding his wrists to its arms. "Your Highness?" He made an instinctive move to stand, but the chains held him fast.

"Yes, it's me." Teodora smiled down at him, then sat down across from him. "I thought it was time we had a chat."

"I hope I've done nothing wrong." He offered a charming, ironic smile, which also appeared quite innocent.

"To be honest Prince, I'm not sure." Teodora smiled back, though she kept it chilly. Let the boy squirm for a moment.

It seemed she wasn't succeeding. Aksel sat relaxed in spite of his restraints, regarding her with friendly and mildly curious blue eyes. She decided the spectacles did nothing to detract from his looks, and in fact made him appear more interesting than he probably was. Faced with an apparent choice between Gauvain Brevard and this rather sweet young prince, she could see why Zofya was smitten.

Finally she said, "It's come to my attention you spent quite a bit of time with the Archduchess Zofya before this." She waved her hand at the barred window.

Aksel's face lit up. "I did. I hope I wasn't wrong in doing so. The archduchess has a sharp mind with a scientific bent. Before this happened, we'd been working on a solution to the—"

"Never mind that," Teodora interrupted. She found science dull and generally useless, unless it advanced military technology. "I don't care how she spends her free time. However, it seems she's fallen in love with you."

From the way Aksel's eyebrows shot up, Teodora guessed this was the first he'd heard of it. Then a flush spread over his face, though it appeared to be embarrassment, not ardor.

"I'm sorry about that," he said. "I can assure you, Your Highness, that I had no intention of leading the archduchess on. I thought we were merely friends."

"I hoped that might be the case," Teodora said. "Zofya is still young, and her head is full of silly romantic notions. You might have heard that she is betrothed to Gauvain Brevard."

"Yes, I knew of that. In fact it was the archduchess who told me. It was some time ago, but she seemed to like the idea of becoming Queen of Galladium."

"Yes, she did, and so do I." Teodora leaned back and fixed her gaze on Aksel. "You seem a reasonable sort—unlike your idiotic brother and fanatical sister—so I don't mind telling you, it's very important that this marriage go forward."

Aksel seemed amused, rather than offended at the insults she'd just flung at his siblings. He leaned forward. "Is that why I'm in here? To keep me out of her way? If so, I can assure you I'll do my best to avoid the archduchess, should you be kind enough to send me back to the temple."

"You're in here because I need your brother to send me money sooner than agreed." There was no point in pretending. "I only found out about Zofya's feelings when she came to plead for your release."

"How sweet of her. Has my brother responded to your satisfaction?"

"It's too soon to say." Teodora shrugged. "Though you might help with that. Perhaps you can write him a letter, letting him know you're safe, but will only remain so if he cooperates."

"What do I get if I write your letter?" Aksel's tone was mild, but his eye bore an amused glint. He didn't seem nearly upset enough about his circumstances.

"Don't be impertinent," Teodora snapped. "You're in no position to negotiate."

"True. I meant no disrespect. But I promise to be the picture of cooperation if you let me out of here."

"We'll see." Teodora stood and walked to the door. "Write that letter, and I'll think about improving your situation." Compared to his older brother, she found Aksel marvelously easy to deal with. Given time, she was sure she could find a use for him.

BRAEDEN

It made sense there'd be soldiers ranged all along that bank of the river. Braeden's only hope now was that a small party watched the ferry, so he and Karil could somehow blast their way through.

"How many?" he whispered, mounting Kazmir and hauling Karil up behind him. They'd have a better chance on horseback.

"Six, I think," Karil whispered back.

"Have they seen us?"

"I don't know. They're standing on the road."

By now Braeden had spotted them too, and was certain they were Mattila's troops. "We'll come up on them quiet as we can. You hold the saber and I'll take the pistols."

In spite of the bumpy crossing, Kazmir acted refreshed. Maybe he was looking forward to some action. Braeden walked him slowly through the trees, keeping the soldiers in view. They acted as though they hadn't seen him, standing around in disorder, some looking toward the river as they talked, others watching the woods on the other side of the road. If they had spotted their quarry, they were hiding it well. Braeden counted six as well.

"We'll run over them once, then come back and finish what's left," he murmured to Karil. A rising wind rustled the needles of the firs, masking any smaller noises. It died down, and Braeden pulled Kazmir to a stop. The moment it rose again, he spurred him to a gallop, and Karil shrieked something ungodly at the top of his lungs. Braeden grinned, recognizing the Marjatyan battle cry.

One soldier turned to face him, so Braeden shot him first. Another went down under Kazmir's hoofs.

"Right!" Karil shouted, and Braeden turned as a woman raised a musket. He shot her, and a scream rang in his ear as Karil caught a man from behind with the saber. These were lightly armored infantry troops; easy to kill.

The remaining two tried to get away. Kazmir danced like a colt, and chased them down. Braeden drew his estoc, and stabbed the man running alongside the road, while Karil got the one trying to turn toward the river.

"That's all," Karil said, once Braeden had pulled Kazmir to a halt.

Braeden turned in the saddle to grin at Karil. "You really are a menace with a blade," he said.

"Thank Prince Kendryk for making me practice every day for two years." Karil wiped the bloody saber on his breeches. They were so filthy by now, a little blood didn't matter.

"Now, we need to find our way, and quickly," Braeden said, squinting up at the sky. The sun had moved high by now, though it hung far to the south this time of year. "East is that way." He pointed into the trees. "I hope we can find a path that will lead us straight into Terragand. It can't be over five leagues. Now let's take cover and reload the pistols, since we made quite a ruckus, and might have raised the alarm for any other troops nearby."

He was right. They hadn't so much as reloaded before they heard hoofbeats in the distance. "Cavalry," Karil said. "Could be it's your friends."

"I hope not. Captain Dura will be watched, so she can't let us go a second time. We need to disappear into the woods."

Kazmir was reluctant to turn away from another fight, but Braeden made him plunge into the dark trees. They had to move both quickly and quietly, and it wasn't long before hoofbeats pounded on the road behind them. Their pursuers stopped to look at the bodies, which slowed them down, but they had to know their prize wasn't far away. Braeden kept Kazmir at a walk, his heart in his mouth. The moment he found a deer trail, he urged him to a trot.

"They're right behind us," Karil whispered. "Shall I shoot at them?"

"Not yet," Braeden said. "Let's try to get away first. How many do you see?"

"Four or five," Karil said. "It's hard to count them between the trees. I think the others have gone down to the river, but they'll be on our trail fast enough."

"Let's speed up," Braeden said, letting Kazmir have his head. Behind him, horses crashed through the trees.

ANTON

Anton's head hurt worse than it ever had from drinking too much wine. He rolled over onto his back and moaned. When he opened his eyes, he saw the light of a fire and people he didn't know sitting around it. He sat up carefully, and noticed his armor was gone. So was his doublet, and his boots. He wondered if he'd been hurt and someone had undressed him. But he wasn't inside a hospital tent or wagon. He tried to stand, but his knees buckled, so he sat back down again.

A few other fellows sat nearby, and he recognized one of them. "Where are we?" he asked. "Where is the count?"

The man looked at him, hollow-eyed. "The count is dead," he said. "And we're prisoners of Brynhild Mattila herself."

The memory of what he had seen rushed back into Anton's mind. "Oh gods."

The man looked sympathetic. "A real shame, the way he went. That gunner had perfect aim; took the count and his horse right with him. Nothing left but a few bits here and there."

Anton tried to speak but choked, and was sick in the grass. He laid back down again, staring up at the black sky. So what he'd seen really was the count and Cid. And all that blood; it had to be from the two of them. Anton was sick again. Then he thought of Skandar, and sat up. "My horse," he said, trying to quell the panic rising in his voice. "Where is my horse? Is he all right?"

"They took our horses," the man said. "I wouldn't be surprised if Mattila takes yours for herself. Even a general doesn't see a battle charger so fine very often."

Anton sprang to his feet, though he still wobbled. "I have to get him," he said. "You have to help me."

The man laughed. "I don't think you understand, boy. We're prisoners of war and we're not going anywhere."

"I don't. What?" Anton fell back into the grass. His legs wouldn't support him.

"Prisoners," the man said. "That's why your armor and most of your clothes are gone. Spoils of battle. You might not see them, but you can be sure there's guards posted all around us."

"So I'm a prisoner of the empress?" Anton was finally making sense of some of this.

"In a manner of speaking, though the general might not agree. Either way, you'd best get used to the idea."

"What will happen to us?" Anton asked. He had to find out what was next, so he could figure out a way to get Skandar back.

"I imagine those of us who are still fit will be invited to join the general's ranks. As infantry, you understand."

"I won't," Anton said. "I won't fight for the empress."

The man laughed again, harsher this time. "You will. If you refuse you die. They've already killed the wounded, and they'll get rid of you too if you're not of any use to them. Best do as you're told. With any luck, the tide will turn, and you'll be captured by the other side."

"I can't fight for the empress," Anton said again.

"Just do it," the man said wearily. "Make it easier on yourself."

Anton shook his head and closed his eyes. Maybe this was a bad dream and he'd wake up in the morning, the count's familiar laugh in his ear, with Cid and Skandar standing nearby. He smelled food and realized he was hungry, though he doubted he'd get any of it. He was right.

A kick to the ribs woke him up before dawn. "Up with you," someone shouted.

Anton sensed another kick coming, and scrambled to his feet before it connected with him again. The others were getting to their feet as well. A big man with a dark, fleshy face paced before them. It was cold, and Anton shivered, realizing he was in nothing but his shirt and breeches.

"I reckon you lot know the drill," the big man was saying. "Our fine general is offering you employment in her army. Say yes and you'll be assigned to a unit, fed and paid mostly regular. Say no, and you travel straight to paradise, though from the looks of you, you're more likely to go the other direction."

The man walked along the line, followed by a skinny girl scribbling on a sheet of paper fastened to a wooden tablet. He took their names and ages, then other men led them off somewhere. Anton was close to the end of the line.

"Remember what I said," the man standing next to him muttered. "Just do this, and might be you'll live to get away."

Anton had to clench his teeth to keep them from chattering. The big man stood in front of him now. "Name?" he asked, looking Anton up and down with a critical eye.

"Er." Anton realized at that moment he shouldn't give his real name.

"Name!" the man barked. "Or are you one of them idiots? Them are the ones what dig privy trenches."

"Oh, er, no," Anton said, His tongue getting in his way. "Beran. My name is Anton Beran."

"Moraltan," the man grumbled. "Troublemaker most like. Age?"

"Sixteen." This lie came more easily since Anton used it on a regular basis.

"Doubt that," the man grumbled. "And skinny as a beanpole too. But you're tall, and might yet get stronger if you're dragging a pike all day. Pike," he barked at the girl and she scribbled. "Off you go." And he waved Anton to the left.

A man who looked like an infantry sergeant said, "You'll come this way. Welcome to the army of Brynhild Mattila. Weber back there says you're Moraltan, so you'll be with your kind. I'm assigning you to the Michalek pike regiment. You'll report to the quartermaster and he'll get you fixed for clothes." Anton must have looked confused because the man shook his head, grabbed him by the arm and turned him around. "Between those tents, to the big one at the end. There'll be a line of your lot."

Anton hurried off, cold mud squishing between his bare toes. He hoped the quartermaster had shoes. Something warm to wear over his shirt would be nice too. And food. It had been too long since he'd had anything to eat.

BRAEDEN

As the crashing behind them grew louder, Braeden let Kazmir go. He'd have to trust him to find his way without breaking a leg. A shot whizzed overhead. "Keep your head down," Braeden said, leaning over Kazmir's neck. "Make yourself a small target."

"I should shoot back," Karil said.

"Not unless they're so close you can't miss. We can't reload, and there are a lot more of them."

Braeden concentrated on finding a safe path for Kazmir, so he could go faster. By his reckoning, they were still too far from the Terragand border to get away, but he could do nothing but try.

More shots flew by, and Braeden ventured a look back. They were right behind him now, with a clear shot if he stopped. He pulled Kazmir toward a thicket, hoping for a way out the other side. If not, Braeden would turn and face them.

In the gloom, the bushes and trees showed no gap, but Kazmir went ahead anyway. Branches lashed at Braeden's face, and he tasted blood on his lip. Their only hope now was that their pursuers couldn't see which way they'd gone, though they'd likely heard them.

"They're Oricians," Karil said in his ear.

"Are you sure?" Light cavalry from the Zastwar borderlands, Oricians were notoriously good trackers. They wouldn't lose the trail for long, if at all.

"I'm sure," Karil said. "Those long red coats and black hats. Can we outrun them? Their horses are smaller."

"Kazmir is too tired," Braeden said. "We'll go as far as we can, then we'll have to fight them off until we can't anymore."

He stopped Kazmir for a moment, and listened. The horse's labored breathing blocked out any other sounds. Braeden wouldn't push him any further. Even if the Oricians killed Braeden and Karil, they'd recognize a great warhorse and take good care of him. He dismounted quietly, helped Karil down, and pushed Kazmir behind the wide trunk of a tree.

With the pursuers so close behind him, he recognized the Orician tongue. A cluster of them stood on the other side of the thicket, and Braeden understood enough to tell they were searching for his trail. The gloom of the thick woods made it hard for them to spot it. Braeden put his finger to his lips, and drew his pistols. He hoped they'd go in another direction. If not, he'd be ready for them.

A torch flared up; they hadn't stopped looking. With that much light, they'd probably find it. They also made better targets.

"Now," Braeden whispered. "At any silhouette." A shape moved into the light and Braeden fired. There was a shout, and a crash as something fell into a bush. A body, hopefully. Light flared from muzzles as they fired back. Wood splintered into Braeden's face as shots drove into the trees around him. He wished he'd sent Karil into the shelter of the big tree along with Kazmir.

Beside him, Karil fired both pistols at the same time and hit at least one Orician, crashing through the bushes now, dead ahead. Braeden fired again, but now his pistols were empty, so he drew a blade and stepped forward. He still didn't know their numbers, or how many pistols they had, but he reckoned he might get one or two, even on horseback, before they took him down.

An Orician thundered down on him, a pistol in one hand, a saber in the other. Braeden jumped aside as he fired, while Karil cried out and fell to the ground behind him. Willing himself not to look, Braeden gritted his teeth and lunged at the horseman. The man tried wheeling around, but the thicket was too small, and his horse balked. Braeden slashed across his back with the saber, hoping the fellow was as lightly armored as most Oricians. The man slumped forward across his horse's neck, and Braeden looked for Karil.

He sat on the ground, and in the gloom, it was hard to tell how badly he was hurt. Karil held a sword, barely fending off another horseman slashing down at him. Braeden ran toward him, and caught the man's saber arm as he raised it for another blow. He shrieked and fell off his horse. Braeden whirled around as another horse bore down on him, threw himself to the side, rolling out of the way, and leapt to his feet as soon as the horse passed him.

Karil shouted, "Behind you," but before Braeden could turn, something crashed into his shoulder and knocked him to the ground.

Braeden tried raising himself up on one elbow, but his arm didn't work. He used the other to roll to a seated position, and looked for his saber. It was impossible to see anything on the dark forest floor. His right arm throbbed, and when he touched his shoulder, his hand came away bloody. A taste of his own medicine, he thought with a grin.

Braeden felt bad about Karil, but reckoned this was the perfect way for a fighter to meet his death. Especially against a pack of ferocious Oricians; no shame in that. Far better than facing an executioner. He used his good arm to pull the dagger out of his boot. He'd take one more down with him before the end.

Braeden struggled to his feet, and looked for Karil, who'd dragged himself against a tree and sat there, still holding a sword. Another horseman came toward him, and Braeden stepped in his path. The arm holding the dagger wasn't as strong as his right, but it was strong enough. He caught the saber's blade with the dagger, dragging it aside, and slashed at the horseman's leg. It didn't stop him, but it got him out of the way. "Give me the sword, Karil," he said, handing him the dagger. For the first time, he felt lightheaded.

"You're bleeding an awful lot," Karil said. "I don't—" Another pistol-shot interrupted him, but this one came from another direction. The Orician, turning to face Braeden again, toppled out of the saddle.

"What?" Braeden and Karil said together.

More pistol-fire came from the east, and the few remaining Oricians turned and headed back toward the road.

"Let's just sit here, and stay out of the way for a minute," Braeden said, slumping to the ground next to Karil. He heard more shooting, but then a loud ringing in his ears drowned out all other sounds while he slid into darkness.

ANTON

Serving in the infantry was very different from being page to a general, and Anton didn't like anything about it. At first, he missed Skandar and Cid so much he could hardly move. He missed the count too, and the life he'd had with him.

Life in the Moraltan pike regiment was hard. Anton had no money, so he had to wear whatever rags the quartermaster doled out. He received two meals a day—horrible stuff—but at least it kept him alive. And he had to walk everywhere, wearing shoes that were both too small and falling apart. Every night before going to sleep, he closed his eyes, hoping that when he woke up he'd be back in the count's camp, with everything the same as before.

He consoled himself with the belief that Skandar might still be somewhere in this camp, and kept an eye out for him. As soon as he found him, he'd make a plan to grab him and take him back to Galladium. But weeks went by, and he didn't see him. In this vast camp, Anton never so much as glimpsed the general or any of her staff. He rarely even saw cavalry of any kind.

The only good in all of this was that he was now a real soldier, a professional who would be paid in real coin as soon as his regimental commander, Count Michalek, came into funds. Anton had no idea when that would be, and no one else seemed to know either.

They marched south slowly through Brandana, near as Anton could tell. But since Anton no longer spent time with the officers who always talked about where to go next and what to do there, he seldom knew exactly where they were.

On the days they didn't march, Anton drilled with all of the other pikemen. It wasn't so much hard as boring, and his pike wasn't heavy, but on the second morning after his first day of drilling, Anton could hardly move, his muscles ached so.

"Bet you weren't expecting that, were you, boy?" his tentmate Stasny asked, grinning. "Harder than it looks."

Anton had made the mistake of saying how easy this was compared to firing a pistol from a galloping horse.

Anton shrugged, even though his shoulders screamed in pain. "I'll get used to it."

"Oh, you will. Though you'll wish you hadn't been born for the next few days." Stasny was all right, as infantrymen went. Anton reckoned he might be about twenty, and had been in the army a good five years, since the beginning of the war. Tall and skinny, like Anton, he never let anyone else make fun of him for that.

The pain was bad for a few days, though Anton welcomed it, since it distracted him from even worse feelings. But once it went away, the days stretched ahead, long and repetitive, while he thought of nothing but getting back on a horse.

He'd been very lucky to become a cavalry page. You could barely live on a regular soldier's pay, let alone come up with the funds to buy a horse, its trappings and all the equipment a cavalry trooper needed. Since he hadn't been paid and had no idea when he would be, Anton reckoned he'd wait for the next city they plundered.

Stasny dashed that hope. "We in the pike seldom get plunder," he groused when Anton asked him about it. "We're always the last to get in, since we have to deal with our weapons before we can enter a city."

"Can't you throw the pike down when the battle is over?"

"Only if you want to get yourself killed. Throwing down your weapon before being ordered is called desertion, and sergeant's allowed to shoot you on the spot if he so chooses. Besides, you put down your pike, you're unarmed."

"That doesn't seem fair." Anton said, wondering if he needed to save up for a pistol long before he considered a horse. Right now he didn't even have a dagger. "How's a fellow supposed to get ahead?"

"Luck and time. Some of Mattila's best officers have come up from the pike ranks, but it takes years of distinguishing yourself in victorious units. If you're smart and lucky, you ought to have a chance."

"I'm smart," Anton said. "And lucky, too. Or at least I was lucky until this happened. I'll be lucky again. But I don't have time to wait around for it."

"The main thing is to survive. It seems easy right now and you're bored, but just wait until your first battle."

"I've been in lots of battles," Anton said.

"Maybe so." Anton liked it that Stasny never questioned Anton's stories, like the other fellows did. No one else believed he'd been Count Orland's page or done anything spectacular, although Anton didn't mention Prince Kendryk's rescue to anyone here. "But it's different when you're down in the ranks." Stasny went on. "When you're standing shoulder-to-shoulder, and can't take a step unless the fellow in front of you does. And that goes for when cavalry is trying to ride over you, or the big guns are tearing your comrades to bits beside you. That's the hard part."

"I know something about that," Anton said, remembering what had happened to the count. Nothing could be worse than that.

BRAEDEN

Braeden woke up, feeling like he had a mouth full of cotton. His head hurt, and his whole right arm was on fire. He opened his eyes to canvas overhead. So he was inside a tent. He wondered if he'd been captured, and cautiously poked at his shoulder with his left hand. The slightest touch hurt, but his hand landed on a bandage, so the wound had been dressed. That was a good sign, unless they were keeping him alive long enough to face the executioner.

He was terribly thirsty, and propped himself up on his good elbow. A pewter pitcher stood on a box next to the cot he lay on, but he had no way to reach it.

"You're awake," a voice said from across the tent.

"Karil?" Braeden tried to sit up, and fell back. He hadn't yet worked out how to manage with just the one arm. "You're all right?"

"Well enough, considering." Karil sounded downright cheerful.

"But you were hurt." He remembered Karil on the ground, blood pooling around him.

"Flesh wound." He heard rustling and thumping, then Karil flopped onto the edge of Braeden's cot. "Got a pistol ball in the thigh. Plenty of blood, and it hurt worse than anything, but didn't hit anything important."

"Thank the gods," Braeden said. "I didn't mind going down like that myself, but it didn't seem right to take you with me."

"I'm hard to kill," Karil said, his voice dropping, becoming stern and manly. "But so are you, fortunately, though your wound is pretty bad."

"Where are we?"

"Trystan Martinek's camp, just inside Terragand."

"How did that happen?" Braeden was both relieved and amazed at surviving such a hopeless situation.

"The duke will want to tell you the whole story, but first I need to tell the doctor you're awake."

"All right," Braeden said weakly. "Might I have some water first?" He'd never had a wound this severe, and hated this helplessness.

Karil poured water from the pitcher into a tin cup, and helped Braeden drink it. That done, he made for the tent door, with a pronounced limp that didn't slow him down much. Braeden was grateful for that at least.

A little later, someone else entered. The face of a young man, long and thin, topped with a mop of dark hair, hovered over him. "I'm Doctor Sarborg," he said in such a mournful tone that Braeden worried he was about to tell him he was close to death. "I'm glad you're awake since I was beginning to wonder ..." He trailed off, peering at Braeden's shoulder, sniffed, and pulled a face. "Smells all right, I suppose."

"Will I get back the use of my arm?" Braeden asked, though he feared the answer. He wouldn't be much use as a fighter without a strong right arm.

"Might be." Doctor Sarborg still sounded mournful. "We must wait and see, while you follow my instructions precisely. At least it doesn't appear to be festering, which is a start."

If this was how the doctor delivered good news, Braeden didn't want to think how he sounded when he told a patient he needed to saw off a limb.

Fortunately, Karil returned before the doctor could depress Braeden any further. "Duke Trystan is on his way," he said. "He's very anxious to speak with you."

"Can you help me sit?" Braeden didn't want to converse on his back.

"I don't know ..." Doctor Sarborg began.

"Help me sit," Braeden barked in his best officering tone, and Karil hurried to his side.

Karil pulled on his good arm, while the doctor made clucking noises and arranged pillows to prop him up. "I won't be held responsible if it starts bleeding again."

"It's fine," Braeden said, doing his best to sound robust, and in the next instant swallowing down a wave of nausea. Sweat sprang out all over his face and he leaned back, breathing hard.

"It's too much," the doctor said. "You must go slower."

"You fuss like my old nurse, Sarborg," came a voice from the tent opening.

"Your Grace." The doctor stiffened as if to attention, and bent into an even stiffer bow.

Braeden almost laughed, but that hurt, so he stopped with a somewhat strangled sound.

A young man stood at the foot of his cot. He didn't look much older than Karil, or much taller. Dark red hair fell to his shoulders and piercing yellow-gray eyes regarded Braeden intently.

"Your Grace," Braeden said, realizing this youngster must be Trystan Martinek, Duke of Podoska.

"Glad you made it, Terris," Martinek said, taking a seat in a camp chair the doctor brought up. "We had trouble finding you until all hell broke loose near the ferry. Then you were so well-hidden in the woods, we almost didn't get to you in time."

"How did you know to look for me?"

"It was the strangest thing." Martinek bent forward and regarded Braeden with a piercing gaze. "A slip of a girl, riding as though she had demons on her back, came flying into our camp, practically bowling over the pickets. An ensign in Mattila's cavalry, bearing a white flag."

Braeden's mouth dried up again. "Dark hair, dark eyes?"

Martinek grinned. "Yes, and rather pretty, if you like 'em skinny and fierce; which I do."

"Trisa Torresia," Braeden said. "The Sanova Hussars. I can't believe—" He fell back against the pillows, nausea rising again.

"Old friends?" Martinek grinned again.

Braeden found that smile unsettling, though he couldn't say why. "She was my page. I'll strangle Dura next time I see her. She should never have risked it."

"Good thing she did, or both you and young Andarosz would be dead. She said you and the boy would try to cross the river ahead of pursuers, and that you'd be looking for us. She told me you'd rescued Kendryk, so I wanted to help you. We waited for you at the bridge, but once Mattila's forces crossed it, we thought you might try the Erzenbach ferry. We took a long time getting there, with imperial troops all over the road. By the time we reached you, the Oricians were pressing you hard."

That was one way of putting it. Braeden felt even weaker than before. "Thank you," he said. "Once I've recovered, I'll try to help you in any way I can. I suppose you're aware that the empress has a price on my head?"

Martinek nodded. "I don't want her money. I want the satisfaction of letting her know that you're alive and well, and aiding her enemies."

"That sounds satisfying to me, too," Braeden said.

ELEKTRA

Elektra loved being back with the general. Even though she hadn't caught Braeden and Karil, Mattila still treated her like a hero.

"It's not your fault," Mattila said to Elektra, after she received the news that Trystan Martinek had snatched the fugitives out from under an attack by a fierce Orician unit. "I suspect Captain Dura tipped off both Terris and Martinek, though I can't prove anything. I'm sure we'll get another chance."

Elektra found she didn't mind too much that her captors had escaped. All that mattered was that she had her old life back, and didn't have to deal with either one of them anymore. Once it became certain they'd escaped, Elektra found the nearest League priestess. She wished for her own priestess, but Luca was far away, and Elektra needed to speak with someone now.

"Might I see you alone, Mother?" Elektra asked, after she'd tracked Mother Dava down to a half-ruined temple in the nearest village. League clerics occupied all of the Brandana temples while they returned their congregations to the true faith.

"Certainly, Your Grace." The priestess had a calm, capable air about her that Elektra knew characterized those with League training. They were nearly impossible to upset, and even harder to argue with. "We'll speak in my quarters straight away." She beckoned over a young priest to finish the lesson she was giving to a group of about twenty sullen-looking peasant women. Perhaps conversion wasn't going as easily as expected, and they preferred being heretics, though Elektra couldn't imagine why.

She escaped their hostile glowers to a drafty study behind the main altar. Mother Dava poured tea from a pot hanging over a small fire in the hearth, and settled back into a camp chair. Elektra sat across from her in an identical one.

"What is it, my child?" she asked. "I can see something troubles you."

"I'm afraid I've done an awful thing." Elektra took a deep breath, surprised at how hard it was to get the words out. "I swore a vow on Holy Vica, and broke it. Even worse, I never intended to keep the vow while I made it."

Mother Dava frowned, but appeared curious rather than angry. "I assume you had a good reason."

"I did," Elektra said eagerly. "I was in a desperate situation with a man who wanted to kill me. My only hope of escape was to swear on an icon of Vica that I would help with his plan."

"Did his plan oppose the will of the Goddess?"

"I believe it did." It didn't seem wise to mention she really wanted her mother dead, but didn't need help from rebels and heretics to do that.

"Then you have nothing to worry about." Dava smiled at Elektra. "But to be safe, after the congregation has gone, pray for an hour before Vica's icon, begging her forgiveness, then make an offering. I'll leave the amount to your discretion."

"I'm happy to do all of that." Elektra's relief was even more acute than when she first realized she'd escaped Braeden's clutches. She feared for the state of her soul, and wanted to curse him for putting it in such jeopardy. She had no money, but hoped to borrow a substantial amount from the general. Perhaps she could give enough to buy a new icon from one of the great Cesiano religious artists. That would be something marvelous for a tiny Brandana temple.

Mother Dava kept smiling. "You have nothing to fear. Vica is loving, forgiving, and wise. She understands you did what was necessary to survive, so you can carry on her work."

"I sometimes felt like she was guiding me," Elektra whispered. "Not all the time. But when I was in the greatest danger, I swear I felt her presence." Mother Dava seemed kind, but Elektra worried at being found presumptuous. Why would Vica bless an ignorant girl of sixteen with no special gifts when there were so many learned and devout clerics constantly praying for such blessings?

"Of course you did. My child, that is why we pray, and why we seek to know the will of the Goddess. In the moments you need her most, she will be there to guide and protect you. No matter the challenges and dangers you face, never forget that she helped you once and she will do so again, as often as you need her."

Elektra nodded, tears starting to her eyes. She tried to blink them back, but suddenly all the danger and deprivation of the past months threatened to overwhelm her. Escaping death so narrowly seemed like a miracle.

Mother Dava was at her side in an instant, handing her a soft linen handkerchief. "Cry as much as you wish, my child. You have been strong for a long time and now you are amongst friends, in the shelter of the Goddess's arms."

Elektra cried and cried, and when she was done, was renewed altogether. If she was strong enough to take on a hardened killer like Braeden Terris and survive, and wily enough to earn the respect of General Mattila, the empress wouldn't be able to stand against her either, when the time came.

GWYNNETH

The summons came from Natalya at midday. "I wonder what's happened?" Kendryk asked Gwynneth as they hurried down the street to Natalya's palace. It was always faster to walk than calling for a carriage, or saddling a horse. "Surely Lennart hasn't landed in Kronland yet?"

"I hope he has," Gwynneth said, praying he had. "Perhaps he went ahead before the entire subsidy arrived."

Natalya met them at the door of her library, her face grave. "Have a seat," she said. "You'll want a drink," she added, and a novice brought cut glass tumblers of brandy to each of them before leaving the room.

"Oh dear," Gwynneth said, before gulping down the drink. Perhaps something had happened to Arryk, or to Aksel. He was the empress's hostage. What if Teodora killed him in retaliation for Kendryk's escape? Her brandy down, she choked out, "My brothers?"

"No, no," Natalya said. "The last I heard, Arryk is restoring his government and acting peculiar, but we can speak of that another time. Aksel has safely arrived in Atlona. Livilla wrote, and said he's set up a laboratory in her palace. He'll be allowed to write to you soon, I'm sure."

"Thank the gods." Gwynneth sank back into the chair's soft cushions, and put her empty glass on a tiny table next to it.

"What is it then, Natalya?" Kendryk asked.

Gwynneth realized he hadn't touched his drink.

"Arian Orland is dead."

"What?" Gwynneth and Kendryk chorused.

"How?" Kendryk added.

"Ambushed by Mattila in Brandana," Natalya said. "She wiped out his entire force, with only a few taken prisoner."

"Wouldn't Mattila want Arian as a prisoner?" Kendryk's voice was soft.

"Perhaps. Though she never got the chance. A cannon ball took him, and that was it. Not even a corpse to return to his family."

"Oh gods," Gwynneth said faintly, not sure what to feel.

"Is it certain then?" Kendryk seemed to be bearing up well. "If there's no body, perhaps he got away. It's happened before."

"It's certain. Several eyewitnesses reported it. I am sorry; I never had much use for him, but I know you were friends."

"In a manner of speaking," Kendryk said.

Gwynneth knew she no longer cared for him, but was sad all the same. And then something occurred to her. "Have you heard anything about his page? Of Anton?" Maryna and Devyn would be terribly upset at the news that harm had come to their friend.

Natalya shook her head. "No. It's likely he was killed as well, but I have no reports either way. Perhaps he got away somehow, but it's best not to cling to false hope."

Gwynneth turned to Kendryk. "What will we tell the children? They were so fond of Anton."

"So was I," Kendryk said heavily. "Let's say nothing for now. Perhaps he'll turn up, and they will have grieved needlessly."

"That's wise," Natalya said. "Before Orland left, I told Anton he was always welcome here. If he escaped, perhaps he can find his way back."

"Gods, I hope so," Gwynneth said.

Kendryk took her hand and squeezed it. "We'll go straight to the chapel and pray to Ercos for his protection."

"That's a good idea," Natalya said. "It's all we can do right now."

TEODORA

"The Orlands, father and son, are finished," Teodora said to Solteszy as they sat in her study early one morning. She had just received the latest dispatches. They'd already heard that Mattila had chased down and defeated Arian Orland. "Now it's certain Arian is dead. Numerous witnesses saw him blown to bits. And now even more good news." She handed the message she had just opened to Solteszy. "Ensden has taken Kaltental from Duke Aidan Orland and chased him off into the countryside. If Lennart thinks to invade, he'll have trouble gaining a foothold without Kaltental." Teodora felt positively gleeful. So many of her opponents were now dead or utterly defeated.

Good news followed on good. Next came a letter from Elektra, saying she was safe, and telling of an incredible adventure. She had been captured by the traitor Braeden Terris, but escaped his clutches and made her way through the wilderness alone until she found Mattila. Teodora was astonished at her daughter's resourcefulness, and decided she might be of some use after all. So she immediately sent a contingent of imperial guards bearing a letter, ordering the archduchess to return to Atlona immediately. With any luck, she'd be on her way soon.

Teodora pondered. Elektra was nearing her majority and it was customary for the heir to be given an important position in the capital. Teodora squirmed in her chair. Her own similar experience had made her realize she could do the job much better than her decrepit old uncle. And ultimately, that realization had led to his death. The last thing she needed was Elektra getting the same ideas. She needed to find some role for her daughter, one that would make her feel important without being a threat.

"What do you think about a marriage with Norovaea?" she asked.

Solteszy looked up, mildly alarmed. "Surely, you're not thinking about breaking the Archduchess Zofya's engagement?"

"Not at all. But Elektra is available and old enough to marry." Livilla had told her about the attempted match with Arryk, and Teodora was disappointed that hadn't worked out. True, Arryk had been upset about Larisa Karsten, but surely he could see the value in a match with the future Olvisyan empress? "And conveniently, Aksel Roussay is here. I've only spoken with him briefly, but he seems reasonable and he's been cooperative enough."

Aksel had written his brother a plaintive letter, and Arryk's response had been ... interesting. Judging by his raving, incoherent tone, it was only a matter of time before he lost his mind altogether, and hopefully his throne along with it. Teodora wondered if she could groom Aksel to be ready to take his place when the time came. Perhaps he'd be happy to marry Elektra—dull as she was—if it meant gaining a kingdom.

But he wouldn't make much of a suitor shut up in the Arnfels. Teodora stood. "I'll be back in a few hours." She called for a carriage and went straight to the fortress. When she saw Aksel this time, in the same little room, he looked a bit worse for the wear.

"You look like you need a change of scene." Teodora smiled.

"Very much." Aksel didn't make an attempt to smile back.

"This is what I propose," Teodora said. "I will have you moved into the Palais Arden. There's plenty of room in the family wing with both girls gone, and I'll see you get a laboratory as well."

Aksel's eyebrows shot up. "You want me to live with you?" He didn't sound excited at the prospect.

"In a manner of speaking. The palace is large, so I doubt we'll see much of each other."

"All right," Aksel said slowly. "What do you want from me in return?"

"Nothing right now." Teodora didn't want to bring up marriage until she had everything else organized. "Your brother has indicated the money is on its way, so as an act of good faith, I thought it would be nice to get you out of here."

"It would be nice." Aksel finally smiled. "Very nice. When can I go?"

"Today," Teodora said. "I'll have rooms prepared for you."

LENNART

The first installment of money arrived from Zeelund, and Lennart set to planning his invasion in earnest. The noble council was easy enough to bring into line, once he showed them the guarantees. He'd also been able to raise a fair amount of enthusiasm across the countryside.

Lennart had laid the groundwork long ago, by making sure every temple received detailed accounts of the atrocities committed by Teodora Inferrara and Brynhild Mattila in the name of the old faith. Special services were held on the anniversary of the fall of Kersenstadt to remember the thousands of innocent believers slaughtered there. So when it came time to call up the provincial militias, everyone of fighting age signed up eagerly. In some areas, recruiters turned away dozens, because a portion of the young and able-bodied needed to stay behind to work the land.

Priests and priestesses in the Estenor temples had preached for months now that Lennart was the long-awaited ruler, chosen by the gods to vanquish the forces of darkness. While Lennart was aware of the confusion around the ruler mentioned in the prophecy, he thought he might be the one. Not that he wanted to place himself above the likes of someone as good and devout as Prince Kendryk, but Lennart realized he fit the prophecy closely enough, with a much better chance of victory than Kendryk ever had. As soon as he'd read the words of Edric Maximus, he realized the gods had chosen him for something special. He intended to not disappoint them.

And the one problem holding him back was now solved as well. Just before the longest night, Raysa came to him mid-morning, in his study, something she never did. She'd had a visit from her doctor, and the look on her face told him all he needed to know. "Meldahl, give us a moment?"

His adviser left the room soundlessly and at speed. The moment the door fell shut behind him, Lennart gathered his wife into his arms. "So it's certain then?"

She'd buried her face in his chest and when she looked up, tears streaked her cheeks, though she glowed with happiness. "Yes, the doctor said the little one will be here before the leaves fall again."

"Thank the gods," he murmured, pulling her close again and stroking her hair. "I'm so proud of you, sweetheart. I knew you could do it."

"It wasn't me, or even us," she said softly. "It was the will of the gods. They are blessing your actions. They want you to go to Kronland."

He sat down in Meldahl's chair and pulled her onto his knee. "That's what I believe too." In the past months, Raysa had read the Holy Scrolls, and while she wasn't completely convinced of the Quadrene doctrines, she at least understood why Lennart believed. He hoped to bring her all the way before long. "And the timing couldn't be better," he said, after they'd grinned at each other for a moment. "I must be in Kronland by spring, and now I can make plans for a regency."

She frowned. "I'm not ready to be regent. And besides, I still want to go to Kronland with you."

"I'm sorry love, it's out of the question now. Once you've had the baby and the two of you are well, you can both come see me. But first I must make some arrangements. The baby will be my heir, but you and Meldahl will rule jointly until it's seventeen, should anything happen to me."

"I hope nothing does," she whispered. "I couldn't bear it."

"I doubt it will. Like I said, I'm lucky, and now I'm certain the gods are looking after me and want me to succeed. While I'm away you won't have to worry about anything. Meldahl will be in charge of day-to-day affairs, and I'll manage the rest with letters and fast couriers. If you feel up to it, you can sit in on council session so you learn what goes on there. How does that sound?"

"Intimidating. But I want to learn so I can help while you're away."

"That's all I need." He kissed her, then said, "We'll announce it at the feast for the Coming of Light two days from now. Sounds right, doesn't it?"

"It's perfect," she smiled again, then kissed him herself, quite a bit longer this time.

BRAEDEN

Feeling so weak was annoying. Braeden had taken a pistol ball through his right shoulder, and though the ball had been removed while he was unconscious, the flesh took far too long knitting itself back together again.

"You move too much, sir," Doctor Sarborg said, looking sad. "It will never heal if you keep moving."

"Never?" Braeden asked in exasperation. He was aware that the doctor was prone to exaggeration, especially of the negative, but he was sick of it.

"Well, not never, perhaps." The doctor wrung his pale hands. "But it might take a long time. And I'm sure you're eager to get back to ... well, whatever it is you do."

"Hmph," Braeden said, and flung himself back against the pillows, tired of staying still. He walked a little every day, though not for long, and the doctor complained when he did. He was also bored. Karil had healed far more quickly, and was already drilling with Martinek's troops. Braeden was eager to get back into the game himself.

"How are you today?" Trystan Martinek asked as he came inside the tent. He stopped by nearly every day, though Braeden wasn't sure why, since he improved so slowly.

"Same as before." Braeden grimaced. "Worse, if you ask the doctor."

Trystan shook his head as he took a seat at Braeden's bedside. "I hoped you'd learned by now not to ask Sarborg anything. You'll never get an answer you like."

The doctor huffed indignantly and left the tent.

Trystan's face clouded over. "I'm afraid I have bad news," he said. "Mattila caught Arian Orland trying to cross the Lera, cut him off, destroyed his force, and killed him."

Braeden felt like he'd been doused in cold water.

"Are you all right, man?" Trystan asked.

Braeden swallowed hard. "Orland dead, are you certain?" he choked out.

"I'm afraid so." Trystan's face was grave. "I'm sorry; I'm sure the two of you were friends." Braeden had told him how they'd planned Prince Kendryk's rescue.

"Of a sort," Braeden said. He didn't want to think of the rest, had to force the words out. "But what's worse, my stepson was Orland's page. I don't suppose there's been any word of an Anton Kronek?"

"That's terrible luck," Trystan said. "I can make inquiries, but from what I've heard, no one survived. There might have been a few prisoners we don't know about, and it's possible stragglers will make their way to us. Don't give up hope just yet."

"The boy always had the devil's own luck," Braeden said, his mouth dry. He fumbled for a cup at the bedside, and Trystan poured more water into it and handed it to him. Braeden took a few sips then said, "But Orland had that same luck. If his ran out—" he couldn't say any more and laid back again, exhausted, and with that same dull heaviness he'd felt after Kersenstadt settling over him. He'd failed Janna and his own children; now he'd failed her son too.

Trystan's normally hard eyes were sympathetic. "We'll keep looking for him, in case he got lucky. Unfortunately there's more bad news, though I hope it's not as personal to you. I've also received word that Ensden attacked Kaltental. He caught Orland the elder unawares, and took the city by storm. Evard Bernotas now holds it, while Ensden mops up the rest of Terragand."

Braeden shook his head. "No word from Lennart yet?"

"None." Trystan looked grim.

"What about Faris?"

"He'll be lucky to hold Birkenfels through the winter. I reckon the best I can do is try to keep Ensden off him."

"Can you?" Braeden asked. "Can we?" He wanted nothing more right now than to get out of bed and go fight Ensden. "I know how to fight him. I've fought at his side often enough."

"I thought you had," Trystan said. "And I'll need your help. But you'll stay in an advisory capacity until you've recovered. And that might take longer than we'd hoped because we need to move out. I want to go today."

"I'm ready," Braeden said, though he didn't know if it was true.

ELEKTRA

Now that Elektra wasn't so frightened of Mattila anymore, she felt more comfortable questioning the general's strange behavior. "I mean no disrespect of course," she said, noticing Mattila's mouth quirk upward. Secretly, she wondered if the general still despised her as much as she had seemed to before her abductions. But aside from a few small gestures, she treated Elektra far better than anyone on her staff.

She plunged ahead. "I'm just curious, since I've read the empress's orders. Why are you not following them? Brandana is subdued, and only Terragand and Podoska oppose you. Why don't you take them on while you are so strong?"

"That's a good question, Your Grace." Mattila waved at her clerk and he scurried out of the room, the door falling shut behind him. Now the weather had turned colder, Mattila had moved her headquarters to a comfortable manor house near Lerania. Elektra spent most days with her in the library, at her own desk, opening correspondence and answering less important letters. At first, she wanted to object to being forced into a secretary's position, but she held her tongue, and soon discovered that she was privy to all of the information that reached the general, officially and otherwise. Tedious as the work sometimes was, she liked knowing what was going on.

Mattila laid her quill down and turned to face Elektra. "You may have noticed by now that your mother and I are engaged in a power struggle."

Elektra nodded. That had always been obvious to her.

"If I subdue Terragand now, and hand Kronland to your mother on a silver platter, she will order me to retire to Moralta. I am not ready to retire." She regarded Elektra with cold gray eyes.

"But isn't Count Ensden conquering Terragand for her?"

Mattila snorted. "He's taken Kaltental, but doesn't have the resources to hold the rest of the kingdom. He'll crumble under any attack by a larger force."

"A larger force like King Lennart's?" Elektra had read intelligence dispatches indicating that the Estenorian king was planning an invasion.

"Precisely. I expect him to make short work of Ensden. Then your mother will need me a bit longer, won't she?"

"I suppose so. Aren't you the least bit worried about King Lennart?"

Mattila shrugged. "Not that puppy. I hear he's smart and eager, but I've met and defeated far greater generals in my time. Lennart is too sure of himself, and needs to be taken down a notch. And for all his reputation, he didn't subdue Sanova, did he?"

"No, I suppose he didn't. So you'll just sit here until my mother begs for help?"

"Perhaps. I haven't yet decided. I'll consolidate my hold on Brandana since I intend to keep it in any event. I'm tired of being sidelined to Moralta whenever there isn't enough work to keep me busy. Your mother can hardly ignore me if I rule Brandana."

"She can't, though she'll fly into the most awful rage." Elektra couldn't suppress a giggle. "She's already angry because you haven't sent me back to Atlona."

"You're free to go anytime," Mattila said blandly.

Elektra was sure this wasn't true, but she pretended it was. Besides, she had no great wish to return to Atlona right now. Since her relationship with the general was more pleasant, it seemed wiser to stay here and learn what she could. She missed Mother Luca, and sometimes remembered Aksel Roussay with a twinge, but they would still be there whenever she returned.

She smiled at Mattila. "I'm enjoying myself. Working with you is far more interesting than temple school."

"Yes, it's time you learned more practical matters. I've told your mother I won't risk sending you across Kronland again unless I can escort you personally. By now, she ought to understand the dangers."

"She doesn't care about the risks," Elektra burst out, surprised at the bitterness in her voice. "She doesn't care what happens to me in the least."

"She'd better care. You're her heir and shaping up to be a rather impressive one."

"It's kind of you to say so, but I doubt she agrees."

Mattila made an impatient noise. "She doesn't agree because she hasn't seen you in several years. When you left Atlona you were only a child, and understood nothing of military campaigns. Now you've been in battle, and you've seen what it's like to run an army of this size." She paused and regarded

Elektra critically. "In fact, it's time you started your military service. You're a little young, but more experienced than your mother was at your age. And you're just as able."

"You think so?" Elektra had been terrified of actual military service, but it had always been inevitable. And now she could take care of herself, it didn't seem as frightening.

"I'm sure of it. How would you like to command your own infantry unit? You can start small, and work your way up. It will do you good to spend time with common soldiers."

Elektra didn't see how, but decided she wouldn't stay long in such a lowly position. She lifted her chin. "All right," she said. "I'm ready."

TEODORA

For this important moment, Teodora called her entire council together. "I realize not all of you know of Brynhild Mattila's misdeeds, but now I have proof, we can discuss them openly. Count?" She nodded at Solteszy, who cleared his throat and began reading from a long sheet of paper.

He started with a list of smaller infractions, beginning with Mattila's refusal to leave Norovaea when ordered. It was a galling reminder of the many instances in which she'd openly defied her ruler, but Teodora knew the idiots seated around this table would demand a legal case before backing her. They murmured unhappily when confronted with Mattila's refusal to invade Terragand, but murmurs turned to shouts of outrage when she unveiled Mattila's real treachery.

"A Kronland ruler is ordained by both the Empire and the Faith," an old duke blustered. "She cannot simply declare herself as one."

"No, she cannot." Teodora had to stop herself from smiling too broadly. Keeping her council in the dark for so long had been wise. Rather than receiving the hints and trickles of information Teodora had endured for the past months, she'd deliver all of it today in one blow. They'd have no choice but to react. "Not only does she violate our dearest laws and traditions, she is threatening the safety of my darling daughter. I've ordered the Archduchess Elektra returned to Atlona, and she has refused to deliver her." Another gasp from the group. "It's time to put a stop to this rebellious behavior."

"*Can* we stop her?" A young Olvisyan count asked rather eagerly. Teodora looked him over, remembering that this was his first council meeting upon replacing his father who'd died recently. A small, dark-haired, wiry fellow, he seemed energetic enough. If he proved himself competent, Teodora might find a use for him.

"We shall." Teodora smiled at him until he glowed under her regard. "But we must proceed with care. Mattila is rich and powerful, with a large army at her disposal. Our first step will be to remove that army from her control. We must also ensure the safety of the archduchess. I've acted already in secret, since Mattila has agents everywhere." She left it unsaid that for all she knew, a few sat on this council.

"King Arryk was kind enough to send the first installment of reparations early. I will use those funds to entice Mattila's officers away from her." It wasn't necessary to mention the uncivil tone of Arryk's correspondence. As long as Teodora had his brother, he'd have to do what she wanted.

"When will you do this? How?" someone asked.

"I'm doing it already." Teodora wanted to laugh at their dumbstruck faces. "Two weeks ago, Livilla Maxima set out with a large sum of money and an even larger force guarding it. She bears my orders to Mattila, relieving her of command and releasing the archduchess into her care."

"What if Mattila refuses?" the young count asked. He looked like he was spoiling for a fight.

"I expect her to refuse." Teodora kept her tone casual. "But her consent isn't needed. She can call herself supreme general as long as she wants, but she will have no army to command. The clerics of the League of Aeternos have already been in contact with every officer under Mattila. When Livilla arrives with my order, they will submit to it publicly, in exchange for suitable compensation, which Livilla will have on hand."

"What will keep Mattila from simply taking the money from her?" The young count was being annoyingly curious, though Teodora reminded herself to be patient. His interest could be useful.

"Mattila has a lot of enemies. She's a brutal bully and most don't enjoy working for her. We are offering hard coin and an opportunity to serve under Count Ensden, who is known for being far more reasonable. Upon a word from Livilla, the bulk of Mattila's army will leave her and move into Terragand to join Ensden. It's all arranged."

"Astonishing, Your Highness," a dried-up old duchess said. "I suppose once she's without an army, it will be easy to remove Mattila from Brandana."

"In time," Teodora said. "First we must deal with the threat from Estenor. Lennart is ready to invade, and will likely do so as soon as the weather clears. I'm sure he had hoped to take advantage of Mattila's inactivity, and is expecting a small, scattered force in Terragand. He'll be in for a surprise when he finds out the hard way that Ensden has been strengthened by the bulk of Mattila's forces. Once Lennart is defeated, we'll take on Mattila and force her to leave Brandana."

Teodora sat back and enjoyed the noises of commendation coming from her council. Useless as they were—she'd had to arrange all of this without them after all—they'd provide an air of legitimacy to everything she did. Even the Kronland rulers would be impressed by this move. Any of them who hoped for Kendryk's speedy reinstatement would be disappointed.

She rose. "We'll reconvene as soon as I receive word from Livilla that Mattila is removed from command, and the archduchess is safe. In the meantime, we prepare for war against Lennart. The sooner we send him back to his icy wasteland of a country, the better."

ANTON

After a few months with Mattila's army, Anton realized he needed to accept that the count and Cid were gone. He had to make plans for life on his own. What he couldn't accept was Skandar belonging to someone else. He'd finally become brave enough to sneak around at night, and located the general's horses. Sure enough, Skandar stayed in a stable near her headquarters. Anton wasn't able to get close, because there were always people around him, but he swore he heard Skandar nicker. He must have sensed his real owner was nearby.

Anton had to content himself with knowing that Skandar was being well cared for, since he didn't know how to break him out. The whole area around General Mattila swarmed with other generals, even more officers, and all of their guards. And Anton looked so ragged, no one would even mistake him for a servant.

He hated not having any money; not even enough to buy a decent doublet or cloak. Surprisingly, he didn't freeze to death, since the wool of his only doublet was so thin. He couldn't afford liquor, and made do with the weak ale served out with regular rations.

Seeing Skandar and knowing he was all right made him understand how hard it would be to get his old life back. Maybe he wouldn't get it back at all.

"You shouldn't be sad on such a beautiful day." A clear voice rang out beside him.

Anton skidded to a stop. He'd been wandering around camp, feeling sorry for himself. "It's not a beautiful day," he said, looking up at the lowering clouds, then at the girl who'd spoken.

She grinned at him. "At least I got you to look up."

"True," Anton said, looking at her with interest. He hadn't paid much attention to girls lately, and they hadn't given him much either. This one wasn't his usual type, but she wasn't bad. Short and round, light brown curls, a snub nose with a dusting of freckles across it, she looked like a maid in the

Maxima's palace. A broad smile revealed a gap between her top front teeth, and her hazel eyes were merry. He almost smiled back.

"I'm Susanna," she said, coming to a halt. Anton saw she'd been dragging some kind of cart. "Aren't you with the Moraltan pike?"

"I am," Anton said, though he didn't volunteer anything further. There was no point in making friends if he was going to leave again soon.

But Susanna wasn't going anywhere. "Weren't you one of those taken prisoner after Count Orland's defeat?"

"Yes." Anton clenched his teeth.

She laughed, something she looked like she did often. "I'm sorry. I'm sure you don't want to talk about that. How do you like serving in the pike?"

"I hate it," Anton burst out. They had stopped in the middle of camp, and she put down her little barrow, stretching her arms. "What's that?" he asked, pointing at the barrow.

"My goods." She pulled a canvas back to show piles of everything from clothes and shoes, buttons and spools of thread, to bottles of liquor, and even a few cheeses. "I peddle these all over camp."

So she was just trying to sell him something. No wonder she was so friendly. Anton didn't even bother looking further. "Sorry," he said. "Don't have any money."

"I offer credit," she said, still smiling. "To friends."

"I'm not your friend." Anton hoped he didn't sound too rude.

She sucked in her lower lip. It showed the gap in her top teeth to advantage, or disadvantage, depending on how you felt about gaps.

"We can be friends, if you want." She smiled at him in a way he hadn't been smiled at in a long time. Anton decided he liked the gap.

He didn't know what she saw in him, looking like a dirty scarecrow. "Hey, Susanna," he said. "You're really nice. But it's better for me if I don't have friends. I'm leaving soon."

"Really? Where? On a secret mission for the general?" He saw from the spark in her eye she was teasing him.

"Hardly." He had to smile just a little. "But I have something important to do, and have to go as soon as I can."

Her eyes grew huge. "But you can't! That's desertion, and you'll be killed when they catch you. You shouldn't even joke about something like that. They caught a fellow a few weeks ago and you should have seen what they did to him."

Anton *had* seen. They flogged the man until he was a bloody mess, then hanged him until he strangled to death slowly. "I won't get caught," Anton said, though he wasn't about to breathe a word about Skandar. He had decided he wouldn't be taken alive.

"You will," she said frowning. "Please promise me right now you won't try it. You must find another way to get an official discharge."

"I can't." Anton had already asked about that, and it involved buying out his five-year contract, which he had entered when the girl scribbled his name onto a piece of paper. He'd also have to come up with bribes for the sergeant, and the officers all the way up to Count Michalek to get them to consider it. Far easier to steal Skandar back.

"Well then, you'll have to make the best of it, won't you? Listen, I understand this life isn't much fun, especially when you're used to better, which I can tell you are."

Anton didn't know how she could tell, but it was probably part of her sales speech. He shook his head, but she went on.

"I can help you. Let's start by finding you some warm clothes. You can pay me back when you get money."

"That might be months. It's already been months."

"Or, you could help me."

"How?" He couldn't imagine that she needed help.

"I can make a lot more money if I visit the tents with all the dice and card games, but it's not safe for me to go alone. If you come with me, I can sell liquor to the soldiers and give them cash for whatever they'll sell me."

"You can do that?" Anton had watched quite a few card games, but never took part because he had nothing to gamble.

"Sure. But when it's a lot of men they can get rowdy, and I have trouble keeping my money, not to mention my honor." There was that smile again. "I need a bodyguard."

Anton thought about it, but he didn't have to think long. "I'll need a weapon," he said.

"That's no problem." Susanna turned and rummaged in her cart, soon producing a dagger with a jeweled hilt and finely etched blade.

"That's pretty," Anton said. "But I'll look ridiculous holding it." It went without saying that such a weapon belonged on a fine leather belt around a velvet doublet, lace cascading nearby.

"True," she said. "But I can help you with that. Give me a few hours and I'll get some nice clothes for you. Don't worry about paying for them, or credit or anything. Consider it an advance on what I'll pay you for helping me out."

"What are you paying me?" Anton realized he hadn't asked about that part of it.

"How about half of all the coin I take in at the gambling parties?"

"That seems like a lot. Aren't you doing all the work?" Anton didn't want to take advantage of her kindness.

"Mostly. But I'll keep all the goods I get. Those can be worth quite a bit. We'll keep the coin we take in separate from what I pay out. I'm good at keeping a ledger, if you want to check it."

"Er," Anton said. He was about to add that he trusted her, then realized that would be foolish. He'd heard about these girls who peddled wares of all kinds in camp, and they were the opposite of trustworthy. Just because she looked and acted kind didn't mean she was. "All right," he said. "We'll go over accounts after every party. My father was a merchant, so I know what's what." He tried to look stern.

"Perfect." Susanna offered a small, plump hand. "Welcome to the business."

BRAEDEN

Karil dropped the wooden sword. "Are you all right?"

"Sure." Braeden forced a smile and wiped the sweat from his forehead. "Just out of practice. I ought to visit Kazmir." Best not to humiliate himself any further in front of Karil's friends.

"We're getting old," Braeden murmured against Kazmir's neck, once the two of them were alone. After he'd caught his breath, he called for a groom, so at least he wouldn't kill himself trying to saddle his own horse. Three months of inactivity had left him weaker than a baby.

By the time Braeden rode out, Trystan had joined him. "I was hoping you'd come out," he said. "It's time we moved again. We've run into a lot of Ensden's skirmishers lately, so he's probably figured out where we are. Are you well enough to ride for a day or two?"

"I believe so," Braeden said, though he wasn't sure at all. He'd barely survived the last move.

"Good. As soon as you're ready, I'd like it if you'd lead patrols. Everyone's demoralized, but having a famous Sanova Hussar at their head would lift their spirits."

"Ex-Sanova Hussar," Braeden said heavily. It had been a hard winter, and not just for Duke Trystan's harried, outnumbered troops. Under Doctor Sarborg's care, Braeden slid into despair. He'd replaced the first wave of overwhelming grief after Kersenstadt with anger, and considerable activity. But with nothing to do but lie in bed, he slid back into the numb lethargy that had plagued him in Allaux.

Karil had done his best to be encouraging, but Braeden sensed him pulling away. Trystan had made him a lieutenant of musketeers, and Karil was busy with his unit, making friends with other young officers. From his bed, Braeden could hear their shouts as they practiced and played in the courtyard below.

This was a force unlike any Braeden had ever been part of. Around a core of young Podoskan officers who'd followed Trystan from his home were the remnants of Seward Kurant's army. After fighting Daciana Tomescu for a year, few of these veterans remained.

The rest of the force was a hodge-podge of Terragand militia volunteers and imperial deserters. They numbered barely two thousand, had no money, no supplies, and little hope of victory. They survived by stealing, first from the local populace, and once all of that was gone, attacking Ensden's supply trains. This was risky; the trains were heavily guarded and every attack—even successful ones—diminished their numbers still further.

"Why don't you go home?" Braeden asked Trystan as they rode along the forest path. "You can't run from Ensden forever. It's only a matter of time before he corners you like Mattila did Arian Orland."

"He might not." Trystan seemed unbothered by the prospect of gory death, hardened perhaps after long experience with the likes of Tomescu. "Though you're welcome to leave if you're afraid."

"I'm not afraid," Braeden said. "I just don't care. Not about this war, not about your cause—whatever it is—not about anything."

"We all have those times," Trystan said, and in spite of his smooth-cheeked youth, Braeden believed him. "What choice is there but going on until someone stops us?"

"I wish you'd let the Oricians kill me," Braeden burst out.

Trystan reined in his horse, then grabbed Kazmir's bridle so he stopped as well. "I know," he said. "Karil told me what happened to your family. I understand you still feel awful, but you kept going when things were worse, didn't you?"

"I did," Braeden said. "But I don't feel anything now. I don't see the point in all of this; I couldn't even tell you what this war is about anymore. I consider Prince Kendryk a friend, but I have other, older friends and they're all on the other side. Even if we win, it means my friends will lose, maybe even die."

"If your friends are half as resourceful as you, they'll be fine," Trystan said as his horse continued down the path. "Inactivity always breeds despair. I felt it myself in those months after Arryk's defeat, stuck at Birkenfels, trying to put this force together. But you'll be happier once you're chasing Ensden's skirmishers through the woods on a crisp morning like this one. Just wait and see."

LENNART

The storm's remnants had passed the previous night, though a bank of dark clouds still hung in the east, concealing the mid-morning sun. Lennart's scientific advisers predicted at least two fine days before the next storm, more than enough to get Lennart to Helvundala, and General Kalstrom to Terragand. On the docks, Lennart gave his final orders to another general, Tora Isenberg, who would head for northwestern Terragand.

"Wait for the next storm to pass, and go as soon as you have a few clear days. You must hurry, in case Mattila gets wind of what's going on. Just hold her off until I get there," Lennart said. He would get Prince Stepan's agreement to an alliance when he arrived, and augment his own armies with several thousand Helvundala veterans. Even with all his forces gathered, Lennart knew he didn't have enough to take on Mattila and Ensden. He'd need help from the Kronland rulers, and he planned to get it.

Isenberg didn't seem worried. "I'll send you a message as soon as I land, and again once I'm in position. I'll deploy scouts right away to find out what Mattila's up to, though I doubt she can get her whole army up north before you arrive."

"No, but she can send a smaller one. Remember what happened to Arian Orland."

Isenberg's long, tanned face split into a grin. "I'm not that dumb."

Lennart shook his head. "Neither was Orland, yet Mattila herded his cuirassiers like a flock of geese to the chopping block."

"I'm not a goose either, Your Highness."

Lennart laughed and clapped her on the shoulder. "No you're not, thank the gods. Still, be careful. I'll send reinforcements as soon as I can."

"You needn't worry about me." Isenberg inclined her head. "Looks like the queen has come to see you off."

Raysa had arrived at the docks with a small escort. The wind was cold, and Lennart didn't want her getting out of the carriage, so her hurried to her. When he climbed in, only Silvya Meldahl was with her. "I'll wait outside," Silvya said, wrapping herself in a long fur cloak and going out the other door.

Raysa looked after her, frowning. "I hope she doesn't freeze out there."

"She'll be fine. It's a brisk morning, but girls from here are used to it. I won't take long." They'd already said their real goodbyes the night before, and early that morning before he left, but Lennart was pleased she'd come to see him off. He moved to the bench next to Raysa, and pulled her into his arms. "I'll be honest," he said. "When I first agreed to marry you, it never crossed my mind I'd be sorry to say good-bye to you when this day came."

She smiled up at him. "I didn't think you would be, either. And I didn't expect I'd be sad when you left." She paused and blinked back tears. "But it's better this way, isn't it? Now you have something to look forward to when you return."

"That's a great way to see it." Lennart had thought that, nice as falling in love with his wife was, it created complications. He didn't want to worry about her; didn't need the desire to return to her anywhere in his mind while he dealt with Kronland. He couldn't afford to have his thoughts pulled toward the queen's quarters in Tharvik while he negotiated with stubborn Kronland rulers and planned battles. But it had happened, and he was certain it was what the gods wanted, since they were making everything else easy for him, too.

"I'll write to you every day," Raysa said. "Though I don't expect you to reply," she added with a laugh, seeing his look of alarm. He'd be lucky to have time to write once a week.

"I'll write as often as I can." He kissed her one more time, then put his hand on her belly, just beginning to swell. "Take care of yourself and this little one, all right?"

"Of course I will. But you must take care of yourself as well. Promise?"

He sighed, then smiled. "I promise."

ANTON

"That'll be six coppers." Susanna put out her hand.

"What if I don't want to pay?" The musketeer leered at her. "What if I want extra for my money?"

Anton pushed forward, and Susanna stepped aside. "No extras. It looks like you've had too much already. You're lucky the lady is selling you this fine brandy. It's wasted on the likes of you."

"Hey." The man stuck his chest out, but he still wasn't as tall as Anton. "I ain't had enough. And you wouldn't call that little slut a lady, if you had a clue what she gets up to when your back is turned."

Anton's hand slid to the hilt of his dagger. "You can take your bottle and leave, or I'll be forced to make you apologize." He took a step forward so he stood almost, but not quite, on the fellow's foot.

"Come on, Kreuzer," a man shouted from a table behind Anton. "What's the hold-up? You're supposed to bring the next round."

Kreuzer huffed at Anton, but stepped around him, and returned to his card game.

Susanna grabbed Anton's arm. "Come on, officers are playing in the next tent. We can sell them the really good stuff."

"At terribly inflated prices," Anton said with a laugh once they left the cloying, smoke-filled air of the tent. "I know what that brandy is supposed to cost. I always got it for the count."

"They're paying for convenience," Susanna said, patting the purse at her waist. "Most don't have pages to run errands for them while they're in the middle of a high-stakes game. You did well in there. I told you it wasn't hard."

It was Anton's first night working with Susana. True to her word, she'd provided him with a slightly used suit of green velvet. It wasn't his best color, but the doublet was well-padded, especially around the shoulders, so it made him look bigger than he was. He'd also perfected a mean-looking scowl that seemed to work so far. "It wasn't hard," he said. "But what if someone wants to start a fight? What if two or more want to start a fight?"

"You can handle yourself, can't you?" Susanna looked up at him, the light from a nearby torch catching the challenging glint in her eye.

"Sure," Anton said, though he wasn't at all sure. It was one thing to be in battle, loaded down with weapons while riding behind the count, and another to exchange blows with Mattila's burly veterans. "It's mostly that we're outnumbered in there."

"We are," Susanna said. "If things get crazy, we'll have to leave in a hurry. But most just want their liquor, and to get back to their game. If there's trouble, that could bring a sergeant, or one of those Quadrene officers who don't like gambling. They don't want trouble any more than we do."

"You're the one with the experience." Anton grinned down at her. "And this beats having to sit around in the cold, listening to Stasny's stories and drinking his horrible beer."

"See the terrible life I've saved you from?" Susanna took Anton's arm after he picked up the handles of her barrow. He felt stupid pulling it in his finery, but it didn't seem right to let her do it when she was such a tiny thing. She looked up at him. "And you're quite a good-looking young man, with the right clothes."

"I know," Anton said, giving her his crooked smile.

Susanna snorted. "Remind me to never compliment you again. Once a fellow has a big head, he's impossible to be around."

"I don't have a big head." Anton made sure to show his dimples. "I can't help it if girls like me." He wondered if she spoke from experience. It was clear Susanna understood the ways of the world. He thought she might be at least sixteen, and while they'd walked through camp earlier, another girl had shouted something at her about a husband. It was probably a joke, but Anton wondered how he could find out more about her without asking directly.

"Ready?" Susanna asked. "This lot ought to be more civilized, though it doesn't always last, once they get into the drink."

"Don't worry," Anton said, lowering his voice. "I'll protect you."

"You'd better," Susanna said, giving his arm a squeeze.

They went back to her tent just before dawn. Anton was shocked at how much coin came out of the little purse when she dumped it onto her table.

"Nice," Susanna said, sliding the lamp closer. "With you standing there, they didn't try bargaining me down as much. Hand me that book over there, will you?"

Anton grabbed a small accounts book laying on a nearby chair. While Susanna tallied up the columns, muttering to herself, he looked around the tent curiously. Even in the dim light, he noticed it was clean and orderly. He looked back at Susanna, bent over the book, and was surprised at how quickly she added up the columns and how neatly she wrote. "You've been to school," he said.

She looked up at him and laid the quill down. "Yes, I have," she said. "Just because I'm a sutler doesn't make me trash."

"Hey," Anton said. "That's not at all what I meant. I'm used to most people in this camp not even knowing how to read, let alone do figures the way you can. I don't think you're trash. Not at all." He looked straight at her until he caught her eye, and held it for a moment. The thrust of her lip turned to a half-smile. "I came from somewhere better too," he said.

"I can tell," she said. "My family wasn't rich, but decent enough. It's obvious from the way you talk, the way you walk—well, everything—that you come from real money."

"Somewhat," Anton said, realizing that he really had been rich, back in Kaleva. He'd been rich most of his time with the count, too. He didn't want to think about that. "So, where is your family?" he asked.

"Dead." Susanna shoved the book at him. "Take a look at these figures, and then we'll settle up."

LENNART

It was a beautiful day for an invasion. Lennart leaned against *Drekir's* rail and enjoyed the sight of his fleet falling into line behind the flagship. After *Drekir,* the next ship sailing out of Tharvik harbor was *Fifa,* holding General Lofbrok, the commander of Lennart's troops in Helvundala. Once the Helvundala force was on its way, the ships bearing Kalstrom's Terragand army would sail west.

Tharvik dwindled into the distance, shining in the weak winter sunlight. Lennart wondered if Raysa was still watching, worried she might catch cold, then shook his head to banish thoughts of his wife. He'd left Silvya Meldahl with strict instructions as to her care, and knew Silvya would follow them, perhaps even improve upon them. She was after all, her father's daughter.

Once the city was ought of sight, Lennart turned toward the quarter-deck. The wind was no longer in his face, and the *Drekir* ran at full sail, the white canvas bellied-out and snapping with each gust. He took the steps to the upper deck two at a time. Captain Brun stood at the rail, peering south through a glass.

"See Helvundala yet, Captain?" Lennart joked.

Kelsi Brun turned to him. "Not yet." She never joked, Lennart had noticed. "But if this wind keeps up, we'll see land in about two hours. Maybe we'll reach Helvundala before nightfall." Captain Brun was new to the navy. Upon Gwynneth's recommendation, Lennart had recruited her to serve under his flagship captain. When the old fellow's heart had failed as he stood at the wheel, mid-voyage, ferrying troops from Sanova, Brun had taken charge with not even a moment's fuss. *Drekir's* other officers and sailors had been unanimous in their approval when Lennart promoted her soon after.

"That's excellent news, Captain. I'd like to have you back in Tharvik soon, so you can head the fleet taking General Isenberg to Terragand."

Brun frowned. "You don't want me to stand off Helvundala in case you need to leave in a hurry?"

Lennart laughed. "I won't leave anytime soon. I don't expect any trouble just yet."

"I hate to say it Your Highness, but it's nice to be back in action. Business is slow during peacetime, and I've missed that little bit of danger we always felt crossing back and forth from Sanova. Not that the Sanovan navy ever gave ours any real trouble." Brun gave a snort, and Lennart laughed again. She looked funny in her captain's uniform, since she insisted on wearing her old fur hat with its ear flaps. Because she was captain, no one but Lennart could order her to remove it, and he wasn't about to.

True to her word, Captain Brun sailed up within view of a flat Helvundala beach in the late afternoon. "We'll anchor here and offload you in the morning," she said. "It will be a nice, calm night and it'll be easier getting onto the beach in daylight."

At dawn, Lennart went ashore in a small boat with a few officers. All was quiet on the beach, but that didn't last. For the next few hours, the place swarmed with soldiers, pack horses and mules, while mountains of supplies grew out of range of the high tide. General Lofbrok was to organize those, and by evening had hired carts and wagons from villages in the area. He also hired as many horses and oxen as he could find to pull the artillery pieces. Lennart had insisted on using smaller pieces to move more quickly, but it still took a lot of animals to pull them all.

Once he saw that the situation on the beach was under control, he left Lofbrok in charge and headed for Prince Stepan's palace. The first order of business was to bring Helvundala into a formal alliance with Estenor. Lennart had hoped to accomplish this through correspondence, but Prince Stepan had firmly refused to commit to anything in writing. That would change now that Lennart was here in person.

The prince greeted him politely enough. "You are welcome to stay as long as you like, Your Highness." Stepan Falk was just as unpleasant in person as he came across in his letters. A tall, thin man of perhaps thirty-five years, he had a snake-like look to him, only increased by long black hair he wore slicked back, and watery blue eyes just a little too wide-set. Since his mother, the Princess Rheda was small and attractive, as well as friendly and cheerful, Lennart assumed that Stepan had inherited his looks and disposition from his late father Bronson, a cranky old fellow by all accounts.

"I don't plan to stay long," Lennart said. "My other generals are setting up in Terragand, and I'll march west with you as soon as you gather up your army."

"You want me to go west?" Stepan raised his eyebrows. "I'm afraid I don't understand. I won't take my army out of Helvundala with both Mattila and Ensden on the loose, with no one to stop them."

"*I'm* stopping them," Lennart said, reminding himself to be polite. "And you'll help me."

"Hmm," Stepan said. "We must discuss it further, I'm sure."

"We've already discussed it." Lennart reminded himself to breathe deeply.

"You're right. Though I don't recall we came to any agreement. Well, we'll talk tomorrow. I'm having a suite prepared for you, and we'll have a big dinner tonight. Naturally, all the local nobility want to meet you."

"Naturally." Lennart forced a smile. Perhaps the prince's neighbors would be less difficult. He'd get their cooperation first, and Prince Stepan's later. For now, he'd be friendly, but that would change fast if the prince didn't budge.

KENDRYK

"Lennart's on his way." Kendryk rushed to Gwynneth's side as soon as word came from Natalya. "What an awful time for me to leave." The baby was due within a few weeks.

"It's all right," Gwynneth said. "We always knew it might be a near thing. And I never have any trouble, so there's nothing for you to worry about."

"You're right," Kendryk said. The household was in a flurry of activity while he prepared to leave. "But that won't keep me from worrying."

"I know." She grabbed his hand and kissed it. "You'll give Edric my love?"

"Certainly." He still found it almost humorous that Gwynneth and the Maximus had become such good friends, though he was glad of it. "I'll find him first, and take him to Helvundala with me."

Natalya's agents in Estenor had reported that Lennart sailed for Helvundala a week before, with another, larger force headed for Terragand. "He hasn't shared his plans with me," Natalya had said, "But I'm certain they involve Kaltental. He'll want to get rid of Evard first. Best you go soon, so he can install you there when he takes it."

"I want to get rid of Evard, too," Kendryk muttered, mostly to himself, though Natalya heard, and smiled.

Official word of the invasion came just a few days later, directly from Lennart. "He's having trouble with your cousin," Natalya said. "Prince Stepan is most reluctant to lend his support."

"I don't blame him." Kendryk had only met Stepan once and hadn't been impressed, though he understood why he might not want to put his kingdom at risk.

"You must convince him all the same," Natalya said, laying the dispatch on her desk. She and Kendryk sat in the small study attached to her personal rooms. No one but the king, Kendryk and Gwynneth ever came here. "Lennart's force is too small to take on both Ensden and Mattila. He can hire mercenaries, but must go far to get them. That's why he needs support from Kronland."

"It's the least they can do to help him," Kendryk said.

"That's the other thing." Natalya clasped her hands on her desk and leaned forward. "This enterprise is risky because Lennart is not only a foreigner, but also because he's made no secret of his ambitions. Left unchecked, he'll dominate all of northern Kronland."

Kendryk's heart dropped into his stomach. "That's unacceptable."

"It is." Natalya's eyes were grave. She seemed tired and preoccupied. Kendryk hoped nothing else was wrong. "That's why your presence is so important. Lennart must be made to understand that, while we appreciate his help, we don't want him meddling in Kronland's affairs once he's vanquished Teodora. His interference is ultimately just as harmful as Teodora's, or mine," she added with a wry smile.

"But we need him right now, and desperately," Kendryk said. "I'm afraid I'm not sure what to do."

"Take as big a leadership role as you can. When he reviews troops, be at his side. When he makes decisions, give him counsel."

"Why would he listen to me?" Kendryk couldn't imagine what advice he could offer someone like Lennart.

"Because you are still senior ruler in Kronland, and the others will listen to you. Thanks to your cousin's stubbornness, Lennart is already getting the message they won't be as cooperative as he'd hoped. If you show him they'll follow you, he'll be forced to rely on you. And that means he won't be able to build unchecked political power on his own."

"I still don't understand why anyone in Kronland would follow me," Kendryk said, leaning back in his chair and staring at the ceiling. For the first time, he noticed it was covered in a most lascivious painting. He flushed, and looked back down.

Natalya noticed his blush, and smirked. "You've faced Teodora and survived; now you've returned with a powerful ally. That's impressive, and others will see it too. When you meet Edric, explain my concerns. Lennart is keen to spread the Quadrene Creed, but I hope Edric will still hesitate to lend unqualified support."

"He will. Devout as he is, he's also concerned with the sovereignty of Kronland, and of Terragand's in particular. I'm sure he'll see things our way."

"I think so too. I haven't written to him about any of this, and I ask that you don't either. I believe Lennart might well have ways of interfering with official dispatches."

Kendryk was becoming more and more worried about what he, Gwynneth, and Natalya had just unleashed. "Is he at all trustworthy?"

"In his own way. He possesses considerable integrity, but he's realistic about the quality of his friends and his enemies. I'm sure you'll like him, but never let your guard down completely."

"I'll remember that." Kendryk's mouth was dry. He was glad he'd have Edric with him when he met his new ally.

ANTON

"I wish there'd be a battle," Anton told Susanna after they'd finished work one evening. Neither of them wanted to sleep, so they shared the rest of a bottle of brandy left over from a party. "I'm sick of sitting here while the general plays games with the empress."

"You'd rather fight than help me out?" Susanna sounded like she was joking, but had a challenging tilt to her chin.

Anton grinned at her. "I like helping you out. It's fun, and nice to make money. But I'm a soldier, and fighting is better than anything." At least that had been true with the count and Skandar. He hoped it would still be true, even while fighting on the wrong side.

"I'll worry about you," Susanna said, folding her hands on the table after pushing aside her ledger.

Anton always went over it with her, and liked how straightforward and honest she was. "You will?" he asked, feeling stupid for asking when she'd already said she would be.

"I will." She looked straight at him. "I've grown fond of you, even though you're dreadfully conceited."

"I'm not conceited." Anton said indignantly. "Just confident."

"Too good for me," she said softly. She finished her cup, and poured more.

"That's not true," he said. "I wish you'd stop saying things like that. Just because I don't drool over you like some of those other fellows..." He'd noticed she had several suitors, though she never paid them any mind. Now he admitted to himself he was glad she didn't.

"No, you only drool a little." She sounded playful, but her face was serious.

"I can't help it; you're really pretty. But we have a professional relationship, don't we?" Even as the words came out, Anton realized he wouldn't mind something more, though he wasn't sure what that meant. Even though Susanna was still mostly a stranger, he liked being around her. She really was pretty, Anton thought, far more than he'd noticed at first. Her eyes snapped

124

and sparkled, her skin was smooth and creamy, with only a few cute freckles across her nose. Even though Susanna was short, she had a deliciously round figure, and showed it off with dresses cut lower than was quite decent. She'd caught Anton staring at her bosom once or twice and only said, "My eyes are up here, silly," which made him blush and stammer an apology. But she never seemed offended.

"Hm." Susanna drummed her fingers on the table. "We could be closer, if you wanted to."

"Really? I'd love that, but you never tell me anything about yourself."

"There's not much to tell."

"There doesn't need to be." He realized it bothered him that he knew so little about her. "You haven't told me how old you are, where you're from, how you came to be here. I've told you all of that about me."

"I don't know how old you are." She looked triumphant.

"I'm sixteen, like I said." Anton reckoned his height made that believable.

"I don't believe you." She leaned back in her chair, and folded her arms across her chest, pushing her breasts up, forcing Anton to look at the ceiling. "I'm almost certain you're lying about your age, though I'm not sure why."

He took a long drink, emptying his cup. The drink warmed his insides, and the knot that had stuck in his chest since his capture loosened up a little. "Pour me some more, and I'll tell you how old I really am." He slid his cup across the table, and Susanna raised an eyebrow, but poured more and slid it back. He took another long drink. "I'm almost fifteen," he said. "I started lying about my age at ten, so the count would take me into battle. Then I got into the habit."

"I was afraid of that." Susanna sighed, then poured the rest of the brandy into her cup. "What a shame; you really are too young for me."

"I'm not," Anton said a little too loudly. "You're only a few years older than me."

"I'm twenty," she said. "And I'm married."

Anton laughed. "That's funny. Where's your husband?"

"I'm not sure." She stared at the table. It seemed she wasn't joking. Anton hoped she wouldn't start crying.

"He's still alive?"

"Perhaps." She looked up, her eyes damp. "He ran off about a year ago with another woman, and I haven't heard from him since."

"Was he a soldier? Did he desert?"

"He was a soldier, but he didn't desert. He just failed to tell me that his contract was up and he was going to Cesiano. I woke up one morning, and he'd disappeared. One of his comrades told me where he went."

"That's awful," Anton said, meaning it. "How did you manage? Though you're doing well enough now."

She shrugged. "He never was much use, so I'd already started selling things. He'd always drink away his pay when he got it." She sighed heavily. "Still, I loved him, and he broke my heart."

Anton couldn't think of what to say. She looked sad, but he sensed that if he said the right thing now, she might see him in a different way. Finally he said, "I've been there."

"You've been in love?" she looked skeptical.

"Yes," Anton said. "And she left, and broke my heart, too."

"Poor little boy," Susanna said, breaking the spell.

ELEKTRA

Elektra was excited when Livilla appeared in Mattila's study, but only for a moment. The Maxima barely delivered her message before the general flew into a rage. "Who does she think she is?" Mattila shouted, overturning the table Elektra had been sitting at. Elektra jumped out of the way, but not fast enough, as a chair toppled over, smashing her little toe. She wanted to shriek out in pain, but bit her tongue until it bled, rather than draw attention to herself. She backed into a corner of the room, keeping one eye on the general, and the other on Livilla.

The Maxima stood calmly inside the door, flanked by imperial guards. Elektra saw more of them clustered outside in the corridor. She hoped they would be enough.

Mattila finally stopped trying to destroy the furniture, and stood in the center of the room, breathing hard. Her face was red, and a lock of her short gray hair fell over her forehead. Elektra had never seen her in such disarray.

Elektra turned back toward Livilla, who put out her hand. "Come my dear, it's time you returned to Atlona."

Elektra hesitated. She didn't want to stay with Mattila a moment longer, but didn't want to return to her old life either. Trapped in a temple dormitory with silly, giggling girls, going over the same dull lessons every day. She'd spent the past several months in command of an infantry regiment, and found she loved it. She loved the drills and inspections, and planning maneuvers with other officers. Their flattery aside, she suspected she was good at it.

"Come," Livilla said, her hand still extended.

Elektra glanced at Mattila; hatred burned in her eyes. It was likely all for her mother, but it wasn't wise to stay and find out. She edged along the wall until she was out of Mattila's reach, and ran to Livilla and the shelter of the guards.

"Stupid girl," Mattila spat, while Elektra cowered into Livilla's arms. "This old hag and your mother will never let you do anything worthwhile. Don't let them turn you into their creature; you can do so much more."

Elektra felt tears welling up, wondering how the general understood her greatest fear, but realized she wouldn't stay. She'd suffered for her mother's actions before, and didn't want to endure that again.

Livilla handed her off to a guard, who hustled her into the corridor. From there, Elektra was unable to watch the rest, but she heard Livilla's voice. "The empress also orders you to leave Brandana and return to your lands in Moralta."

"And if I don't?" Mattila's voice was firm, though Elektra recognized the rage boiling under the surface.

"Nothing will happen right now," Livilla said. "The empress has other concerns. But be assured she will take care of you later. She will not allow treason to go unpunished."

"Treason," Mattila said with a snort. "I think not. You can tell Teodora she hasn't seen the last of me. Not only will she be sorry she's done this, she'll come crawling back soon enough. She hasn't a clue—you and I know that better than anyone, and the little archduchess here is about to learn it. We'll talk again soon. Now get out of my sight, old woman."

And Elektra was swept along with the guards until they were outside the house, and Livilla was beside her again. "That went well, my dear, don't you think?"

"I don't understand what happened." Elektra tried to keep her voice from quavering.

Livilla pulled Elektra along by the arm as they walked down the street. "Your mother just removed Mattila from command over her armies. All but one regiment are now in imperial pay and will join Count Ensden in Terragand."

Elektra didn't understand how all of this had been accomplished, but she never doubted Livilla. She came to a stop. "I don't want to go back to Atlona," she said.

Livilla stopped as well. "Your mother has ordered it."

The tears she'd held back earlier now overflowed. "But I can't. I have my regiment. I'm responsible for it, and can't leave it." She was blubbering now, even as she realized that tears were hardly the stuff of an infantry colonel.

Livilla smiled. "I understand. I'm afraid I can't go against your mother's orders, but perhaps I can arrange a compromise. I agree that you should not abandon your military duties, so you'll bring your troops along."

Elektra imagined riding through the gates of Atlona at the head of her own shining, well-drilled force. That would impress her mother. She brightened. "I won't have to go back to school?"

Livilla smiled, though she looked a little sad too. "No, your school days are behind you," she said.

GWYNNETH

Once her time drew near, Natalya insisted that Gwynneth and the children move into her palace. Gwynneth didn't see why, but Natalya said, "I promised Kendryk I would take care of you, and I can do that best in my home. The doctor will also stay with me until it's time."

"But I never have trouble," Gwynneth protested.

"Good." Natalya smiled, though there was steel in her voice. Gwynneth realized arguing was pointless. So her third daughter arrived on a stormy late winter night, with a Maxima there to bless her the moment she arrived. Gwynneth had to admit it was nicer than giving birth in a tent, which was where Stella had been born.

Kendryk and Gwynneth had already decided to name a girl Renata, after Kendryk's mother. It was a relief to have so much help, with Natalya providing an army of servants and nurses. So Gwynneth appeared at court only a few days after the baby's birth. She decided it was important to not be away too long, since King Gauvain and Natalya seemed constantly distracted by matters that wouldn't further Kendryk's cause.

Natalya seemed altogether preoccupied. She always looked tired, and Gwynneth noticed her eyes appearing strange and glassy, as though she were under the influence of some potion. But she laughed off Gwynneth's concerned questions, so Gwynneth decided not to pry further.

"We must put pressure on Stepan Falk," Gwynneth said, sitting in Natalya's study.

Natalya shook her head. "I don't see how. If Lennart is as effective as you say, he will convince him, or carry on without him. We don't have time to worry about it right now, since we have to send more troops to the Dallmaring Provinces, and Maladena is making noises about Zeelund."

Gwynneth frowned. "Isn't the populace in the Dallmarings in favor of Galladian rule?"

"Not really." Natalya sighed, pushing aside the letter she'd been reading. "They were always against Olvisyan oppression, and looked to us for help. But they wish to govern themselves, and see an opportunity right now."

"Govern themselves? What a ridiculous idea. They must realize that Gauvain will treat them far better than Teodora ever did."

"People don't always know what's good for them." Natalya gave a half-smile. "So I suppose we must show them the hard way. But that's far from the only thing weighing on my mind. " Natalya stood, stretched, and walked over to a window. "The more I study the Scrolls, the more I understand Edric didn't go nearly far enough with his ideas. And there is no time to lose in making the changes the gods require."

Gwynneth got up and joined her at the window. In spite of the gradual coming of spring, a cold wind blew even colder drops of rain against the tall windows. Gwynneth watched a drop run all the way down the pane. "I'm afraid I don't understand. How could Edric possibly go any farther than he did? He risked everything to bring about his reforms."

Natalya turned toward Gwynneth, her eyes grave. "Oh, I'm not faulting anything Edric has done. We owe him a great debt for his accomplishments and his steadfastness. But we must do much more. Or perhaps someone else needs to carry on what he has started to its final conclusion."

Gwynneth was beginning to understand. "Someone like you."

Natalya smiled. "You think me power-hungry."

"I know you are." Gwynneth smiled back to show she didn't mean it as an insult. "It's one of the things I love about you. But this can't go much farther until Kronland is free of Teodora's influence."

Natalya took Gwynneth's hand and led her to a cushioned bench near the window, then said, "You had the right idea when Arryk first came, converting all of the people before enlisting their rulers as allies."

"That didn't work out, did it?"

"No, it did not, but it wasn't because the people were lacking in faith. They lacked a leader who shared their convictions."

Gwynneth sighed. "It's obvious now that Arryk was not the right leader for that task."

"He was not, though I appreciate his efforts, and he provided vital protection for Edric in those early days."

"Isn't Lennart a whole other matter? I have every reason to believe his faith is strong."

"It may be. But once he's defeated Teodora, he cannot stay in Kronland. No, the rulers must look to one of their own."

"Kendryk." Gwynneth leaned back.

Natalya nodded.

"He hates the idea."

"I know." Natalya looked sympathetic but no less resolute. "It's a terrible burden, but one he must shoulder. It will come to him naturally once he's back in Terragand. Everyone there still sees him as their leader."

"But what can he do there? If anything, he's in a much weaker position than when he first started."

Natalya's eyes settled into a faraway gaze. "Not necessarily. He has Lennart behind him now, but it must be made clear to everyone—Lennart included—that a foreign king can be only a tool of the gods, and a servant to the chosen leader."

"Lennart hasn't said as much." Gwynneth chose her words carefully. "But why should he not believe he is the chosen one?"

Natalya laughed. "Oh, I'm certain he does; why would he not? But I'm sure he is wrong."

"I still don't understand how Kendryk can make him do what he wants."

"By getting Kronland behind him. Make it clear they fight for the Quadrene faith first, Kendryk second, and the rest of the Kronlanders after that. Lennart is only a useful ally."

"The faith first then." Gwynneth hadn't missed that.

"Yes." Natalya looked straight at her. "That's the whole point of this. The outcome of this war will determine which creed prevails. But the gods don't mean for us to win by strength of arms alone. The prophecy is plain in this. First comes faith, then comes victory."

"It sounds nice," Gwynneth said. "But how can this be done?"

"Very simply," Natalya replied. "By eliminating all enemies of the truth while purifying our own worship."

ANTON

"I don't understand what's happening," Anton said when he found Susanna. "Count Michalek gave the order to get ready to march to Terragand tomorrow."

"It's strange," Susanna said. He had burst into her tent, and found her packing her things. "But everyone says they're going to join Ensden." She put down the blanket she'd been rolling up, sat down on her cot and patted the spot next to her.

Anton sat. "So General Mattila has finally given in to the empress?"

Susanna shook her head. "Apparently not. Again, this is all a rumor, but I heard that Livilla Maxima herself appeared at the general's house and relieved her of command."

"What?" Anton couldn't picture anyone being able to do that.

"Hard to believe, isn't it? And yet, all the officers are suddenly throwing money around. Livilla must have paid them off so they'd abandon Mattila. Perhaps you'll get paid soon." She gave Anton an elbow to the ribs. That he'd never received so much as a copper while serving as a soldier bothered him, even though he made plenty working with Susanna.

"So we're leaving Mattila and going to Terragand?"

"Yes. Maybe you'll get to fight, as you've been wanting to for so long." Her lip curled, and her eyes narrowed.

"Could be. But—" Anton suddenly remembered Skandar, and dropped his head into his hands.

"What is it?"

"I can't go. General Mattila has my horse. If I leave here I'll never see him again." He'd kept Skandar a secret from everyone. The fewer who knew about him and what he meant to Anton, the better.

"Have you lost your mind? You must follow your commander. And you don't have a horse."

Anton took a deep breath, looked at her puzzled face and clear hazel eyes, and decided to tell her everything, starting with saving King Arryk in battle. It was hard to tell if she believed him, but she was silent while he spoke, her eyes never leaving his face. "So you see why I can't leave him," he finished.

Susanna was quiet a while longer, then said, "That's a crazy story, especially the part about Prince Kendryk." She breathed in, then sighed. "I believe you, but that doesn't do you any good. There's nothing you can do about it."

Anton clenched his fists in his lap. "There is. I can steal Skandar tonight and run away. Will you cover for me?" He looked at Susanna anxiously.

Her eyes grew wide. "You can't be serious. You'd not only be a deserter, you'd be a thief."

"He's my horse, and no one else's."

A flush spread over Susanna's face. "I'm sorry Anton, but he isn't. Not anymore. He belongs to the general now."

"She stole him from me." Anton was already wishing he hadn't said anything. He should have waited for darkness, and gone to find Skandar alone.

"He was a spoil of war. How many times did you take things that didn't belong to you during a sacking?"

Anton opened his mouth, then closed it again. "That was different," he said, fully aware that she was right.

Susanna shook her head. "You know it's not." She took one of Anton's hands, still balled into a fist, and tucked it between hers. "I'm so sorry, but you must give him up. I won't let you take him. I can't bear to think about them catching you."

"They won't catch me," Anton said. "At least not alive."

"Don't say such awful things." Tears stood in her eyes now, and she held his hand so tightly it hurt. "Please. And besides." She looked down for a moment, before meeting his eyes again. "I can't do without you."

"Yes, you can." Anton was surprised at how rough his voice sounded. "You were fine before I got here, and you'll be fine after I leave. You don't need anyone."

"That's not true," she whispered. "I couldn't bear it if anything happened to you." She sounded convincing, but Anton was sure she was only saying that so he wouldn't go.

He pulled his hand away and stared at the floor. As long as he looked into her eyes, he felt himself getting soft inside, and that wouldn't do.

Susanna sniffled, but he refused to look at her. After a while she said, "I have an idea. You kept most of the money you made, didn't you?"

Anton nodded. He'd been saving up to buy out his contract, since he was earning enough money to make it a possibility before too long.

"I've got quite a bit put by." She took his hand again. "Why don't we do this? We'll put together everything we have, you can go to the general, and offer to buy your horse back."

Anton's breath caught, since he knew how hard Susanna worked, and how much she prized her independence. "I can't take your money," he said. "And I doubt it will be enough."

"Consider it a loan," she said. "With a horse you can be a cavalry trooper, and ought get a lot more plunder, not to mention better pay. You can pay me back when we sack a rich Terragand city."

"But I don't even know what a horse like Skandar costs. I've only got three hundred Kroner." That had seemed like a fabulous sum before, but it wasn't enough.

"That's a good start." Susanna's face broke into a smile. "I have eight hundred."

"You can't be serious." Even as he said it, Anton had a feeling she was.

"I am. And with what's just happened, I doubt the general will say no to that amount of money."

"You keep it in here?" Anton looked around the tent.

"Gods no, that would be stupid. The Moraltan quartermaster keeps a bank, and I'm sure he'll be flush with coin today. I'll go get it right now." She stood and reached for her cloak.

"You can't go alone," Anton said. "Someone will rob you."

"Then come along," she said. "You're my bodyguard. Let's go get my money, and then you can get your horse."

LENNART

Prince Stepan jumped as Lennart slammed his fist on the table, then said. "Really, Your Highness. There is no need to lose your temper."

"Yes there is." Lennart slammed his fist down again, knocking over an inkpot, then stood up so quickly the legs of his chair screeched as they scraped against the parquet floor. He hoped they left a deep gash. "I've been here for nearly a month, spending enormous amounts of money, while Count Ensden tramps all over Terragand. I need to stop him before he takes Birkenfels, and I need to do it now, but I'm not going until I have a few Kronland rulers with me. This is your fight."

"It's Terragand's fight." Stepan's voice sounded hollow behind him. "My cousin started this, and it's his problem. Where is Kendryk anyway? Will he bring no troops to your aid?"

Lennart whirled on him. "Your cousin has done plenty to help, and he'll do more. But he and I can't do this alone. I won't do it alone." He was sick of looking at Stepan's ugly face, so he turned and stomped out of the room.

General Lofbrok had preceded him, and stood waiting in the corridor. "Come, Your Highness," he said. "Let's return to your quarters. Perhaps it's time we made other plans."

Lennart shot him an angry look. To make other plans at this point was tantamount to admitting defeat. How could he succeed in a mission to unite Kronland when the first prince he encountered refused to cooperate? Lennart wanted to make clear he was no foreign invader, and to do that, he needed to build a coalition of Kronland rulers.

"I know," Lofbrok said, his broad, plain face affable as always. "I'd love to murder the fellow in his sleep too, but that won't do." They settled into a brisk pace until they'd reached Lennart's quarters. Prince Stepan had provided him with an entire wing of his palace, so there was room for Lennart's household, his senior officers, and all of their servants and other staff. Once buzzing with

136

activity, the area now felt like a sickly beehive, the drones turned lethargic from inactivity.

Lennart waited until they were both seated in his study behind closed doors. "I'd gladly do away with the fellow myself, but it's not the best way to inspire confidence around here," he said. "I must find a way to work with these Kronlanders."

"Perhaps we can find a less difficult one," Lofbrok said, pouring both of them a drink. Princess Rheda had been kind enough to place cut glass decanters of the finest Sanovan brandy in every room.

"I'm beginning to think there aren't any," Lennart said, tossing the drink back and putting the glass onto a table with a bang. "I'd heard tales of their stubbornness, but I didn't think it could be that bad. Turns out, it's worse."

"What about Ummarvik?" Lofbrok took a small sip, then set his glass aside. His sobriety was one of the things that made him a good general. Or maybe it was the self-discipline that led to the sobriety. Lennart wasn't sure, and was somewhat suspicious of an Estenorian who wasn't also a drinker. "We're hearing interesting rumors from Brandana," Lofbrok went on. "If it's true that Mattila no longer works for Teodora, we might be able to take advantage of the chaos."

"Is that possible?" Lennart wondered. "I don't see how Teodora can get rid of her so easy. She'd need money, and I'm pretty sure she hasn't got any."

"Unless Natalya is funding her behind your back."

"What?" Lennart held his glass out for another drink, and Lofbrok duly poured. "Why would she provide money to two opposing sides? How does that serve Galladium's interest?"

Lofbrok shrugged. "She backs the winner either way."

"True." Lennart downed this glass a little more slowly. If Teodora had come into funds, he had a problem, a much bigger one than a stubborn prince. "I suppose you're right. We have to make a move, Prince Stepan or not. But I'm not ready to admit defeat just yet." Lennart paused and looked out the window, then turned back to Lofbrok. "Call the other officers to meet in a quarter hour, and I'll send for Princess Rheda. I know what to do."

KENDRYK

They stopped for the night at an inn near the Brandana border. Captain Dorais, the head of Kendryk's guard, thought they should find out where Mattila was before deciding on their approach to Terragand.

"Oh, she'll stay in Brandana for the time being," the talkative innkeep said, once he learned that Kendryk wanted to avoid her. "I don't suppose you've heard the latest."

"Seems not," Kendryk said, settling onto a bench with a trencher full of stew, and a large mug of beer. He preferred dining with his guards, rather than taking a solitary meal upstairs. "Please tell me she hasn't invaded Terragand."

"Oh no," the innkeep said, bending down, so his voice was audible over the din of the busy room. He was a tall, lanky fellow, and looked oddly grasshopper-like with his elbows stuck out at an angle as he rested his hands on the table. "Not at all. No, the empress herself took Mattila's command away from her."

Kendryk nearly choked on his beer. "She what?" he asked, once he'd recovered.

The innkeep nodded, pleased he'd made such an impression. "Sent that old Maxima after her with several wagon-loads of coin. She spent the night here both times, coming and going. The Maxima might be old, but I wouldn't tangle with her. So she went to Brandana and paid off all of Mattila's officers, who've gone to fight for Ensden."

Kendryk frowned. "So Mattila's army is in Terragand, even though she's not."

"In a manner of speaking. It's a slow business, getting all of those units where they're supposed to be, since no one's sure where that is. No doubt Ensden will get them organized before Lennart leaves Helvundala, if he ever does."

Once the innkeep had gone, Kendryk called over Captain Dorais. "Brandana might be safe," he said. "But how will we get through Terragand unnoticed?"

Dorais looked grim. "We won't. Might be we'll have to fight our way through."

"We can't." Kendryk's escort numbered exactly fifty.

"Not alone. But we know Duke Trystan is operating somewhere in western Terragand. We must find him."

"Yes, I believe you're right. Once we do, we can decide how to get Edric Maximus. I won't even worry about Lennart until that's done." Kendryk wondered now if he should have taken ship to Helvundala instead. "Send out messengers tonight, to ask about Duke Trystan at every inn and temple. With any luck we'll find him before enemy troops finds us."

A message from the duke reached them before they crossed into Terragand. Kendryk read it, then handed it to Dorais. "He says it's safe for the first twenty leagues over the border. Most of the imperial troops went north and east, to defend Kaltental and threaten Birkenfels." Kendryk sighed. "We must relieve Faris before looking for Edric. I hope he's safe now that Terragand's swarming with hostile armies."

"We'll find a way." Dorais looked up after reading the message. "The Maximus has many friends who'll shelter him. Let's meet Duke Trystan first, and then we can plan."

They crossed the border without incident, but found conditions in Terragand appalling. "What happened here?" Kendryk asked as they rode through a town. Most of the buildings stood, but all were deserted. A few human and animal corpses lay in the open, though judging by the work the crows had done, they'd been there for several weeks.

They passed through several more villages in similar condition before Duke Trystan's outriders found them. As he led them to a well-hidden camp, a young cavalry officer explained. "There's only been a little fighting here, but the armies took everything. We've been living off the land all winter, so we'd already picked the area clean. Then several thousand of Mattila's lot came through two weeks ago and finished 'em off."

"What happened to all the people?" Kendryk couldn't believe the condition of his kingdom, for it was still his, no matter what Teodora said. Guilt at what he'd done rose inside him. He swallowed it down and hardened his face.

"Gone," the officer said. "A plague of dysentery swept through last month and killed a lot of 'em. Took a lot of ours too. The rest ran off, I imagine."

"Where can they go?" Kendryk asked.

"Who knows? There's scarcely any safe parts of Terragand now there's soldiers everywhere, most of them enemy. We've got to break through to Birkenfels, but we haven't figured that out yet. I reckon you and the duke can chew that one over."

"I suppose so," Kendryk said, trying to push down the horror that would overwhelm him if he let it. Everything he'd feared happening to Terragand if he didn't act, had happened because he *had* acted. And now he had to repair it. If he could.

BRAEDEN

"He's here." Karil stuck his head in the door of Braeden's room, then ran off. Braeden followed more slowly. His wound always troubled him the first hour after waking. By the time he reached the courtyard, Kendryk had dismounted and pulled Karil into an embrace. He smiled when Braeden appeared. "You're the last people I expected to find here," he said. "What happened?"

"Long story." Braeden clapped Kendryk on the shoulder. He looked well, though tired, with a sad shadow over his eyes. "But first, you'll meet the duke. Did you have any trouble getting here?"

"No," Kendryk said, hurrying to catch up to Braeden as they entered the dilapidated manor house Duke Trystan had turned into his headquarters. It had been abandoned for some time, and was off the main road, so no enemy soldiers passed this way. The woods grew thick all around, and only a few locals knew of it. "We spotted a small artillery detachment on the road south of here, and waited until after dark to move. I don't think they ever saw or heard us. There are remarkable woodsmen in this army."

"Terragand seems to specialize in those," Duke Trystan said, striding down the corridor toward them. He had mud on his boots, and his cloak was damp, so he'd likely taken a round of guard duty. Braeden liked that about him.

Trystan paused and bowed in front of Kendryk, reminding Braeden that he'd treated the prince like a junior cavalry officer.

"Your Grace," Trystan said, "Welcome back to Terragand."

"Thank you," Kendryk said, extending his hand. He smiled, but his eyes were grave. "It's good to be back, though I confess I'm appalled at the state of the countryside."

"Yes, it's terrible." Trystan led them into a room that might once have been a parlor. As one of the few rooms with covered windows and a working fireplace, it now served as his study, meeting room and dining hall. "And I'm afraid we've contributed to it, though we had little choice."

"I would never blame you," Kendryk said, taking a seat in the best chair as Braeden pulled it up for him. Karil immediately perched on the arm, beaming in spite of Trystan's frown. "In fact, I wish to thank you for keeping the faith when so few others have. I hope your loyalty can soon be rewarded."

"I wish for no reward," Trystan said, once he and Braeden were seated. "Only to see your rule restored, and imperial troops removed from all of Kronland for good."

"Then we have the same goal," Kendryk said. "And help is at hand, with Lennart in Helvundala and part of his army besieging Kaltental."

"He's here?" Trystan's eyes lit up while Braeden grinned, relieved. In their isolated position they had heard only rumors of Lennart's arrival, but had no concrete signs of it.

"It's why I'm here," Kendryk said. "We received word several weeks ago that Lennart himself landed in Helvundala, while sending two of his generals to hold what bits of Terragand shore they can. But Lennart can't persuade Prince Stepan to ally with him and march on Ensden."

"Coward," Trystan spat. "I know he's your cousin, but he's not worthy of his crown. He won't lift a finger to help you, or anyone trying to help you."

"We bear each other no love, it's true," Kendryk said mildly, "though his father was loyal enough. But I fear without Stepan's support, Lennart will get no other in Kronland."

"My mother will help," Trystan said. "She's not afraid of Teodora or any of her toadies. That's why I'm here too. But I've been pinned down while Mattila's troops flooded in from Brandana, since I'm not strong enough to break through. I'm happy to meet with Lennart and offer a formal alliance with Podoska."

"My plan was to collect Edric Maximus from whichever temple he might be at, and find Lennart in Helvundala," Kendryk said. "I imagine the lot of us might persuade Stepan. Your resoluteness ought to shame him, if nothing else."

Trystan frowned. "Karil," he said. "Go find a servant and order refreshments."

"But—" Karil said.

"You can return here after you've done it. But you must sit properly, and not perch like a monkey on the prince's armrest."

"I don't mind." Kendryk smiled after Karil's retreating form. "We shared imprisonment in the Arnfels for several years, and he's like a son to me."

"How nice," Trystan said. "But his manners need improvement all the same." He didn't miss the grin Kendryk and Braeden shared, then snorted. "Amazing you lot are old friends. You two have some catching up to do."

"The quartermaster brews an atrocious cherry brandy," Braeden said. "We'll share a bottle tonight."

"I look forward to it." Kendryk grinned. "But hadn't we best make a plan before you addle my brain with liquor?"

"I agree," Trystan said, as a soldier came in bearing a tray with mugs of weak beer and some cheese. "I apologize for the food, but we're on short rations. If you hadn't come within the week, we would have been forced to move east to rob provisions off the enemy."

"Then we'll go soon," Kendryk said. "I must find Edric Maximus. I believe he'll be key to gaining the support of the Kronland rulers."

"Finding him may be difficult, if he still lives," Trystan said. "The clergy accompanying Ensden's army are diligent in spreading their poison to every temple, and they're backed by considerable force. All those preaching Edric's work have been killed, or gone into hiding. It's possible a few temples in the east are untouched, but we can't be certain."

Kendryk couldn't hide the shock on his face. "I see," he finally said. "I trust the gods will keep Edric safe somehow. But this means we must make for eastern Terragand without delay. Is there any chance we can reach Birkenfels before Ensden takes it?"

"Perhaps, with luck." Trystan took a long drink. "Until Mattila's forces came this way, Ensden couldn't hold Kaltental, occupy the larger towns, besiege the castle, and deal with me. That's changed. Now there's no way I can stop him, although he's in some disarray until he absorbs Mattila's army into his own."

"We must go," Kendryk said. "Right away, if you don't mind."

LENNART

It was already spring, and Lennart had hoped to be well into Terragand by now, but at least there would be no further delays after today. He visited Prince Stepan in the prince's private study one morning, and was pleased to find him alone. "I've come to say good-bye," he said.

There was no mistaking the relief on the prince's face, though he tried to cover it with a gracious nod. "So you have decided to conquer Terragand without me."

"Yes." Lennart smiled. "I've decided I don't need your help to carry out my plans."

"I agree," the prince said, with his characteristic oily smirk. "I'm sure you will have better luck recruiting in the other kingdoms."

"Perhaps, though few can match the fine force your father built up, and which you have so well maintained."

"True." Stepan inclined his head, then fumbled with a quill and inkpot. "I wish you luck, Your Highness. I'm sure your campaign will be a great success."

"So do I." Lennart stood.

Behind him, the door opened, and Princess Rheda entered the room. Lennart stepped aside, so she and the contingent of guards could approach Stepan.

The prince jumped out of his chair. "What is the meaning of this, Mother?" he screeched.

Princess Rheda was perfectly calm. Lennart noted with approval that she wore an elaborate cuirass over her starkly cut dress. For all her tiny stature she looked formidable. "I'm removing you from the throne of Helvundala," she said.

"You cannot." Stepan was sputtering. "This is treason."

Rheda stood in front of his desk. "I can, and it's perfectly legal. Helvundala's charter states that an incompetent ruler can be removed in favor of his heir. Your unwillingness to acknowledge and act on a clear threat from the empire makes you incompetent. Since your heir is only eleven years old, I will serve as regent until he comes of age. You will now go with the guards."

Stepan brought his fists down on the desk with a bang. "The only threat to my kingdom comes from this foreigner." He pointed at Lennart, hatred in his eyes. "As long as he remains, the empress will consider us rebellious."

"She already does." Lennart was enjoying himself. Once he had discovered that Princess Rheda considered her son a threat to the security of the kingdom, it was easy to persuade her to take this step. She had insisted on getting the support of the aristocracy first; hence the delay.

"After my father died, we engaged in no further acts against Teodora. In fact, I'm on the verge of reaching an agreement with ..." Stepan trailed off, as if he realized what he'd just said.

"Perhaps I was wrong before," Princess Rheda said, her eyes steely. "You are not merely incompetent, you are also engaged in treason, negotiating with the empress without consulting the council."

Stepan opened and closed his mouth, but no sound came out. He looked so ridiculous, Lennart almost laughed.

Rheda continued. "Until a moment ago, I was going to handle you gently. You are my son after all, though not a terribly good one. I planned on sending you to live in comfort in the countryside, and you'd have no further trouble if you stayed out of politics. But if you've been talking to Teodora behind all of our backs, I'm afraid you will need to be kept in a more secure place." She nodded at a guard. "Take him to the dungeon."

Stepan's hands scrambled in a drawer of his desk, and he pulled out a pistol. Lennart lunged at him as soon as he saw the motion, but wasn't fast enough, and Stepan fired straight at his mother before Lennart could tackle him. The princess's shriek cut off as she crumpled to the floor. Lennart wanted to go to her, but holding Stepan down until the guards got to him was more important.

"Someone see to the princess and send for a doctor," Lennart bellowed. "The rest of you come here, and take this idiot to the dungeon."

ANTON

Anton was jumping with excitement. In a matter of hours, Skandar would be his again. The quartermaster had established his office in the back room of a decent-looking tavern not far from the general's headquarters, and Anton and Susanna hurried straight there.

They had to wait for three officers ahead of them, but it didn't take long. Susanna fished a piece of paper out of a little bag she always carried. Anton was well-acquainted with the quartermaster, and didn't care for the man one bit. He was a corrupt liar who never hesitated to take advantage of someone else's misfortune. Until Anton had made his own money, he owed him a huge sum for clothes and food that were worth little.

Anton narrowed his eyes as soon as he saw him. The quartermaster sat at a table, looking much like a smug toad, though Anton doubted that toads had three chins. Behind him stood two heavily armed guards, ensuring the chests full of coin standing against the back wall remained undisturbed.

The quartermaster beckoned to the one other chair at the table, and Susanna sat down. Anton stood at her shoulder, his trademark scowl in place.

"Madame Stengel," the man said, and Anton realized he hadn't, until that moment, even known Susanna's last name. "You brought your last deposit only a few days ago. Don't tell me the Maxima paid you off as well."

Susanna offered a half-smile. Anton saw she kept her cloak wrapped tightly around her shoulders, even though the room was warm. "I wish to make a withdrawal," she said.

"Indeed." The quartermaster returned Anton's hard stare. "Would it have anything to do with this young scoundrel here?"

Susanna sniffed, and sat up straighter. "That's hardly any of your business." She handed over the slip of paper. "I'd like all of it please."

The quartermaster raised his eyebrows. "All of it? Are you buying out your boyfriend's contract? I'd advise against that."

146

Anton bit his tongue. Susanna could handle this.

"I'm not asking your advice." Her tone remained cool. "I'm asking for my money, with interest."

The man hesitated for a long while. Anton never broke his stare, and slid his hand to the dagger at his belt. He wouldn't have much chance against those guards, but they were there to protect the money. Maybe they'd let him stick the quartermaster if he deserved it.

Finally, the man turned to a guard, and handed him the slip. "Get it out," he said, and turned back to Susanna. "I'd have thought you'd be smarter about this by now, Madame. After what happened with your husband."

Susanna's cheeks were bright red, and Anton hoped she wouldn't lose her temper.

"I'd prefer not to discuss personal matters," she said. "My money, please."

Anton took a step forward, pulling the dagger slightly out of its sheath with an audible chink.

"Just trying to make conversation," the quartermaster grumbled, taking a bag of coins from the guard. "Shall we count it?"

Anton paid close attention, though knew Susanna wouldn't miss a trick. The quartermaster handed it over to her after counting, then she counted again.

"Eight hundred sixteen Kroner," she said at last. "Good. But you owe me another thirty in interest."

The man's face turned red, but he waved to the guard, and had him hand over the rest.

"Thank you," Susanna said primly. "I'll be back when I have more to deposit."

"I doubt you will," the quartermaster said to their retreating backs.

"Is he always like that with you?" Anton asked, once they were outside and walking down the road toward the general's quarters.

"He was much better today, probably because you were there," she said. "Usually he's very suggestive, and once even chased me around the room. I had to bring a friend the next time I made a deposit."

"You should bring me with you from now on," Anton said.

Susanna slowed down a little. "How are we going to do this?" she asked. "I doubt we can go straight to the general and ask to buy one of her horses."

"We should see her Master of Horse first," Anton said. "He'll be able to manage it. If he gives us any trouble, we'll figure out how to see the general."

"I hope you know what you're doing," Susanna said.

"I'm going to get my horse, thanks to you." Anton grinned down at her. "I can't wait for you to meet him. I'm sure he'll like you."

Susanna laughed. "You talk about him as if he were a person."

"He is a person, in a way." Anton couldn't stop smiling.

When they entered the stable yard, Anton spotted the master right away, working with a fine young gelding. He waved at him, then waited until he handed the horse off to a groom. Anton was wearing his best clothes, so he looked important enough to be given attention.

"What is it?" the man asked, once he came over to Anton and Susanna, wiping his dusty hands on his breeches.

"There's a horse here I'd like to buy," Anton said. "A young Norovaean battle charger. I'm sure you only have the one."

"Popular horse," the man muttered, then said, "I had one, but he's gone now."

Anton's heart fell into his boots. "Gone? How?"

"Sold," the man said. "Last night."

Anton's voice caught in his throat. "Who?" he finally croaked. "Who did you sell him to?"

"You really want that horse, don't you?" The master shook his head. "Well, it might be you can still find him, though I doubt she'll sell him so easy." Anton's face must have looked awful, because the man seemed to feel sorry for him. "I sold him to an officer in the Sanova Hussars, a young woman with red hair. Didn't get her name, though I'm sure you can ask around."

Anton still stood there, thunderstruck, when Susanna took his hand and said, "Thank you. We'll look for her," then dragged Anton out of the stable yard. "We'll find her," Susanna said.

Anton was still feeling numb, but Susanna asked her way through camp until they reached the Sanovan section. They stood at the edge of camp, staring at the vast empty space that might have once been a meadow. Nothing remained but churned-up mud and a few broken tent stakes. Susanna dragged Anton over to a ragged-looking woman picking through the mud, looking for gods-only-knew what. "Where are the Sanova Hussars?" she asked.

The woman straightened up. "Gone," she said.

"When?" Susanna asked.

The woman shrugged. "Their vanguard moved out at dawn, the last of their wagons a few hours ago."

"To Terragand?" Susanna persisted.

"I reckon so. You might try to chase them down, though from what I could gather, they had orders and were moving at speed. You'd want a fast horse to catch up to them."

KENDRYK

It was dangerous here, on the banks of the Velta river. Kendryk rode next to Trystan, showing him the way. "All we have to do is follow the river north."

Trystan shook his head. "Ensden will have people watching the road. They'll be expecting me."

Kendryk smiled. "We won't need the main road. There's another way. It might be slower, but we'll have help from the country folk, and I doubt the enemy will know it." He turned to Braeden, riding on his left. "I'm sure you remember the gap between the hills across from Birkenfels."

"I remember," Braeden said, his face grim.

Kendryk still only had a foggy recollection of the battle fought there five years before. He remembered lining his forces up in front of those hills, watching the enemy—Braeden included—advance through the mist, and that was all. Only a few hours after that, his horse had landed on his leg when Teodora shot it, and he was taken prisoner. He hadn't regained consciousness for nearly a week, and still had trouble remembering much from that awful time.

"We'll come at the castle from that gap," Kendryk said. "It will be easy for us to hide on the other side to scout out the enemy before we approach it."

"What if Ensden has besieged it?" Braeden asked.

"There might still be a way," Kendryk said. "I'll tell you once we get there." His father had shown him the secret years ago. Kendryk was barely twelve, but became heir to Terragand when his older brother died. Only the ruler of the kingdom was aware of this old escape route, and Kendryk regretted that he'd never shown Gwynneth. She and the children might have gotten away without ever involving her brother in the war. He resolved to show Maryna at the earliest opportunity.

Following Kendryk's instructions, Trystan's forces left the river, and headed into the hill country. The woods grew deep and dark; the only way to pass was along narrow winding trails cut through heavy underbrush. Few people lived here, but those few remained undisturbed by the chaos consuming the rest of the kingdom. In the four days of their journey through here, Kendryk's party came upon only three dozen cabins and a handful of tiny hamlets. Whenever they passed one, the few folk nearby came and stared. Most had never left these woods, or seen over fifty people at one time. An army of nearly two thousand was hard to comprehend.

"Are they loyal?" Trystan looked down at one burly young woodsman standing alongside the path, his jaw nearly on the forest floor.

"As loyal as any in Terragand," Kendryk said. "I'd be surprised if they've ever heard of Edric Maximus, or of any of the changes in the rest of the land. But these woods have always provided refuge and support for the rulers of Terragand. We can count on them now." He hoped it was true, since they were in desperate straits. They'd left the western frontier with virtually no food, and so far had survived by hunting game, which was scarce and skinny this time of year. One raid on an imperial supply train had yielded enough bread to get them this far, though they'd lost more than a dozen soldiers in the attack. Kendryk had only a stale crust in his saddlebag, and was certain he'd been given more than anyone else. They needed help now if they weren't to starve.

He looked down at the young woodsman. "We need food," he said. "Just enough for a meal or two, and we'll be on our way."

The young man clapped his mouth shut with an effort and nodded.

"I know who you are," another young man standing beside him said. This one was a lot smaller, but seemed quicker. His dark eyes sparkled and his smile was ready.

"Do you?" Kendryk asked. He swung down from his horse, and the young man sketched a bow.

"I seen you once, years ago. You was traveling through the forest, on your way to a trial in Berndorf, at the edge of the wood."

Kendryk had traveled through many forests to many trials, so it seemed likely. He smiled. "Then you must tell me your name."

"I'm Nik," the young man said. "And this here's Stiva." He elbowed the bigger man in the ribs. "We ain't got much food here, but if you can wait a day, we can round up fresh game for you. I'll go around to all my traps. Stiva's a good shot with a matchlock, but we run out of powder months ago."

"That's no problem," Kendryk said. "He's welcome to the best of our muskets." He felt bad, taking food off people who came by it so hard, but he

151

could pay them in coin, and ask Trystan how much powder and shot he could spare.

Nik led them to a clearing where they could make camp, and soon more people emerged from the woods. Word had gotten out that the Prince of Terragand was here, and everyone was curious. Tired as Kendryk was, he held court near an enormous oak tree in the middle of the clearing. He realized these were just about the only citizens of Terragand he'd seen who weren't terrorized refugees. He hoped they'd stay that way.

The folk here lived crude, poverty-stricken lives, but they shared the little they had with Kendryk and Trystan's troops. At midday, someone built a large fire, and brought an enormous iron pot in a cart pulled by a skinny donkey. Several country folk along with the camp cooks set to peeling and cutting a mountain of half-rotted potatoes and carrots. A few hours later, Nik appeared, triumphantly bearing a dozen scrawny rabbits. Behind him, Stiva carried still more, in addition to several squirrels and hedge-hogs.

"They don't taste so great," Nik told Kendryk after leaving them with the cooks. "But my mother knows how to season a stew. You'll never know they're in there."

Kendryk watched the woman skin a squirrel, and his stomach growled even as he shuddered. He turned to smile at Nik. "I don't mind one bit."

The stew was surprisingly good. Trystan sat next to Kendryk at a fire and sighed happily. "I don't think I've eaten this well since I last left Birkenfels. Perhaps we should stay a few days."

"We can't." Kendryk shook his head. "There are only a few hundred folk who live here, and I'm sure we've cleaned out their reserves. If we break out of Birkenfels, I'll see about sending some food their way so they survive to the harvest."

"You're right," Trystan said. "But I'm afraid it will be no better later on. We must accept that many people who haven't already starved, will do so soon."

Kendryk stared into the flames. He was still hungry. "I'm sure you're right. But I don't like it. And as ruler of Terragand, I'm responsible for everyone, not just these soldiers. I must do what I can."

The next morning, Kendryk was awakened by several musket shots nearby. He jumped out of his bedroll and hurried out of the tent, pulling on his clothes as he went. Braeden appeared at his side, pistols drawn, but put them away again when he saw Trystan approach them, smiling. "They're shooting our breakfast," he said. "Some of the woodsmen went out with my best sharpshooters before dawn. Said they could find wild boar and deer. They'll be tough and skinny, but there'll be meat on their bones. They'll need time to dress and cook the meat, but we'll have a little something to take along."

"And we'll see Birkenfels in another day," Kendryk said. He almost hoped there'd be a besieging army that might have food they could steal.

GWYNNETH

"Gwynneth, is there any way you can help me?"

Gwynneth and King Gauvain sat alone in her library. She had moved back to her own house a few weeks after giving birth to Renata. The king came to her back door with only a few guards, but he was clearly desperate. She sighed. "I can try, but you know how Natalya is. Once she's decided on a path, it's hard to make her reconsider."

Gauvain put his head in his hands. Gwynneth felt sorry for him. He'd come to her after Natalya decided her affair with him was displeasing to the gods, and that it must end. He looked up, his eyes bloodshot. "I can't live without her."

"She's not making you live without her," Gwynneth said gently. "She'll just no longer share your bed."

Gauvain made a strangled sound, and Gwynneth feared he might cry. "I don't understand," he said in a small voice.

"I don't understand either," Gwynneth said. "But surely she knows better than any of us what the gods want. I am certain she loves you as much as ever." But she wasn't certain of that. In fact, she was certain of very little right now. Ever since Natalya decided that Edric's reforms hadn't gone far enough, much had changed in Allaux.

"She doesn't show it anymore," Gauvain whispered, almost to himself. He stared at the wall for a moment, then turned to Gwynneth again. "It's like she's turned into another person."

Gwynneth agreed, though she didn't say so. The changes had been many and rapid. Natalya started by kicking the king out of her bed, but that was only the beginning. She removed every lascivious painting and sculpture from her palace, and those in the king's palace were next. She forbade the drinking of wine except for at mealtimes, and dancing at any time.

Natalya herself exchanged her traditional white Maxima's robes for severe black dresses with high white collars. They did not become her, but the severity of the look ensured no one—not even Gwynneth—breathed a word about it. When Gwynneth mentioned that she missed seeing her favorite sculpture in the garden, Natalya had all but snapped at her. "The gods do not approve of such displays," she said, her eyes cold.

Later, Gwynneth asked her how she knew the gods disapproved.

Natalya's tone softened. "I've had several dreams these past weeks, and many obscure passages in the Holy Scrolls are now clear to me. I will explain more soon." Gwynneth wondered if she was using a potion reserved for the higher clergy to lend clarity to their dreams. It might explain her altered appearance and behavior.

"And that's the other thing," Gauvain said. "I'm not sure I approve of what she's about to do to the temples. I realize she is Maxima, and they are in her jurisdiction, but it seems excessive." Natalya had informed the king that praying to icons directly contradicted the Holy Scrolls, and that all icons in Galladium's temples were to be destroyed. In a country known for its beautiful temples and fabulous icons, such an act might start a revolution.

Gwynneth breathed out and pondered. In such a situation, the king was within his rights to overrule a Maxima, but it was hard to picture Gauvain doing any such thing. "I can't advise you on that, either," Gwynneth admitted. "The last time I told a ruler to override a Maxima's wishes, as I did with Edric Landrus, it didn't end well." Edric was her friend, but in her darkest hours, Gwynneth had more than once wished he'd never been born.

"I can't do it—I won't do it. Still, it would all be bearable if only she'd come back to me."

Gwynneth said nothing to that, but offered a sympathetic smile. It would be good for Gauvain to assert himself against Natalya, but he seemed unready to do so.

"I have it!" Gauvain's face suddenly lit up. "I'll marry her. I can't make her queen unless she gives up her post, but once we're husband and wife ..." he trailed off, his smile fading.

"What about Zofya Inferrara? Surely you don't mean to break that alliance at such a delicate time."

"I don't care about that. I'll happily return the Dallmaring Provinces. We got Kendryk back, so we don't need Teodora for anything else."

"My brother—" Gwynneth began.

"Aksel is a hostage for Arryk's good behavior, not ours."

Gwynneth swallowed. "You're right, of course. But supposing you marry Natalya. How will that change anything she has planned?"

"It won't. But I'll have her back at my side where she's meant to be."

"Hm," Gwynneth said, not wishing to encourage him. Privately, she was certain Natalya wouldn't agree, but she didn't want to be the one to break it to the king.

Gauvain stood. "I'll do that." He already looked much happier, grabbed Gwynneth's hand and kissed it. "Thank you for your good advice."

Gwynneth was sure it wasn't much good at all, but it seemed the king needed to learn that for himself.

It went even worse than she'd feared. That evening, Natalya stormed into Gwynneth's drawing room, unannounced. Gwynneth had been entertaining a few guests, but excused herself, and led Natalya into the dining room, as far from the others as possible. She hadn't so much as shut the door behind her when Natalya exploded.

"How dare you give the king advice concerning me!" Her voice was low, but trembled with anger. Her eyes blazed.

Gwynneth backed away. "I did no such thing," she said, struggling to stay calm. Natalya had never been angry with her before.

Natalya raised an eyebrow and huffed.

Gwynneth assumed she should continue. "The king came to see me. He was distraught about your decision, and wondered how he might sway you."

"And you told him to propose?" Natalya took only one step, but it was enough to make Gwynneth shrink into a corner.

"I didn't." Gwynneth reminded herself that Natalya had no right to speak to her this way. She lifted her chin, and took a step toward Natalya. "He brought it up, and I raised every objection I could think of. I didn't tell him not to do it, but it wasn't my idea to start with. I remembered what you told me when you left me to study in Atlona all those years ago."

Natalya's face softened just a little. "I told you I would never marry, since men only ever create complications." She threw her hands up. "And I was right, wasn't I?" She looked around for somewhere to sit, finally pulling a chair away from the table. She extended her hand to Gwynneth, pulling her down beside her.

"I suppose you were." Gwynneth had to smile.

"Of course I was." Natalya tossed her head. "Just look at all the trouble Kendryk's caused you. If you had never married, you'd likely be Queen of Norovaea right now."

"Perhaps," Gwynneth said, "but I'd rather have Kendryk."

"I know." Natalya looked Gwynneth in the eye. "But I'm not like you." She sighed. "I've always had big ambitions, and a great vision for Galladium. But you must believe me when I tell you that until recently, I was going about it all wrong. The gods are showing me the right way now, and I must trust them. In turn, you and Gauvain must trust me. Can you do that?"

"I can." Gwynneth looked straight back. "The king trusts you too, but he misses the way things used to be."

"All things change," Natalya said. "Even the good ones."

BRAEDEN

"It's here somewhere," Kendryk said, though he seemed puzzled. He'd been looking for a cave hidden in the woods for several hours now. "But it's been almost fifteen years since my father brought me here, and the area has changed a great deal."

Braeden looked around. They stood on a hillside, the same one from which Kendryk's guns had once blasted at him. They were deep in a thicket of tall fir trees grown close together, making it feel like dusk in here, even though it was nearly midday.

Their party had come up on Birkenfels, and found an unfriendly army camped around it. Trystan had gone to scout the numbers and positions, but their only hope of getting into the castle without a fight was Kendryk's secret passageway. If he ever found it. Braeden tried not to worry about how they'd get out of the castle once they were inside.

"Should we try a different area?" Braeden finally asked, after Kendryk sat down on a fallen log with a defeated sigh.

"Yes, perhaps. I was certain I had a view of the castle back then, though small trees grew all around, and I thought they might have grown enough to obscure it by now."

"Might be," Braeden said. "Or maybe we should try a completely different spot." He didn't want to put too much pressure on Kendryk, but they had no time. If they didn't find a way into the castle today, they'd have to raid the enemy for food, and then everyone would know they were here.

He'd thought he was hungry the past autumn while bringing Elektra to Mattila, but hadn't realized how lucky he'd been to travel during the harvest time. Aside from midwinter, this was the thinnest time of year in the countryside. Things were growing, but weren't ready to eat. Berries wouldn't be ripe for another month or two, and the game hadn't fattened up yet. Braeden had never been so hungry. And hungry soldiers didn't fight well, at least not for long.

"All right," Kendryk said, standing up. "Let's go over here."

Braeden went ahead, using one of his older, duller swords to hack at the underbrush. Not even a deer could get through here. It must have been a job for Kendryk's forces to lug all their cannon up here. He remembered something. "Do you recall where Count Faris put his guns?" he asked. "Back at the first battle?"

"Further north," Kendryk said, slightly out of breath behind him. "Where it's more open, with a clear view down." He chuckled. "Of course. Seeing the castle is easy from that spot. I know where to look now."

Braeden grinned, and kept hacking away until they reached a clearing. From here, they looked almost directly across at the castle, the tents of the enemy forces spread out below. Braeden wondered how long they'd been there, and how long the castle would hold out.

Kendryk paused and looked out at Birkenfels. "I haven't seen it in such a long time. It's the only home I have now, though not a safe one."

"I reckon it'll be yours before long." Braeden didn't want him sliding into melancholy right now.

Kendryk turned back toward the hillside, and a smile spread across his face. "Over there, on your left." He pointed at what looked like a wall of limestone.

Braeden turned, and peered at it more closely. Thick brush grew in front of the chalky cliff, but behind that, he saw a long crack.

"Come here," Kendryk said. "If the gods are with us, the way is still clear."

What looked like a crack turned out to be one wall overlapping another, with a narrow entry-way leading into the cliff. "We'll need light," Braeden said. "And weapons. Who knows what's inside."

"You're right," Kendryk said. "I'll wait here and you can get the others."

Braeden didn't like leaving him alone, but he was well-hidden in the trees, and their rendezvous point wasn't far away. By the time he reached it, Trystan had returned from his scouting. "It's not a big force," he told Braeden as he led him back to Kendryk. "Only four thousand, and they haven't been here long, since they're not well dug in."

By now they'd reached Kendryk, and Trystan sent a few men into the cave with torches to see if at least the first bit was passable.

"How many soldiers might Count Faris have inside the castle?" Kendryk asked as they waited.

Trystan shook his head. "When I left him, there were only a few hundred. Even if he still has that many, we'll be outnumbered."

"We must attack at night," Braeden said. "It's the only way we can keep them from knowing how few we are."

You're right," Trystan said, and they finalized plans before Kendryk led three hundred soldiers into the tunnel.

LENNART

Once the guards led—or rather, dragged—Stepan away, Lennart hurried to the princess. By now a doctor had come at a run, and Lennart broke through a cluster of guards surrounding her. When he'd finally shouldered his way through, he found her propped up, still sitting on the floor.

Lennart took a deep breath and knelt next to her. "Thank Ercos you're alive, Princess," he said. "I am very sorry I wasn't able to stop him in time."

Rheda turned to him with a thin smile. She was white as paper but appeared unhurt. "Fortunately, I was ready." She put a pale hand on her cuirass, now significantly dented.

"You expected him to shoot you?" Lennart couldn't hide his chagrin.

"I considered the possibility." Rheda's eyes were sad. "I believe my son cares for me, but he cares for power far more."

"I am very sorry about that," Lennart said, and meant it. Rheda was so pretty and sweet, he wouldn't have minded having her as his own mother. He'd never been close to his, although much as she had annoyed him, he couldn't imagine ever wanting to harm her. "But now he's out of your way. You must take great care to ensure he can't contact his friends and plot against you."

Rheda shook her head. "Fortunately for us, he has no friends. His personality was such that ... well, I believe you can judge that yourself. And I intend to give the citizens of Helvundala no cause to miss him. Will you help me up, Your Highness?"

Lennart shot the doctor a questioning glance, but she shrugged and said, "Her Grace had the wind knocked out of her, and will have a great bruise on her chest. She can try standing, though she should lean on you."

"I'll be sure not to wear low-cut gowns for a while," Rheda gasped as Lennart helped her to her feet. He chuckled, fully aware that the princess only ever wore the highest lace collars. He didn't recall seeing so much as an inch of her neck, let alone any bosom.

With Lennart on one side and the doctor on the other, they walked the princess to another room, and put her down on a cushioned bench. Lennart was glad to see some color had returned to her usually rosy cheeks. "Send for Prince Toland," Rheda ordered a guard, and he disappeared down a corridor.

She leaned back against the cushions, patted the spot next to her, and Lennart sat down. "Does your grandson know what's going on?" he asked.

Rheda shook her head. "I didn't want him to worry, though it will be quite a shock. But he isn't close to his father, and his life will change very little. I'll take care of everything for the time being."

"Thank the gods," Lennart said, then stood as the heir to Helvundala entered the room. "Prince Toland," he said to the pudgy blond boy who bowed before him. "I congratulate you."

The boy shot Lennart a puzzled look, then asked, "What's going on, Grandmother?"

"I have overthrown your father and put you in his place."

The boy gasped, his brown eyes wide. "I don't understand."

"It's simple my dear." The princess went on. "Your father was an idiot, refused to deal with King Lennart—an ally sent to us by the gods—and worst of all, engaged in treasonous negotiations with the empress herself."

The boy swallowed hard. "What have you done to Father?"

"Nothing too dreadful. He'll stay in the dungeon for the time being, though I suppose the council and I will have to investigate his treasonous activities sooner or later. You can visit him if you like."

"I'd rather not," the boy said. He looked around the room, as if unsure that what he wanted to say ought to be said in front of everyone. Then he swallowed again and said softly, "I'm sure you did the right thing, Grandmother, though I haven't the slightest idea what I'm supposed to do now."

Lennart gave him an encouraging smile as Rheda said, "You needn't do anything my dear. I'll rule in your name until you turn seventeen. If you're interested, you may sit with me and join the council meetings, as long as you finish your lessons first."

Toland's eyes lit up. "I don't have to wait until I'm twelve? Father said—"

"Never mind that now," Rheda said sharply. "You don't have to wait until you're twelve, though you can if you want to."

"I don't want to," the boy said eagerly. "Wait, I mean. I'd like to start learning now."

"That's what I thought," the princess said with a fond smile. "I always knew you'd make a better ruler than your father." She turned to Lennart. "Toland takes after his mother in just about every way. She was a dear, clever girl, and I miss her terribly. Such a shame she still isn't with us."

Toland hung his head, and Lennart wondered how old he'd been when his mother died.

"You may go back to your lessons," the princess said. "There's nothing you need do right now. I'll come see you this afternoon, just like I always do."

"Yes," Toland said. "And Grandmother, thank you." He beamed at her before bowing to Lennart again, and leaving the room.

Once the door had shut behind him Lennart said, "I like him. Are you sure he belongs to Stepan?"

"Quite," Rheda said tartly. "Though I'm relieved he doesn't resemble him at all. But now you and I must talk. I wish to give you as many troops as I can, though I will not be leading them myself. I will send for the Baron Manier, who will take our forces to Terragand with you."

"Geffrey Manier?" Lennart said. "I know him." The young infantry colonel had already impressed Lennart as one of Stepan's most competent officers.

"He's a good man and a brilliant strategist," Rheda said. "I hope you can make use of him. In the meantime, I'll send for refreshments and we'll discuss your invasion of Terragand as soon as he arrives."

ANTON

"Come on," Susanna said, tugging at Anton's arm. They had been staring at the remains of the Sanovan camp for several minutes. "It looks like rain. We should go."

Anton couldn't speak, but stumbled after her. He was glad Susanna said nothing for a while, since he was trying to think. He couldn't accept that Skandar might be gone for good. How would he get to the Sanova Hussars without deserting? And once he'd found them, what then? March up to Skandar's new owner with a bag of coin? An officer who had spent most—if not all—of her payout from Livilla on a horse was unlikely to want to give him up.

Susanna dragged Anton along, all the way through camp, much of it already being taken down and loaded into wagons. From the look of it, every unit was leaving. They walked along an endless string of wagons, and a long line of artillery being hitched to six-horse teams. Normally, Anton would have stopped to admire the big guns and joke with their crews, but today he barely noticed them.

It started raining. Susanna yanked on his arm and they went faster. She took him to her tent since it was closer than his, but by the time they'd reached it, they were both soaked. Anton fell into a chair while Susanna hurried to close the flap and light a lamp. "It's so cold," she said. "I'll start a fire."

Anton nodded, numbness creeping over him, though it wasn't only the cold making him feel that way.

Susanna shed her wet cloak and hat, and set about starting a fire in the little brazier. Once she had it crackling merrily, she came to Anton and took his hand.

"Come sit by the fire. And take off that wet doublet. Here."

She helped him peel it off, and hung it over the back of a chair. For the first time, Anton noticed how cold he really was, and shivered. He slumped to the floor in front of the fire cross-legged, while Susanna bustled around.

When she returned to sit beside him, she had a bottle of the best liquor from her cart and two mugs. "We'll figure out what to do later," she said, handing Anton a rather full mug. "But first let's have a drink or three."

Anton drank it down fast, sighing as the warmth spread through his middle and out to his fingers and toes. "I can't think of what to do," he said, as Susanna topped off his mug.

She took a few sips of hers and said, "You can't do anything right now. But fortunately, we're sure to run into the Sanova Hussars again."

"We never even saw them when they were here." Anton drank more in big gulps, hoping to get drunk faster.

"We weren't looking for them before." Susanna put her mug on the floor, then tugged at her hair, pinned up at the back of her head, until it fell down around her shoulders. It was damp, but sprang into little curls as it dried.

Anton realized he'd never seen her with her hair down, and wanted to tell her how pretty it was, but was too miserable. "So we find them," he said. "Then what?"

"It shouldn't be too hard to find a red-headed female officer. There aren't many women amongst the Sanovans. I hear they're dreadfully old-fashioned." Susanna shook her head. "We find her and offer to buy him."

"She won't want to give him up." Anton drained his mug again and held it out.

Susanna shook her head. "You need to slow down. I'll get you some water."

"No," Anton said. "More of this." He realized he sounded like the count. "I need to get really drunk."

Susanna sighed and poured a little more. "You'll be sorry when you're on the march tomorrow."

"I don't care. The thing is, she'll love Skandar, and she won't give him up for anything. Even when I was close to starving, I wouldn't have sold him for any amount of money."

"You'll have to ask anyway," Susanna said. They were both silent for a moment until she turned to him, sliding closer. "Oh, Anton," she said, "I'm so sorry." She put an arm around his waist and rested her head on his shoulder. "I wish you'd told me about your horse sooner. We might have been able to get him weeks ago."

Anton rested his cheek on top of her head. Her hair was almost dry now and very soft. "I should have told you," he said, "Even though you never tell me anything, Madame Stengel."

That made her laugh. "You're right," she said. "I don't know when I became so suspicious of everyone."

"When your husband left you, no doubt."

She shook her head, damp curls tickling Anton's nose. "No, it was before that. Once I realized I'd have to live in a military camp and make my own way, I decided it was better to trust no one but myself."

"I don't blame you," Anton said. "It must be hard for a girl alone, especially a pretty one like you." He was drunk now, and a little happier. He might not have Skandar, but he hadn't even seen him in months. What he did have was Susanna, practically in his lap. He slid an arm around her waist and pulled her even closer. When she looked up at him, he kissed her. She hesitated, but kissed him back. Her lips tasted like brandy as Anton ran his tongue over them. She made a little noise, and pushed her tongue toward his.

Just as he started to really enjoy himself, she broke away. "Anton," she said. "We're drunk. This is probably not a good time."

"According to you, it's never a good time," he said, a little angrily. Then he gave her his best sad look. "Please Susanna." He stroked her cheek softly. "I like you a lot, and I really appreciate how you tried to help me today. I doubt you'd give all of your money to a fellow for a horse unless you liked him a lot."

"I do like you a lot," Susanna said. "But you're too young."

"Do I kiss like someone who's too young?" Anton asked, glad he'd had practice already before trying something like this.

She flushed, a deep pink, which spread rather adorably across her cheeks and nose. Anton kissed the tip of her nose, then nibbled softly on her jawline before moving to her neck.

Susanna whimpered.

Anton took that as a sign to go ahead, and lifted her onto his lap with one smooth motion. But he was drunk, and she was heavier than he'd expected, so her weight knocked him over. He pulled her onto the floor with him, and she didn't resist.

KENDRYK

The darkness took Kendryk's breath away. A torch went ahead of and behind him, and a whole line of them stretched back into the distance. But they seemed like tiny, fragile flickers in the oppressive blackness. He pushed down the panic that flared up, realizing this reminded him of the Arnfels dungeon. Then he told himself this was nothing like that. He was free now, leading a troop of soldiers who would help liberate his home and his friends.

Once inside the mountain, the way sloped down quickly. The soldier holding the torch in front of him kept it close to the damp and slippery ground. The passageway was tall enough for someone of Kendryk's height. Braeden would have had to duck. Kendryk wished he were here too, but he was needed to help carry out their plan elsewhere.

Here inside the mountain, the way was clear. A tunnel had been carved into the limestone and it remained in good condition. They went down for what felt like hours. Finally, the tunnel straightened out, though now it became more dangerous. They must have reached the bottom of the hill, and were now underneath the meadow that lay before Birkenfels. Here, the tunnel went through thick clay, so wooden supports held it together. No one had touched these for the better part of a century—Terragand had been at peace for so long. Now they sagged, rotting and broken in many places.

Kendryk found he was holding his breath, hoping the way hadn't collapsed altogether. He didn't want to think of making the climb to go all the way back. More importantly, he hoped it wouldn't collapse now, with several hundred men tramping through it. They went slowly, picking their way across a muddy floor, and stepping over pieces of fallen wood. Yet another thing Kendryk might add to his list once he was restored here. He resolved that this route must always remain in good repair.

After what seemed like hours—and one heart-stopping moment in which several large beams needed to be cleared away before they could go forward—

the tunnel changed again, turning to stone and becoming taller and wider. "We're under the castle now," Kendryk said, and a relieved murmur went up behind him. He was sure they'd emerge in a cellar, but wasn't sure which one.

At last they reached a heavy wooden door, bound with iron. As Kendryk's father had told him, it latched from the tunnel side, in case of pursuit from the castle. No one else would know about the entrance on the hillside, though Kendryk realized with a wry grin that the secret was out now. No matter; he would worry about that some other time. Today, the tunnel had served its purpose.

The latch had rusted, and Kendryk used the hilt of his dagger to pound it open. He pulled, and it opened slowly, the rusty hinges shrieking. He wondered if anyone inside the castle heard, and hoped they'd look before shooting the intruders. The door opened to blackness, so Kendryk grabbed a torch and raised it high. A wooden wall blocked their way. His heart fell into his feet. Had the entrance been boarded up? Exhausted as they were, they'd have to cut their way in somehow.

Someone large loomed up behind him. "Let me try," the man said, grinning down at Kendryk.

"Can you break it?" Kendryk asked.

The man took a few steps back and ran at the wall, shoulder first. There was a great crash of wood, a shrieking noise, and then the wood fell forward, big fellow on top. It smashed onto the stone floor of the cellar, and they were in. The man stood, dusting himself off. "Guess it was just a shelf," he said with a grin. "And an empty one at that."

Kendryk almost laughed with relief, though an empty shelf was never a good sign in a besieged castle. He clapped the man on the shoulder. "Thank you," he said. "But I'll go first, in case someone thinks we're attacking."

He wasn't wrong. A few seconds later, footsteps pounded on the stairs, the cellar door burst open, and Merton nearly fell into the room, sword drawn.

As soon as he saw Kendryk, he stopped short and stared. "Is it? What?" He shook his head.

Kendryk hurried forward and grabbed his hand. "It's me," he said. "I've come to get you out of here." He realized he hadn't seen his old friend in over five years after leaving his family in his care before going into battle. And through all of that, Merton had always held Birkenfels. Kendryk's trust had been well-placed.

For a moment, he worried Merton would cry, but he recovered and was soon grinning widely. "We'd heard about your rescue," Merton said. "But we expected you to stay in Galladium until Lennart made a move."

"I can't wait for Lennart," Kendryk said. "He's having trouble in Helvundala, and I hoped to gather up allies to encourage him." Behind him, men streamed into the room out of the tunnel.

Merton stared. "I had no idea this was here."

"No one does but me. Well, now it's me, Duke Trystan and these three hundred good men."

Merton frowned. "I doubt three hundred will be enough to break out. We have only that many ourselves."

Kendryk couldn't stop smiling. "Trystan waits out there with another fifteen hundred. We'll get out tonight."

Now they were climbing the winding stairs leading to the castle courtyard. "And then what?" Merton asked.

"I must find Edric Maximus," Kendryk said. "Wherever he goes, I'm sure we can gain allies. But they say there's trouble in the temples." He gnawed at his lower lip, hoping it wasn't already too late. "I don't know where he is."

Merton stopped short. "He's here," he said. "He came not five days ago, right ahead of that army you see camped around us."

"So he's all right then? Unhurt?"

"Yes, he's fine. He had some trouble, but he made it here, and now we can keep him safe."

"I must see him right away," Kendryk said, his heart pounding. There was no one in the world he wanted to see more right now.

"Edric Maximus is in his study, just like the old days," Merton said as they entered the castle living quarters.

It was a long climb, most of the way up the tower, but Kendryk took the stairs two at a time, even though his wounded leg ached. The door to Edric's study stood ajar, and Kendryk pushed it open. Edric stood with his back to Kendryk, leaning out the window, watching the commotion in the courtyard as Kendryk's men streamed in. "Has someone come to relieve us?" he asked, without turning his head.

"I have," Kendryk said, feeling suddenly shy and overwhelmed as he stepped into the familiar room. Memories of a happier, more carefree time rushed back at the sight and smell of it, and Kendryk swallowed down a lump in his throat. By then, Edric had crossed the room and pulled him into a firm embrace. Kendryk repressed the urge to burst into tears on his shoulder.

When they pulled apart, Edric's eyes shone. "Thank the gods," he finally said, his voice husky. "I worried I'd never see you again."

"So did I." Kendryk's voice wobbled, but he steadied it and smiled. "Though it seems the gods spared me for some reason, and now I'm going to get you out of here."

Edric smiled back. "I know exactly why the gods spared you, and it wasn't to rescue me."

"Maybe so." Kendryk thought his face might split from grinning. "But I'll do it anyway. You might as well pack up your things, and prepare to move back into your palace."

ANTON

Someone was shaking Anton's shoulder.

"Wake up," a soft voice whispered in his ear. Hair tickled his cheek.

Anton screwed his eyes shut and grinned. "Don't want to."

Susanna shook him again. "Come on. Michalek's pike is moving out in a few hours, and I'm sure your things aren't packed. You need to get going."

Anton opened his eyes. Susanna sat on the edge of the cot, already dressed, with her hair still down.

"You have pretty hair," he said. "I wanted to tell you yesterday, but worried I'd sound too forward."

"Hmph," she said. "Groping me the way you did was a little bolder than a compliment."

Anton propped himself up on his elbow. "You didn't seem to mind too much, as I recall." Then he frowned. "What exactly happened? I remember being on the floor, but how did I get ..." He trailed off, since he had just noticed that even though he lay in Susanna's bed, he still wore his breeches.

She grinned at him. "You were really drunk," she said. "And once we got into bed, you fell asleep before much of anything happened."

Anton flopped back onto the pillow, feeling like an idiot. "Too bad. I doubt you'll ever give me another chance."

Susanna stood. "Are you sure about that? Why don't you stop by tonight, and find out?"

Anton jumped out of bed, though his head throbbed. Rain drummed on the tent, so the march today would be especially miserable. But he didn't care. "What are you saying?" He realized he should try to act more casual—the count had always told him appearing too eager put women off. Except he *was* eager, and it was too late to hide it from Susanna in any case.

Susanna pinned her hair up now, her little hands moving deftly, as if she didn't even have to think about it. "I'm saying, you should come by after we make camp tonight. And I don't mean to work. We'll take the evening off, and become better acquainted." She finished her hair, then handed Anton his shirt and doublet, nearly dry by now.

"Acquainted how?" Anton pulled his clothes on quickly. It had to be near dawn, and he had a lot to do before leaving. He hoped Stasny had already taken down their tent.

Once he was dressed, Susanna came up to him and put her hands on his shoulders. "I'll tell you all about myself—anything at all. I might have a few questions for you too."

"I've told you everything." Anton smiled down at her. In spite of his headache, he wanted to dance a jig.

"There are a few more things I'd like to find out," Susanna looked up at him, her eyes grave. "Like who the girl was; the one who taught you to kiss like that."

"Oh that." Anton gave her his special smile. "That comes naturally."

Susanna shook her head, though she was smiling too. "Well, you can tell me everything tonight." She stood up on tiptoe, and kissed him softly on the lips. "Oh, and tell your sergeant to put a new recruit in your tent. You'll stay with me from now on."

Anton's breath caught. "Are you sure? You want me to live with you?"

"Why not? We already spend all of our free time together. And it would be more convenient, since we work together too."

"Yes, very convenient." Anton swallowed hard, his head swimming with possibilities. "I don't want to go," he whispered.

"I know. But you must. Bring your things with you when you come tonight." One more little kiss, and she shoved him out of the tent and into the rain.

Anton reached his regiment just as Count Michalek had gathered them for a speech of sorts, which he almost never did. He said the empress had ordered them to Terragand, where they would join General Ensden in the fight against King Lennart, who had already invaded Helvundala. Anton found he didn't care about King Lennart, and wasn't as unhappy about fighting for the empress as he had been before. In fact, he didn't care about much at all except seeing Susanna again as soon as he could. Fortunately the speech didn't go on long, because Count Michalek was drunk, and it was raining hard.

Anton should have been miserable that day, but he couldn't stop grinning. Stasny was very grumpy when Anton told him he was moving out. "I've been trying to get a nice girl for years," he said. "Now you show up and snatch up one of the best ones after just a few months."

"Told you I was lucky," Anton said. "I can't help it if women love me." He happily marched all day, in the rain, with an awful headache.

The rain fell in a steady drizzle, creating a mist that covered everything, so it was impossible to see where they were going, besides down a muddy road. He'd rather be on horseback, but marching in step like this wasn't too bad, with stout fellows on all sides of you, the sergeant leading them in marching songs with words that used to make Anton blush, though they didn't anymore.

When they briefly stopped around midday to eat biscuit and cheese, Anton found that Stasny and the sergeant had already spread the word. His comrades looked at him with new respect, and considerable envy. Susanna was popular with the soldiers, but had a reputation for being picky about her men.

"Thinks she's too good for the likes of us," one man sniffed. "Can't think what she sees in a little squirt like you." He glared at Anton, who tried not to grin, but failed.

"It might be my looks," Anton said, "or my charming personality, my fashion sense, my courage in battle, or my intelligence, but it's most likely my love-making skills." It was hard to say that last bit without feeling embarrassed about the previous evening, though he kept a cocky grin firmly in place. To be honest, he enjoyed the good-natured ribbing, and it made him feel like he'd become a real man at last.

BRAEDEN

Braeden's stomach growled so loudly he was sure the enemy heard it. He'd eaten nothing but a little bit of left-over stew early that morning. They'd waited at the tunnel entrance for hours, until a messenger returned through it saying Kendryk and his men had reached the castle.

"Can't everyone get back out that way?" Trystan asked.

Braeden had wondered about that. It would be so much easier if all of them could sneak out of the castle without the enemy knowing about it.

The messenger shook his head. "There's a dangerous stretch under the meadow where the support beams have collapsed. We barely made it through the first time, and they chose me to come back because I'm so skinny. I had to crawl through a few holes so small even I got stuck."

"I see." Trystan frowned. "We'll stay with our original plan then." He nodded at Braeden. "Terris, you take the cavalry to the south end of the valley."

Braeden hurried back around the hill where the small troop of cavalry waited. They numbered only a few hundred, and weren't close to the Sanova Hussars in experience or skill, but Braeden had drilled them hard, and they would do well enough tonight.

The rest of Trystan's troops, including Karil's musketeer company, would be deployed along the edge of the wood at the base of the hill. Whoever commanded the enemy troops had been lax, and wasn't keeping an eye on the woods. Braeden wondered if they weren't expecting anyone, or if it never occurred to them that a large force might get here without being noticed. Without Kendryk's knowledge of the countryside, they would have been forced to take the main road and attracted attention.

Braeden led his troops single file along a deer trail at the edge of the woods until they reached a clearing. He sent his most sharp-eyed scout ahead, and he returned quickly with word that the enemy outposts lay a quarter-league distant and out of sight.

"We'll cross the clearing at a walk," Braeden ordered. "We're more likely to be heard than seen, so do what you can to keep your tack and weapons from jangling."

Braeden's nerves stretched taut as his force strung out, exposed for a good twenty minutes until the woods concealed them once more.

As afternoon wore into evening, Braeden made sure everyone received a few hours' rest in shifts and was at the ready. He could expect a signal after dark. He'd posted a lookout on a small hill to his rear with a clear view of its crest. Once the sun dropped behind the mountains and the sky turned dark, a few lone stars blinking into view, he ordered his troops into formation. He mounted Kazmir in full armor, weapons ready, and watched the hill intently.

Twilight turned to complete darkness, and it took a while for Braeden's eyes to adjust. It was quiet, except for the croaking of frogs at a nearby pond. A slight breeze rustled the new leaves, and Braeden shivered. The nights were still cold and damp. He stared at the hill until his eyes crossed, wondering if something had gone wrong.

Those inside the castle would light a beacon when they were ready, and that would be relayed to all of Trystan's forces surrounding the valley. Braeden was last in line. If anything went wrong along the way, he might never find out when to attack.

He had just started formulating a different plan, when light flared up from the hillside. "Advance," Braeden whispered to a lieutenant, and the command went down the line. He rode to the head of the force, then made for the road, everyone following in two long columns.

As soon as he came out of the trees onto the road, sounds of battle drifted on the air. Behind him, someone drew a saber.

"Steady," Braeden said. "We wait here. I know it's hard, but it's part of the plan."

"Won't be any left for us," someone muttered.

Braeden chuckled. "We're outnumbered two to one. That won't be a problem."

They didn't have to wait much longer. The least stalwart of the enemy troops, and several camp followers came down the road at a run. When they saw the horses standing in their path, they stopped, then ran into the woods on either side of the road.

"Let them go," Braeden said. "They're not fighting us, but mind the rear in case they regroup."

He spurred Kazmir lightly, and they advanced along the road. Now he saw more and more of the enemy. Trystan and the others had surprised the sleepy camp, while Kendryk and Count Faris led out the six hundred soldiers from the castle. They'd easily overrun the guards, and everyone else was asleep or otherwise unprepared. Most of the soldiers Braeden caught retreating along the road carried few or unloaded weapons. He sent several dozen of his troopers to round up prisoners and disarm them.

His main task was more important. They were in the enemy camp now, moving quickly through fleeing soldiers and camp followers. Even in the dark it wasn't hard to know when they'd reached the baggage train.

"Secure all the wagons," Braeden said. "Guard those holding food most carefully, then those holding powder and weapons." All this was for nothing if they were still starving at the end of the night.

By the time Braeden found Trystan in the center of camp, he was accepting the formal surrender of Alona Brynner, the colonel in charge of the siege. A short, sturdy veteran of many Zastwar campaigns, she recognized Braeden as soon as he stepped into the circle of light outside her tent.

Her pudgy face split into a smile. "Terris!" she said. "This really is too bad. If I'd been more careful, I'd be rich from collecting the bounty on that scruffy head of yours."

Braeden grinned. "Too bad for you. It's good to see you, old girl. Maybe we can catch up later." He turned to Trystan. "Baggage is secured, and my men are rounding up a good many prisoners. There's a lot of food out there."

"Thank the gods," Trystan said. He turned toward Brynner. "Reckon I can get the prisoners to fight for me?"

She shrugged, as Trystan handed back her sword. "Depends on how well you pay. Everyone was flush for a few weeks after Livilla Maxima paid us off, but I used most of mine to lay in supplies for a month-long siege. I imagine the others have gambled theirs away by now."

"I have nothing," Trystan said in that forthright way he had. "But we're going to meet King Lennart, and he's got a lot of coin and is looking to hire."

"Think he'd have a place for me?" Brynner slid her sword back into its scabbard. "Ensden won't be happy that I've botched this."

"I'm sure he would," Trystan said, and just like that, Alona Brynner and her army joined the ranks of Kendryk's allies.

ELEKTRA

Even though she hadn't wanted to return at first, Elektra was glad to see Atlona again. She'd been away for over three years, and it really was different, passing through the big gates on her splendid charger, at the head of her own regiment. Livilla had been careful to arrange it so her mother was present when Elektra approached the parade grounds in front of the Palais Arden.

On the long journey from Brandana, Elektra explained to Livilla why impressing her mother was so important to her.

"She doesn't think me capable," she'd said. "And I know I am."

"I know you are too," Livilla said with a kind smile.

"But I'm afraid Mother will make me go back to school, and give my regiment to someone else."

"I doubt she's given it much thought," Livilla said, "so we must do our best to show her how different you are now. I'm certain she found the story of your kidnapping and escape marvelous, so she shouldn't be too surprised to see how you've changed."

"I have changed a lot, haven't I?" Elektra had, at least outwardly. Even at her worst, she'd always known she was made of the stuff to be empress, though she hadn't been so good at showing it. But now she looked the part.

Perhaps she wasn't as tall or as attractive as her mother, but she carried herself well. She had grown taller, and lost the baby fat that lent her face a childish pudginess. Her skin had cleared under a light tan, while her hair thickened and darkened to a rather pleasing dark brown with a slight reddish hue. A few men even looked at her in the way men looked at pretty women, and that gave her confidence too.

Above all, Elektra realized she could take care of herself, and that she was a good leader. Her arguments with Karil had taught her there were better and worse ways of handling one's subjects. She'd learned that grace and tact went further than a domineering manner. When she was empress, people would obey, no matter how she gave the orders, but she wanted more than the grudging, fearful obedience her mother commanded. She wanted to be loved and respected, and was well on her way to accomplishing this. Once she got rid of her mother, everyone would realize that Elektra was by far the better ruler.

These pleasant thoughts had led to a rather inappropriate grin on her face as her mother's suite approached. Elektra replaced it with a cool, slightly haughty look that always worked well on stubborn officers. Somehow, Livilla had persuaded Teodora to review Elektra's troops, which were in top condition. Elektra had received a large sum from Livilla as official payment for leaving Mattila, and borrowed even more. She used the money to outfit the entire regiment with new clothing, matching tabards bearing the Inferrara crest, a suit of half-armor for each soldier, and finely crafted modern weapons from Zeelund. Then she used every spare moment to drill them mercilessly, until they moved like one enormous, glittering creature. All that remained was to prove them in battle.

As Teodora came near, Elektra urged her horse forward. "It's good to see you again, Your Highness," she lied.

Teodora pulled her horse to a stop. "I'm glad you finally came home. Why did you disobey my orders?"

Elektra wondered if her mother even noticed the magnificent troops ranged behind her, and willed the flush rising up her neck to disappear. "I received no orders from you, I'm afraid," she said, keeping her face expressionless. This was technically true, since orders went straight to Mattila. Elektra never so much as received a personal letter from her mother.

"Hmph," Teodora said, frowning. "I suppose Mattila kept them from you."

"Probably." Elektra shrugged, trying to conceal her shock over how much worse her mother looked. Her dark hair bore gray streaks, and wrinkles creased her forehead and the skin around her mouth, while her eyes looked flat and lifeless. Elektra realized she'd been away for several years, and a great deal had happened in that time. "I'm back now, but just for a short time."

Teodora raised an eyebrow. "Is that what you think?"

Elektra did her best to stay calm. "I have orders. Count Ensden needs me in Terragand."

"Ridiculous," Teodora said. "He needs those soldiers, not you. They're very pretty. I recall you liked dressing up your dolls too."

Elektra swallowed down her indignation. Everything depended on showing her mother she was an adult who couldn't be pushed around. It would do no good to lose her temper like a helpless little girl. "I don't believe you ever paid enough attention to me to remember what I did with my dolls. If you had, you'd recall I enjoyed beheading them." Elektra narrowed her eyes and stared straight at her mother.

Teodora burst out laughing. "You're right. I can't abide children—so dull. But I must confess, I like that you've grown a spine. You were quite ridiculous last time we spoke."

"I'm an adult now," Elektra said quietly.

"We'll see about that." Teodora's face changed to one of false friendliness. "But come. We haven't seen each other in years, and I'm sure you have a great deal to tell me. Send these fine fellows to the barracks, and give them a week's leave. You'll come stay with me, and we'll discuss everything."

Elektra nodded, not knowing what else to do. Her officers and troops would welcome the time off in the city— many had family here—and she couldn't defy her mother in front of everyone. It would just end in embarrassment. She'd have to find another way, and hope to get help from Livilla.

"You'll stay in the guest wing, since you're old room is occupied," Teodora was saying.

"Did Zofya take my room?" Elektra frowned. She wouldn't have minded staying near the nursery, with her little brother, who probably wasn't so little anymore.

"Zofya is at the temple school now, and so is your brother. No, your rooms have been taken over by Aksel Roussay and his laboratory."

That was good news, and Elektra didn't try to hide her smile. "How nice. He and I are old friends."

Her mother looked pleased. "Really? You must pay him a visit."

KENDRYK

"We must continue to hold Birkenfels somehow," Kendryk insisted. Trystan had been in a rush to make for Helvundala, and proposed abandoning the castle for now. "So little of Terragand is ours, but as long as Birkenfels is safe, we have a rallying point."

"Can we spare the soldiers?" Trystan asked, frowning. They had gathered in Birkenfels' small dining hall to make plans. "Now Brynner has joined us, we're doing better, but I doubt we can spare a garrison here."

"We must," Kendryk said firmly. "We'll keep it small so their supplies last longer; no more than fifty."

Trystan raised his eyebrows. "Is that enough?"

"That's all we had during the original siege," Kendryk said. "All the rest were civilians. The walls are strong, it's nearly impossible to storm the gate, and it's difficult to position big guns to strike it with any force."

"We can spare fifty," Trystan said.

Kendryk realized he could give the order, and Trystan would have to comply, but he preferred to keep things friendly. Besides, he valued Trystan's expertise. He'd spent most of the past several years fighting imperial forces at terrible odds, and succeeding surprisingly often. Aside from Braeden and Count Faris, he was the most experienced person here.

"Please don't leave me here again." Merton spoke up from the end of the table.

Kendryk smiled at him. "Tired of this castle, are you? I understand. You'll come with me, but I'd like it if you personally picked the soldiers for the garrison."

"Be glad to," Merton said with a grin. He'd barely set foot outside the castle walls since the first siege over four years before.

"I propose we make for Helvundala as quickly as possible," Kendryk said, now that had been settled. "I'm certain our appearance will sway my cousin, and give Lennart support."

"I agree," Count Faris said. He looked down at the map spread across the table, and pointed at a spot. "The fastest way is through here. I'm sure you're familiar with the Garsten Gap."

Braeden snorted rather loudly. "Best watch yourself before going in there."

Faris looked at him. "I take it you have experience with it?"

Braeden shook his head. "We came from the other side, and Duke Evard's small force of musketeers stopped us cold. Though at the time I was sure you were in charge there," he added with a nod toward Faris.

"I remember," Kendryk said, though he hated to think of that awful time. "I was impressed by my uncle, and grateful that he kept your lot away from Birkenfels just a little longer. Though it turned out to be Gwynneth's plan, and she forced him to carry it out." His cousin Balduin still sat in the dungeon here, but Kendryk hoped he might be used for leverage against Evard; he just hadn't figured out how.

"So if the enemy reaches it ahead of us, we might not get through?" Faris asked.

"If they can get in, and position muskets on top of the stone outcroppings on both sides of the road, I doubt anyone can get through," Braeden said.

"We must get there first then," Faris said. They'd spent nearly ten days here after taking the castle back, scouting out the area, trying to learn which way the bulk of Ensden's force was headed. "In fact, if we can get there soon, we can position our muskets as Evard did, then head for Helvundala and get Lennart. It will be the fastest way for him to get into Terragand."

"That sounds like an excellent plan," Kendryk said. "I'll send a message to Lennart, telling him we're on our way, and that we'll hold the gap for him."

After the group broke up, Kendryk made his way up the winding stone staircase to Edric's study. Edric sat at his desk as usual, but it was large enough that Kendryk used the other side for his correspondence. He might have chosen a room of his own, but he enjoyed spending time with Edric. It didn't make up for the years apart, but it was nice to be together now.

"We'll leave for Helvundala tomorrow," Kendryk said, sliding into his chair. "Will you be ready?"

"Certainly." Edric shuffled papers around.

"What are you working on?" Kendryk asked.

"Nothing right now." Edric had changed a great deal since Kendryk had first met him. His blond hair had turned mostly gray, he'd grown thin and gaunt, the bones of his face appearing skeletal in dim light. His pale eyes had lost none of their fire, but they looked sometimes tired and always sad. "I've finished all the letters to the temples that remain, but I can't think of what to do next." He looked up at Kendryk and attempted a smile. "That's never happened before. I used to fear I would die before I finished all the work I needed to. I haven't finished it all, but I'm questioning if there's any point to it."

Kendryk stared at him, stunned. He'd never known Edric to express any doubt at all. He said, "Surely, you are tired. And the last months have been difficult. Perhaps you should take time off from your work until we've met with Lennart. Once we reconquer Terragand, you'll have much to do in the temples."

"That's the problem. I was sure that by now, our faith would prevail to where the enemy couldn't defeat it through force of arms. I'd hoped the people would stand firm no matter what happened on the battlefield." He buried his head in his hands.

Kendryk swallowed hard. He was not accustomed to being the one to comfort Edric, since it was usually the other way around. Still, if he needed comfort, Kendryk would try to provide it. "Many stood firm," Kendryk said finally. "And I'm sure many still do, just not in the temples." Aside from a sliver on the eastern edge of Terragand, and in the near vicinity of Birkenfels, all temples were under the control of the League of Aeternos.

Edric looked up. "True, many stood firm, and most of those died. Those who remain are not as brave, not as convinced. Will they hold to their beliefs under the relentless pressure of the League?"

"You told me once we are all at different levels of faith. Those who were strongest are now dead. But perhaps the less strong will become so in time, and take their places."

Edric's eyes were sad. "Will there be time for that before the enemy roots them out and kills them too, or forces them to falter in their faith?"

"There will." Kendryk smiled, and didn't have to force himself to do so. "Soon we'll meet with Lennart, and whether or not my cousin cooperates, we'll bring an army here, and make Terragand safe for the true believers once more."

Edric wasn't able to manage a smile, but a light flickered in his eyes. "I hope you're right, and I thank the gods every day for your steadfastness."

ELEKTRA

After settling into her suite in the palace's guest wing—much nicer than her own room, she had to admit—Elektra washed, changed her clothes, and went in search of Aksel. She told herself she put on her prettiest gown because she'd be dining with her mother and the court later, but deep down she knew it was only Aksel's opinion she cared about.

The children's wing of the castle was silent and deserted. The last time Elektra had been here, it resonated with Zofya's lively chatter and Rudofo's boisterous shouts. She hadn't thought about her siblings often in the past few years, but now she was here, she missed their presence. She would be sure to pay them both a visit at the temple school. The nursery made a good spot for a laboratory, so Elektra went there first. She found Aksel perched on a high stool behind a table, staring at the wall.

"Hello," she said, walking into the room.

Aksel's face lit up. "Your Grace!" He jumped off the stool and hurried over to her.

She extended her hand. He took it, bowed over it, then kissed it. He didn't linger the way General Barela always had, but it was still much nicer than the usual way courtiers minced and slobbered over it.

"I'm so glad you're safe," he said. "I was worried when I heard of your kidnapping."

That made her happy. She smiled at him. "Do you have time to talk?"

"Of course." He led her to a bench pushed up against the wall. Elektra recognized it as old nursery furniture. Once they sat side-by-side, he said, "You must tell me everything that happened. Zofya said you had an incredible adventure."

"I did." Elektra told him the real tale, the one she hadn't told her mother. She'd hoped Teodora would be more impressed if she'd escaped Braeden right away, and then made her own way across war-torn Kronland. In truth, she knew she never would have survived without Braeden. Much as she hated him, she had to give him that.

She loved talking to Aksel, because he always listened so carefully, and with such interest. He asked few questions, but she saw he paid close attention. She'd been ashamed of her broken vow to Vica, but told him about that too, hoping he wouldn't judge her too harshly.

When she finished, there was a long moment of silence. Aksel looked thoughtful, and Elektra held her breath, praying he didn't find her too horrible.

Then he said, "How brave you were, and how very clever, too."

Elektra's insides warmed.

"A bit wicked too, I must say." He turned to her with a grin, showing he didn't mean it. "But I understand why you did that. And of course, I hold to the Quadrene creed, so any vow made on Vica alone shouldn't be taken too seriously. Everyone knows you must swear on the Holy Family if you really mean it."

Something heavy dropped in Elektra's middle. "You're a Quadrene? A heretic?" A flush rose over her face, and this time she didn't try to make it go away.

Aksel smiled again. "According to my priests, you're the heretic, although I'm in favor of finding a way to meet in the middle. Just don't tell my sister."

"I ..." Elektra wanted to blurt out he must realize how wrong he was, and that he must go to the temple at once, confess his heresy, and receive instruction from a League priestess. "I think you're wrong," she said at last.

"I know," Aksel said.

She couldn't understand how it didn't bother him. "But can't you see why you are?" she asked.

He shook his head. "I wonder that you can't see your way is wrong."

Elektra wanted to be angry, but she was far more sad. She liked Aksel so much, and worried he would be cursed and condemned forever. She forced a smile. "I hope you come to find the truth. I will pray for you."

"Thank you." He seemed most sincere. "And I will pray for you."

Elektra worried that a heretic's prayers might bring something awful down upon her, but hoped she could save him before things went much further. She'd have to consult Livilla.

She changed the subject, asking Aksel to show her around the laboratory.

"Your sister and I were working on this," he said, showing Elektra a peculiar device made of several layers of glass lenses mounted on a thin wooden frame, with an eyepiece at the top.

"Zofya?" she asked, feeling a surge of jealousy, even though she supposed her sister was far too young to interest Aksel.

"Yes," he said, looking sad. "But your mother decided she didn't want us spending time together."

That was even worse. "I wonder why?" Elektra asked as innocently as she could.

Aksel hesitated, then said, "She was convinced Zofya had developed a crush on me, though I'm sure she was wrong."

"Hm," Elektra said, certain her mother was right. At least she'd stopped it, hopefully before anything happened. "And did you like her too?"

His laugh reassured her. "Zofya was a good friend, and has an excellent mind. She had such a good idea when I was struggling to put this device together. She remembered a book in the temple library, written by a scientist in Cesiano, which has made all the difference. I'm close to having something I can use. But that's all it was. I had no intentions toward your sister, and fortunately your mother believed me when I said so. It was bad enough she threw me in the Arnfels when she was having trouble with my brother."

Elektra had already heard about that from her maid, and said, "She's so horrible; I'm sorry she put you through that," while she tried concealing her annoyance at his admiration for Zofya's intelligence. She'd always been quick, with an academic bent Elektra didn't have. She gave Aksel her brightest smile. "You must explain it all to me. I'm sure it's brilliant. But I must see my mother now. She wants to talk for a while before dinner; no doubt to grill me all about General Mattila's activities. Will you join us later?"

"If you're here, certainly," Aksel said. "Most of the time I have a tray sent up so I can keep working, but I'd love to help celebrate your return."

"Knowing my mother, it won't be much of a celebration," Elektra said, all while knowing that having Aksel at her side would be more than enough.

BRAEDEN

They made it to the gap ahead of Ensden's troops, but barely. Trystan had taken care to send scouts in all directions, and they soon heard what the enemy was doing. The gap was less than a day's march from Birkenfels, but by now they had nearly six thousand soldiers to get through the narrow defile before imperial troops caught up to them.

Braeden and Trystan hurried ahead to make plans before the rest of the force arrived.

"Look familiar?" Trystan asked, as they came to a halt at the base of the hill, the road ahead of them disappearing into the dark trees.

Braeden nodded. "This end looks much like the other. Most likely, the outcroppings go all the way through on both sides of the road, so we can position soldiers along them."

"How far to the other side?" They were riding into the forest now, a hundred cavalry troopers at their backs.

"I don't know," Braeden admitted. "We didn't get in very far before we decided it was best to find another way."

Trystan chuckled. "I can't picture your lot retreating."

Braeden hated being reminded of it, though he knew Novitny had made the right decision. And Janna had fallen all over him upon his safe return, which made the whole expedition worthwhile, as far as he was concerned. In fact, that had been the day he became certain they'd spend the rest of their lives together.

"You all right?" Trystan turned toward him.

"I'm fine." Braeden shook his head, banishing that memory. He turned his attention to the rocks rising straight up from the sides of the road. He guessed they stood about twenty feet tall, with plenty of trees and brush growing on top.

"Perfect for an ambush," Trystan said. "They can try to shoot back, but they won't hit much. We'll do what we can to keep our lot well-hidden. Just because our numbers have increased doesn't mean I want to lose any more soldiers."

"I agree," Braeden said. They rode in silence until they reached the other side, the road opening out onto flatter land.

"We can make good time from here," Trystan said. "Kendryk sent Lennart another message, and with any luck he'll get here in a few days. Can we hold it that long?"

"We will," Braeden said. "We have to."

By the time they returned to the western side, the rest of the force had arrived. So had a scout, with worrisome news. "They're coming down the road along the river, only two leagues from Birkenfels," she said, her eyes wide. She and her horse were spattered with mud. A gentle rain had fallen for two days, and she'd ridden hard.

Trystan's eyes hardened. "How many?"

Braeden always admired his calm and the steel under it. Those two qualities came together rarely, but when they did, and combined with a keen intelligence, the result was usually a brilliant commander. He hoped Lennart would detect Trystan's quality, and give him the responsibilities he deserved.

"Two, three thousand, as far as I could see, though there might be more. They came down the road eight abreast, and I could only see the end of the column from the top of the castle. Those are a lot of stairs when you're taking them fast. I'm almost as tired as my horse," the scout said, dismounting. "Would someone please rub down this poor creature? He's the only one I've got."

Trystan waved his hand, and a groom came running to take the horse. He turned to Kendryk. "Will they try for the castle?"

"We'd be lucky if they did," Kendryk said. "But I'm sure they're coming for us instead. They've failed so often to take the castle, they'd rather trap us in the open."

"They would." Trystan folded his arms across his chest and scowled. Braeden recognized the posture; he was thinking.

"We need to move now," Braeden said. "Send everyone through the gap, Prince Kendryk and Edric Maximus first. No matter what happens, they can't be caught."

Kendryk opened his mouth to protest, but Trystan stopped him. "Commander Terris is right. The two of you must get through to Lennart at all costs. We'll be right behind you."

Kendryk still looked unhappy, but Edric Maximus came up beside him. "Please, Your Grace, the duke is right. Lennart's success depends on his alliances in Kronland, and they won't happen without you."

Once Kendryk and much of the infantry had disappeared into the gap, Trystan turned to his officers. "I want all pike going in now. And most of the muskets. We won't need more than six companies, don't you think?" He turned back to Braeden.

"That should do it," Braeden said, though his heart sank as Karil sprang forward.

"Please, Your Grace," Karil said to Trystan. "Please let my platoon take the forward position."

Braeden opened his mouth to protest, but Karil shot him a pleading look before he spoke. Much as he hated having Karil in harm's way yet again, he understood. He'd been the same way at that age, when there was nothing worse than the prospect of missing out on the hottest action.

Trystan grinned. "As long as your captain says it's all right." He turned to Captain Rieser, a man Braeden knew held Karil in high regard.

"Sure," the man said. "Usually best to have the little hot-heads out front. Give the enemy what-for." He winked at Karil, who beamed, saluted and ran off to gather his unit.

Braeden found his throat was dry, cleared it, and said to Rieser, "Make sure you leave off their armor, or cover it. It's hard to see through the trees, but those little glints will give them away." Especially now as the rain had stopped, and the sun peeked through. "And tell them to stay well away from the edges. If they can't get a clear shot, let them pass. With as many muskets as we'll have lined up, someone's sure to get lucky. And we'll be waiting inside for those of the enemy who make it through."

Captain Rieser nodded. "I'll tell them. And you needn't worry about Andarosz; he's a smart lad."

"He's also brave to the point of stupidity," Braeden said, mostly to himself, then excused himself before he got emotional. He still had plenty to do without worrying about Karil yet again.

ANTON

"What are you grinning about?" Susanna asked, as she and Anton strolled back to her tent after a supper around the campfire. The days grew longer now as they headed north, with songs and laughter when everyone came together after a long day's march.

"Nothing," he said, tucking her hand under his elbow. He liked being on the move as they headed for the Terragand coast to take on one of King Lennart's generals. Even though Anton was still unhappy about Skandar, the rest of his life was pretty good. Marching all day beat sitting around in camp or drilling, although he and Susanna had less opportunity to work the gambling parties. Or maybe they had less interest in spending their evenings dealing with drunken soldiers, when they could be getting to know each other better in Susanna's cozy tent instead.

Anton felt like an adult, living with a woman as though they were married. A lot of soldiers lived that way, though a fair number got married in time. Anton didn't worry about it, because Susanna didn't seem to mind, though his mother would have disapproved. She would have disapproved of Susanna in any case, with her low-cut gowns and saucy smile. But his mother wasn't here now, and Anton had to make a life for himself. Besides, he was happy— happier than he'd been in a long time.

He didn't have to work too hard, or do things that made him feel bad later, like he sometimes had with the count. He had money too, though he and Susanna put their combined riches back with the quartermaster. Much as Anton hated the man, he seemed reliable. And best of all, he had Susanna. He'd tried to puzzle out if he loved her the way he'd loved Lora, and decided this was different. Lora had been mostly a dream, but Susanna was real.

Inside the tent, Susanna tied off the flap, while Anton rummaged in her cart, parked in the corner. He pulled out a bottle, and poured some for both of them after sitting down at the little table.

Susanna shook her head. "You drink too much."

"You're one to talk." Anton smirked after tossing down his, though he noticed she hadn't touched hers.

"I'm serious, Anton," she said, looking at him across the table. "I worry about you. You're too young to have that kind of problem."

Anton shrugged. "It's not a problem. It's not like it keeps me from doing my job, and I don't spend all my money on it."

"I know. I just remember..." she trailed off, and Anton figured she was thinking about her husband, who really had drunk too much.

"I'm not like him," Anton said, wishing he had a way to make her forget about that idiot once and for all.

"I never said you were. In fact, you're better in every way."

Anton agreed, though he didn't say so. "Well, I'll never leave you for another woman and run off to another country."

"Don't say never." Susanna's usually merry eyes were serious. "You're still so young. You'll probably fall in love ten more times before you're my age."

Anton scoffed. "Who would I fall in love with? You're the prettiest and the best girl I've seen in this whole camp."

"The world is a lot bigger than this camp."

"I know that. I've seen much of it." He banged his cup down a little hard. He hated it when she reminded him how much younger he was.

Susanna dropped her head to the table. Her shoulders shook.

"Oh gods, Susanna." Anton hurried to her, and put his arm around her as he knelt on the floor. "What's wrong?"

She raised her head slowly. Tears brimmed in her eyes, though they hadn't yet spilled over. Susanna never cried.

"What did I do?"

She managed a smile. "Nothing. I'm just a little out of sorts. The closer we get to the coast and that Estenorian army, the more I worry about you. I've become very fond of you, even though we haven't been together long." She leaned into Anton, and he put both arms around her.

"You needn't worry," he said. "I'm lucky. I mean, bad things have happened, but I always get away. Even when the count was killed." He paused and swallowed, surprised at how much he still hated talking about that. "Even when the count was killed with me right there, I wasn't even hurt. So I doubt anything will happen when I'm standing in the middle of a big block of pike. No one will get to me."

190

"That won't keep me from worrying," Susanna said, pulling away and wiping her eyes. "I'm not sure what's come over me. I've never fussed over anyone like this."

"You probably haven't ever liked anyone this much before," Anton said, giving her his special smile.

"Liked? I'm afraid it's gone further than that." She turned to face him. "I'm very sorry, but I've fallen in love with you."

"Why are you sorry?" Anton couldn't stop smiling now. "That's a good thing, isn't it?"

"Only if you feel the same way." Her eyes were more serious than he'd ever seen them.

He smiled at her some more, until she smiled back, then said, "You're as lucky as I am, Madame. It turns out I do feel the same way."

ELEKTRA

Even though it was nice to not be stuck in the temple school anymore, Elektra still looked forward to a visit. She had a few old friends there, and wanted to see her sister and brother. Elektra had also learned Mother Luca was here, and couldn't wait to be reunited with her. She would discuss Aksel Roussay's deplorable spiritual state with her and with Livilla. They would know what to do.

The moment Elektra stepped into the common room of her old dormitory—lessons were over for the day, and all the girls were studying at long tables—her best friend saw her, and ran to her with a squeal.

"Elektra! I hardly recognized you," Silia Raverna said, once they'd hugged and shed a few tears.

"I hardly recognized you either," Elektra said, looking down at Silia, who was as short as ever, though she had filled out in a way Elektra had yet to. "I suppose we've both grown up, and I worried you might not be here anymore." Many girls left the temple school at seventeen, either to pursue an occupation or further study. A few of the sillier ones got married. Silia had always grumbled she'd be forced to work in her family's banking house, even though she had no head for figures.

"I was sent back," Silia said, grimacing. She and Elektra took two chairs in the corner of the room, while other girls clustered around.

"What happened?" Elektra asked. "I worried when you stopped writing."

Silia's dark face flushed. "It's too embarrassing. I went to work in our counting house with my older sister, and made a terrible mess of things. After two weeks, my parents decided I'd have to find another vocation, and sent me back here. I never heard the end of it from this lot." She glared at the girls gathered around.

Elektra was sure she didn't mean it, because Silia was the most popular girl in the school, and everyone loved her. She knew her dormitory was pleased to have her back, though there had no doubt been some good-natured teasing. "So what will you do?" she asked her friend.

"I don't know," Silia said. "Livilla said I should try serving in a temple, though that seems dreadfully boring."

"What about a military career?" Elektra asked. "I'm always looking for good officers."

"Do I look like a fighter?" Silia laughed. "I'm more likely to be stepped on than hurt anyone."

"No, I was thinking I need an assistant," Elektra said. She was making this up on the spot, because she hadn't expected Silia to be available. "Like a secretary. You'd have military rank and pay, but you wouldn't be expected to fight."

"So you're not staying here?"

"I don't plan to," Elektra said. "My regiment has orders to report to Count Ensden in Terragand, and I intend to go with it."

All right then." Silia was grinning widely. "I'll come with you if you go. It would be marvelous to have an adventure together."

"I agree." Elektra smiled back. "Though I hope the next one doesn't involve kidnapping. I'll send for you soon, and we'll discuss everything. I'm sure Livilla won't mind."

"Mind? She'll be pleased to be rid of me for good."

Elektra smiled happily, then remembered another reason she'd come. "I must visit Mother Luca. I've missed her so much."

One girl gave her directions to Mother Luca's private study, and Elektra found her looking over lessons with a little girl. When she saw Elektra, she said, "I'll send for you later. Run along now, my dear."

Elektra smiled down at the girl, who stared up at her wide-eyed, before finally leaving and closing the door behind her, then turned to Luca.

To her surprise, Luca started sobbing. "Oh my dear child," she said, pulling Elektra into her arms. "I feared I'd never see you again. I've never forgiven myself for letting you out of my sight."

"It wasn't your fault," Elektra said. "You weren't my guard. And I'm all right now. See?" She pulled back and smiled at the priestess.

"Yes, thank Vica." Luca wiped her eyes, then led Elektra to a chair. "You must tell me everything."

Though it had been nice to tell Aksel her story, telling it to Luca was even better, since she'd been the one Elektra wanted to unburden herself to in the first place.

When she had told it all, Luca smiled gently. "I'm so glad Dava was there to help you. She is one of the most committed and knowledgeable in the League, and she offered you good advice."

"I still wished for you instead," Elektra said. She looked around the cozy little room. It was a fine spring day, and the windows stood open to the temple gardens, a warm, fragrant breeze rustling the papers on the desk. "I plan to return to the field soon," she said, "and was hoping you'd come with me. If you don't want to, I understand; I'm so pleased Livilla found a place for you here, and I'm sure the students love you."

"I'll come, if you wish it," Luca said. "I enjoy my work here, but find a military camp rather exciting by comparison."

"Thank Vica," Elektra said, surprised to find she'd been holding her breath. "Silia Raverna is coming as my personal secretary. This time, I want to have people I can count on close to me at all times. The world is such a treacherous place," she said, her voice wobbling a little. "There are some very wicked people about." She thought of Braeden, of General Mattila, and of her own mother.

Now she was back at the school, she realized for the first time how much she missed it. She still didn't want to come back as a student, but she'd forever look back on the simplicity of life here with a little yearning.

"There are," Luca said softly. "But you're right—it's important to have your friends around you. When do you plan to leave?"

"I don't know yet," Elektra said, frowning. "My mother doesn't want me to go, but I hope Livilla can help me work something out. I will go to her now."

LENNART

Lennart was ready to leave Helvundala. Both Kalstrom and Isenberg were holding firm in northern Terragand, but Ensden was pressing them hard. He had absorbed the bulk of Mattila's army, and now that he was organized, might split his forces, sending armies into at least three directions if he so chose.

Lennart wanted to head back to the coast, then march around the mountains ,and along the shore to Kaltental. He was nearly ready to go, when a message came. "It's from Prince Kendryk," Lennart told General Lofbrok, looking up after reading the letter. They stood in the stable yard at Oberfeld while Lennart oversaw the preparations to move out. "He's headed this way with a force of over five thousand, and has already relieved Birkenfels."

"That's excellent news," Lofbrok said. "But why is he coming here?"

Lennart frowned. "He'd heard I was having trouble with Prince Stepan, and hoped he might help persuade him. He's joined up with Trystan Martinek's force, and they've added a few thousand more under the command of an Alona Brynner. She worked for Ensden until they beat her at Birkenfels, and she decided she'd rather help us."

"Extraordinary," Lofbrok said. "I would never have guessed that Kendryk could pull together a force of that size so quickly."

"I'm impressed too." Lennart grinned. "And what's more, he has recent intelligence on Ensden's movements. It seems he is throwing almost everything at Kaltental, since he's expecting us to attack it. But he's also sent a smaller force to the Garsten Gap, in case we try to get into Terragand that way."

Lofbrok frowned. "If we get through there with a smaller force, we can attack Ensden from the rear, while the bulk of our army marches on Kaltental."

"That's a good plan. But here's the best part: Kendryk's force will hold the gap for us until we can get there."

"Any idea how long he's been there?"

Lennart looked at the letter. "Not long. He wrote this three days ago."

"If we go right away we can relieve him."

Lennart folded the letter and put it in his pocket. "I agree. But I still want you to take all of our troops directly to Kaltental if Ensden is pushing that way. I'll take the Helvundala forces to meet Kendryk, and then we'll come up from the south. Ensden has a large army, but maybe we can trap him between our two forces."

Lennart couldn't stop smiling. He went straight to see Princess Rheda.

"Change of plans," he said, bursting in on her in the library.

She looked up from the book she'd been reading. "Judging by the look on your face, I'm guessing it's a good change."

"It is. I've had a letter from Kendryk." He pulled it out of his pocket and handed it to the princess, then paced the room while she read it.

"Thank the gods," she said, putting it down. "I was so worried when I'd heard he left Galladium. I understand why he needs to do this, but part of me wishes he'd stay somewhere safe until this is over. We can't risk anything happening to him."

"I'll take good care of him," Lennart said, after she handed back the letter.

"I'm sure you will. But this says he's holding the Garsten Gap against Ensden. Isn't that dangerous?"

"Might be. But we can get there quickly." He finally sat down, seeing he was annoying the princess with his pacing. "I'll send Lofbrok to join the others near Kaltental, but I'll take Baron Manier and your troops to meet with Kendryk. If we leave today, we should be able to reach him in two days."

Princess Rheda jumped to her feet. "Yes, please go quickly." She paused, and wiped an eye. "You must think me rather soft to worry about Kendryk so."

"I know you're not soft, Princess." Lennart grinned at her.

She sighed. "It's just that Kendryk was always my favorite nephew. I can't tell you how many times I wished he'd been my son instead of Stepan. When he was hurt and captured, I feared my heart would break. He was such a sweet, gentle soul, and I hated the thought of him at Teodora's mercy. Now I worry he's put himself in harm's way again."

Lennart walked over to her and took both her hands in his. "I've never met Kendryk, but he seems very brave. Few stand up to Teodora, and live to tell about it. The gods made his escape possible, and have a plan for him. They're watching over him even now."

"I hope you're right." Rheda pulled her hands away, then smiled. "Well, there's no use standing around here worrying. Let's do everything we can to get your force on its way today."

GWYNNETH

Gwynneth was no longer enjoying herself in Allaux. Natalya was implementing her reforms with a heavy hand, and though the people hadn't revolted against the changes she forced in the temples, the popular mood was ugly. Gwynneth and the children never went out without a full complement of guards, and she worried that someone would recognize her as Natalya's close friend, and take their anger out on her or one of the children.

There were no more brilliant parties at Natalya's palace, and even the king seldom entertained. Gwynneth worried about him the most. These days, she hated confronting Natalya—she had become so strange and serious—but the king had once again pleaded with her to intervene.

"Gauvain says you no longer visit your daughter," Gwynneth said as casually as she could manage. She sat with Natalya in her study one evening, the two of them writing letters together, just as they had when they were girls.

Natalya looked away. "I doubt she misses me. She has three nurses, and Gauvain is forever hovering over her. It can't be good for her."

"Of course it is." Gwynneth struggled to keep her tone light. She was not terribly maternal, but couldn't imagine spending no time at all with her children. "It's good for children to see their parents often, and know they're loved."

Natalya was silent for a long time, but Gwynneth held her tongue, not wanting to push her. Finally Natalya said, "I do love Joslyn."

"I never questioned that," Gwynneth said softly.

Natalya sighed heavily. "It's just that whenever I see her, I'm reminded of the mistake I made, getting involved with the king."

"You truly see it as a mistake?" Sadness settled over Gwynneth like a fog. "When I first came here, you two looked so happy. I remember how much joy it gave me, seeing you like that." She had to struggle to keep the tears from her eyes. For there was no doubt that Natalya was no longer happy.

Natalya's eyes flashed, and Gwynneth worried she'd offended her. It was too easy to do these days. Natalya huffed angrily and said, "One thing I've learned of a certainty, is that the gods do not care for our happiness. They care about how we honor them in the way we live."

"I'm afraid I don't understand. Are you saying happiness is a sin?"

"I wouldn't go that far." Natalya folded her arms on the desk and looked straight at Gwynneth. "I don't understand it perfectly myself, but I know this. Happiness in itself isn't wrong, but it can lead us astray. Doing things that are wrong or bad for us can make us happy too. It's no guarantee of righteousness."

"I never thought of it that way," Gwynneth said. "But how can you tell what's bad and what isn't?"

"Oh come Gwynneth, that should be obvious," Natalya said in such a patronizing tone that Gwynneth stared at her, startled.

Now Gwynneth's anger rose. She laid her quill down and said, "No, it isn't obvious. My understanding has been that if we pray with good intentions, and try to keep the will of the gods in mind, they will guide our actions."

"That's pleasantly vague, isn't it?" Natalya snapped. "And makes it all too easy to justify all sorts of bad behavior."

"Bad behavior?" Gwynneth shook her head, remembering the king. "How can love be bad?"

"It can be, if it distracts you from more important things. And that's what happened with me and Gauvain. I became so concerned for his happiness, I neglected the work I was meant to do as Maxima."

"But you've always fulfilled your duties," Gwynneth protested. "You've always served the Temple and Galladium perfectly."

Natalya gave a short laugh. "My work has been far from perfect. No, as difficult as this is, I'm convinced it's right."

"Don't you care about him at all?" Gwynneth whispered, not knowing if she should feel more sorry for the grim stranger Natalya had become, or for the king, who still loved her to distraction.

"I do care," Natalya said, though neither her tone nor her demeanor softened. "But that means I must do what's best for him, and stay away from him. He must focus on Zofya Inferrara, who is to be his wife, and not on me. I don't approve of his attachment to Joslyn, but I suppose I can allow it for now."

"Oh please do," Gwynneth said. "If not for his sake, then for your little girl's."

Natalya looked at Gwynneth for a while, clearly thinking. "I have an idea," she said at last. "Wouldn't it be nice if Joslyn came to live with you? She's of an age with Stella. I'll pay for her upkeep of course."

"I—" Gwynneth didn't know what to say. "I ought to ask Kendryk."

Natalya made an impatient noise. "He's far away, and it'll take forever. I'm sure he won't mind, since he loves children."

"Yes he does, but what about Gauvain? I cannot keep the king from seeing his own daughter." Gwynneth wanted to refuse—every bone in her body vibrated with the wrongness of what Natalya was doing. And at that moment, she decided that no matter what Natalya said, she'd make sure Joslyn spent time with her father.

"I'd never put you in that position." Natalya offered a half-smile. "But if she's not in the palace, it'll be easier for him to detach himself. Because that is what he must do, sooner or later."

ELEKTRA

It seemed Livilla was very busy after being away from Atlona for so long, so it was several days before Elektra was able to have a private chat with her.

"Come, my dear," Livilla said, standing up from her desk. "We'll have a walk in the garden, since it's such a lovely day." She turned to the young priest sitting at a table in the corner of her study, scribbling his way through a pile of papers. "Get something to eat. I'll meet you here in an hour."

He looked like he wanted to protest, then nodded and put his writing things away.

Livilla took Elektra's arm, and led her through the tall glass door opening to the garden. Once they were away from the building, Livilla said, "One of your mother's spies, I'm afraid."

Elektra stopped short. "She spies on you?"

"Of course she does." Livilla didn't seem the least bit bothered, and kept walking. "Or at least she tries. And I have my spies around her."

"I—" Elektra didn't know what to say to that. "But you love each other. I'm sure she sees you as a mother."

"We do love each other," Livilla said. "But we don't trust each other entirely. It's better that way, don't you agree?"

"It's dreadful." Elektra yanked her arm away, and hurried ahead down the garden path. She couldn't imagine ever spying on Luca or any of her friends, and she was certain they wouldn't spy on her either. The idea upset her.

She heard Livilla's steps slow, then stop behind her. She sighed, and turned around. Livilla had taken a seat on a sun-warmed stone bench at the edge of an expanse of red flowers. Elektra walked back slowly, and sat down next to her. They were both silent for awhile, the only sounds the splashing of a nearby fountain, and the hum of bees in the flowers.

"It's hard to understand when you're young," Livilla said, laying a hand on Elektra's knee. "I do not doubt that your mother loves me, but I know her well, and understand that her largest concern is the power of your family and that of the empire. She must always be certain that I'm acting in accord with her."

"But you always do," Elektra said. "How can she doubt you after all these years?"

"Your mother trusts no one, especially after what happened with General Barela. Can you blame her?"

"I still don't believe he tried to kill her," Elektra muttered. "Though I can understand why he would." The words were barely out before she wished she hadn't said that. Maybe Livilla was right, and you really shouldn't trust anyone.

"The general was an attractive, charming man who at one point really loved your mother. It doesn't change the fact he also conspired against her; that is beyond question."

"How could he love her, but then want to kill her? I would never want to hurt anyone I loved." She tried to imagine doing to Aksel what her mother had done to Barela, and couldn't. It was impossible.

Livilla sighed. "Love can turn to hate quite easily. That's something you have yet to learn, though I pray you will not have to experience it directly. For now, when it comes to your mother, it's best to realize that she does not trust you, even though you're her daughter."

"I would never hurt her," Elektra said, though she'd been telling the truth when she assured Braeden she wanted her dead. "Even if I wanted to, I have no power."

"Not yet. But before long, you have the potential to become a great threat to her, even if you don't see it that way. If she dies, you are first in line for the throne. And you'll soon be of age, so you won't be answerable to anyone when the time comes."

"I'd still want your advice," Elektra said. "I'm sure I'd need it rather badly."

"I'd do my best to help," Livilla said. "But please Vica, that day is still far away, and you have time to learn and enjoy your own life. And that brings me to another matter. Your mother hasn't yet spoken of this, but as I said, I have a spy close to her."

"Why? I suppose I understand that she doesn't trust you, but why must you spy on her?"

Livilla chuckled. "For moments like this, I suppose. I like to be aware of what she's planning, so I can anticipate how best to advise her. Your mother can be impulsive; even unwise. It's much easier for me to react if I know what she's going to do."

"And what is she planning?"

Livilla turned to her. "She wants you to marry Aksel Roussay. And she wants you to do it now, before summer is here."

A strange combination of feelings washed over Elektra. Joy was one of them; it was hard to imagine anything nicer than being married to Aksel. Panic came next. If she was married, her mother would want her to stay here, or ship her off to one of her country estates, where she'd rot until something happened to Teodora.

"I-I can't," she choked out.

"Don't you like him? From what I saw when he joined us for dinner these past few evenings, he seems to like you too."

"I do like him." Elektra had been trying to take deep, slow breaths, hoping to quiet her pounding heart. "I think he likes me too, though he's nice to everyone. Zofya is convinced he's as much in love with her as she is with him." That was another thing; her little sister would be devastated, and that was unbearable too.

"Yet you are unhappy at the idea."

"I'm only sixteen, and not ready to marry. If I do, I'm sure I'll become useless again. I like Aksel, but if I marry him, it should be in a few years, after I've helped defeat Lennart and Mattila. I want to be part of that so badly I can hardly stand it." She turned to Livilla and grabbed her hands. "You must help me, please."

"It's hard to dissuade your mother once she's put her mind to something," Livilla said, "but perhaps we can delay it with a legal reason. Maybe I can discover an old law that requires King Arryk's consent, which I doubt would be forthcoming."

Then Elektra remembered why she'd wanted to see Livilla. "There might be something. I didn't realize Aksel was a heretic, and was hoping you could ..."

Livilla's eyes lit up. "He follows the Quadrene creed? Interesting."

"It's not interesting. It's dreadful. I was hoping you might help me show him the true path."

"It can be done. I shall send a League priest to advise him. But in the meantime, I believe we've found a way to delay the marriage, since you cannot be married to a heretic."

"Mother wouldn't force him to convert, would she?" That would be worse than anything.

"She cannot." Livilla smiled. "That is my jurisdiction, and she'll defer to me. As long as she knows he's being instructed by a League priest, she cannot protest. And that instruction will take time." Livilla stood, pulling Elektra up with her. "Say nothing of this to you mother, and leave it to me."

BRAEDEN

They saw no sign of imperial troops for quite some time. Braeden wondered if they'd guessed wrong, and those troops were making another try for the castle. No matter; they had to get everyone to the other side of the gap. With the road so narrow, the infantry marched only three abreast, and it took a great deal of time. Still, they had nearly everyone through before word came of imperial infantry on the road ahead.

Trystan turned toward Braeden. "I'll go now, and try to make them hurry. Don't take any unnecessary risks."

Braeden snorted, and Trystan grinned at him. "I had to say it, with you being such a mother hen about young Andarosz."

Braeden had to smile at that, and waved at Trystan before he and his horse disappeared into the trees. If the worst should happen, and Ensden's troops broke through, he'd hold them off until Kendryk got away, or Lennart arrived. But Braeden wouldn't let that happen. He had picked two hundred of his best cavalry, and placed them at the mouth of the gap.

Drums, and the tramp of thousands of marching feet sounded in the distance, but the enemy was not yet in sight. Braeden took Kazmir into the gap and yelled, "Hey, Karil." The dense foliage swallowed the sound, but leaves rustled, and Karil peered over the edge of the rock. He'd smeared his face, and the rest of him, with mud. Trystan had hit on the idea as a way of making it easier for the musketeers to blend into the woods. Their clothes were already so ragged and dirty, they didn't look all that much worse, and after the rain, mud was plentiful.

"What is it?" Karil asked.

"Just a reminder," Braeden said, remembering his own youth. "Hold still, and not a word or a shot until we've drawn them in. Got it?"

"Yes, sir," Karil said. "Please don't kill them all before I get a chance."

Braeden shook his head and grinned. "You don't have to worry about that. Just shoot at those you can see, try not to hit any of ours, reload fast, and for

Ercos' sake, stay out of sight. One way or another, I'll get you back to your mother in one piece."

Karil nodded, then disappeared.

Braeden rode back out into the clear, and, at last, the enemy came into view. He wouldn't be able to fight them for long, but he could draw them in, and distract them from the ambush.

"Lances ready!" he shouted. These troopers were not experienced lancers like the Sanova Hussars, but he'd trained them well enough for a short action like this one.

The enemy moved into position quickly. Well-drilled troops then; probably had been Mattila's.

"Forward!" he called out, and urged Kazmir to a gallop. They would be upon the enemy in seconds. "Lances down." Braeden dropped his into position, wincing at the strain on his injured shoulder, and gave Kazmir the spurs, though the old fellow was so eager he didn't need them. He'd kept his visor up to keep an eye on the others, and was pleased his front line held steady. He'd put all the young nobles with tourney experience into it. Many had never been in this kind of fight, but at least they knew how to knock people over with a long stick.

The pike held firm, but only until Braeden skewered one of them. Out of the corner of his eye, he watched others go down. Aside from the Sanova Hussars, lancers were so rare these days, most pike didn't train to deal with them. Braeden ran down a few more rows, until the next ranks tripped over each other, trying to get away. Braeden wanted to keep going, but that wasn't part of the plan. He dropped his lance on the ground, then peeled off to the right while drawing his saber. He cut down a few more enemy soldiers before heading toward the gap. The rest of his cavalry thundered after him.

It would be a few minutes before the enemy got organized, but an experienced commander wouldn't take long to send muskets forward while the pike sorted themselves out. Braeden waited near the entrance to the gap, letting his cavalry pass. He kept one eye in Karil's direction, though the leaves remained motionless.

He followed his troops in, until the light from the mouth of the gap nearly disappeared. The shouts of confusion and cries of the wounded faded as the silent woods closed around him. It wouldn't be long now. He hoped they came before the light faded so much that Karil and his soldiers wouldn't be able to see. But with the days so long now, the sunlight filtered through the dense trees, even as it slowly set.

Braeden raised his pistols and licked his lips. He heard shouted orders, followed by marching as the first ranks entered the defile. They feared what was on those rocks, as they should have, so they were looking up, and didn't spot Braeden until it was too late. He spurred Kazmir with a shout, and charged forward. As soon as he came in range, he fired one pistol, then the other. In the same instant, the musketeers up high began shooting. Their shots were steady; after one rank fired, they scrambled back to reload, while another rank moved forward. By the time a third row had fired, the first was ready again.

Braeden and his cavalry retreated slowly, drawing in as many of the enemy as they could. Before long, he knew none would get through, and wondered how much punishment they would take before retreating. Those that survived the first few onslaughts tried to run away, but stumbled over bodies strewn all over the narrow road, and became even easier targets. None escaped.

TEODORA

"That's not good enough," Teodora said. "I want the girl married, and I want it done now." She drummed her fingers on the arms of her chair while she glared at Livilla.

Livilla as always, seemed unaffected by her anger. "Then you must find someone else for her. I spoke to the young man myself, and he's unapologetic about his beliefs. They can be changed, but it will take time."

"I don't have time," Teodora snapped. "He's entirely in my power; I'll order him to embrace the true faith, and that will be the end of it."

Livilla shook her head. "I strongly advise against such a course. It's one thing to force commoners to convert, but quite another to do it to a king's brother. And consider this: if he marries Elektra while paying only lip service to the faith, you will have a resentful family member, who will undermine you when given the chance. Why not allow the time necessary, and have him friendly instead?"

"I want Elektra married now." Teodora wondered if she should confide all of her reasons. She had gotten the real story of Elektra's escape from her source in the temple school, and knew the tale Elektra had fed her was largely untrue. Why would the girl lie? "She's more than old enough."

"She's barely old enough," Livilla said with a gentle smile. "And while it would be a good match, she still has a great deal to learn about the world."

"Let her learn it as a married woman." Teodora stood, and resumed her pacing. She understood, from personal experience, that Elektra was old enough to be a threat. Seeing her daughter at the head of her own army, poised and confident, had been a shock. Teodora had always considered her weak and frightened, but she clearly no longer was.

Livilla sighed. "The fact remains, she cannot marry Prince Aksel in his current spiritual state."

Teodora turned to face her. "What do you plan to do about it?"

"It's already arranged. I've sent Father Marcus to assist him in his laboratory."

"Who is Father Marcus?"

"He's a young Olvisyan noble. He's had an excellent scientific education, has a pleasant manner, and I'm sure he and the prince will get on well. I've told Marcus to go slowly and without pressure. Once they've become friends, it'll be easier for him to influence Aksel."

"Clever. But that might take months."

Livilla shrugged. "True. But imagine Arryk's devastation when he learns his little brother has been converted by none other than a priest of the League of Aeternos. It ought to upset Princess Gwynneth even more."

Teodora sat back down. "That alone might be worth it." If only she could find something to upset Kendryk just as much. "What do I do with Elektra in the meantime?"

"Let her join Ensden in Terragand. You received similar experience at that age, and it did you good."

"I don't want her to leave so soon. She's been away for years, and now she wants to go again. You'd think she didn't care for her family at all."

Livilla smiled. "That's not true. But like you at that age, she has the desire for adventure, and to distinguish herself on her own."

That was exactly what Teodora didn't want, but preferred not to tell Livilla. "I'd rather keep her here. I can give her a position in the guards if she insists on military service, but I want her married the moment Aksel has converted."

Livilla inclined her head, and Teodora could tell she didn't agree. Teodora wondered if Livilla knew the real story of Elektra's Kronland adventure, and if she did, why she hadn't mentioned it so far. It really would be nice to have just one trustworthy person in her life.

KENDRYK

Kendryk hated leaving Braeden and Karil behind while he advanced in relative safety. It was an uncomfortable reminder of his escape from the Arnfels. He'd stood anxiously on the ship's deck at Capo, waiting for them to return, while the captain made noises about sailing without them, in spite of Kendryk's orders to the contrary. And now, even on the other side of the gap, he wanted to be there when they appeared again.

Trystan had other ideas. "I want you to ride for Helvundala," he said. "Take Edric Maximus, your Galladian guard, and another hundred of mine. The way ought to be safe, but you never know. I'll stay here, and make sure the enemy doesn't break through."

Kendryk bit his tongue. He wanted to protest, but understood the importance of meeting Lennart and returning as quickly as possible.

"You seem troubled," Edric said, as they turned to ride east.

"I'm worried about my friends."

"Of course. But the situation seems to be well in hand. Commander Terris got you out of the Arnfels alive. To my knowledge, no one's ever accomplished that. This seems a far easier task."

"It's more straightforward. But I don't know if I'll ever get used to people putting themselves in harm's way for my sake. I don't deserve it." Kendryk stared hard at the road ahead, not wanting to meet his friend's eyes.

"Perhaps none of us deserve all the good we receive, or the bad either. That's not up to us, however. This is part of the gods' plan, and we only see a bit of our small part in it."

Kendryk shook his head. "None of this makes any sense. I don't understand why things looked so promising before that first battle, and why they went bad so quickly. I still consider my escape a miracle, but fail to understand its purpose even now. Everything—good and bad—went on well enough without me."

"I'll keep saying this until you believe it." Edric's voice was firm. "You have been chosen for an important work, and the gods will guide your steps until you accomplish it. Your path has been difficult, but that will make your success all the more rewarding."

Kendryk had to smile, secretly relieved his friend's usual optimism had returned, even if he didn't share in it.

They rode in companionable silence for a while. They were still far from the border with Helvundala, but Kendryk hoped Lennart was on his way. He didn't want to leave Trystan and the rest unsupported any longer than he had to.

Only a few hours later, a scout came with a report. "There's a large force about three leagues ahead. It just turned our way at the crossroads."

Hope leapt up inside Kendryk. "Is it Lennart?" He'd made sure all of his scouts could recognize Estenor's standard.

The scout shook his head. "No, only Helvundala's colors. It must be Falk."

Kendryk had to laugh. "So he persuaded my cousin to come. Let's go meet him." He was disappointed that he wouldn't meet Lennart just yet, but supposed he had other battles to attend to. He also didn't look forward to seeing his cousin, though he was pleased he'd finally come through.

But when he spotted an army up ahead, Estenor's banner flew beside the lead horsemen. The scout must have been confused, although as they came closer, Kendryk noticed a great number of the Falk standard as well. His captain of the guard insisted on riding ahead to make sure it was safe, and returned to Kendryk with the head of the force.

"As the ruler of this land, you must receive him; not the other way around," Captain Dorais said with a sniff. The captain was a snob, and appalled by the lack of protocol he'd seen in Kronland so far.

Kendryk realized he looked rough after several months on the road, but he hoped Lennart—if it was him—would understand. So he drew his horse to a halt, and did his best to look dignified as a small group of men came near.

There was no question the man riding at the head of the group stood out. Even on horseback, his height and bulk were obvious. Kendryk had seen few men approach Braeden for size, but this one came close. Though the royal banner of Estenor flew right behind him, Lennart was not dressed like a king. He wore a plain doublet of blue wool over black breeches, and tall riding boots. He appeared to wear no armor at all, and a breeze ruffled unruly brown hair, uncovered as well. Kendryk suddenly didn't feel so bad about his own plain appearance, and was rather glad he looked rough and battle-weary.

Once he reached Kendryk, Lennart dismounted and gave a brief bow. "It's good to meet you at last, Your Grace."

Kendryk hurried to dismount, bowing as well. There were those who thought one should never bow to a fellow head of state, but Kendryk didn't see the harm, especially as Lennart had gone first.

Lennart grinned at him, bright hazel eyes twinkling. Kendryk would have felt uncomfortable at being looked over in such a familiar fashion, except Lennart appeared entirely friendly and good-natured.

"Shall we sit over here and talk?" Kendryk asked. Someone had already hurried to set up a table and camp chairs, while someone else brought ale. "Where's my cousin? I suppose we ought to include him."

Lennart laughed. "Your cousin isn't here."

"But this looks like his army."

"It was his army. But now, it's your Aunt Rheda's army. Much has changed in Helvundala in the past week. Let me tell you about it over a tankard of ale."

ANTON

"We're getting close to the coastline now," the sergeant told Anton on a bright June day while marching northward. "And when we do, we'll deploy so we push Tora Isenberg onto the beach. She'll have to fight or flee."

"Where would she go?" Anton asked.

"The Estenorian fleet is standing just off the coast, so they'll send boats if she needs them."

"She'll go back to Estenor?"

The sergeant shrugged. "I doubt it. The ships might take her across that little sound to the west, into Ummarvik."

"How will we chase her there?"

"We won't. But if you lot do your job, there won't be much left to chase. General Ensden's made sure she'll be seriously outnumbered."

Anton just hoped the fight would be long enough for him to see action. He worried about his regiment being held in reserve, and missing out on everything.

By the time they came upon Isenberg, the ocean was in sight. Anton hadn't been this close to the water since he and the count stole the ships, though he recognized the smell of the salty air.

"I'd like to take you down to the beach," Anton said to Susanna after she told him she'd never seen the ocean.

"Isn't the enemy there?"

"They're close at least. Maybe after the battle."

"I'm sure the beach will be lovely, covered with corpses." Susanna was making an effort not to seem worried about him, but Anton knew she was anyway. Since they'd made camp and the orders had come down for getting ready for battle, she hadn't been the same.

"Might be we won't fight on the beach," Anton said, though he thought that might be interesting.

"I wish you wouldn't fight anywhere," Susanna said, "but I know you have to."

"It's my job," Anton said. "I wish you wouldn't worry. I've had a lot of experience, and my regiment is really well-trained. We've drilled so long, I can do all of those maneuvers in my sleep."

"I think you do, the way you sometimes thrash around at night." Susanna gave a half-smile.

"That's something else," Anton said shortly. "Bad dreams." Now that his life had become calmer, only his sleep was haunted. Things he hadn't thought about in years returned to him as nightmares. The burning farm in Moralta, being held on the ground, unable to help, while his mother screamed and screamed. When he closed his eyes, the bridge at Lerania crashed over him night after night, sweeping him and Skandar down a river, until a cannonball took the count and Cid from right in front of him. Maybe it was a good thing, to finally be on the winning side, so bad things could stop happening.

"I worry about you, too," he said to Susanna, the morning they were to go into battle. She was helping him strap on his armor. Since he had money now, he'd bought a sturdy cuirass, a fine crested helmet, and a brace of pistols.

She raised her eyebrows. "Whatever for? I'll be fine back here in camp. I don't think there's any chance of the Estenorians breaking through."

"They won't if I have anything to do with it." Anton felt better with all of his gear on, even though it was heavy. He hoped they wouldn't have to walk too far. "But if the worst happens, head straight east until you get to Anglestein castle, and ask to be taken to the countess. She's Count Orland's widow, and I'm sure she'll remember me and help you. She's very nice."

Susanna shook her head. "I doubt any countess would want to see me."

"Tell her you're Anton Kronek's wife—that's the name I used back then— and I'll find you as soon as I can. Please Susanna, promise me you'll do this."

"All right," she said, putting her arms around his neck, pulling him down for a kiss. "If the worst happens, I'll look for that countess, if you insist."

"Good." Anton smiled down at her. "That makes me feel better."

The air around Anton crackled with excitement as his regiment marched toward the shore. He couldn't see anything, with rank on rank of pike all around him, but it was fun to be part of something so big. He wished they weren't in the reserve, and worried they'd never see action before it was all over.

"It's not so bad in the reserve," Stasny said, "and you're more likely to live to fight another day. There'll be plenty more battles before this war is over. My first engagement, I worried about that too, but that was five years ago, and I've been in more battles than I can count since then."

Anton grimaced, but said nothing. He hated it when Stasny made it sound like he was more experienced than Anton, which he really wasn't. Though it was true he'd done a lot more infantry fighting.

"You'll be sorry you're carrying those pistols," Stasny went on. "Heavy as they are, you'll drop them on the ground after we've marched a league or two."

"Not a chance," Anton said. "I'm better with pistols than anything, so I won't do without them." It was true they were heavy, but he didn't like being unprotected if his square broke. And he didn't plan on running either, no matter what happened.

They didn't march too much longer before coming to a halt. It was late morning, and the sun had broken through a fog as it rose in the sky. Anton's helmet became very hot, and he pulled it off, at least until they moved again. He hated not knowing what was going on. At first, he'd heard only the distant rumble of the ocean, but then the crackle of musket fire came over that. The front lines must be engaging. Anton shifted onto his other foot, and gripped his pike.

TEODORA

"Shall we go for a ride together?" Teodora asked Elektra after sending for her. "I never have time to enjoy the spring weather otherwise." She also hoped getting Elektra out of the palace and into the fresh air would put her in a better mood.

"If you like." Elektra's tone was flat. After several weeks in Atlona, she no longer seemed as confident as she had at her arrival. Perhaps that was a good thing.

Teodora waited until they had ridden out into the shady paths of the forest outside the city's eastern gate. "Did you know Arian Orland launched his attack from this very spot?" she asked.

"Hm," Elektra said, apparently uninterested.

Teodora shrugged. It wasn't as though she enjoyed revisiting that awful day, but anything that reminded her of Arian Orland, and that he was now dead, made her happy.

Teodora pulled ahead, just out of earshot of the guards, and Elektra followed. "I've been wanting to have a chat," she said.

"All right," Elektra said, her voice dull.

"I've decided you're to marry Aksel Roussay."

Elektra raised her eyebrows and was silent. She didn't seem nearly as shocked as Teodora had expected her to be. Perhaps she'd caught wind of a rumor.

"Don't you like him?"

"I do." Elektra turned toward her. "But I don't want to marry him."

"Why ever not? He's attractive, intelligent, and seems to like you. He might also become King of Norovaea before long."

"Oh gods." Elektra pulled her horse to an abrupt halt. "Is that what you want? To send me to Norovaea where I'll be out of your way forever?"

"Goodness, no. I want you to be Queen of Norovaea. Wouldn't you like that?"

"I don't see how Aksel can be a king anytime soon, and no, I don't want to be a queen."

Teodora waved at the guards to stop before they came closer. "Why not?"

"I want to be empress someday. And it would be terrible to have a husband I like but never see, because he's in some faraway country."

Teodora snorted. "You won't be empress for a long time." Even as she said it, a chill crept through her bones. Perhaps she was right to suspect Elektra of having unnatural ambition.

"I realize that." Now there was more force in Elektra's voice. "But in the meantime, I want a military career, not to be shunted off to Norovaea. And if I marry Aksel, what will I do instead? If something happens to King Arryk, his sister and her children are next in line, not Aksel. It seems unlikely he'll ever be king."

"I'm sure I could arrange it," Teodora said with a smirk.

Elektra shook her head, color spreading across her face. "I don't want you to arrange it, and neither does Aksel. He doesn't want to be king. You should stay out of Norovaean politics anyway."

"Oh, is that what you think?" Teodora barked an unpleasant laugh. "Well, you understand little enough about the affairs of state, so you'd be far wiser to listen to me. After all, I have your best interests at heart."

"That is a lie." Elektra said in a furious whisper. "You don't care about anyone but yourself." She spurred her horse, and made off down the path at a smart canter.

Teodora let her go, keeping her horse at a walk. A few minutes later, she reached a bend, and when she came around it, saw Elektra, her horse standing in the middle of the path. Teodora raised an eyebrow. "You should apologize. What did I do to deserve such ugly treatment? Really, I raised you to have better manners."

"You didn't raise me at all." Elektra's voice was louder now, but the guards kept a discreet distance. "You paid no attention to any of us until you needed us for something. Zofya told me she hadn't laid eyes on you in three years before you told her she was marrying Gauvain Brevard. I doubt you even remembered you had children most of the time." She was talking fast now, her face furious. "In fact, Braeden said—" she stopped short, likely realizing what she'd just given away.

Teodora laughed. "Oh, it's Braeden now? I had a feeling you became friendlier with him than you ever let on. Tell me, did you plot with him to kill me?"

That was just a guess, but a lucky one, since the look of astonishment on Elektra's face told her everything.

"I—I did no such thing," Elektra said, though her voice lacked conviction. She took a deep breath. "I left a few things out of the story I told you."

"Apparently," Teodora said, unable to hide her glee, thrilled she had finally cornered the sneaky little weasel.

Elektra's face reddened. "I wanted to impress you, and telling you that Braeden Terris delivered me to Mattila like a sack of potatoes was not that impressive."

Now it was Teodora's turn to be confused. "Braeden worked for Mattila?"

"No. That's what I thought at first, but he was acting on his own. His wife and children died at Kersenstadt, in the fire, and he wanted to kill me as a way of taking revenge on you."

"But he didn't, clearly." At the moment, Teodora was rather wishing he had.

"No, he didn't. I convinced him that killing me wouldn't bother you in the least, and he agreed." Color flooded Elektra's face, and she was breathing hard.

"Insolent wretch," Teodora muttered.

"I told him I hated you and wanted you dead." Elektra was talking faster now, as if the truth was pouring out of her.

"And is that true?" Teodora had no interest in making this easy for the little liar.

Elektra bit her lip so hard it bled. "Sometimes, I do hate you," she said, "but I don't want you dead."

Teodora raised an eyebrow, and said nothing.

"The only way I could stay alive was to pretend I'd help him kill you. I told him Mattila would help us, but as soon as I got back to Mattila's camp, I turned him in. I swear it." Elektra stared at her, eyes wide, as if willing Teodora to believe her.

"That's quite a story," Teodora said. "But the fact remains he got away. How did you arrange that, and why? Do you hope he'll get another chance at me?"

Elektra shook her head. "He got away because Mattila made a mistake. She sent one of the Sanova Hussars after him, expecting they'd be happy to have his head. I suppose they were still friends, because one of them must have helped him escape. You must believe me, Mother." She was pleading now. Much better.

Teodora took her time responding. It wouldn't hurt to let her suffer for a while. "I'm not sure I do. In fact, this story is so different from what you first told me, I don't know what to believe." She turned her horse back toward the city, and Elektra followed.

"I'll write to Mattila," Elektra said, her voice very small now. "She'll tell you it's the truth."

Teodora laughed. "You think I'd trust a word that woman says? You clearly don't know me at all. She was probably in on your conspiracy until Terris escaped, for whatever reason. No, that won't do at all."

"That's why it's best if I leave," Elektra was saying now. "I'll head for Terragand tomorrow."

Teodora whirled on her. "There's no way I'm letting you out of my sight now. We're going back to the palace, where you'll be confined to your room until Aksel is converted and you can be married. And when he becomes king, you'll go to Norovaea with him. In fact, from now on, you'll do everything I say without question, is that understood? One peep from you, and you'll go to the Arnfels."

Elektra gasped and looked around wildly, but at a gesture from Teodora, the guards had drawn close around her. She wasn't getting away.

LENNART

Once Lennart explained the situation in Helvundala to Kendryk, they rode west at speed. Kendryk told him that Martinek and the rest were holding off an unknown number of enemy, so there was no time to lose. They could talk on the way. Kendryk took the news of his cousin's overthrow with good humor. Lennart wasn't too surprised, since he doubted Kendryk found Stepan any more likable than he had.

"Try not to worry," Lennart said, though it looked like Kendryk would anyway. "Our numbers combined with yours will be more than enough to overcome any resistance. If Ensden is throwing the bulk of his force at Kaltental, I doubt he's got much to spare to oppose us here."

"But if they take the gap, we won't be able to get through." Kendryk's eyes were wide and anxious. Lennart had to admit that the prince was an appealing young fellow, but much too serious.

Lennart shrugged. "We'll find a way. And you've already told me about your friend holding it. I'll be very surprised if anyone gets around him."

Kendryk seemed to attempt a smile, but he was clearly still worried. Lennart thought he understood well enough. This was his land, and he'd already seen much of it devastated. Lennart tried to picture Estenor wracked by war, and shuddered. Far better to take the fight to foreign soil.

Still, this part of Terragand wasn't bad. Lennart liked the look of the tidy farms—the fields just now being sown by sturdy-looking country folk—and the pretty villages. He was a little disappointed they'd see no larger towns in this area, but when he said so, Kendryk, replied, "That's what's spared this region so far. Ensden has concentrated all of his efforts on bigger places, and isn't too concerned with the countryside. He still strips it bare on his way to the towns," he added, bitterness plain in his voice.

"Well, we're putting a stop to that now, aren't we?" Lennart asked.

"I hope so." Kendryk offered a weak smile.

Lennart hoped he'd find a way to cheer him up, or they were sure to have a depressing time as they reconquered Terragand. As they rode, he assessed Kendryk still further. He could hardly admit to himself that he considered him a rival for Gwynneth's affection. Not that he was interested in Gwynneth that way anymore, at least not too much. He told himself she was just a friend, and he wished only for her happiness.

Lennart understood why she had fallen in love with Kendryk. In spite of his sadness, he was very good-looking, with luminous blue-green eyes, and a kind, open manner making it impossible to dislike him. Lennart was certain he was an attentive husband, and likely an excellent father. "How many children do you have?" he asked, hoping to cheer him up.

That worked. A smile spread across Kendryk's face as he said, "Gwynneth just had our fifth a few months ago; our third girl. I can't wait to meet her."

"Queen Raysa and I are expecting a baby later in the summer." When he said it like that, Lennart felt inordinately proud, though he reminded himself that Raysa was doing the hard part. He felt a sudden pang, missing her.

"That's marvelous," Kendryk said, still smiling. "I think you'll find there's nothing nicer than being a father. I only wish I hadn't missed so many years of my own children growing up." His face sobered again.

That gave Lennart pause. "I suppose I'm likely to miss a few years, though I hope it won't take too long to defeat Teodora and her toadies."

"Aren't you at all worried?" Kendryk asked. "By my best guess, you're outnumbered by Ensden now he has all of Mattila's troops. Are you sure you'll be able to defeat him?"

"Very sure. Now I've got you along, I imagine at least a few of the other Kronland rulers will send us troops."

"I hope so," Kendryk said, though he didn't sound convinced.

So Lennart told him about his military innovations, and how he hoped to implement them. "I'm convinced that more effective artillery can even out great odds, though I'd rather not face them to begin with."

"I hope you're right," Kendryk said. "I'm looking forward to seeing your ideas put into action."

Riding with Kendryk was the famed Edric Maximus, who'd started all of the religious changes. His greeting to Lennart had been friendly, though reserved. Lennart didn't blame him for having doubts, though he hoped they'd have time to talk at length before too long. If it turned out Edric believed Lennart was the prophesied ruler, it would do much to strengthen his cause.

But the first order of business was relieving Trystan Martinek's force. They came upon them early the next morning, camped in a meadow against a series of low, steep hills. The road led into what looked like a dark hole in the trees—no doubt the entrance to the feared gap. The pickets had already alerted Martinek, so by the time Lennart rode into camp, the duke hurried to meet them.

"Your timing is excellent, Your Highness," Trystan said, after he'd invited them to his tent for breakfast. Lennart regarded him intently, and liked what he saw. Edyta Martinek's youngest son wasn't tall, but he looked strong and resolute. His penetrating gaze no doubt unsettled some, but Lennart saw behind it a kindred spirit. More than anyone he'd met so far, he was sure he and the young duke would get on well.

"I'm assuming from the way you're camped here that you still hold the gap," Lennart said, after he, Kendryk and Trystan were seated around a small table in Trystan's tent. It's furnishings had once been luxurious, but now everything had a battered, worn look. It had been several years since Trystan had been home to re-equip.

"We do. It's gone exactly as planned. The enemy is camped on the other side, but doesn't dare venture in. Commander Terris has reported that the first quarter-league of the road is clogged with corpses."

Kendryk brightened. "So Braeden and Karil are well?"

"Yes. I received a dispatch only an hour ago with a list of casualties. We have suffered no deaths, although one musketeer broke his ankle while running through the woods, and one cavalry trooper fell off his horse. Our problem remains that while they cannot get in, we cannot get out, unless we want to march over dead bodies."

"Do you have a map?" Lennart asked.

Trystan nodded, pulled one from behind his chair and unrolled it on the table, pushing dishes aside.

"I know a way we can take out that force on the other side," Lennart said, happy that he'd studied his maps of Kronland so carefully before coming here.

GWYNNETH

"I'm so sorry, Your Highness," Gwynneth murmured, unable to look the king in the eye. "This was not my choice, though I love Joslyn and will take good care of her." That wasn't strictly true, since Joslyn was rather unfriendly and difficult for such a small child, but it was clear Gauvain adored his daughter.

"I understand," Gauvain said, then gave a weary sigh. He had come to see Gwynneth at home, likely as soon as he heard of what Natalya had done. "I realize I could order her to come live with me in the palace, but I don't want to anger Natalya."

"You shouldn't be afraid of her," Gwynneth burst out. "I mean, we shouldn't be afraid of her."

Gauvain caught her eye and chuckled. "You're right. But it's hard, isn't it? She's always radiated power, but now she's so stern and forbidding, she really is frightening."

Gwynneth wished the changes in Natalya would help the king get over her, but she doubted it. He was loyal to a fault. "You're the king," she said, keeping her tone gentle. "Any power she has outside the temple has been granted by you. You could take it away, you know." She felt a pang, as if she were betraying her friend, then told herself that Natalya had changed so much, she was a different person now.

That made the king laugh. "You're right, of course. But I can't do that. Even though we're not as close as we used to be." He paused and swallowed. The pain in his eyes was so obvious, Gwynneth had to look away. "She's still invaluable to me for political matters." He went on. "No one else sees matters so clearly."

Gwynneth disagreed. "You would let her drag you into war with Maladena?"

The king's eyes widened, and Gwynneth held her breath, hoping she hadn't gone too far. Worry about war looming on Galladium's southern border consumed many of her waking hours of late, though she'd been afraid to confront Natalya about it.

"We have no quarrel with Maladena." The king's voice was bland, though his eyes betrayed him. Lovely as those eyes were, their openness was not helpful for a sovereign.

"They seem to have a quarrel with you," Gwynneth said lightly. "My sources at Queen Beatryz's court say she is convinced of Natalya's heresy, and will do anything to keep it from spreading to her lands."

"Natalya has done nothing to spread her reforms beyond the borders of Galladium. Though really, Gwynneth, I wish you'd tell me when you receive such information. It might help me a great deal."

"Certainly." Gwynneth wondered if there was a way to spin this to her advantage. "I assumed your sources were at least as good. Natalya has the most amazing spy network I've ever seen."

"True, though she doesn't share everything with me." The king looked thoughtful. "Perhaps we can help each other. I don't wish for war with Maladena, though I fear Natalya will provoke it. Can you think of any way to convince Queen Beatryz that we mean her country no harm?"

"That's a tall order, I'm afraid."

"I understand. But at least consider it. Perhaps we can find a solution."

Gwynneth sighed. "Natalya is the solution. If only she'd temper her ardor, perhaps be less extreme ..."

"That's unlikely to happen soon," Gauvain said sadly. "We must do this without her, or in spite of her. I hope you don't consider it disloyal on either of our parts."

"I don't," Gwynneth said, letting anger creep into her voice. "She's hardly been loyal to either one of us, has she? I bear her no ill will in spite of everything." That wasn't exactly true, but Gwynneth wanted to be charitable. "But it can't come as a surprise to you I'm especially interested in preventing war with Maladena."

"I understand. You don't wish us distracted from what's happening in Kronland, though Lennart has the situation well in hand." Word had finally come of the Helvundala coup, and Kendryk's victory at Birkenfels. Gwynneth had been so proud when she read the letters. Kendryk's own account of the action had been modest, but she'd also received letters from Count Faris and Lennart, both of whom praised his courage and creative thinking.

"It's going well now," she said. "But will you still be able to send him money when you have your own war to worry about?"

"That's a good question," Gauvain said. "And the answer is, we can help a while longer, but if a war with Maladena drags on, I can't be sure of anything." "I'm sure we can come up with something," Gwynneth said, as she stood. "Come, I'll take you to see Joslyn. She and Stella have divided and conquered the nursery. Everyone's been forced to pick sides."

Gauvain chuckled as he followed Gwynneth into the corridor. "I'm sure she got that from Natalya. I'm very sorry to cause trouble in your peaceful household."

Gwynneth turned to smile at him. "Any household containing Stella is never peaceful. What's a little more trouble? And besides." She fell in beside Gauvain and took his arm. "No one will think anything of it, if you come to visit Joslyn every day. We'll have plenty of opportunity to discuss everything." She hoped he understood what she meant.

"You're right." Gauvain patted her hand. "I'm sure between the two of us, we'll find a way to keep the peace, both in your house and in my country."

ANTON

Anton's hands were slippery with sweat where they gripped the pike, and he wiped first one hand and then the other on his breeches. No one wore gloves, since the pike slipped against the leather. By now, Anton's hands were so callused, he no longer noticed the the wood.

"Nervous?" Stasny grinned at him.

"No," Anton said, though something hard knotted in the pit of his stomach. "It's just hot." A breeze rustled the flags flying over each company, but it didn't reach into the ranks of tightly packed soldiers.

Stasny opened his mouth to say something, but stopped at the rumble of distant thunder.

Anton knew that sound, and hurried to clap his helmet back on. "I wonder if those guns are ours or theirs?" he asked, trying to sound calm, even as his heart hammered in his chest.

"Probably both," Stasny said, "though it's true we don't have so many. Hopefully the enemy doesn't either."

Within seconds, the most awful sounds rose from the front lines, carried on the salty breeze. Anton didn't know which side was being hit. He gripped the haft of the pike until his knuckles whitened, winced, and forced himself not to duck as a cannonball shrieked overhead.

"Guess we're in range," Stasny said.

His tone was casual, but Anton noticed his voice shaking a little. It was hard to say if that made him feel better or worse.

Anton wanted to reply, but only managed a brief "Hm," since his lips were pressed together so tightly.

Though there was a small break after that first ball, the aftermath behind him was awful. Anton didn't dare turn around. Judging by the shrieks and shouts, that last ball had landed only a few rows behind him. It did no good to look, or even imagine what had happened. There was nothing to be done about it.

225

Sweat poured down Anton's face, and he wanted to be sick. Now he wished to be on horseback more than ever; at least he'd be able to move somehow. He wondered if Skandar was nearby, though rumor said the Sanova Hussars had gone east. He hoped it was true, and that Skandar was out of harm's way.

More balls shrieked, but this time they fell a little to Anton's right. The ground shook at the impact, and out of the corner of his eye, blood and wood exploded into the air. The shock of it made him bite his tongue, while his mouth filled with blood. "We have to move," he said to Stasny, through gritted teeth. "We can't just stand here while they kill us."

"We can't move," Stasny said, his face set and pale when Anton dared to glance at him. "There's nowhere to go. We have to wait until we get the order to move forward. Or perhaps our front ranks will overrun the enemy guns."

"How can they, when they're shooting like this?" Anton tried to keep his teeth from chattering. He wasn't sure if he'd ever been so scared; even when riding into cannonfire with the count that last time. He was sure such rapid fire wasn't possible. How many guns did Isenberg have? Or were her crews inhumanly fast re-loaders? Wouldn't they run out of shot before long?

More cannonball hit, one so close in front of Anton, he closed his eyes against the spray of blood, then nearly screamed from the terrible pain in his cheek. When he dared to open his eyes, he had to look away, because the man in front of him lay on the ground, and not altogether in one piece. Anton wiped blood from his eyes, while more blood rushed into his mouth. He poked at his cheek with his tongue. Something had pierced the side of his face, probably a splinter from a pike.

He probed it carefully, since figuring out what had happened to his face beat looking at, or thinking about, the mess in front of him. From somewhere very far away, the sergeant shouted something about holding firm. Anton didn't have much choice. He would have to stand here until he died. At this rate, that was likely to happen long before they marched in any direction at all.

"That looks nasty," Stasny said next to him. "Hope your girl will still love you, with your face no longer so pretty."

Anton wanted to say he hadn't been pretty to begin with, but between the blood in his mouth and the splinter in his cheek, couldn't get any words out. Cannonballs continued dropping around him, but maybe the breaks between them were longer. He had no way of telling. Now the first shock passed, and the pain came in waves. He worried he might fall, so he held onto his pike, after making sure he'd forced it far into the sandy ground. He closed his eyes. Better not to know what was going on around him.

After an eternity, Stasny gave him a sharp nudge in the ribs. "We're moving," he said. "Can you march?"

Anton nodded and opened his eyes, still not trusting himself to speak. He concentrated on the sergeant's voice, shouting out the orders, same as always, and put one foot in front of the other. The cannonballs now flew overhead more often than not, and gradually, the awful sounds receded into the distance. Every few paces, Anton stepped over or around the results of the bombardment, but he kept his eyes straight ahead, while using his pike to feel his way along the ground. Not everyone he passed was dead, but he wasn't able to help in any case.

He hoped that moving forward meant they were winning. They marched on, heavy smoke filling his nose with the acrid scent of burnt powder, while the sun still shone warm above. They topped a ridge before their way sloped down to the wide beach. Anton opened his eyes to see the guns that had beaten his regiment to a pulp. The captured pieces stood on the ridge, still too hot to touch, judging by the way troops milled around them. Their own crews had spiked some of them as they retreated. Imperial infantry ranged all across the beach, while small boats swarmed the water between the beach and four huge ships standing out a bit further.

"They're getting away," Anton said out of the corner of his mouth, though by now he had no wish to chase after anyone.

"What's left of them," Stasny said.

Anton was so grateful his comrade had survived, he wanted to throw himself at Stasny and cry all over him. He blinked, and stared out to sea.

Imperial musketeers fired at the small boats, though Anton couldn't tell if they'd hit anyone. Before long, one of the big ships moved forward, then sideways, and smoke puffed out from its side in two rows. By now, Anton wasn't able to see or hear very well, and he wondered if he'd entered one of his nightmares, as hundreds of musketeers crumpled onto the beach under those terrible guns.

Anton remembered the count worrying about the pirated merchantman firing on them. He hadn't been able to picture it then, and didn't want to see it now.

Someone called back the troops on the beach, and Anton's group was ordered to stand down. He and all the others dropped their pike into the stringy grass and sat. Those with stronger stomachs pulled food and water out of their packs, while Anton concentrated on not being sick. He heard Stasny shouting at his side, but couldn't hold his head up or respond. His head nearly hit the ground when someone grabbed him, then laid him down carefully. He opened his eyes to see someone looming over him, blocking out the sun.

"This is going to hurt," a deep voice said.

BRAEDEN

Braeden was happy to be called back to Trystan and the others. Spending one night camped on the road with all of those dead bodies was more than enough. He needed air. As he and Karil's battalion came out, Trystan sent another group in to relieve them. Cavalry wasn't necessary now, as long as someone blocked the road and held the high ground.

He found Trystan flanked by Kendryk—clearly relieved to see Braeden—and a man who had to be Lennart. It had been awhile since Braeden had met a man tall enough to look him in the eye. He sensed Lennart assessing him carefully as he delivered his report, but Braeden wasn't worried. The mission had been an unqualified success. "Right after I sent the last message, Your Grace," he said to Trystan, careful to address him correctly in front of the king, "An enemy envoy approached. There's a Maladene colonel in charge there—a Tavio Sora—and he asked for a truce so they can retrieve the bodies of their dead. I told him I'd check with you, and send a reply before noon."

Trystan scowled. "Let them rot a bit longer."

"No," Kendryk said. "Absolutely not. What does having all of those bodies lying on the road accomplish? We're not barbarians."

Color rose in Trystan's cheeks. "As long as those bodies block the road, they can't get past."

"They can't get past anyway," Kendryk said. "Please, Duke. I don't wish to order you to agree to a cease-fire, but I will if I have to."

Braeden shifted, conscious of Lennart's amused gaze. It was the worst kind of luck that Trystan and Kendryk were having their first real disagreement in front of the new fellow. Braeden agreed with Kendryk—he didn't want anyone else to have to spend another night in there with the dead—but he'd as soon stay out of it.

"Then you will have to give the order," Trystan said, his eyes sparking yellow. Braeden was uncomfortably reminded of Daciana Tomescu.

"If I may, I have an idea," Lennart said. "We've discussed traveling around the mountains and surprising the enemy on the other side. I'd hate to do it as they're burying their dead. We might surprise them, but it doesn't seem right." He looked at Braeden. "Do you know how long it'll take us to go that way?"

"If we leave now, we'd get close by nightfall tomorrow, and attack the next morning. We'd have to leave the baggage and big guns behind, though."

Lennart put a hand on Kendryk's shoulder. "I understand why you want this done quickly. Those poor fellows in there—I don't like it either. But if we attack day after tomorrow, they'll only be there two more nights. No doubt we'll add to the body count anyway."

Kendryk looked unhappy. Braeden felt bad for him, but a truce would delay things and give the enemy time to regroup. Then he thought of something, and sent a page in search of Alona Brynner. When she appeared and had been presented to the king, Braeden asked. "What do you know about Tavio Sora? Seems he's in charge on the other side."

"Oh, him." Brynner gave a disdainful laugh. "He's Maladene, and as arrogant as they come. Competent enough I suppose, but never expects anything unexpected. Though I shouldn't throw stones on that score," She added with a sheepish grin.

"Do you reckon he'll expect us to outflank him?"

"Gods no. He'll expect you to send a messenger with terms he can't agree to, and that you'll go back and forth for several days."

"Excellent," Lennart said. "That's our solution. We'll send messages, and let the commander inside deal with the replies. Let him dawdle and delay while we come around the other side."

It was nice to ride at the head of a large force once more. Between the Helvundala army, led by the clearly competent Geffrey Manier, Lennart's Estenorians, and Trystan's and Brynner's combined forces, they numbered a good twelve thousand. You could do something with an army that size.

Kendryk insisted on riding at the head of the Terragand force with Trystan, but Braeden quietly put himself between them. He sensed that Trystan was still angry with Kendryk for pulling rank in front of the king, and Kendryk was embarrassed at being overridden, even though Lennart had done it tactfully, Braeden thought.

They hurried south along a road flanking the hills, a path familiar to Braeden since he'd taken it on his way to Birkenfels the first time. But it had been autumn then, and now it was spring, so it looked different enough he pretended not to remember it well. The problem with being in this part of Terragand, was that everything reminded him of Janna.

Lennart had insisted on leaving a substantial force behind to hold the gap indefinitely. "We might need it again, and we don't want the enemy to have use of it," he said. "And now it's ours, it should be easy to hold onto."

Braeden was glad; he never wanted to see the inside of that place again.

They traveled with only the cavalry and the infantry marching double-time. They'd be tired when they reached their destination, but would sleep through the night before surprising the enemy in the morning. The artillery and baggage followed, and would meet them a day later.

Braeden noticed that both Faris and Trystan deferred to Lennart, who took over the whole operation as if it were the most natural thing in the world. It was probably better that way, since Kendryk didn't seem to mind either. Clearly, Lennart had a core of iron, and his ability was beyond question. Braeden liked having someone so strong in charge again. He appreciated a good leader, and was glad to be on his side.

The attack went even better than expected, since Sora and his troops were demoralized by their many casualties, and distracted by the endless messages going back and forth. Lennart led the attack just after dawn, and it was over before the sun had risen above the tree tops. Most of the enemy troops simply surrendered, and soon Tavio Sora followed Alona Brynner into Lennart's service.

As soon as it was over, Lennart called for Braeden and Trystan. "Your work here has been invaluable," he said. "But now I have another mission for you."

TEODORA

"I was hoping you could help me," Teodora said after taking a sip of wine. She had called Countess Biaram to her private study.

The countess took a long drink, nearly draining her glass.

Teodora raised an eyebrow, but supposed she didn't blame her. It must take nerves of steel to deal with a bad-tempered empress every day.

"Excellent vintage," the countess said, looking at the empty glass with longing. "The northern Cesiano riverlands, '21, if I'm not mistaken."

"You're right," Teodora said, then took another small sip of hers. The countess would have to wait for a refill.

"How might I help you?"

"What kind of contacts do you have in Galladium?" Teodora asked. "I can no longer trust anything I hear from Natalya."

"It's been some time since her information has been reliable," the countess said with a sniff. "We should have developed more diverse contacts in Allaux."

Teodora ignored the implied scolding. "Please tell me you have someone else there." She drained the contents of her glass before she realized it.

"I do," the countess said, then refilled both their glasses, even though Teodora hadn't asked. "But I'm afraid it's become increasingly difficult for them to get close to the Maxima, since she and the king are no longer intimate."

"I can't say I blame her." Teodora grimaced. "Though it's annoying for us. I need someone who can give me detailed reports on Princess Gwynneth's activities."

"That will be difficult. What precisely do you need to find out?"

Teodora wasn't sure how much to divulge, though as far as she knew, Countess Biaram was trustworthy. She took a deep breath. "I need your assurance that what I'm about to tell you will go no further. Not even Count Solteszy or Livilla must learn of what I'm planning."

The countess beamed, apparently pleased to be taken into imperial confidence. "You have my word."

Teodora dropped her voice, even though no one else was present. Someone might be listening at the door. "I must get rid of Princess Gwynneth, and all of her children, preferably."

"Get rid of, as in, dead?" The countess didn't look terribly shocked, though she took another long drink.

"Yes, dead." It was a relief to finally say it out loud, since she'd been thinking about it forever. "I need to clear the way for Aksel Roussay to become King of Norovaea." Instead of sending the next shipload of coin when it was due in the early spring, Arryk had sent a messenger with a small chest of silver accompanied by a vague, rambling note filled with excuses about why it was impossible to send the full amount. It was time to replace him with someone more reliable.

"I see." The countess finished her glass again, with a remarkably steady hand. "Though I don't wish to question you, I don't understand why the children must also be killed. It's one thing to assassinate a princess, and quite another ... I'm sure you realize."

"I do." Secretly, Teodora relished the idea of getting rid of all of Kendryk's offspring. They were likely to grow up as troublesome as their father. And even better, annihilating his family would be a fitting revenge for his escape, and everything else he'd done. "The problem is that, even with Gwynneth dead, the Duchess Maryna will be next in line for the Norovaean throne."

"I understand that, but, she's still a little girl, and it's unlikely Kendryk will allow his heir to go to Norovaea alone. Perhaps he would agree to it if Aksel were to be regent until she comes of age."

Teodora leaned back in her chair. Aksel holding all of the real power in Maryna's name might be acceptable. But then Teodora realized she wouldn't accept the possibility of Kendryk's daughter becoming queen. She wanted nothing left of that family. "No, that won't do," she said. "I need Aksel to become king soon, and it must be certain."

"What about Arryk? Do you have plans for him as well?" The countess wore a decidedly nasty grin.

"Arryk will take care of himself. Recently, he's dismissed his ruling council, and replaced all of his advisers with—as far as I can tell—peasants and minor nobility from gods-know-where in the countryside. The Norovaea aristocracy is on the brink of revolt. It's only a matter of time before they get rid of Arryk for good." Teodora didn't feel she needed to mention that she had already sent agents to Norovaea to help stir things up.

"So it's likely they'll depose him?"

"At worst." Teodora shrugged. "If we're lucky, they'll kill him. But even if he's deposed, they will next look to Gwynneth to replace him. And if she's no longer alive ..."

"Interesting. I'll see what I can do. It'll be difficult to get close to her, but my contact has proven himself resourceful in the past. I'll get in touch, and report back to you as soon as I can."

"It won't take too long, will it?" There was no time to waste. If the way to the Norovaean throne was clear, she'd just as soon marry Elektra off to a heretic if she couldn't get Aksel to convert. Then her untrustworthy child would be thousands of leagues away while, with any luck, Aksel turned out to be a tractable puppet.

"We will have to be patient, Your Highness." The countess was smiling, probably pleased to be given such an interesting, sensitive task. "It will take time for messages to reach my source and return. But I should hope we'll have information we can use before winter."

Teodora could only hope Gwynneth would stay put in Allaux that long, though if she joined her husband in Terragand, she'd be far more vulnerable. Teodora decided to send Ensden a letter telling him to keep an eye out for the princess, and if she were spotted, make it clear that no one would be upset if she were killed accidentally. No one but Kendryk, that is.

ELEKTRA

For the first few hours after being locked up, Elektra felt like a wayward little girl sent to her room without supper. But then supper came, borne by an unfamiliar servant, who smiled politely but refused to answer questions.

Elektra forced herself to eat, hoping her mother wouldn't keep her here for long. Just in case, she opened her window and looked down. She was four floors up, and the walls stretched smooth on all sides, the neighboring windowsills nearly flush with them. Even if she'd been brave enough to climb, she doubted she could get a foothold. She looked up. The roof was much too high. Climbing either way was out of the question, but perhaps she would come up with something else.

The next morning, a different unfamiliar servant came with breakfast and water for washing. A little later, a maid came for the dirty dishes and the chamberpot. No one would speak to her.

Elektra needed help if she was to get out of here, but she couldn't think who might pull it off. Mother Luca? Aksel? She hoped both of them would want to, but neither one of them had any power, or was familiar with the palace. There was only one other person, and Elektra wasn't at all sure of her. She wasn't certain that Livilla hadn't betrayed her to her mother.

The very thought made her sick, and she struggled to keep despair at bay as the day wore on. She worried that her mother would order her troops into the field without her, since they'd been in Atlona for nearly a month by now. She had to come up with something, and by the time supper arrived, she was ready. As soon as the servant, an older man with a pale, stern face, put the tray down, she thrust the note at him. "You must deliver this to the Maxima," she said, using her most commanding tone. "You will, of course, be compensated for your trouble."

A fleeting smile crossed the man's face as he pushed Elektra's hand aside. He shook his head and said, "I'm sorry, Your Grace, but I have orders. No messages."

"Please," Elektra whispered. "You must help me. What if the empress kills me?"

"I'm certain she means you no harm." The man's voice was gentler than his face. "But I'm sure you understand that I must follow orders."

Elektra nodded, dropping the note to the floor. She cried herself to sleep that night with the hopelessness of it all. Most likely, no one else had any idea where she was. Her friends would wonder what had happened, but her mother would probably make some excuse for her, and they'd accept it.

She spent much of the next day praying to Vica. The goddess had helped her when Braeden was ready to kill her, and gave her the words she needed to save herself. Surely she could find words to persuade the servants to help her.

Several days of praying and pondering passed, but after nearly a week had gone by, her mother came to see her. The empress acted as if she were paying a normal social call, taking a seat at a little table, and beckoning Elektra to join her.

"You are well, I hope?" she asked, her tone friendly and conversational.

Elektra stared. "What do you think? I must get out of here, Mother. Please." Tears came to her eyes and her voice wobbled, but Elektra let it happen. Appearing tough in front of her mother hadn't helped her cause. Maybe tears would do it.

"Why?" Teodora looked around. "This is a lovely room. The ambassador from Moralta stays here often. So much nicer than the Arnfels, isn't it?"

"I wouldn't know." Elektra tried to keep the panic from her voice.

"I don't suppose you'd want to find out." Teodora leaned forward, propping her elbows on the table. "Though it might not hurt you to have the experience. I sometimes wonder, if I'd been more familiar with the place, I might have been able to prevent ..."

"Prevent what?" Elektra welcomed anything that might distract her mother from sending her there.

"Prisoners escaping, that sort of thing." Teodora's voice was flat, her eyes hard. "But I don't like the idea of sending my heir there. Even though you're right; I don't care for you in the least."

While Elektra had always known this, it hurt terribly to hear it from her own mother. But she mustn't let it show if she was going to outwit her somehow. "The feeling is mutual then." She forced a smile. "But that doesn't mean we can't work together, does it?"

"Of course not." Teodora stopped short, and Elektra held her breath. Then Teodora continued, "But working with you means I'd need to trust you at least a tiny bit, and after your little revelation, I'm afraid I can't."

"I see." Elektra tried to keep her voice from trembling. "So, what must I do to get out of here?" She raised her chin, and looked Teodora in the eye. As little good as showing backbone did, crying and sniveling seemed to be even less effective. And maintaining one's dignity had to count for something.

Teodora shrugged. "Nothing right now. It will do you good to stay here longer and think about things. Consider especially how you might regain my trust. You'll never have all of it, but I'd like to at least know you can follow orders."

"I can," Elektra said, a little too eagerly. At this point she was willing to agree to just about anything.

"Perhaps." Teodora stood. "I don't need you yet. Aksel's conversion is proceeding rather slowly, and until he cooperates I have little use for you."

"Let me talk to him," Elektra said, suddenly realizing she wanted nothing more than to see Aksel, even for a few minutes. "I'm sure he'll convert if it means getting me out of here." A friend who would do something like that for her was beyond all of Elektra's hopes, but she allowed herself to dream anyway.

Teodora swept past her to the door and knocked on it. "I'm afraid you overestimate your charms, my dear," she said, looking Elektra over condescendingly. "No one will do anything like that for you. We'll talk again in a few weeks, I'm sure."

"A few weeks?" Elektra shrieked, but the door had already closed behind her mother.

ANTON

Anton awoke briefly to something pouring down his throat. It burned, and Anton tried to struggle, but warmth washed through him, and he slumped back against whoever held him.

"Hold his head steady," the same deep voice said, and large hands grabbed him by the chin and forehead. Anton struggled some more, but it did no good at all. Someone held his legs down too. Panic spread as he wondered if they were getting ready to cut off a limb, though he didn't remember being hit. He was in pain, but couldn't quite tell where it came from, especially as the liquor numbed his whole body.

A moment of blinding agony was followed by a sustained stabbing, and blood flooded his mouth again. He spit it onto the grass before sliding into blackness.

When he woke up, it was nearly dark and he still lay in the sand, his head in someone's lap. He looked up with an effort, and saw Stasny, asleep. Or at least he had his eyes closed, because they came open the moment Anton made a sound, his throat so raw and dry he wasn't even able ask for water. But Stasny seemed to know, grabbing a flask from somewhere, and pushing it between Anton's lips. He gulped it down fast, then felt sick.

Once the wave of nausea had passed, Anton tried speaking again, even though moving his mouth made pain shoot through his head. "What happened? Are we prisoners?" Though he didn't like fighting for the empress, being taken by the other side now meant separation from Susanna, maybe forever.

Stasny laughed, sounding almost the same as usual. "We won. Chased Tora Isenberg back into the sea, though we got a fair number of her troops before they got away."

Anton breathed in deeply. "But they killed so many of ours."

"True, we took a few casualties, but not as many as it felt like when those cannonballs dropped on us like rain."

"Where are we?" Anton still wasn't able to think straight.

"Still on the field. The doctor stitched your face up, and I waited for you to wake up so we can get back to camp. Think you can walk?"

Anton nudged his right cheek, and when he did, noticed the bandage that wound around his head, holding the dressing in place. He didn't dare touch the inside with his tongue. At least it hadn't taken his eye. Only two inches higher, and he would have looked more like the count than he ever wanted to. "I'll try," he finally said, though he was very weak. But he really needed to get back to Susanna, since he knew she'd worry.

Stasny hauled him to his feet, and Anton stood there for a moment, swaying. He leaned on Stasny, and took a few deeps breaths. With the smoke of the battlefield blown away, a breeze came off the ocean, fresh and cool. Anton gulped it down and watched the sun, now a bright orange ball hovering on the distant horizon.

"It's late," he finally said.

"You were out for a few hours," Stasny said cheerfully, "though I think that was more from the brandy they gave you than anything else. We'll go slow, though I'll try to get you into camp before dark."

Anton found that his head cleared as he walked, and the pain in his cheek turned to a dull throbbing. "Thank you for taking care of me," he said to Stasny, once they'd reached the edge of camp.

"You'd do the same for me. There was no way I'd leave you lying in the sand."

"I'm glad you didn't." Anton grinned, then yelped when he realized one side of his face wouldn't move without extreme pain. "And you're right; I'd do the same for you, though I hope I never have to."

Anton stumbled along in silence, Stasny's hand on his elbow. He wondered if they'd ever get to their part of camp. Torches flared up, lighting the paths between the tents, and Anton had to stop a few times, feeling weaker. He hoped he could make it.

From somewhere ahead of him came a shriek, and a moment later a crying Susanna flung herself at him.

"Oh gods, I thought you were dead when you didn't come back."

Anton put an arm around her, but sagged.

"Hey, easy there," Stasny said. "He's on the wobbly side. Can you help me hold him up?"

Anton almost grinned down at Susanna as she came around to his other side, then remembered he shouldn't. She was still crying, but at least she was helping support him.

"What happened?" she finally asked.

"Just a splinter through the cheek," Stasny said. "The doctor's already taken it out, and stitched up the hole. You'll need to help him keep it clean, and make sure he has a shot of brandy to help him sleep."

"That'll take more than a shot," Susanna grumbled, though she pulled Anton even closer.

Anton wasn't sure he'd make it much further, when they finally reached the tent and he collapsed onto the cot. "So dirty," he moaned, realizing he had to be covered in blood and worse.

"Never mind that," Susanna said, then turned away for a moment.

Anton heard her murmuring at Stasny. There was a rustle and a laugh, and Stasny was gone.

"Thank the gods for that man," Susanna said, kneeling at the side of the cot, while she pushed Anton's hair away from his forehead. "I gave him a bottle of my best brandy for taking such good care of you."

She cried a little more, though Anton didn't know quite how to comfort her. Then she got some water, and after he'd had a long drink, she started cleaning him up.

"Thank the gods for *you*," Anton said, wishing he could smile.

LENNART

Lennart read the message and swore as he flung it to the ground.

"Bad news?" Kendryk asked, looking worried. He rode beside Lennart as they led the combined force, heading deep into Terragand.

Lennart nodded. "Ensden defeated Tora Isenberg on a beach in northwestern Terragand." This news followed Kalstrom losing his foothold on a spit of land in Kaltental harbor when Ensden launched a night attack. Kalstrom had fallen back to join Lofbrok a few leagues off on the northern shore without too many casualties, but it was a significant strategic loss.

"Oh gods." Kendryk turned pale. "How bad is it?"

"Not as bad as all that." Lennart sighed, already recalculating his plans. "Most of my fleet was standing off the coast there, since I worried about Isenberg being cut off from everyone else. She could save nearly all of her army, though she had to abandon much of the artillery. Not that Ensden will know what to do with it."

"Where is she now?"

"Ummarvik, though she says Prince Ossian is less than thrilled at hosting her. Princess Floreta is also there, and is trying to persuade Isenberg to use her troops to move on Mattila in Brandana."

"That would be a mistake," Kendryk said. "We barely have enough to take on Ensden."

"You're right." Lennart looked at Kendryk, then paused. He might as well ask him. "I have other ideas about Brynhild Mattila. How do you feel about a trip to Brandana?"

"You want me to negotiate with her?" It was clear from the look on Kendryk's face he'd never considered it, and didn't much like the idea.

"Why not? We have little to lose if she says no, and much to gain if she agrees. If she could gather even a small force, she might make all the difference."

"True," Kendryk said, "but I don't want to condone the way she's usurped the throne of Brandana."

"You needn't. I won't ask you to treat with her as an equal; as far as you're concerned, she's just another general you're trying to get on our side."

"I don't want to leave Terragand," Kendryk said, a stubborn set to his jaw. "I don't want to risk missing out on any major action."

"If you can bring Mattila in before we engage with Ensden, it might well turn the tide."

"I doubt I can do it in time," Kendryk said.

"I'll wait." Lennart smiled, knowing he could answer any objection. "We can manage well enough through the summer, and I wouldn't mind seeing if I can get reinforcements from further south in the meantime. The more Kronlanders we have on our side, the better."

Kendryk frowned. "What makes you so sure any Kronlanders will join us? The only reason you got support from Helvundala is because my aunt now rules there, but I can't imagine anyone else will be interested in helping me."

"It's not only you they're helping." Lennart slowed his horse. Now was as good a time as any to have this conversation. "They all benefit if I can run Teodora out of Kronland once and for all."

"She'll come back when you leave."

"Not this time. If she survives this fight, she'll still lose it. And when she loses, she'll sign a treaty with the two of us."

"What kind of treaty?" Kendryk suddenly looked more interested.

"She must agree to political and religious freedom for all of Kronland." Lennart couldn't hide a triumphant grin.

A smile spread across Kendryk's face. "That would be marvelous." He paused, and his brow creased. "It's hard to imagine right now." The smile fled. "And there's something else." He shifted in the saddle. "I don't want you to think I'm ungrateful for everything you're doing. But I can't help but wonder why you're doing this. What do you hope to gain from this venture?"

"A strong, independent Kronland benefits Estenor too," Lennart said. "If Teodora overruns you completely, she'll be lurking at my doorstep, cutting off my access to the sea, and no doubt engaging in all kinds of villainy."

"No doubt," Kendryk said wryly. "You want us to provide you a buffer."

"Only as you usually have. Estenor has nearly always been friendly with Helvundala and Terragand to our mutual benefit. I want to make that permanent by defeating Teodora so thoroughly she'll never dream of attacking

Kronland again. I'll tie her up with as harsh a treaty as I can manage, and guarantee it all with a permanent army minding the Olvisyan border."

"Sounds ambitious." Kendryk still looked dubious, but interested. "And expensive. Who will pay for this standing army?"

"Teodora will." Lennart grinned. "Just like she's sucking your brother-in-law dry with reparations payments, I'll do the same to her. And that's if she's still alive at the end of this. I'm assuming her replacement will be more cooperative."

"Anyone would be more cooperative." Now Kendryk was smiling again. "And I won't deny I'd love to see her dead. But forgive me if I still have trouble believing that you're going to all of this trouble, risk and expense for the sake of an independent Kronland alone. What else do you want?"

"I want to see the Quadrene creed spread through all of Kronland," Lennart said quietly. They'd talked religion more than once, but he'd never explained what he hoped for. "I want the empire and the old faith to guarantee they won't interfere with it."

"That will never happen." Kendryk shook his head. "I like the idea, but the empire and the faith will go down in flames before they allow tolerance."

"So they'll burn." Lennart shrugged, and waited until he'd caught Kendryk's eye. "I've read all of Edric's writings and I've read the Scrolls. I know this must be done before it's too late." A strange excitement rose inside him, as it always did when he remembered his real reason for being here.

Kendryk nodded slowly. "You're right." He smiled again. "And I'm very pleased about your plan. I was grateful you were willing to help restore Terragand, but I was sure you did that out of friendship to Gwynneth. That you wish to do far more is the answer to many prayers. Knowing that, I'm happy to negotiate with Brynhild Mattila on your behalf."

Lennart grinned. "And imagine the look on Teodora Inferrara's face when she learns her former general is now working for us."

TEODORA

"Out of the way," Teodora screeched, cracking the whip at an old woman in the street. The woman stumbled against the wall of a house, narrowly missing the horse's hoofs. After that, the rest of the traffic cleared a path for her quickly enough.

Alarmed by Livilla's uncharacteristically cryptic note, Teodora was in a hurry to get to the Maxima's palace. Rather than taking the imperial carriage with its six horses and many guards, she'd asked for a two-horse buggy, and insisted on driving it herself.

"Your Highness, please," said the guard sitting next to her. "This is dangerous. We cannot risk—"

"It's these idiots who are in danger," Teodora said, settling back into the seat as the street widened. The square in front of the Maxima's palace lay straight ahead. "Don't be such a ninny." She had to laugh at the guard, her knuckles white as she clung to the seat. Though she couldn't see the three sitting behind her in the buggy, they probably weren't any better off.

Teodora kept the horses at a smart trot, slowing only as the courtyard gate swung open ahead of her, then leapt out of the seat before they came to a stop. "Where is the Maxima?" she asked a servant who'd been standing in front of the stable.

"In her private study, Your Highness. Please follow me."

Teodora knew the way, but it didn't do to fling oneself into the Maxima's presence like a schoolgirl. The bright heat of the summer's day turned suddenly cool and dark as she entered the palace. The gray floors and black pillars—all in marble—lining the great hall gave an impression both forbidding and impressive, a fitting demonstration of Livilla's power.

By the time she reached her destination, Teodora had cooled off, though she was still anxious. Livilla never sent for her like this unless the news was bad. She breathed in deeply, steeling herself for whatever lay ahead.

Livilla rose from a seat in the shadows as Teodora entered, the door falling shut soundlessly behind her. This room, though relatively small, was also lined in black marble, broken only by white silk curtains billowing at the open windows.

"Come, child," Livilla said, walking up to Teodora and taking her hand. "You must sit down and have something cool to drink."

Teodora sat in a silver chair, upholstered in black silk. "I don't want a drink," she said. "Is it very bad, whatever you're going to tell me?"

"I'm not sure," Livilla said, pouring what looked like white wine into two small crystal glasses, and handing one to Teodora. "Both bad and good, I think."

It was impossible to tell anything from Livilla's tone, so Teodora took the glass and tried to relax into the chair, sipping at the cool, sweet drink.

Livilla sat down across from Teodora in an identical chair, set her glass down and then took what seemed like an eternity arranging her robes around her. Did she always move this deliberately?

"I'll start with the good news," she said at last. "Daciana Tomescu is alive."

Teodora jumped out of her seat, cold wine spilling onto her lap even as the glass shattered on the floor.

"How? Where? Are you certain?"

"My dear, sit down please, and I will tell you everything."

"Is she here? I must see her." Teodora looked around wildly, as if she expected Daciana to stride out of the shadows at any moment. As the shock receded, she was still frightened, mostly because Livilla's face was so grave. "She's hurt, isn't she?" Teodora sank back into her chair.

"She is," Livilla nodded. "Someone found her floating in the harbor after Prince Kendryk's escape. They took her to the temple in Capo, where she lay near death for many months. It's only been in recent weeks she's been able to remember who she was, and the priest sent us word."

"Is she there? I must go to her." Teodora jumped up again.

"Yes, she is still there," Livilla said. "The priest in Capo doesn't wish to move her yet. She had many injuries, and not all have healed. He said ..." Livilla trailed off, then stood and took Teodora's hand. "He said she'd been shot in the head and badly burned. It's possible we will not recognize her."

"Oh gods." Teodora yanked her hand out of Livilla's grasp and turned away. "I don't believe that. I will always recognize her. I must go to her right away. Surely we can help her somehow."

"Perhaps we can," Livilla said. "I don't know what kind of care she has had there. I think it's best if you come along, in case certain decisions have to be made."

"What kinds of decisions?" Teodora forced herself to look Livilla in the eye as dread twisted in the pit of her belly.

"I don't know yet. But we must be prepared for anything." Livilla put her hands on Teodora's shoulders. "You've heard the rumors about Daciana, that she can't be killed."

"Of course. I thought she started those, and I did my best to help them along." Teodora caught Livilla's eye. "Oh gods, are you saying it's true?"

"It's possible. In my studies I've come across a few such cases, and there's no explanation except for intervention from the Mother herself. Those few were unable to die, but sometimes their wounds were so terrible, it would have been better ..." Livilla paused, her eyes full of sympathy. "There is something I might do in that case, but I will need both your help and permission to do it."

"I can't give you permission," Teodora whispered, blinking back tears. "Not until I see."

"I understand," Livilla said. "Let's go right away."

GWYNNETH

"I hadn't expected to see you in the middle of the day." Gwynneth did her best to look as if she welcomed an unexpected visit from Natalya, though dread washed over her. Natalya never paid social calls anymore.

"I wanted to see my daughter." Natalya smiled, though her eyes were cold. "And it might be nice for us to catch up."

"Certainly. We haven't seen enough of each other lately," Gwynneth said, leading the way to a group of chairs near the window in her sitting room. "Do you want me to send for Joslyn?"

"Not right now." Natalya said shortly. "I understand her father visits every day, or so I've heard." She looked directly at Gwynneth, who had to force down a shudder.

"He does." Gwynneth smiled. "He's very devoted."

"Hmph. To her at least." Though she might have been mistaken, Gwynneth thought she saw a shadow pass over Natalya's eyes.

"And to you too," Gwynneth said softly. "He still loves you very much. I'm sure he always will."

"Ridiculous." Natalya shook her head, then looked at Gwynneth, her eyes boring into hers. "We need to talk."

"We do." Gwynneth reminded herself she'd done nothing wrong, though she she cursed the color flooding to her cheeks.

"The king comes here every day. That is a fact."

"It is," Gwynneth said. "Did you expect anything less from him?"

"I had hoped for better sense, but he always disappoints." Natalya gave a disdainful sniff. "I suppose it's natural he'd spend time with Joslyn, but I have it on good authority he spends a great deal of time closeted with you."

Gwynneth stared straight back at Natalya, hoping she appeared calm even as her heart thumped wildly. She should have known Natalya would place spies in her house, but pushed her indignation down. "Closeted? That sounds rather sinister. I offer the king refreshment whenever he comes to visit, not that

I need to justify myself to you." So much for keeping the indignation at bay. Now she'd done it, she added a head toss for good measure.

To her surprise, Natalya laughed. "You're right, of course, and I have no right to spy on you."

"You spy on everyone." Gwynneth continued her challenging stare. Maybe it was better to have it out.

"True." Natalya looked amused. "I'm afraid I can't help myself." Then she sighed. "I don't mind if you and the king are on good terms. He needs a friend he can count on. And if you're carrying on with him, you're doing it discreetly. I can't begrudge him a bit of—"

"You think the king and I are having an affair?" Gwynneth had trouble keeping her voice down. On one hand, she was relieved, but on the other, she wished she could be above suspicion, even all these years later. Now she regretted having confided in Natalya about Arian Orland one evening after too many glasses of wine.

"I don't mind." Natalya shrugged. "I won't lie; I'm a little offended he got over me so quickly, but I'm sure it's for the best."

Gwynneth chewed on her lip, unsure whether to laugh or cry. "I don't expect you to believe me, but the king and I are just friends." That was true. "We spend all of our time talking about the children." That was a lie, though the king had become fond of Gwynneth's children.

"Hm." Natalya looked at her carefully. "I suppose that makes sense. It makes me uncomfortable, knowing that the two people I care about most are spending so much time alone without me. Especially since neither one of you likes what I'm doing."

Gwynneth sighed. "It's true, we don't like what you're doing. But you will do it anyway, so you can't blame us for commiserating about how difficult you are." She smiled a bit at this last, hoping to lessen the sting of her words.

"I suppose not," Natalya said dryly. "Just so long as you're not plotting against me. That would be terrible." The look she gave Gwynneth was sad, and so far from threatening, that Gwynneth softened.

"It would be," she said firmly. "But I don't wish to become involved in Galladian politics. I'm happy to listen to any concerns the king might have, but, I always advise him to follow your lead."

"The king has concerns, does he?" Natalya's eyes hardened again. "Perhaps you could tell me about them."

Gwynneth cursed her stupidity. "I doubt it's anything you don't already know about."

"I wouldn't count on that." Natalya leaned forward. "Why don't you tell me, and I'll let you know."

For the first time, Gwynneth was afraid, though fear mingled with anger. Natalya was putting her into an impossible situation. "I won't pass on things the king has told me in confidence," she said, aware of how lame that sounded.

Natalya stood abruptly. "Gwynneth," she said. "You must decide. Are you loyal to the king or to me?"

"Both." Gwynneth stood and faced her. "Why can't I be loyal to both of you?" To her chagrin, her voice wobbled a little.

"That's impossible." Natalya shook her head. "You will choose." She walked to the door. "And you'd better do it soon."

The anger boiled over. "Are you threatening me, Natalya? Really?" Gwynneth followed her to the door. "After everything we've been through?"

"What kind of monster do you take me for?" Natalya's voice sharpened. "I need to be assured of your loyalty in these treacherous times. And if you're not loyal? Well, I'll be hurt, but I won't do anything to you except perhaps confide in you less."

"You don't confide in me at all," Gwynneth whispered, letting tears wet her eyes. "Not anymore."

"That's because you so obviously disapprove of what I'm doing. I suggest you spend more time praying and reading the Scrolls, and less time coddling the king. It'll do both of you good."

Natalya swept out of the room, the door banging shut behind her.

Gwynneth sat back down, her legs shaking. Perhaps it was time to leave Galladium, though she didn't know where to go. She offered a quick prayer that Lennart and Kendryk would soon secure Terragand so she could go home.

ANTON

Anton got a few days to recover before the army marched out again. As far as everyone knew, Tora Isenberg had sailed for Ummarvik, where rumor said she planned to meet a large army of mercenaries from Anglana.

"We were lucky they didn't reach her before we did," the sergeant said as they all sat around the fire one evening. "It might have been a much fairer fight."

Anton shuddered at the idea of it being even worse than it had been. He rested with his back against a log, Susanna in his lap, her arms wound tightly around his neck, her head nestled under his chin. Since he'd been hurt, she'd been very clingy, though he didn't mind too much.

"Won't she attack us from there, once she regroups?" someone asked.

"Don't know." The sergeant shrugged. "Not our problem. We'll leave a regiment behind to guard the beach in case she comes back, but we're making for Kaltental. Lennart is finally marching out of Helvundala, and we want to defeat his general who's besieging the city. Hopefully we can take him out before Lennart arrives. Ensden is using everything he has to defend Kaltental. We'll have a bit of a march, since we need to dodge unfriendly territory. Duke Orland still holds the lands near the river, and we'll steer clear of him."

"Why don't we clean him up while we're at it?" someone else asked.

"He's got his troops scattered through the woods along the river, and it'll take too long to root them out. Easier to mop him up after Kaltental is secure."

Anton shivered, and Susanna squeezed him a little harder. "Any relation to your count?" she whispered.

"The duke's his father." Anton remembered all of the shouting whenever the count visited. "The father is as fierce as his son was, so we're better off staying clear."

"Good." Susanna snuggled closer into his arms.

After that, they marched a little each day, but took their time so the wounded could catch up. Fortunately, Anton was able to walk just fine, though his face still hurt if he talked too much, or ate anything that required much chewing. Susanna fed him porridge diligently, and Anton was getting sick of it, even though she added all kinds of good things like fruit and honey to make it taste better.

It occurred to Anton that he'd never had a chance to fight at the beach, but now he wasn't sure he wanted to. In fact, it seemed infantry fighting was no good at all. He needed to figure out a way of getting back into the cavalry.

But when he told Susanna, she didn't agree. "It won't make any difference," she said. "You might still be stuck somewhere in a crowd of troops, not able to move while those guns fired at you. And as long as you're facing Lennart or his generals, it won't get better," she added gravely.

"What do you mean?" Anton asked.

"I overheard officers talking the other day when I was selling the colonel material for a new cloak. They said that Lennart's army has hundreds upon hundreds of those guns, like the ones you saw on the beach."

"They seemed small once I got close to them," Anton said.

"They *are* small, according to the colonel. But there are a lot of them, they fire fast, and they're easy to move. You will run into them at every battle most like."

"I'd rather not think about that," Anton said, then was silent as Susanna cleaned his wound and put on a fresh dressing. In a few more days he could leave it off altogether. "That's going to leave a huge scar, isn't it?" he asked.

"I think so." Her eyes were soft as she finished wrapping the bandage around his head. She touched it gently. "But it'll make you look ever so dashing, don't you think?"

"I wish," Anton grumbled. He hoped she was right, but what worried him more than the scar, was getting his courage back before the next battle. He hated to admit it, but for the first time since he'd started fighting, he was afraid.

251

TEODORA

Teodora left Atlona quietly. Until she knew exactly what was going on, she didn't want it known that Daciana might still be alive. She told Count Solteszy she had urgent business in the countryside, and to take charge until she returned. He merely raised his eyebrows and agreed, asking no further questions.

"If I'm needed, send a message to the temple in Capo. They will know how to find me," she said, hoping she would return before Solteszy had to deal with any crisis. If all went well, she'd be back with Daciana in a few days. Now she knew her friend was alive, she refused to believe anything but that she would nurse her back to health, while keeping her close for as long as it took.

Teodora and Livilla rode south on horseback, a contingent of guards at their heels. Teodora had ordered them to remove the imperial livery and dress as ordinary soldiers. She needed protection, but preferred not to be recognized. The road to Capo was not long, for which Teodora was grateful, though as they neared the port, she was sick with fear at what she might find.

Livilla led the way to the temple, a modest building in an unpleasant part of town, near the harbor. The pungent odor of fish, smoke, and varied types of excrement hung in the still air, and reminded Teodora of a military camp.

Even though Livilla had sent word ahead, the priest was excited and nervous at the sight of Teodora. A small, round man with a rosy face, he had prepared a speech, one Teodora didn't have time to listen to.

"Yes, yes. That's all very well." She flapped her hands at him as he tripped over flowery words. "Now please, take me to her."

The priest hesitated, but Livilla nodded and he led them down a dark stone corridor, lit only by the lamp he carried. After the light and bustle of the harbor, it was like walking into a tomb. A silly thought, no doubt brought on by the foreboding which haunted her since she'd received Livilla's message, Teodora did her best to shake it off. She had to be strong now, for herself, but most of all for Daciana.

The priest fumbled with a key, then turned it in a huge lock hanging on the door.

"Why is she locked in?" Teodora demanded.

He turned to her, looking apologetic. "It's for her own protection, Your Highness. She's been overcome by madness a few times, and once ran into the street, raving. The townspeople set upon her, certain she was a demon, and it was all I could do to save her from them."

"Gods," Teodora murmured, then squared her shoulders as the door swung open. Dim light came from a window, though there were bars across it. It didn't matter. She'd soon have her out of here.

It took a moment for her eyes to adjust to the gloom. The priest left, the door falling shut behind him. Livilla stood at her elbow. Someone sat at a table facing the window, her back to Teodora.

Teodora swallowed hard. "Daciana?"

A woman turned to her, a shock of curly black hair surrounding a face that was familiar, and yet not quite.

Teodora breathed out, relieved. Daciana looked the same, though her hair was much shorter. But the dark eyes staring back at Teodora were blank and strange.

"It's me," Teodora said, trying to keep her tone light. "And the Maxima. We've come to take you home."

"Home?" Daciana rasped. "I have no home."

"You'll come to Atlona with me. Stay as long as you like, until you're well."

"Who are you?"

The question, combined with the complete lack of recognition in the eyes struck Teodora like a punch to the face. She gasped for breath, conscious only of Livilla's hand on her elbow, leading her aside and pushing her to sit down on a little cot.

While Teodora swallowed down the bile rising in her throat, Livilla spoke. "I am the Maxima of Olvisya," she said, "and this is Empress Teodora, your oldest and best friend."

"I have no friends," Daciana said.

"Then why did you send for me?" Teodora finally forced the words out.

Daciana shrugged. "I didn't. No doubt it was that priest fellow. He's all right, for a religious sort, though I'm not sure I can put up with a Maxima." She smiled at Livilla, her fangs showing.

Teodora shuddered, hoping she hadn't made a terrible mistake in coming here unguarded. She clenched her teeth, forcing herself to stand. "You will," she said, taking a few steps forward, so she stood between Daciana and Livilla. "We're here to help you," she added, doing her best to soften her voice.

"No one can help me." Daciana's voice dropped to a whisper. She turned toward the window, and raised her arm so the sleeve of her robe fell back.

Teodora gasped. The light revealed terrible scarring as far up the arm as she could see.

"That's not all." Daciana stood, unfastened the robe, and dropped it to the floor.

Teodora barely stopped the whimper that threatened to burst out, while Livilla gasped behind her. Daciana took a step toward the window so the light fell across her emaciated body, revealing a web of angry pink and white scars from her neck down to her feet. When a sob caught in Teodora's throat, Daciana laughed, and pulled her hair away from her face. Scars went up her cheek and puckered around her right eye. Just above that, a long, seamed scar left a jagged line on her forehead.

"How did you survive?" A tear slid down Teodora's cheek, and she didn't try to stop it.

"I shouldn't have." Daciana bent down, pulled up her robe, and covered herself again. "When the priest learned I was still alive, he nearly lost his mind. He worried I'd been possessed by evil spirits, and nearly killed himself saying prayers over me. I wished I was dead, but that wasn't enough. I even tried it myself a few times." She ran a finger across a long scar circling her throat. "Didn't work." She shrugged. "So here I am, no good to anyone, with pain that never ends."

"You're my friend," Teodora said. "I will help you; I swear it."

BRAEDEN

For the first few days of their journey to Podoska, Trystan was in a terrible mood.

"Lennart thinks I'm too young," he grumbled. "He'll give my command to someone else."

Braeden didn't agree, though he didn't know what was on Lennart's mind. "I reckon he'll give you an even bigger command when you come back with other allies."

"Oh come on." Trystan's tone was impatient. "Why would he give me anything when he has experienced commanders like Geffrey Manier, Count Faris, Alona Brynner or Tavio Sora? It makes little sense."

"It makes plenty of sense. You're the only one who's had a recent victory. Faris might have won at Birkenfels with Arryk, but that was years ago. You're the only one who kept the fight alive in Terragand. And Lennart respects you a great deal; I can tell."

"You're just saying that," Trystan said, though Braeden could tell he was pleased.

"I'll repeat all that to your mother," Braeden said in a teasing tone, though judging by the way the flush rose on Trystan's cheeks, that might not be a bad idea either.

"I doubt my mother will remember who I am," Trystan said.

"How many children ahead of you?" Braeden was sure it was many, but couldn't recall the exact number.

"Eleven." Trystan scowled. "Five sisters and six brothers. Podoska isn't big enough for all of them, and certainly not for me."

"You reckon your mother will want to help Lennart?"

"I hope so." Trystan sighed. "She was eager enough when Arryk invaded, but I haven't been home since then. Who knows what's going on now."

Trystan fell quiet as they approached the spires of Berolstein, Princess Edyta's seat. Braeden had never seen a castle quite like it. Built on a flat hilltop taller than any others nearby, countless small towers sprouted from the sprawling walls, maybe one for each of the children, Braeden thought. They seemed very tiny, even up close. The overall effect would have been cheerful and fairytale-like, except the whole edifice was made of dark granite, with even darker slate rooftops. As Braeden and Trystan rode up to it, black clouds and thunder rolled overhead, and Braeden felt a cold shiver.

"Don't you worry about lightning with all those towers?" Braeden asked, grateful to be in the shelter of the gate before a downpour started.

"Not really," Trystan said. "Every tower has been struck several times, and nothing too terrible ever happens. There've only been a few fires." He was clearly nervous as they rode into the courtyard. "Tell the princess I'm here," he said to a servant who had come hurrying out and recognized Trystan.

By the time they'd reached the great hall, teeming with activity, everyone knew he'd returned. For someone with such a big family, it was a peculiar homecoming. One young man was happy to see him, and a girl just a bit older than Trystan flung herself into his arms with a squeal, but the rest of the group seemed uninterested, and perhaps resentful. Braeden ignored that, and focused instead on the imposing woman seated at the head of a table stretching along one side of the hall. This was the famous Princess Edyta, the most unconventional and unpredictable of the Kronland rulers.

"Have a seat, little one." She waved Trystan to a chair near her. "And your scruffy friend too." She looked Braeden over condescendingly.

Braeden bowed before sitting down, though the princess didn't seem to care what he did.

"I'm surprised to see you after all this time." The princess had strange yellowish eyes, much like Trystan's, though they were far less friendly. "I was beginning to think you'd never come back."

Trystan shrugged. "It's the first chance I've had. We were hard-pressed in Terragand for some time. But now that King Lennart's here—"

The princess interrupted him with a loud, insincere laugh. "Oh please, don't tell me you're here on that idiot's behalf."

Trystan jumped up so fast his chair fell over. "Don't be disrespectful, Mother. Lennart is a king, and the only ruler to do anything of note to save Kronland from Teodora."

"Sit down, sit down." The princess snickered, and Trystan sat, though he still looked angry. "I'm just annoyed with you for being gone so long. Did it never occur to you that I've missed you terribly?"

"No," Trystan said, his eyes hard. "You never paid me any attention before I left, so I assume you didn't miss me much."

"I noticed you weren't here from time to time. And you are my littlest one, so you're special to me." The princess stared at her son in what Braeden guessed was supposed to be maternal affection, but the effect was all wrong.

Trystan rolled his eyes. "That won't do, Mother. I'm not little anymore, and if you're going to be difficult, Commander Terris and I will leave and find allies elsewhere."

"I doubt you will. Who else would follow you?"

Braeden cleared his throat. "Oltena definitely, and probably Lantura too. We also have high hopes of Isenwald and Aquianus. They helped King Arryk when he came, and Lennart has a far better chance of success."

The princess turned and fixed her unpleasant gaze on Braeden. "He speaks! A lot of nonsense, but still. I know who you are, and yes, I'm impressed. Somewhat." She drummed her fingers on the table. "Since you pulled off such a famous rescue, why aren't you in charge of this operation? You have far more experience than this puppy here."

Trystan made an angry noise, and Braeden was annoyed on his behalf. If the woman hadn't been a princess, he might have slapped her. He did his best to keep his voice calm. "Your son is an excellent commander who's proven himself time and again. Lennart trusts him with good reason, and so do I."

"Oh very well then." The princess huffed. "I can see the two of you are going to stick together. How annoying. Now go off to your rooms, and we'll meet again for dinner so you can get acquainted with the rest of the family. Most of them are nicer than I am, so you needn't worry."

"You're such a liar, Mother." Trystan stood. "I apologize," he said to Braeden. "I'd hoped things had improved here, but they clearly haven't. You can see why I left as soon as I was old enough."

ELEKTRA

Elektra was going mad with boredom. At the time of her imprisonment, her room only held two books—a life of Vica, recommended by Luca, and an infantry manual. After several weeks, she had them memorized and was sick of both. As the summer wore on, the temperature grew hot, and even with the windows wide open, the room was unpleasantly warm.

She spent her days sleeping, or pacing the length of the room to keep up her physical condition, while trying to figure out a way to escape. At one point, she'd knotted together all of the sheets and blankets, hoping to create a climbing rope, but right after she realized it wasn't long enough, a maid had come in and seen it. The next time a servant appeared, he took all of the bedding except for one sheet, and a blanket so thin it was see-through. She would need to get help, but after two months stuck here with no visitors besides her mother, she began to despair of that. She would have to wait for her mother's return and then agree to her terms.

It was hard not to lose hope. By now Aksel had likely converted, and there'd be no obstacle to their marriage. Elektra told herself that being married to Aksel would be nice, and she'd have to make the best of it. Being queen of Norovaea might be nice too, and she'd have to see it as practice for being empress later. Her mother wouldn't live forever, so Elektra would bide her time and await her chance.

Resignation didn't make the time go by faster, but it diminished her frustration, at least a little. It was much more fun to daydream about marriage to Aksel than to fruitlessly scheme about how she might return to the army. And perhaps once they were married, Aksel would make use of her military talents for his own army. She asked a servant for a Norovaean dictionary, and to her surprise, received it immediately. Perhaps her mother saw that as acquiescence. At least memorizing lists of foreign words gave her something to do.

So when help came, Elektra was unprepared for it. She'd been sound asleep in the middle of the night, a light breeze blowing through the open window, when her door opened suddenly and a light flared up. Elektra sat up right away. Who would sneak in at this hour? The servants never appeared after sundown.

"Shh, Your Grace," a woman's voice said, then a small lamp appeared on the table next to Elektra's bed. The light flickered up to reveal the face of Countess Biaram.

Elektra gasped. She'd always considered the countess one of her mother's worst toadies, and wondered what she was doing here.

"Please get dressed, Your Grace," the countess said. "We must go quickly."

"Go where?" Elektra asked, though she scrambled out of bed. "To my mother?" She wasn't keen on that, but it was better than being stuck here.

"No." The countess was rummaging through Elektra's wardrobe, and pulled out a plain shirt and breeches. "I'm taking you to your officers."

"My regiment is still here?" Elektra was wide awake now, and hurrying to pull on her clothes.

"No; it received orders to join Ensden in Terragand, and is already marching north. A few officers loyal to you remain in the city, and will help you get out so you can join the rest of your troops."

None of this made any sense to Elektra. If her officers were loyal, why had they taken so long to help her. "Why now?"

The countess turned toward her. "There was not much point in springing you until they were ready to leave the city. It took time for them to work out who could help you inside the palace."

"You're the last person I expected to do this," Elektra admitted. "Why are you helping me?"

"Because you will be empress someday." The countess threw a cloak over Elektra's shoulders. "Your mother wants us all to take sides, but I don't see why I can't be of help to both of you. If you are to be a strong ruler, it makes more sense for you to be independent now than under your mother's thumb."

"I won't argue with that," Elektra said, as the door swung open silently. To her surprise, the corridor was unguarded.

"I tampered with the guard schedule," the countess said. "The next round will be here in a few minutes, but your door will be shut and they won't suspect anything. There'll be confusion among the servants in the morning, so with any luck, your disappearance won't be noticed until evening. "

They silently hurried along the palace's vast corridors, down a back stairway and into rooms Elektra had never seen before.

"Servant's quarters," the countess explained as she opened another door leading into what looked like the kitchen. The light from the lamp caught the glint of copper pots hanging from hooks, and Elektra's shoes padded softly on the stone floor.

The countess opened another door, and they entered a little garden. A gate creaked, and they stepped onto a street outside the palace. A horse nickered nearby, and Elektra stifled a scream as three shadowy figures appeared out of an alleyway. But then she recognized one of her officers, a Major Linser. She knew the two others behind him—a man and a woman—though she couldn't recall their names, her head pounded so hard. "Thank the gods." She swallowed down a sob of relief.

"A horse, Your Grace." Major Linser waved it forward. "It's not yours, but the finest we could get under the circumstances."

"It's perfect," Elektra said, though she could discern only the animal's ears in the shadows. She reached for the reins, then turned to Countess Biaram. "I'm so grateful," she said. "Anything I can do for you, just ask."

"Nothing right now." The countess smiled. "But I trust you'll remember this the next time you hear from me."

"Oh, I will," Elektra said, as she swung into the saddle.

"And now we go," the major said. "We must get as far as we can before the alarm is raised."

"Will they chase us?" Elektra asked, her euphoria fading as she realized she was still in danger.

"Not if I can help it," the countess said. "The empress is not in the capital, and I will order pursuit in a different direction. By the time Teodora returns, you will be over the mountains and well into Kronland."

"Where is the empress?" Elektra had a sudden nightmare of meeting her on the road.

"In Capo, so you needn't worry about running into her. I'm sure by the time she returns here, I can persuade her to leave you alone. She has other things to worry about." The countess's tone was ominous.

Elektra shuddered, thinking she'd rather not know what those things were. "Let's go." And their horses moved quietly down the deserted streets, straight to the northern gate, which swung open after the major gave a password. It was only once they were on the road outside the city that Elektra realized she'd been holding her breath.

LENNART

A few hours of writing letters in one day was more than enough, as far as Lennart was concerned. He put his quill down, clapped the lid on the inkpot, and handed a stack of letters to the secretary.

"Get these to the messenger," he said. "I'm going to visit the Maximus."

He strode into the corridor, and waved to the guards who accompanied him everywhere.

"Not going far," he said, stepping out into the street.

It was a sunny day in Heidenhof, something Lennart had learned to appreciate since coming to Kronland, where it seemed to rain constantly, no matter the time of year. He whistled as he sauntered down the busy street, dodging carts, horses and children.

Things were finally going well again. General Kalstrom had recovered from his defeat and was helping Lofbrok fortify the northern shore of Kaltental harbor. They wouldn't take the city from there, but Ensden couldn't threaten them either. Isenberg was regrouping, and expected to be at full strength by the time Lennart needed her.

After sweeping southeastern Terragand clear of imperial influence, Lennart had decided to spend a few weeks in Heidenhof. He installed Edric Maximus back in his palace, and himself in the burgomaster's luxurious mansion. He cared little about its comforts, but wanted to be easily reached by messenger, since Raysa's time was near. Lennart wrote to her every day now, replying to the letters she'd written daily ever since he'd come to Kronland. In some ways, he felt closer to her now than ever, and missed being near her at such an important time with an almost physical ache.

He'd also written to all of the Kronland rulers, letting them know his plans, and asking for their support. He hoped a letter, followed by a personal visit from someone like Trystan or Braeden might do the job. But there was one more thing he wanted to accomplish during this little respite.

Lennart wandered through the marketplace, happy to see at least half the square was filled with stalls. Even though times were bad, there were still a few farmers and merchants with goods to sell, and having a well-paid army garrisoned here meant they had customers with coin. Lennart wished Kendryk were here to see things were looking better, but hopefully it wouldn't be long before matters improved all over Terragand.

He stopped at a stand to buy a pastry, winked at the pretty girl working there, smiled at her blush, and walked on. By the time he'd reached Edric's palace, he realized he had crumbs all over his doublet, so he paused at the main entrance to brush them off.

"Here to visit the Maximus," he said to the guard, knowing he'd be recognized.

The contrast between the brightness outside, and the gloom as soon as he stepped into the palace was so great he could barely see for a moment. As he stood in the entryway, blinking like an owl, someone appeared before him.

"The Maximus is busy," a pleasant, though slightly sharp feminine voice said.

"I imagine he is." Lennart smiled, especially now that he made out a young priestess. "And you are?"

"I am Mother Leiza."

Now he saw her a little more clearly, she wasn't as young as he'd first thought. Perhaps around Lennart's age, with a plain, serious face.

"I manage the Maximus's household. It's best if you make an appointment with me and come back later."

Lennart chuckled. "The Maximus told me to drop by anytime, but didn't mention the lioness guarding his den."

"Oh dear," Mother Leiza said, clearly embarrassed. "I didn't realize. I mean … I didn't recognize you, Your Highness."

"Quite all right," Lennart said. "No reason you should." He likely would have made a better impression if he'd brought a few guards, and perhaps changed his shirt.

"I'll take you to him right away. I'm sure he's eager to see you." Leiza led him down a long corridor, then paused in front of a door. She turned to Lennart, frowning. "I'm not sure how to say this Your Highness, but I feel I must, before you go in to the Maximus."

"Go ahead," Lennart said. "I'm not easily offended." Perhaps she wanted to tell him to take a more formal tone with the Maximus.

"It's just—" Leiza's hand came to her chin. "You've got crumbs in your beard ... I'm terribly sorry ..."

"Not at all." Lennart had to chuckle as he brushed at his beard. The pastry had been flakier than it looked. "Thank you for telling me." He almost winked at Leiza, then remembered she was a priestess, and decided it wouldn't be proper.

She smiled, clearly relieved, and opened the door after a brief knock. "The king is here," she said, beckoning Lennart in.

The room was light, with the tall windows opened to the garden. The Maximus rose from a desk pushed off to one side.

"Welcome, Your Highness," he said, "and thank you Leiza. You can keep everyone else out for the time being. I'm glad you've come," the Maximus said to Lennart as he led him to a chair. "We have a serious matter to discuss."

BRAEDEN

"I hate to leave you here with this lot," Braeden said to Trystan as he prepared to leave.

Several weeks of arguing had finally persuaded Princess Edyta to offer Lennart her support. But she insisted on placing her eldest daughter and heir, Karolyna, in command of the new army, to which Trystan strenuously objected.

"Don't worry." Trystan looked like he was trying to smile, but his lips twisted into a grimace instead. "I'm used to it. And it's past time to gather other allies. Harvest is fast approaching, and rulers won't be keen on levying troops right now."

Braeden shrugged. "I'll do my best to bribe them with Lennart's money. He won't mind." Having had his own taste of King Gauvain's largesse, Braeden reckoned Lennart would be awash in Galladian funds for the foreseeable future. Might as well spend it locally. Braeden carried little actual coin, but his pockets bulged with papers drawn on bankers scattered across Kronland. Any cooperative rulers might find themselves flush rather quickly.

He hesitated, not sure about giving Trystan any further advice. "I've said it before." He climbed into the saddle, feeling creaky after weeks of rest, then looked down at Trystan. "Let your sister command Podoska's army. Lennart will give you a bigger one; I'm sure of it."

"Well, I'm not." Trystan frowned. "I appreciate your confidence in me, but how will it look if I show up in Terragand with the requested army, but with someone else at its head?" He shook his head. "It won't do. I'll just have to fight it out."

"Best of luck to you then," Braeden said. "We'll see each other soon, I'm sure." As he and Kazmir plodded down the road, a small contingent of guards trailing behind, Braeden pondered that he was always leaving a youngster behind somehow. First Anton in Allaux, and then it had been Karil, his regiment assigned to one of Lennart's officers while he organized the fight for

Terragand. Karil had been happy enough to stay near the action, but Braeden hated leaving him behind. Now he was leaving Trystan as well. Braeden could hardly consider him a boy, considering all he had accomplished, but at barely nineteen, his youth was more apparent among his many older siblings.

Braeden shook his head. Aside from Trystan, he never warmed up to the Martineks; difficult and prickly, the lot of them. Lenora, only a year older than Trystan, appeared sweet enough until she opened her mouth. Braeden had known few soldiers with her vocabulary, and none who used it as cuttingly. Karolyna, the eldest, was close to Braeden's age, but was also the most hostile, no doubt seeing him as her brother's closest ally. Braeden shrugged, then patted Kazmir on the neck. "Glad to be rid of the them, aren't we?"

Braeden made for Oltena, where Kendryk's aunt, Princess Galena Sebesta, welcomed him in a most friendly way. Everywhere Braeden went, his reputation preceded him. With most of Kronland poised to jump in Kendryk and Lennart's direction, that was a good thing. People liked Kendryk, and now he had real force behind his cause, they were glad to welcome his rescuer.

"I've commissioned a song," Princess Galena said, as they sat at a formal dinner in Braeden's honor. "It's about Kendryk's rescue. My singer will perform it after dinner."

"How nice," Braeden said, downing most of his wine at once. He hated folks making a fuss over him, and he'd learned that the story of the Arnfels rescue had been blown all out of proportion. Sure enough, this song was the worst he'd heard so far. The singer had a sweet voice, so it was pleasant to the ear, but Braeden turned redder with each verse. First, it told how he broke into the castle in the middle of the night. "It was broad daylight," Braeden muttered to the princess.

"You were even braver then." She beamed at him, patting his arm. "I'll have the singer make the change."

Next, it was all about how Braeden slaughtered over forty strong men, fighting his way through to Prince Kendryk with his trusty cavalry saber. "There were only three guards," he said. "And that was knife work; no place for a saber."

"What kind of song would that make?" The princess never stopped smiling. "I think the singer knows best how to tell it. See, everyone loves it."

And truly, the nobles sitting at the table looked enthralled, and when the song had ended, much of the applause was for Braeden. He doubted he'd turned redder in his life, and was grateful his beard covered most of it up.

Princess Galena had been the older sister of Kendryk's mother, but Braeden saw little of the prince in her. Her blond hair was now mostly gray, her pale face long and very refined, and her eyes, though blue, were slightly slanted, and nothing like Kendryk's. She'd likely been a handsome woman in her time, and clearly still considered herself as such. So Braeden did his best to play the courtier, managed a few tame jokes she might or might not take for flirtation, and got her to help without handing out too many of Lennart's banknotes.

By the time he left Oltena, Princess Galena promised to raise her own militia and hire a few mercenaries from Briansk, if she could get them.

"Send all of them to Terragand," Braeden said. "Right now there is no threat from the south and if Lennart can beat Ensden, your kingdom will be secure by winter."

"I hope you're right." The princess gave Braeden her hand and he kissed it, adding a little pat for good measure. She'd been very kind. Or maybe he'd become used to Martineks by way of contrast. Now if only the other rulers he needed to visit fell into line as easily.

TEODORA

"I refuse to accept that nothing can be done for her," Teodora said. She and Livilla had been in Capo over a week and had made no progress. After their first mostly lucid conversation with Daciana, she had relapsed into a blank, sullen silence interspersed by fits of violence if anyone tried to approach her.

"I believe we can help her," Livilla said. She looked flustered and wearier than usual. "But she must let us near her. I have prayed to the goddess, and she's shown me a way, though I hesitate to use it."

"Why?" Teodora got up to start her usual pacing, though there was space for only a few steps in her tiny temple quarters. The priest had given her the largest room, but it was still much smaller than what she was accustomed to. "Why do you hesitate?"

Rather than answering that question, Livilla asked, "Does Daciana have anyone close to her besides you; any friends or even distant relations that you know of?"

"No one comes to mind. Her family died when she was taken as a little girl. As far as I know, I'm her only friend, though perhaps she was close to some of the members of her band of marauders."

"Can you find any of them?"

"Probably not. Most were killed in the explosion after Kendryk's escape, and if any survived, they melted away after that whole debacle." Just as well, for Teodora would have killed any survivors in her anger and grief. "It doesn't matter. I'm not foisting her off on someone else to take care of. She's my responsibility, and I will help her." Even though Livilla seemed uncharacteristically hopeless, Teodora refused to lose faith.

Livilla sighed and stared at the wall. "I didn't want to consider this, except as a last resort. There's a chance she can be fully restored to herself, but it will cost you dearly. Too dearly, I fear."

Teodora sat back down, pulling her chair close so she could look directly at Livilla. "I'll do it. I don't care what it is, if it helps her. Aside from you, I have no one left and I refuse to give up on her."

"Your loyalty is admirable," Livilla said, her voice soft and her eyes sad. "But there is a chance that even this significant sacrifice will not be enough."

"I'll try," Teodora said, then licked her lips, aware that her heart was beating faster. "Just tell me what I must do."

"I will do most of the work," Livilla said, "but I must draw the strength I need from you."

"I'm strong," Teodora insisted. "I don't mind giving up some of it."

"It's more than a little." Livilla seemed to not want to continue, passing her hand over her eyes. Teodora had seldom seen her so troubled.

"Tell me," Teodora said, panic rising against her will.

"It will cost years of your life," Livilla said at last.

Teodora's mouth was dry. "Years? How many?"

"Hard to say," Livilla whispered. "At least ten; maybe more."

"I don't understand. How can anything take so much life without killing me? Only the gods can do such a thing."

"Yes. And they will. I'm merely a vessel to transfer your life force to Daciana. I fear it will take a great deal to restore her." Livilla leaned forward and took Teodora's hand, anguish in her eyes. "Please my child, of all people you must not do this. You are too valuable to the Faith and the empire to throw your life away."

"Can someone else do it?" Teodora's mind was clearing a little. She was determined to do this, but wanted to find a less costly way. "I could get a prisoner, someone who will die anyway."

"No." Livilla looked down. "It must be one who loves her. That's why I'd hoped for someone else."

"I can't stand to see her suffer like this," Teodora murmured, mostly to herself. Daciana was tough, but it was clear her pain was nearly unendurable, and there was little respite. The priest had made an herbal concoction that provided a little relief, but never for more than an hour or two of each day.

"Think about it," Livilla said. "Pray. For at least a day and a night. I will pray as well, and if the gods have mercy, they will send us an answer."

Teodora nodded and closed her eyes, even though she dreaded the images that passed before them when she did. For years now, she'd kept the memories at bay, but she couldn't any longer. At this moment, Daciana needed a supreme sacrifice from her. And Teodora owed her one.

GWYNNETH

"I can't stay in Galladium much longer," Gwynneth said the next time she saw the king. She told him about her last conversation with Natalya.

Gauvain frowned. "I'd hate for you to leave, though I won't force you to stay. But I promised Kendryk I'd take care of you and the children, and now I feel terrible that Natalya has made you unwelcome."

"Not unwelcome exactly," Gwynneth said. "But there's no question matters are awkward between us. With everything going so well in Terragand, I don't want to risk becoming embroiled in intrigue here." That made her smile. "Those are words I was sure I'd never say."

"I don't blame you." Gauvain looked worn and somber. "You have your own problems. Although, if you were willing, I might find a job that would take you out of the country for a time."

"You would? And Natalya would approve of this?"

"Probably not." Gauvain sighed. "But after your success in brokering peace between Estenor and Sanova, I'd love to send you on an embassy to Maladena."

"Maladena?" That had never occurred to Gwynneth. "I wouldn't know how to begin." Even though she needed to stay focused on Kronland, she was intrigued and rather flattered at Gauvain's trust in her abilities.

"Very much as you did the last time," Gauvain said. "With an offer of marriage."

"Yours?" Gwynneth was puzzled. "Isn't the treaty with Teodora still in place? And who in Maladena would you marry?"

"I'd be willing to break the treaty with Olvisya," Gauvain said. "Teodora has little to offer at this point. I'd willingly return the troublemakers in the Dallmaring Provinces to her, and she can't threaten us as long as Lennart remains in Kronland. And I've just received word that Queen Beatryz has chosen a new heir, her niece the Princess—now the Enfanta—Lucrecia."

"I know of her." Gwynneth was trying to remember details of the Maladene court. "A quiet, retiring type if I'm not mistaken. And older than you. Are you sure she is still of an age to bear children?" It was hard to look at Gauvain, he seemed so depressed, but Gwynneth had to. She worried he wasn't thinking clearly, and likely to make a terrible mistake.

"She's older than me, but not that old." Gauvain managed a half-smile. "And she's unlikely to be as difficult as any daughter of Teodora's."

"Would Beatryz agree to it? Will Natalya?"

"Beatryz might, but I'm sure Natalya won't. That's why you must do this for me. You're the only person here I can trust, Gwynneth." The king gave her a pleading look.

"I'll have to consider it carefully. Going behind Natalya's back is tantamount to treason, and it would be a terrible betrayal of our friendship."

"Betraying *me* would be treason," the king said, though his tone was gentle. "But you're right; it's a very serious thing I'm asking of you. Just consider this: if I cannot avert war with Maladena, I cannot support Lennart for more than another year, maybe two."

"I hope the war will be over by then," Gwynneth said, though she hardly dared to hope for it.

"So do I. But I want you to be aware of the possibilities and the risks, if we can't manage peace."

"I understand," Gwynneth said. "But suppose I agree to do this. What about my children?"

"I'll keep a close eye on them, and if there's the least hint of trouble, I'll have them brought to the palace. But perhaps, once you've returned I'll have Joslyn stay with me."

"Won't that create difficulties when you marry?" Gwynneth wasn't terribly fond of Joslyn, but she pitied the little girl; neglected by one parent, and an embarrassment to the other.

"There's no need to worry about that," Gauvain said. "And of course, no one in Maladena needs to know anything about it for the time being."

"Of course not." Gwynneth shook her head. "Though I'm not sure I can do it. It's a terrible time for me to leave, since Kendryk expects to hold Terragand again by winter."

"As much faith as I have in his and Lennart's abilities, I would be very surprised if they manage it that soon. But if you leave now, you'll have time to get to Maladena, spend a few weeks there, and return here before winter sets in."

"In theory." Gwynneth smiled. "Though I recall the last time I went on a similar mission with similar plans, I was gone for nearly a year."

"Even a year is worth it if it means peace, don't you agree? And you will of course be compensated."

"It probably is worth it," Gwynneth said, though she still hadn't decided. "You needn't pay me, though I'll need help with expenses." She hated being in a penniless position, still dependent on Natalya.

"That goes without saying. And you'd receive a salary—something like what I pay my ambassadors. It seems only fair. I'm sure you'd enjoy having an income of your own." Gauvain was far too perceptive.

"You're right; I would." She smiled at him. "May I have time to think about it? You make a good case, but I can't make this decision lightly."

But even as the king took his leave, Gwynneth had nearly made up her mind.

KENDRYK

Once Kendryk neared Mattila's seat in Brandana—Princess Floreta's former castle—he stopped at an inn and cleaned up, taking care to put on his best clothes. The few things he'd brought were creased and worn from hard use in the past months, but they would have to do. He also ordered the troops who accompanied him to polish up, though from what he knew of Mattila, she'd appreciate the battle-worn look.

By the time he approached the castle, it was clear he was expected. That he'd gotten this far without being challenged meant he wasn't seen as a threat. Kendryk decided he'd see it as positive. Perhaps she'd be interested in negotiating with him.

Mattila met him at the castle's main entrance, and though her welcome was polite enough, Kendryk noticed she didn't bow, nor did she address him as Your Grace. Count Faris stiffened up next to him indignantly, but Kendryk shot him a glance, hoping he'd understand not to say anything just yet. Mattila was still Teodora's creature and might still consider Duke Evard the rightful ruler of Terragand.

"We can talk now," she said, "unless you're just paying a social call, in which case we'll catch up at dinner."

"Let's talk now," Kendryk said, amused at paying someone like Brynhild Mattila a friendly visit. He tried not to show how intimidating he found her. At least a half-head taller than Kendryk, she was every inch the grim, battle-hardened veteran. Next to her, even an old warrior like Count Faris looked soft. There was nothing of the courtier in her, which Kendryk wasn't certain was a good thing either. He'd become accustomed to protocol while ruling Terragand, and found he worked best within its bounds. The formality of a court like Galladium's was excessive, but he didn't mind some friendly nonsense before getting to the meat of a conversation, giving him time to read the situation. But in Mattila's case, there was no nonsense to be had.

"Do we need him?" she asked, nodding in Faris's direction as she led Kendryk into a cluttered library.

"He's called Count Faris and yes, Countess, we need him," Kendryk said, his tone icy. It was one thing to offend Kendryk, but quite another to treat his loyal friend shabbily.

"All right then." Mattila's mouth quirked up at the corner. "Have a seat." She flung herself into a chair behind a desk piled high with ledgers.

Kendryk took a pile of papers from another chair, and placed them on the desk before sitting down.

"Ugh, I forgot about those," Mattila said. "No one ever tells you how much paperwork is involved in running a kingdom. I'll bet you don't miss it."

"I never minded the paperwork," Kendryk said, reminding himself that she was likely trying to goad him. But he was no Teodora, and wouldn't lose his temper so easily.

"I suppose not, considering all the trouble you're going to, trying to get it back."

Kendryk swallowed and stayed silent.

"Well? Isn't that why you're here?" Mattila leaned forward across the desk, fixing her cold eyes on Kendryk. "Lennart's errand-boy, as it were."

Kendryk bit his lip and counted to ten, hoping Count Faris would hold his tongue. He heard a snort from his direction, but nothing further. When he was sure he could speak calmly, he said, "Not at all. I'm here on my own behalf, as ruler of Terragand. I hoped we might have a civil conversation."

"Calling yourself ruler is rich, though it's true you're a lot nicer than Teodora."

"Everyone's nicer than Teodora," Kendryk said before he could stop himself.

That brought a dry chuckle. "True. I've never met a more disagreeable person, and I'm relieved to be rid of her, at least for the time being."

"Why not be rid of her for good?" Kendryk thought he should take the opening, when offered.

"I'd love that, but how do you propose to do it?"

"Remove all of her options. Ensden's days are numbered, and once he's gone, no one stands between my armies and Teodora."

"So that's the plan then? Lennart will defeat her, and make himself emperor."

"That's not the plan," Kendryk said, though he wondered if he ought to discuss that honestly with Lennart when he saw him again. "Once Teodora is

273

defeated, and Kronland has received guarantees of political independence and religious freedom, Lennart will return to Estenor. Olvisya can choose a ruler who is not an Inferrara."

"And you believe Lennart will leave when all of this is done? I don't."

"I don't blame you," Kendryk said, "but surely you don't mind if Teodora is defeated and deposed. What happens after that can be negotiated when the time comes."

"Perhaps." Mattila looked at him shrewdly. "So what do you want? Me to enter the fight on Lennart's—oh, excuse me, your side—or my promise of neutrality?"

"We'd prefer you to fight on our side," Kendryk said, looking directly at her, "but failing that, a guarantee of neutrality would be acceptable."

"Oh it would, would it? For a fellow with no kingdom and no army, you're much too demanding. And if you're only speaking for Lennart, you're still high and mighty for my taste."

"I'm sorry if my manner offends you," Kendryk said, his tone making it clear he felt no such thing. "I am not making any demands; I'm merely here to negotiate."

"Just one Kronland ruler to another then?"

Kendryk flushed, annoyed. This woman had no right to complain of anyone else's manner, considering how unpleasant hers was. "I'm sure you realize I cannot acknowledge you as a Kronland ruler, at least not while Princess Floreta and any of her heirs still live."

Mattila pulled a face. "Gods, you lot are so stuffy. But that will change soon, mark my words."

Count Faris finally spoke up. "Is that a threat?"

"Not really." Mattila shrugged. "But before we negotiate, perhaps we need to make a few things clear."

TEODORA

Teodora lay awake, listening to the temple bell toll midnight. She had to decide tonight. She couldn't bear to see Daciana in this state any longer, and she needed to return to Atlona. It had been weeks now, and while no new emergencies had arisen, she knew it was only a matter of time before the next crisis.

Deciding meant calling forth memories she'd tried to bury long ago, but she forced herself to do it now. Tears leaked from her eyes, so she screwed them shut all the tighter. It had been nearly thirty years, but the terror of that moment returned quickly, if she let it.

She, Teodora Inferrara, Archduchess of Olvisya, Duchess of Trest and Marova, third in line to the imperial crown, was being stripped and bound to a post, like a common criminal. Teodora had stood there, frozen and terrified, unable to believe this was happening to her. She didn't dare look up, because she would meet the cold eyes of Brynhild Mattila.

Mattila's jailer pushed her to her knees and Teodora fell, scraping her cheek against the rough wood of the post. The muscles of her shoulders screamed as all her weight sagged from her wrists, tied to a beam over her head. Teodora struggled to her feet to take the pressure off, but a knee pressed into her back, pushing her down again. She pressed her lips together. No matter what happened, she wouldn't make a sound, wouldn't shed a tear. She'd never give Mattila the satisfaction.

Teodora realized she was responsible for walking into an ambush near the Zastwar border, but losing most of her company seemed punishment enough. And besides, it was her first real engagement. She was only eighteen, and not even the senior officer. She hadn't made the decision to take the fatal route, but the captain who had was dead. Still, it wasn't fitting punishment for the crime; Teodora was certain of that. She'd heard of similar things happening to other officers, and their punishments—if they happened at all—were fines or temporary demotions. This was so far out of bounds, so unjust, Teodora knew it was only because Brynhild Mattila hated her.

She didn't understand the hatred. Teodora had tried to be friendly, listened to all advice, and followed orders scrupulously. But none of that made any difference, and in later years, Teodora wondered if she'd been sent into that ambush deliberately, not expected to survive.

The lash fell for the first time, and Teodora bit her tongue to keep from screaming. Blood filled her mouth and she spat it out, then looked up. Mattila's gaze bored into her, and Teodora looked straight back, hoping she showed no fear, even though terror nearly overwhelmed her. The lash fell again and again, and Teodora willed herself not to scream or faint. She would not appear weak. She felt ill after the fifth stroke, but then there was a pause and a collective gasp from the assembled troops.

Teodora heard the crack of the whip, and a shriek behind her. She turned her head as far as she could, and saw a skinny little girl, wearing what looked like a ragged sack, wrapping the whip around the jailer's fat neck. The jailer's eyes bulged, his face turned purple, and a horrid gurgling sound came from deep within his throat.

The girl pulled tighter and said, "Cut the young lady down or I kill him." She spoke heavily accented Olvisyan, and her eyes flashed yellow, like a cat's.

"You can't be serious," Mattila said, her voice flat, though two red spots burned on her cheeks. "Let him go right now and I might spare your life, slave."

"Please, let him go," Teodora whispered, trying to catch the girl's eye. She couldn't bear someone dying while trying to defend her, for whatever reason.

The girl shook her head. "No. This is wrong and I refuse to allow it." This coming from a tiny, skeletal ragamuffin who was also apparently a slave would have been amusing, but for those frightening eyes. She yanked harder on the whip, and the jailer passed out. He had turned some awful color, and Teodora hoped he was still alive, not for his sake, but for the girl's.

Mattila moved so quickly Teodora almost missed it, but an instant later, the girl lay on the ground while Mattila pushed the jailer away with her foot. He flopped over, unconscious or dead. Now Mattila held the whip, but when it came down, the girl was gone. Teodora strained her neck, trying to see what was happening behind her. There were sounds of a scuffle, and a shout from Mattila. The girl danced around in front of Teodora, who fell to the ground as the rope holding her wrists was cut. Where had she gotten a knife?

Teodora rolled over, slipping in her own blood, the pain forgotten, trying to scramble to her feet. Mattila loomed over her, blood dripping from her arm. Before Teodora could get away, Mattila grabbed her by the hair with the other hand, and yanked her to her feet. Then she felt cold metal at her throat.

"Put the knife down and surrender," Mattila said to the girl, her teeth gritted. "Or I'll cut the young lady's throat."

Teodora tried desperately to catch the girl's eye. She stood near, but not close enough to get to Mattila before she killed Teodora. And Teodora knew Mattila would welcome the excuse.

While the girl hesitated, two of Mattila's guards jumped on her, throwing her to the ground.

Mattila dropped the knife, and pushed Teodora away. Then she spoke to the guards. "Take that thing to the woods and kill it."

"No," Teodora's throat was so raw, almost no sound came out. "No!" she finally shouted. "I order you to let this girl go."

Mattila scoffed. "You order me. You have no authority over me."

Teodora looked at the girl, her head still up, her eyes blazing in spite of the boots on her back. "Not militarily," she said. "But I'm the Duchess of Marova, and you Countess Mattila, are my subject. I order you to let—what is your name?" she asked the girl.

"Daciana Tomescu," the girl said, her voice firm.

Teodora turned to Mattila and caught her eye. "I order you to let Daciana Tomescu go. She was merely defending me." Teodora had never wanted to take advantage of her position, and even in her worst moments, refused using it to save herself. But she would happily do it now, and would insist on the emperor backing her, if necessary.

"She doesn't belong to you," Mattila said, though she no longer sounded as certain.

Teodora looked down at Daciana. "Who do you belong to? You're a slave, aren't you?"

"An escaped slave," the girl said with a smirk. "I belonged to no one. But now I belong to you."

ANTON

"I worry about you," Susanna murmured, one night as Anton drifted off to sleep after polishing off the better part of a bottle. For a while after the battle, he'd cut back on drinking so much, mostly because he wanted to make Susanna happy. But once the horror of the battle receded, the bad dreams came back, and Anton needed a fair amount of brandy to get any sleep at all.

"Nothing to worry about," he said, trying to move his lips as little as possible.

"You're not happy," she said. "I can tell. You were better before the battle. Does your face still hurt very much?"

"Not really," Anton said. In truth, he hardly noticed it at all.

Susanna propped herself up on her elbows so she could look down at him. "Something is bothering you and you won't tell me."

"It's embarrassing," Anton said, feeling drunk and a little reckless.

"You can tell me anyway." She ran a finger down his cheek; the good one, as he now called it.

"I don't like fighting as much as I used to. It used to be the best thing in the world. Now I hate the idea and don't want to do it anymore."

"Don't then," Susanna said. "Between us, we have enough to buy out your contract."

"And then what?"

"Keep working with me. You make a lot more money from that than you ever have from soldier's pay. We'll get serious about it; start a real business. Perhaps even set up a shop somewhere when the war is over."

Anton remembered his grandfather's shop in Kaleva and smiled.

"You like the idea?" Susanna looked a bit anxious.

"I do. I can't picture how it might happen, but I do like it. My mother's family had a shop—they probably still do. I always liked going in, looking at all of the goods, hearing the customers chat with my aunts and my grandparents."

"You could go back to them."

That hit Anton like a shock. "I'd never thought of it, but you're right. Maybe I could, someday. They're all the way in Kaleva, though."

"I don't speak Moraltan."

"I'll teach you." Anton grabbed Susanna's hand and kissed it, suddenly much happier. If he wasn't cut out to be a soldier after all, it was nice to know he had another choice.

Susanna kept looking at him, breathed in, then frowned a little as she exhaled. "I have to tell you something."

"You're full of ideas tonight." Anton smiled at her sleepily.

"I'm pregnant." She said it quickly, then gasped and held her breath.

"What?" Anton was wide-awake in an instant. He sat up and pulled her up next to him. "Are you sure? Don't you drink that awful-tasting tea every day; the one you got from that strange-looking doctor?" Anton was pretty sure the man was no real doctor, but that's what everyone called him.

"I was." Susanna licked her lips. "It doesn't always work. You're not angry, are you?"

"Why would I be angry? I'm surprised yes, and a little worried. It's such a bad time to have a baby, right in the middle of the war."

Susanna drew her eyebrows together. "I realize it's a terrible time. If you want, I can go back to that doctor. He knows what to do if the tea doesn't work."

"No," Anton said, more sharply than he meant to. "No," he said again, more softly, and stroked her cheek. "Please don't do that. We'll manage somehow." He still wasn't sure what to think. On the one hand, he was unprepared to be a father; far too young, with life so uncertain. On the other, a thrill of joy ran through him, picturing Susanna holding his child in her arms.

"So it's all right then?" She leaned into his hand.

"More than all right," he said, surprised at how happy he was. "But maybe it's best if we don't change anything else right now. I'll stay in the army, we'll keep working together as long as you're able and save as much money as we can. I imagine you'll have to take time off when the baby comes."

"A little, perhaps." She was smiling now.

"And you know what else?" Anton grinned at her. "I've stopped drinking as of right now." He wanted to be a good father and he'd need a clear head to manage it.

TEODORA

The cart bumped down the road, much too slowly for Teodora's liking. It took only a few hours to travel between Capo and Atlona on horseback, but Livilla wanted to move in secret, so Teodora had to ride in a farmer's cart. Like a peasant. Livilla was right; she wouldn't be recognized, sitting next to the farmer, the hood of her cloak pulled up in spite of the heat.

Livilla had insisted they return to Atlona before attempting to heal Daciana. "You will be very weak afterward," she said, "if you survive the ritual."

Teodora shuddered at those words, but there was no going back now, she'd decided.

"Before we start," Livilla went on, "you'll want to be certain of your succession, should the worst happen. I'm not saying you need to release Elektra, but she must be prepared to take over."

That brought the gravity of the situation home. "She's not ready," Teodora said. "Not to mention I can't trust her."

"I'd still be regent for a time," Livilla said. "She'll listen to me."

"I hope so, but I refuse to die. I know this is dangerous, but I will survive it, and so will Daciana."

"I'm sure you will." Livilla's eyes were shadowed, and the skin of her face had sprouted a hundred wrinkles overnight, but her voice remained firm as ever. "I wouldn't agree to do this if I weren't sure of your survival. The gods have sent me dreams the past few nights, and I'm certain Vica will carry you through this. And that's another reason to do it in the capital. I'll have your doctor nearby, and you will have everything you need close at hand."

Teodora couldn't argue with that. She was sick and tired of the deprivation of living in the tiny Capo temple. What was the point of being empress if she couldn't enjoy a few luxuries?

She'd worried about getting Daciana to agree to the move, but Livilla had a simpler solution. "I'll put something in her porridge," she said. "She'll sleep for

280

at least twelve hours; more than enough time to transport her, and prepare her for the ritual. If all goes as hoped, she'll wake up already healed."

They left Capo before dawn, and slow as the cart moved, still reached Atlona before noon. It was strange to enter her capital so anonymously. Teodora looked at the city with new eyes; the eyes of a commoner. Without being high up on horseback, or enclosed in a carriage, she saw the faces of her subjects as never before. Tired, cheerful, angry, preoccupied. She marveled at their variety and, for the first time in her life, wondered what all these people were thinking. She hoped they didn't hate her too much, though she suspected they didn't think much about her at all.

Two little boys ran alongside the cart, begging the farmer to throw them an apple. In her other life, Teodora would have whipped them for insolence if she hadn't ignored them altogether, but this was different.

"I'll pay for these," she murmured to the farmer as she reached back into the wagon, and grabbed two apples from the barrel behind the seat. Daciana lay in the wagonbed, Livilla sitting next to her with barrels all around concealing them from the view of most.

Teodora tossed first one apple, then the other, to the boys. A lump rose in her throat when one of them doffed his cap, and the other blew her a kiss, shouting. "Thank you, pretty lady!" She couldn't think she looked pretty to anyone anymore, but maybe the Scrolls were right, and acts of kindness transformed a person.

By the time they reached the Maxima's palace, the wagon pulling around to the kitchen door, Teodora was trembling. She wondered what had come over her. It was as though she started changing from the moment she decided to do this, and was changing still. Perhaps she was to die soon, and the gods were offering brief moments of joy and clarity before taking her to them.

Teodora jumped down from the wagon unassisted, and pressed silver into the farmer's hand. Livilla had already paid him handsomely, but Teodora wanted to do more. He looked down at the coins, puzzled. Then a broad grin transformed his plain face. "I thank you, my lady. May the gods bless you."

Teodora smiled at him, unable to speak. Before entering the palace kitchen, she looked up at the sky, the clear, deep blue of late summer. It would be harvest soon, and Teodora offered a quick prayer that she would still be alive to enjoy its fruits. "I don't know what's wrong with me," she murmured to herself, stepping inside and waiting for Daciana to be carried in by two strong footmen. Livilla had already hurried ahead to receive any messages she might have missed while away.

Teodora looked down at Daciana's face, walking alongside as they carried her down the corridor on a stretcher. In sleep, her face was soft and peaceful, almost girlish again, the scars barely visible in the shadows. Teodora clenched her fists at her sides. She would restore her friend to health if it was the last thing she did.

Once she'd seen Daciana safely placed in a pleasant bedchamber, Teodora sent for Sybila to watch over her and went in search of Livilla. They had to start soon if they were to complete the ritual before Daciana awoke.

KENDRYK

In Mattila's dusty study, Kendryk shifted in his chair. If he had to choose who was the more unpleasant, he'd consider it a dead tie between Teodora and her former general. He decided to do what he did best, and made sure his face was completely devoid of expression. His tone, when he spoke, was flat.

"What do you need to make clear before we go ahead?"

Mattila leaned forward, fixing her chilly eyes on his. Kendryk wanted badly to look away, but didn't. "I have goals," she said after a lengthy pause that was no doubt meant to make him squirm. "And I see no reason at all to ally myself with you unless you can help me meet those goals."

"I see," Kendryk said, and though he guessed what those goals were, he let her have her say.

"I want to be a Kronland ruler, with the same status as the rest of you. Unlike you, I plan to keep my kingdom."

Kendryk raised an eyebrow. There was a limit to the insults he'd endure, and she was reaching it quickly. "I don't see how I can help you gain legitimacy." Not that he wanted to.

"You can't." Mattila smirked. "But if Lennart can defeat Teodora, then he can do it. All it takes is an imperial charter, if I'm not mistaken."

"And hereditary rights. You must be descended from one of the original twelve families who received their charters from the first Olvisyan emperor." There was no manufacturing that kind of status.

"Such snobbery." Mattila shook her head. "My family is just as old and noble as yours."

Kendryk didn't agree, but said nothing and kept his face impassive.

"What if I married into one of those families?"

"I don't know if that would work," Kendryk admitted. "But aren't you married already?"

"Yes." Mattila shrugged. "Though I'm sure he'll agree to a divorce if I make it worth his while. I haven't seen him in four years, and unsurprisingly, haven't missed him at all."

Kendryk nearly said that he doubted her husband missed her either, but bit his tongue at the last second. Angry as she made him, he was determined to stay on the high road as long as he could manage it.

"So that's no great obstacle." Mattila went on. "All that remains is for me to find a suitable person to marry, and I imagine there are enough unmarried younger sons of the ruling families running about. It's only a matter of finding the one I like best."

Kendryk couldn't hold back a shudder, and Mattila didn't miss that.

"You think I'd make a terrible wife?" She looked amused.

"I have no idea, and I don't care to find out if you have well-hidden charms." Just saying it made his skin crawl.

"Perhaps I do." Mattila smiled.

To steer the conversation away from such an unsettling topic, Kendryk asked, "So you'd agree to ally with Lennart if he guarantees your right to rule Brandana after defeating Teodora?"

"Perhaps. I'd want to speak with him first."

"He's busy," Kendryk said, ready for the conversation to be over, even if it meant the failure of his mission. "That's why I'm here, remember?"

"Unless you can make the guarantee in writing on Lennart's behalf, I'm afraid I can't agree to help you. Tell him to come here if he's serious."

Kendryk stood up quickly. "He has more important things to do, I'm afraid." He'd had enough, and could no longer keep from showing it. "What you're asking is impossible, and you know it. Please forgive me for assuming you are not negotiating in good faith. I'll take my leave." Kendryk turned to Faris. "We have better ways we can spend our time."

Faris jumped up. "I agree. Let's go."

Mattila rose more slowly and didn't appear the least bit bothered. "I won't keep you, but before you go, know this. If Lennart can't grant my request by the time he engages with Ensden, I will not stay neutral."

Kendryk whirled on her, angry now. "Are you saying you'd go back to Teodora?"

A smile quirked at Mattila's lips. "If I must. If she's desperate enough, I'm sure she'll promise me anything."

"Well, we're not that desperate," Kendryk said. "Far from it, in fact. But now I've spoken with you, I can assure you your request is unlikely to be granted by either Lennart or Teodora." No more needed to be said, so Kendryk hurried out of the room.

Count Faris waited in the corridor. "That went about as well as expected," he said. "I don't understand why Lennart bothered sending you."

"I think he might want to be rid of me," Kendryk said, as they burst out the front door of the castle, servants scurrying before them, handing over hats and cloaks.

"I doubt that very much," Faris said.

Kendryk had the distinct feeling he was patronizing him. "He won't manage that so easily," he said, wishing they'd hurry in bringing his horse.

"Back to Terragand then?"

"Not yet," Kendryk said. "Since we're in the neighborhood, I thought we'd go to Ummarvik. We can return to Terragand with Tora Isenberg and her army." If his hunch about Lennart wanting to sideline him was correct, he'd make a better impression appearing at the head of a large force. "We'll talk to Prince Dahlby as well. Maybe he'll be willing to help."

TEODORA

Teodora found Livilla standing in the middle of her study, holding a sheet of paper.

"We should get started," Teodora said. "Before I lose my nerve."

"Elektra is gone," Livilla said.

"What do you mean, gone?" Teodora had made certain there was no way for her to escape on her own, and everyone who came in direct contact with her had been thoroughly intimidated.

"Gone, as in escaped. Left the country in fact, a week ago already."

"How? And why wasn't I told?" Teodora snatched the paper from Livilla. It was from Solteszy, and addressed to Teodora at the Capo temple. "Why didn't it reach me?"

"Hard to say." Livilla shook her head. "There must have been some kind of mix-up." She looked so blank and confused, Teodora banished the momentary suspicion that Livilla might have had something to do with it.

"I'll find out." Teodora snapped. "Someone will pay. But in the meantime, she must be stopped. Which way did she go?" She tried reading the note, but the letters blurred, hopefully not from tears.

"To Kronland, at the head of her regiment." Livilla offered a thin smile. "It seems her officers had a hand in this, and got her out."

"Why would they do such a difficult, not to mention treasonous, thing?" Teodora now shook with rage.

"She was on good terms with her officers. Several of them had considerable respect for her abilities."

Teodora snorted. "Ridiculous. The girl has no idea what she's doing."

"Perhaps not. Although she learned a great deal from Mattila—"

"Shut up!" Teodora screeched. "Never speak that name again." After the past few days of dredging up horrible memories, Teodora couldn't bear to think of the woman. But that reminded her. "Oh gods." She clutched at her head. "Daciana. We have to do something soon."

Livilla shook her head, as if trying to wake herself up. "Yes we do. Elektra will have to wait until this is over."

"But I need my heir here," Teodora whispered, renewed fear washing over her. "What if—?"

Livilla took Teodora's trembling hands in hers. "She won't be needed, since you will survive this. But if something goes wrong, it's no great matter to call her back. And your subjects will be more impressed if their new empress was busy heading an army, rather than confined to her room," she added with a wry smile.

Teodora saw the sense in that, though she'd never admit it. She took a deep breath. "All right. Let's do this thing." No more distractions. "Then I'll deal with my daughter."

Now that it was time, she shook from head to toe as she followed Livilla back to the room where Daciana lay. Sybila was there already, and marched straight up to Livilla as they came in.

"Maxima, I must protest," she said. "I cannot allow this to go forward. Little can be done for this young woman, and putting Her Highness at risk in the attempt is unacceptable."

Livilla had sent word ahead to Teodora's doctor, telling her a significant ritual was about to occur, though she hadn't gone into detail.

"I understand you don't approve," Livilla said, gently pushing Sybila aside. "But Her Highness has decided."

"Please." Sybila turned pleading eyes on Teodora. "Please don't do this."

"It'll be all right." A strange calm washed over Teodora. "Just be here when I wake up, all right?"

Sybila nodded, though a tear ran down the side of her nose. Daciana might have been Teodora's closest friend, but Sybila was one of her oldest. They'd known each other since they'd started at the Temple school together as girls of eleven.

Livilla had drawn the heavy curtains and lit a small lamp. She opened a little bag she'd brought from her study, and started putting things on the table. Teodora wondered what they were, but her eyes weren't focusing.

"Please get undressed, my dear," Livilla said, her voice gentle. "Crawl into bed beside Daciana, and pull the sheet over both of you. I will do the rest."

Teodora did as she was told, hoping she wasn't doing the wrong thing, maybe even an evil thing. Earlier, she had questioned Livilla about the ritual, but Livilla cut her short. "The less you know of this, the better. I'll take full responsibility for what I bring forth."

That sounded ominous, but Teodora was frightened of the look in Livilla's eyes, and found she didn't really want to know any more. Surely the gods wouldn't condemn her for being involved in something she didn't fully understand? She didn't worry about Livilla, for the gods had given her knowledge beyond all others, except perhaps the Imperata. Surely she wouldn't know how to do things the gods didn't approve of?

Teodora tried to stop her thoughts as she crawled into bed, the sheets smooth and cold against her skin. Daciana lay next to her, breathing lightly, still sound asleep. Teodora grabbed her hand, almost ready to weep with relief over its warmth. If she died right now, she couldn't ask for a better companion.

Livilla's face appeared over her, almost impossible to make out in the dim light. "Take a bite of this, my child," she said, "and don't worry about a thing."

Teodora bit down on something soft and bitter. It tasted terrible as it dissolved in her mouth, leaving an acrid film on her tongue. Even as she grimaced against the awful flavor, her body loosened and sank into the mattress.

Livilla chanted something, sounding very far away, and smoke swirled above Teodora's head. She tried to follow it with her eyes, but couldn't keep them open. She tried to remind herself to be afraid, and gripped Daciana's hand even tighter. But she felt only peace, even as a cold blade sliced along her arm, and blood gushed out of it like a fountain. Almost asleep, Teodora smiled. She had life enough to spare, enough to give a friend.

LENNART

Though Lennart had much to occupy his mind, the knowledge that Raysa's time had already passed was a constant worry. It would take at least a week for a message to reach him, but even allowing for that, it was still much too late. A small, fast ship waited in Tharvik harbor to run across the sea, depositing a messenger who'd come overland to Heidenhof. If she'd had the baby when the doctor said she would, and all had gone well, Lennart should have heard by now.

Lennart sat at a table in the little study adjoining his bedchamber, a large bottle of liquor at his elbow. Drinking too much wouldn't improve matters, but it seemed to be the only way to loosen the tightness in his chest, if only temporarily. He'd completed his duties for the day, spoken to everyone who wanted to see him; he'd earned a respite.

Lennart poured another glass before the lone candle burned out, and didn't bother lighting another. He'd opened the window earlier and stared out at the patch of sky, dark blue, and growing lighter as a half-moon rose. That same moon should be visible in Tharvik, if at a different position. If the liquor hadn't already clouded his mind, he would have done a quick calculation for the fun of it.

He thought of Raysa, so thin and frail. Perhaps the doctor had been humoring him when he told her she was strong enough to bear a child. He'd known for years now that folk told kings what they liked to hear. Lennart trembled with rage, imagining how he'd confront the doctor who'd lied to him, and imagined a suitable punishment. That didn't help, so he took a long drink.

He slammed the glass back on the table. Dreaming about punishing some poor doctor was all very well, but in the end, this was all Lennart's fault. He should have known from the moment he first saw Raysa that she wouldn't survive bearing his child. But he'd been so selfish, so fixated on his goal. And to be honest, he'd taken one look at her, even as she trembled at the first sight of him, tears welling up in those beautiful eyes, and decided he wanted her. And then nothing would stop him from having her.

Furious with himself, Lennart threw the glass against the wall. It shattered loudly, and he hoped it wouldn't bring a servant running. But now there was nothing left to drink. He laid his head on the table, trying to order his fuzzy thoughts into a prayer. Only the gods could forgive him for being a selfish ass, and only they could help Raysa. The right words wouldn't come, but he hoped the gods understood anyway. "I'm doing your work," he muttered. "Please help me. Help Raysa. Keep her safe, and our child too. I'll do anything, even if it means leaving Kronland."

Drunk as he was, he knew that wasn't what the gods wanted. They wanted him to stay, to continue what he had started, and to finish it, no matter the cost. And at last he understood it. Long ago, he'd told Gwynneth that he'd do this, even if it meant his death, but now he saw that death right before his eyes. He watched a horse, a dappled gray, one he didn't know, galloping across a battlefield, blood dripping from the empty saddle. He saw his soldiers weeping, even as they fought. And finally, his own body, limp and bloodied.

When Lennart opened his eyes, they were wet with tears. His head pounded, but seemed a little clearer. He got up unsteadily, and walked over to the window. A breeze came in, and he realized he was soaked with sweat. At first it felt good, but then he shivered, finally closing the window and turning away. He stood in the middle of the room, wondering if he should call a servant to bring him another glass. After that dream, he doubted he'd be able to sleep again anytime soon.

He jumped at a pounding on the door. "Come," he called, his voice hoarse.

A young officer entered, his face weary and covered in dust from the road. "A message from Tharvik, Your Highness" he said, handing Lennart a small leather pouch.

Lennart grabbed it, but then stared at the man anxiously, hoping he could tell from his face what the news might be.

The officer's face broke into a smile. "It's a girl, Your Highness. The news was all over Tharvik when I left."

Joy washed over Lennart, but he had to know one more thing. "The queen?" he asked, almost afraid of the answer.

"She's well." The officer looked almost as happy as Lennart felt at those words. "If all goes as planned, she'll appear at the temple tomorrow to have the Maximus name and bless the child."

"Kataryna," Lennart murmured, sinking back into the chair to open the message. He and Raysa had decided on the name before he left. Relieved as he was, his hands still shook as he opened the pouch. "Go to the kitchen and get a bite to eat," he said, remembering the messenger still standing at attention. "Then get some rest. I'll want you to take a message back to the queen in the morning."

Once Lennart was alone again, he took his time reading the letter from Meldahl, explaining in the most business-like terms that, though the queen had labored long and with some difficulty, she was recovering well, and the baby was large and healthy.

A shorter message came from Raysa, her weariness clear in the script that was usually so neat, now wandering all over the page. "I am well, and our daughter is beautiful. I love you."

Lennart folded it up after reading it at least five times, then closed his eyes. A shadow passed in front of them, leftover from his earlier dream. But it no longer frightened him the way it had while he dreamt it. For now, if the worst happened, his line was assured.

He opened his eyes again and whispered "Kataryna," as a smile spread over his face.

BRAEDEN

"You say there's no threat from the south, and yet I'm certain there is."
Prince Benda slammed his mug onto the table, though the quaver in his voice
gave him away.

"What have you heard?" Braeden asked. He didn't blame the old prince for
being nervous. His lands had taken a real beating during Arryk's adventure in
Kronland. Lantura was rich because of its size, and because it stretched from
the Cesiano Sea on the west to Sanova on the east. Trade brought the kingdom
a lot of money. But that also meant all sides needed to march across it in
wartime, which they had, many times in the past several years.

"I've received word from a friend of mine in Tirilis," the prince said,
waving a servant over for more ale. Braeden's mug was topped off whether he
needed it or not. "An army crossed the Galwend mountains a week ago, flying
the Inferrara banners. A fine army too, from the sound of it; infantry with all of
the latest equipment. There's a rumor it's led by the Archduchess Elektra
herself."

Who was leading the army shouldn't matter, but it did. Though Braeden
still hated Teodora and wanted her dead, he wanted at least that much for
Elektra. He understood why she'd betrayed him, but that didn't mean he'd
ever forgive it. Her actions had put his friends in the Sanova Hussars at risk,
and had nearly cost him and Karil their lives. He'd welcome a confrontation,
now that he thought about it. Hoping his face didn't betray him, he said,
"That's interesting. I'm well-acquainted with the archduchess."

"Not in a friendly way, I hope." The prince scowled into his mug.

"I wouldn't call it that." Braeden had to chuckle. "In fact, I'd love to see her
defeated. Dead, preferably."

"So really not friendly." The prince looked a little happier. "How would
you like to lead a force against her?"

"It's tempting," Braeden admitted. "But I can't take the time right now. I
need to move on to Isenwald as soon as I can."

"But you won't go until you have my agreement to help Lennart." The prince's eye held a canny gleam.

Braeden sighed. "At least not until I've given it my best try."

"How about this?" The dried-up old prince was becoming positively animated. "You lead an operation to thwart the Inferrara whelp, and once you've defeated her, I'll agree to raise an army for you."

"Maybe." Braeden reckoned he shouldn't commit to anything until the terms were completely clear. "What army can I use to do this? I've only brought fifty of my own soldiers."

"You can have as many of mine as you want." The prince smiled, revealing toothless gums.

"What's the size of the enemy force?" Braeden wanted to be certain of victory.

"My scouts report a full-size regiment."

The thought of that silly girl in charge of even that many made Braeden shake his head. He couldn't imagine Elektra being much of a threat, though she might do well if she had competent officers under her. "Let me take a look at your troops." He wanted to be sure they were in usable condition. He didn't want to throw green or under-equipped soldiers against Elektra if he was to do the job right.

Prince Benda introduced him to his general, a seasoned, gouty old veteran. Braeden was familiar with the type, and reckoned if he lived a few years longer, he might end up looking similar.

The general was happy to have Braeden review his little army. "We lost most of it when Mattila defeated Arryk, but I've done my best to build it back up again. I've only got two thousand, but they're well-trained, with many veterans among them."

"The imperial regiment will likely number only a thousand, or fifteen hundred at the most," the prince said.

"We'll have more than enough to take them on. Which road are they taking?" Braeden asked.

"A less-traveled one. Seems they're avoiding Kersenstadt."

The others weren't looking at him just then, so Braeden hoped his grimace went unnoticed. Pain still rushed over him whenever he heard the name of that city. He swallowed it down and said, "That means they'll be coming through the woods before they reach the border."

Prince Benda nodded. "It'll be hard for them to know our numbers until they're upon us."

"That's good," Braeden said. "We can make them think we're weaker than we are; encourage them to fight their way through. Elektra's numbers are small enough I reckon she'll try for a soft spot. We'll give her one." Braeden had an idea. "I need an officer of yours," he said, turning to the general. "Someone brave, who's willing to put up with a few hours of captivity."

The general's craggy face broke into a grin. "I have someone who'd be perfect for that kind of operation. She's just come to us recently, but she's always on the lookout for a bit of adventure."

Braeden had prepared a stern, yet friendly look when the young woman appeared, then worried his heart might not handle the shock when he recognized Trisa Torresia.

"You'd better have a seat, sir," she said, leading him over to a bench. She seemed just as surprised to see him, but at her age, she might be able to handle it better.

"Might we have a moment, Your Grace?" Braeden choked out. The prince and his entourage drifted to a discreet distance.

Braeden couldn't think where to begin. He wanted to know how Trisa came to be here, but even more, hoped that her father—one of his oldest friends—hadn't come to harm. Then he remembered something else. "You saved my life," he finally said. "When you told Martinek where we were. He found us just in time."

A grin spread across her face. "I gathered that, once I saw you. I heard you escaped, but were wounded."

"I was," Braeden said, "though I'm all right now. I'm still mad at Franca for sending you on such a dangerous mission."

"I wanted to do it, sir," Trisa said. "And I'm glad I did. I suppose you're wondering what I'm doing here."

"You've got that right." Braeden scowled.

She sighed. "Papa was furious when we were forced to fight for Ensden and Teodora again. So he retired to Atlona with Mama and my sisters." Her dark brows drew together. "The two of them decided I wasn't old enough to be left alone."

Braeden snorted.

"I know. I told them they were being ridiculous. I was getting a commission and everything. Clearly I'm old enough." Trisa tossed her head, flinging a long braid over her shoulder. "But Papa can be so stubborn, and Mama always backs him up. So they dragged me along with them until I ran away."

"Oh gods," Braeden said. "Do your parents know you're all right?"

Trisa rolled her eyes. "They do now. I waited until I had a position in Prince Benda's army, then wrote to them in Atlona. Now I'm committed, of course I can't leave."

"I can't believe the prince took you on," Braeden said, "You can't be a day over sixt—"

"Don't you dare tell them how old I am," Trisa said in a furious whisper. "I told them I'm nineteen, and since I have my own horse and gear, and am good at what I do, no one's questioned me."

"All right, all right." Braeden shook his head, though now he knew Reno and Senta were well, he couldn't keep from smiling. "Your secret's safe with me. Now, are you going to help me catch Elektra Inferrara?"

TEODORA

Teodora opened her eyes carefully. After a moment, she remembered where she was and what had happened, but even as it all came back, she was afraid to move. At least she was alive. She squeezed Daciana's hand, still resting in hers. Still warm, still alive.

Teodora breathed in deeply, and ran her hand over her face. It felt odd, though she didn't know exactly what was different. But it seemed that whatever had happened, hadn't been all that bad.

An instant later, Sibyla's anxious face hovered over hers. "Oh gods," she said, horror in her eyes.

"What?" Teodora asked, her voice strong as ever. "Surely ..." she trailed off, as she ran her fingers through her hair. Something was different. She lifted a hank. The room was light now, the curtains open, evening sun slanting against the walls.

Teodora gasped. The hair she held in her hand was still smooth, still heavy, but it was white. "How bad is it?" She dropped the hair and stared back at Sybila.

Sybila swallowed hard. "At least you're alive. And you don't seem terribly weakened in spite of the blood loss. It's just ..."

"My face." Teodora sat up, remembering how strange it had felt. "Let me see." She'd look at Daciana in a moment, but not before she'd seen the price she'd paid.

Sybila sucked in her lower lip while handing Teodora a small mirror.

Teodora held it up. Her mother, much as she'd looked in the year of her death, stared back at her. Bile rose in her throat, but she forced herself to calm. Her dark hair was white now, her skin as wrinkled as a grandmother's, but her eyes were still dark and resolute and her jaw forceful as ever. As long as her mind still worked like before, she would bear it somehow. "It's not so bad," she said, willing herself to believe it. "Did it work?"

Sybila's eyes sliced away from Teodora's, and across to Daciana.

Teodora followed them. Under both of their intent gazes, Daciana opened her eyes. "I had the most incredible dream," she said.

Teodora tried to smile, but nearly wept instead. It had worked. Daciana's skin was clear and free of scarring, though a small blemish remained on her forehead. Teodora touched it carefully. "Does it hurt?" she asked, pressing down ever so gently.

"No." A smile spread across Daciana's face. "It doesn't. Nothing hurts." She sat up, raised her arm and looked at it. No scars there, or anywhere on her body. "I don't understand." She turned toward Teodora and gasped. "What happened to you?"

"Never mind that," Teodora said, strangely light. All the fear, the strange feelings, the despair at Daciana's condition, had been worth it. Somehow, Livilla had healed her. "Where is the Maxima?" she turned toward Sybila, who was also smiling as she looked Daciana over.

"She's gone to rest," she said. "The ritual tired her greatly."

"She's all right, isn't she?" Teodora was suddenly worried that perhaps this had cost Livilla just as much. And she didn't have ten years of life to give.

I think so." Sybila frowned. "In spite of these incredible results, I can't approve of any of this."

"Of what?" Daciana asked.

"The Maxima performed a ritual that drained Her Highness of nearly all her blood. It seemed she called upon the gods and some dark forces to transfer their life force to you. She didn't allow me to stay in the room, but what I heard was dreadful. I didn't expect to find either one of you alive when she let me back in."

Daciana turned to Teodora, looking her over carefully. "Oh gods." She grabbed Teodora's hands. "This is my fault, isn't it?"

Teodora smiled. "I've repaid a debt. I'm so happy I could do it."

"I don't understand." Daciana shook her head. "I was in some kind of nightmare, then it changed to this peculiar dream and now I really am awake."

"What do you remember?" Teodora asked. Livilla had explained that if all went well, Daciana would have little memory of her most troubled time.

Daciana frowned. "A boy on a big black horse, holding a pistol. A ship, pain and fire. And after that, nothing."

"I have a great deal to tell you then," Teodora said. "But we have time. For I want you to stay with me always. I don't want you out of my sight ever again."

"Are you certain?" A sly smile quirked on her lips. The old Daciana was back. "I'm likely to cause you a great deal of trouble."

"You already have." Teodora smiled back. "I don't mind."

"But I want to be useful to you." Daciana sprang out of bed and put on the robe Sibyla brought her. "You must let me do something. I know you said you've repaid a debt, but I don't understand. We've always been equal, been friends who've helped each other. I want to keep helping you."

Teodora wanted to get up, but found her limbs stiff and unwieldy. Sybila helped her out of bed, and Daciana brought Teodora's dressing gown.

"We can talk of all that later." The problem of Elektra flashed through her mind, but she didn't want to think of that now. "But first, I want to celebrate your return." She'd worry about what she'd seen in the mirror later. It was the only way she would keep from losing her mind.

GWYNNETH

Gwynneth told herself she was doing the right thing, but that didn't keep her from feeling guilty. For she was on her way now, as Gauvain's special ambassador to Maladena. Few people knew she was leaving Allaux, and even fewer where she was going or why, but those were still too many. Preparing for such a lengthy journey without attracting attention was difficult—perhaps impossible—with Natalya's spies everywhere.

Gwynneth didn't even tell the children. Only Maryna knew she was leaving at all.

"If Natalya asks you where I've gone, tell her I'm visiting a friend in the countryside," Gwynneth told Maryna the morning of her departure.

"I will. That's not where you're going?" Maryna cocked her head. Usually, Gwynneth enjoyed her daughter's intelligence and curiosity, but it was inconvenient right now.

Gwynneth furrowed her brow. She hated lying to her children, but didn't want to put Maryna in danger with any knowledge. "Not exactly, though it's better if you don't know. It's possible Natalya will be angry that I've gone so suddenly."

Maryna regarded Gwynneth with grave blue eyes. "I hope you're not doing anything very dangerous, Mama."

"Not at all." Gwynneth smiled down at her reassuringly as she fastened her cloak. "Say goodbye to the other children for me."

"You won't do it yourself?"

"They'll just be upset." Gwynneth tried to smile, but wasn't able to manage it. "It's better this way."

"I'll tell them," Maryna said, though Gwynneth saw she didn't approve. She grabbed Gwynneth's hand. "Please be careful, Mama."

"I will." Gwynneth bent down to kiss Maryna's forehead. She didn't have to bend far; her little girl had grown so tall.

She left Allaux several hours before dawn, in a hired carriage. Someone would surly notice, but Gwynneth hoped she would throw them off the trail. As the carriage rolled out of the city's southern gate, Gwynneth whispered a prayer that Gauvain keep her children safe. She'd only agreed to this mission with his assurance he'd stand up to Natalya, so she wouldn't use the children as hostages to force Gwynneth's return. She was grateful that she hadn't seen Natalya since she'd agreed to do this. That way she hadn't been forced to lie about anything, though she doubted that would help her cause when Natalya found out.

She told herself this was the right thing to do, even if it hurt her friend terribly. Peace with Maladena was of paramount importance, and since Natalya had failed to secure it, it was Gwynneth's duty to do what she could. Gauvain's plan was solid, and Queen Beatryz had expressed cautious interest in a series of encrypted letters. Gwynneth only needed to finalize the deal.

She leaned back against the cushions of the carriage, watching dawn break over the yellow-leafed trees lining the road. With the harvest in full swing, Gwynneth looked forward to reaching the wine-growing country further south. Perhaps seeing pretty villages and merry peasants would help distract her from her terrible anxiety.

"It'll be all right, Your Grace." Catrin had been asleep, curled up in a corner of the bench against the carriage wall, but as the sun slanted in she awakened. Gwynneth had decided she needed no other companion, and more than anyone, she could trust Catrin to keep her mouth shut when it came to sensitive matters.

"I hope so." Gwynneth offered a weak smile. "Though I worry about the children."

"The king will keep them safe. Oh, I can't wait to get to Maladena. I've heard it's so lovely and warm there, with oranges growing on all of the trees."

Gwynneth found it helped to think about her destination, and thanked the gods for Catrin for the hundredth time.

When a whole day passed without incidence, Gwynneth relaxed a little. They switched to a plain post coach at the first mail stations, changed two more times after that, spent three nights in pleasant inns, and even briefly enjoyed a village wine festival in the south of the country. From there, it was only four days to the Maladene border.

The weather turned rainy, which slowed the coach down, though they continued steady progress southward.

"Terrible for the harvest," Gwynneth murmured to herself, looking out the window as they lumbered down a muddy road. She consoled herself with the thought that even though her progress was slowed, pursuers would be slowed as well.

One day from the Maladene border, the road became steep, winding up mountainsides around hairpin turns. Gwynneth and Catrin stayed glued to the window, staring at Galladium spread before them like a miniature kingdom.

"This is what it must be like to be a bird," Catrin said. "To see the whole world from so high."

"Aren't you frightened?" Gwynneth asked. "If something happens to the coach, it's a long way down."

"Nothing will happen, " Catrin said. "People travel this way all the time."

"True." Gwynneth sat back and tried not to worry. They couldn't be more than a half-day from the Maladene border. It would be heavily guarded, but she had a letter of safe passage, bearing the king's seal. There shouldn't be any problems.

The coach moved slower and slower as it neared the top of the mountain. Fog rolled in, and there was nothing to see, so Gwynneth finally fell asleep. Perhaps when she awakened, they'd be at the border.

ELEKTRA

"The scouts report hostile troops just over the border, Your Grace," Major Linser said.

Elektra stared at him, disbelieving. She never dreamed of running into opposition so far south. "What kind of hostile? Mattila?" Even though all reports indicated that Mattila was staying in Brandana, Elektra still worried about her.

"Hard to say, though they don't look organized like Mattila's."

"Who could they be?"

"Locals, I imagine. Lantura militia maybe."

"But …" Elektra swung down from her horse, and waved at a page to set up a table. "I thought all of southern Kronland swore loyalty to my mother."

"They did," Major Linser said, waiting for Elektra to take a seat at the little table, then unrolling the map onto it. "But some of the rulers claimed oaths made under threat aren't binding. They can't be trusted."

Elektra stared at the map. She had to get through Lantura if she wanted to join Ensden soon. The only way around was hundreds of leagues out of her way through Sanova, and she didn't have the time. She was certain Ensden would engage Lennart before winter. The rising wind blew cold, and Elektra shivered, drawing her cloak around her. "What can we do?"

"Send scouts to get what further information we can. Then we must choose a spot and fight our way through. The Lantura border is long; I'm sure we can find a weak point."

"We don't have time for that." Elektra stared at the map even harder, as if that would yield new information.

"Don't worry yet, Your Grace." As usual, the major's optimism never flagged. That quality was likely the same one that made him believe Elektra's rescue was possible.

She smiled at him. "I don't want to miss the big battle."

Linser smiled back and sat down across the table from her. "Why do you expect a big battle? Lennart is outnumbered. He will pick at Ensden around the edges, trying to draw him into a disadvantageous position. It might take months, or might not happen at all. Ensden is too canny to give in to provocation. And in the meantime, if southern Kronland has risen against us, there is useful work we can do here. If we engage and distract Lennart's allies in the south, they can't join him in the north, can they?"

"I suppose not." Out of long habit, Elektra glanced over her shoulder. Even though she'd left Atlona over a month ago, she still worried about pursuit.

Linser understood. "If no one has come after you by now, they likely will not."

"She's waiting for me to let my guard down." Elektra shuddered, remembering the conversation in the woods when her mother had trapped her. "That's what she does."

"Perhaps. But even if someone comes, we won't let them take you."

Elektra still didn't entirely understand why her officers had thrown themselves on her side, risking treason. When questioned, they all said she belonged at the head of their regiment, having taken such good care of them. In private, Major Linser confided that Countess Biaram believed Elektra might become empress before long, though he didn't know her reasons. Had Teodora been weakened in a way Elektra didn't yet grasp? Elektra wished she'd learned more from the countess.

She managed a half-smile for Linser. "I know, and thank you. Now let's figure out how to go forward."

That night, under cover of darkness, Elektra led fifty troops deep into the woods. Her officers objected, but she wanted to do this. She hated always receiving information second-hand, and it felt better to lead the action than sitting in camp stewing, waiting for something to happen. Once they neared the enemy lines, Elektra dropped to her belly, and motioned to the others to do the same. They already had their orders, so now all they had to do was creep forward and carry out the plan.

They were lucky that night. The wind had picked up, rattling dry leaves on the birch trees, and rumbling through the firs. The pickets were spread far apart, and everyone sneaked past them with no incident. Whoever had planned the camp's security had been careless. Elektra ordered everyone to spread out into the woods on both sides of her to keep an eye on the rest of the camp while she got closer. Now she saw the lights from the cook fires and the outlines of tents. She still didn't know how large the force was, but would learn that soon enough.

Elektra was getting cold, lying on the dry leaves, but fear helped warm her as she got close enough to overhear conversations. She needed to find an officer, someone who could give her information. Only common soldiers sat around the first fire, so Elektra crept sideways through the brush until she neared another. It was frustrating to be confined to those at the edge of camp. If she'd been braver, she would have disguised herself and wandered in as if she belonged there, but she wasn't that brave, at least not yet. And until she was, she couldn't ask anyone else to do it.

The wind rose again, the leaves rustled, and the crescent moon seemed to have stuck in its spot in the sky forever. Elektra wondered how much time had passed. It felt like hours, but probably wasn't. She was about to give up at the second fire when she got lucky. A tall young woman paused to warm her hands, and one of the men referred to her as Lieutenant. Elektra grinned, and motioned to the troops waiting behind her. She pointed at the woman, then to the right, and whispered, "Over there." If her guess was correct, the officer was heading toward the privy trenches, which judging by the smell, were very near.

She jumped to her feet, then ran along the edge of the woods, crouched as low as she could. If anyone looked away from their fire, they'd see her, but they weren't looking. Several people laughed at a joke, and a man started singing.

"Sing louder," Elektra muttered to herself.

She kept her eyes on the officer, who had now disappeared behind a mound of dirt. Her guess had been correct. "Now," Elektra whispered, and they pounced. The officer's shriek was cut off quickly, then someone stuffed a rag into her mouth, and put a bag over her head. Uncomfortable memories rushed over Elektra, but she shook her head, banishing them. She'd never be captured like that again. It was someone else's turn tonight.

BRAEDEN

Braeden smiled when he heard Trisa's screech, cut off abruptly. He had just glimpsed the archduchess herself skulking along the tree line. He couldn't believe his good luck. It had never occurred to him that Elektra might lead a reconnaissance mission herself, but it would make his job easier. The wind in the trees obscured the sound of the ensuing scuffle, and he hoped Trisa was following his orders.

"Don't fight too hard," he'd told her. "I don't want them hurting or killing you accidentally."

"They won't." Trisa was fearless as ever. "They need information from me, don't they?"

"Yes, but don't give it up too easy, or they'll be suspicious." Braeden frowned. His plan was solid, but he'd never forgive himself if something happened to Trisa while carrying it out.

"I can handle a little pain." Trisa smiled, as if looking forward to it.

Braeden shook his head. "Don't take any unnecessary risks, all right?" He offered a stern glare, though he suspected she was secretly laughing at him. Braeden told himself he was much too old for these kinds of antics, and resolved to consider retirement once he'd rounded up allies for Lennart. Surely he wouldn't be needed in any further fighting.

After Trisa's capture, Braeden crouched behind the first row of tents, and forced himself to count to one hundred twice. As planned, the soldiers sitting around the fires made a big show of calling good night to each other while dispersing to the tents, some even pretending to be drunk. It seemed everyone but Braeden was having a grand time. He was cold and his knees hurt, so he focused on the flames dying down as darkness settled over the camp. It shouldn't be much longer now.

He'd nearly counted to one hundred again before they came out of the trees. Perfect. He motioned to his lieutenants to wait. The more enemy they could draw between the tents, the better. Braeden, his eyes now accustomed to the dark, kept them peeled for Elektra. He wasn't the praying sort, but thought if there was any justice, the gods would send her his way. He'd make it quick, but would make sure she realized he was the one doing it. She'd know why.

The first rank came toward him, spear-tips glinting in the starlight, the crescent moon providing little light. Braeden held a pistol in each hand, every nerve strained, waiting for them to reach the tents. At that point, they'd have to break ranks to go around them. Knowing Elektra, she would have drilled this lot relentlessly, and they'd fight well enough in formation. Braeden wanted to be certain they never got that chance.

"Now!' he shouted, firing both pistols at the same time. He hit two soldiers; one of them slumped against a tent, and the other fell face-first into the dirt. Everyone around him had fired, and now there was pandemonium. Braeden drew his saber and ran forward. He had kept Kazmir back in case things didn't go as planned.

After being beaten so thoroughly by Mattila, this little army needed a victory, and Braeden intended to give them one. Elektra's well-trained troops fell back in orderly fashion when they saw they'd been ambushed. But that wouldn't help them. As they retreated into the woods, the company that Braeden had sent to outflank them, caught them from behind. With any luck, they'd already retrieved Trisa.

Shots blazed between the trees, and Braeden kept walking forward, looking everywhere for Elektra. She had to be here somewhere. Now the enemy was falling fast, a few throwing down their weapons when they saw all was lost. "Find the archduchess," Braeden shouted over the din. "I want her alive." With any luck at all, she was already a prisoner on the other side of the woods. He'd just have to be patient.

"Secure the prisoners," he told an officer who'd been keeping pace with him. "Keep them out of the fight."

He marched straight into the woods, aware of the danger, though he was flanked on all sides by highly alert soldiers. He couldn't count the bodies on the ground, or the prisoners, but they had to number several hundred. Perhaps Elektra was among them. He kept going until he met his troops coming from the other side. He breathed a sigh of relief when he spotted Trisa, her face bloodied but joyful. "Where are the rest?" he called.

"The rest?" another officer asked. "We got all of 'em, didn't we?"

"It doesn't seem like enough." Braeden looked around. "There must have been a thousand enemy."

"Patience, sir." Trisa wiped blood from her chin. "We haven't counted all the bodies yet."

"You're right." Braeden tried not to worry. Elektra's would surely be among them.

ANTON

As Anton's regiment made its way toward Kaltental, he felt happier again. Maybe he was looking forward to the baby, though that was still months away. Or maybe it was that he had stopped drinking everything except weak ale. His head was clearer, and when he felt sad, it didn't last nearly as long.

"You're sure you're not too tired?" he asked Susanna as they readied the cart for a big gambling party in a major's tent. The major had decided he liked Anton after he'd been wounded in battle. So when he hosted a party, he let Anton know before any other sutlers got a chance.

"I had a nap this afternoon, though it wasn't much fun without you." Susanna shot Anton her saucy grin, and he got weak in the knees, even after all this time. He wished someone had told him how nice it was to be in love and living together like this. The count had always made it sound like a lot more bother.

Susanna threw a rug over the cart, and they made their way slowly through the camp. By now, Anton knew many fellow soldiers, and was on friendly terms with most of them. Once he'd gotten done feeling sorry for himself, he found he enjoyed life a lot more if he made friends.

The Michalek Pike and several other regiments had crossed the Velta River, fording at a shallow spot, then making camp on the right bank, awaiting further instructions from Ensden. Anton for once enjoyed the crossing, wading through chilly ankle-deep water. He liked not worrying about bridges held by the enemy, or being swept away in deep, fast water.

Vineyards covered the steep river banks, but much of the grape harvest was dying on the vine, since the country folk had fled the approaching armies. In an attempt to salvage it, the wine-loving Count Michalek and a few other commanders released their soldiers to help pick grapes on the terraces rising above the river. Anton did his share and enjoyed the work, though he'd been sore after struggling to stay upright on the steep slopes all day.

He liked the views from so high, looking up the river toward Kaltental, and down toward Birkenfels, as it wound between the bright yellow vineyards like a blue ribbon, small towns and castles at nearly every bend. But after his experience with white wine the previous year, he didn't care to sample the finished product.

Other soldiers liked it well enough, so Anton and Susanna had stocked the cart with twenty bottles Anton bought from the vintner whose land he'd worked. The man gave him a good discount in gratitude for his help. Anton felt a little bad, because the farmers wouldn't have had problems in the first place if the army hadn't come tramping all over their land, but he hoped his help made a little difference. With any luck, the coin Anton provided for the wine would help the vintner make it another year.

Officers crowded the major's tent, many of them already drunk, and very happy to see Anton and Susanna. Once word of Susanna's pregnancy had gotten out, the men treated her more respectfully, but Anton was the target of endless good-natured ribbing.

Working with drunk gamblers could be boring, but tonight Anton saw a lot of high-ranking officers, so he hoped to get information about plans for the next action.

"We'll be on the march soon, mark my words," a mustachioed colonel said. "Lennart is only forty leagues south of here, and we already know Ensden doesn't want us to engage him. He'll call us north to get us out of harm's way."

"Why shouldn't we engage?" Anton asked. Now he felt better, his enthusiasm for fighting was returning. Surely not every battle would be as bad as the last one.

"Ensden doesn't want to fight Lennart if he doesn't have to. He's better off sitting pretty in Kaltental, while Lennart spends all of his coin and goodwill, keeping his armies fed through the winter."

"What if Lennart wants to fight in the winter?" Anton asked, remembering what the count had said about Estenorians not being bothered by the cold.

"Then Ensden might have a problem." Maybe it was because the colonel was drunk, but he didn't seem too worried at the prospect. "Lennart will still need to draw him out of Kaltental, make him stand and fight. And Ensden is too experienced to respond to provocation. He'll draw Lennart in close, then let him rot through a few months of winter. Once his army is weakened by disease and desertion, we'll strike. Ought to be an easy win, when the time comes." The colonel looked up at Anton and winked. "You'll just have to cool your heels. Might be your little one will come before the next big battle."

Anton couldn't decide if that would be a good thing or not. He worried about Susanna, but once a baby came, he'd worry about it too. He wished he could find a spot to shelter his little family, then shuddered, thinking of how his mother had died in a place Braeden had been certain was safe.

KENDRYK

The weather held, making Kendryk's journey to Ummarvik pleasant and fast. In spite of Mattila's unfriendliness, she did nothing to hinder his passage, so he, Count Faris and their small escort took their time crossing the kingdom. Kendryk had good reason for his leisurely pace. He was curious about how well-established Mattila was in Brandana, and wanted to learn as much as he could while he was there. He made a point of inviting himself to the homes of all the nobility on his way north, and learned from them that Mattila was both feared and unpopular.

"She collects taxes in a way Princess Floreta never did. I'm sure it's illegal," a countess whispered to Kendryk as they sat at dinner in her pretty manor house. Located just north of the Lera River and south of the Ummarvik border, the countess's lands were particularly vulnerable if Princess Floreta decided to reconquer her kingdom.

Kendryk wondered why the countess was whispering. Did she expect Mattila's spies in her own household? "I'm sure once Lennart has dealt with Teodora, he'll set things right here," Kendryk said, offering an encouraging smile. He was not certain of this, but if Mattila refused to ally herself with Lennart, he'd have no use for her, especially once he'd rid the empire of Teodora.

"I hope so." The countess stared into her soup. "Everyone I know is very unhappy with Mattila. If only we could overthrow her."

"Why can't you? I heard Teodora left her with only a regiment."

"It's true." The countess nodded, still looking around furtively. "But she's recruited from here and there, and she's got plenty of money, especially after bleeding us dry. So we can't recruit, but she can."

"How many troops does she have?" Kendryk reckoned this might be useful information for Princess Floreta, whom he expected to see when he reached Ummarvik. He hadn't seen much military activity himself, but Mattila was unlikely to share information with him.

"It's hard to say—she never invites me to her castle—but the Baron Kretzhof told me he counted at least eight thousand when he stopped there last month."

"That's not so much," Kendryk said, thinking of the force Lennart would assemble in a few months. "I will ask Lennart to intervene as soon as possible. Aside from her illegal activity, I found Brynhild Mattila quite an unpleasant character."

The countess shuddered. "I agree—so barbaric. She's Moraltan, you know," she added as if that explained everything.

When Kendryk reached Ummarvik, he was greeted coolly by its ruler Prince Ossian—who turned over a pile of letters from Gwynneth—and rather sentimentally by old Princess Floreta, who wanted to spend hours with Kendryk, commiserating over the loss of their kingdoms.

But Kendryk had no time for that. He left the princess with polite assurances, then went in search of Tora Isenberg. He found the general camped near the coast with a large force. After her defeat at Ensden's hands, she'd replenished her army with troops recruited in Zeelund and a mercenary force recently arrived from Anglana.

"I have at least fifteen thousand here," she told Kendryk as they toured the vast camp. "Though I'd be happy to take on more if you can convince Prince Ossian to help."

"I'll try if you like," Kendryk said. "Though he seems intimidated by Brynhild Mattila."

"Ridiculous," Isenberg said, turning away from camp, and striding down a path leading to the beach. Kendryk had to hurry to keep up. Isenberg was no taller than he was, but had long legs, moving rapidly everywhere she went. "Mattila is no threat to us right now, even if she won't support us. She will sit there and see how things go, before throwing her weight on the winning side."

"That might be bad," Kendryk said.

"Not if we're the winning side." Isenberg grinned at him. She walked out onto the beach, then stopped. Though the sun was warm, a chill wind blew and the beach was deserted, but for a few soldiers digging for clams, or checking traps set for crab and lobster. Not too far out, eight warships lay at anchor. "If the weather holds, they'll take us to Terragand." Isenberg nodded in their direction.

"And if it doesn't?"

"Quite the optimist, aren't you?"

312

Kendryk had to smile. "Can you blame me?"

Isenberg chuckled. "No, I don't blame you. But you must expect things to get better from now on."

"Will Lennart take on Ensden before winter?" Kendryk stared at the ships, thinking he'd enjoy a short journey on one of them.

"I hope so. He knows Ensden doesn't want a fight, but Lennart will do his best to provoke him."

"Ensden won't fall for that," Kendryk said.

"Might not." Isenberg shrugged. "But Lennart might get lucky. He often does."

"That's true," Kendryk said, remembering his aunt's coup in Helvundala. "I wish him all the luck in the world."

Rather than enjoy Prince Ossian's chilly hospitality, Kendryk stayed with a cousin of his, Duke Arvus Dahlby, who lived in an old castle not far from Isenberg's camp. He wanted to become better acquainted with Isenberg's force, while trying to wring a few thousand troops out of Prince Ossian.

"My cousin is a fool," Arvus sniffed. "It's obvious Lennart will win this war, and those who support him now will benefit the most."

"Would you be willing to send an army of your own?" Kendryk asked.

"I'd be willing all right." The duke grinned. He and Prince Ossian shared long, craggy faces, but while the prince wore a permanently dour expression, the duke's eyes were merry, and frequent laughter traced the lines on his face. He sighed. "But I can't send any of my troops overseas without Ossian's permission."

"Terragand is hardly overseas," Kendryk said. He'd be willing to march the duke's forces overland if the technicality helped him.

Arvus shook his head. "I know it's not. But my cousin has forbidden any of us to take troops beyond Ummarvik's borders without his permission."

"I'll try to get it then," Kendryk said, sounding more confident than he felt.

He took his first chance to read Gwynneth's letters, and as he worked through the bundle, ordered by date, felt a growing sense of dread. In an hour's reading, Natalya went from difficult to sinister, while Gwynneth had agreed to undertake a delicate mission for Gauvain.

Kendryk had endless faith in his wife's abilities, but feared her running afoul of Natalya. Gwynneth had been vague as to the nature of her mission, but Kendryk could guess at it. He didn't want Galladium at war with Maladena either, but even more, he wanted Gwynneth and his children safe.

It was all he could do to stop himself from dropping everything and going straight to Allaux.

ELEKTRA

The moment Elektra realized she was trapped, all she could think about was saving her army. "Fall back!" she shouted, wheeling her horse, and riding along the ranks. "They were waiting for us," she explained to Major Linser when he appeared at her side. "We've got to get away."

"We can try." The major was breathing hard. "A second enemy force is outflanking us. They'll be upon our rear in a few minutes."

Elektra stared at the major in confusion. "How will we escape?"

"We won't all," the major said. "Although you must. Take the cavalry and the dragoons, and make for Arcius. Princess Zelenka will help you."

"But the infantry," Elektra wailed. They were her pride and joy, though not much longer, judging by the sounds coming from the camp.

"I will try to save as many as I can," the major said, already turning away. "Those of us who survive will follow, and meet you in Arcius. Now go, before someone catches you. The enemy knows you're here. I heard one of their officers call out that he wanted you alive."

Elektra's heart fell into her feet. Who besides her mother might want to take her alive? The answer came to her in a panicked rush. She didn't know why Braeden Terris would be here, but now her mind had turned to him, she certainly sensed his presence. He would have known exactly how she'd deploy her infantry, and she'd held her small cavalry back just as he'd explained it to her and Karil, one evening around the fire.

She put the spurs to her horse, looking around wildly, seeing Braeden's massive form in every shadow. If he caught her, there was no telling what he might do. She forced her horse to gallop in spite of the dark and uneven forest trail. Falling off and breaking her neck was still better than being caught by a man who had to want revenge for what she'd done.

On her left, the enemy engaged her company of dragoons. "Fall back, fall back!" she screeched. "Follow me." She turned without waiting to see if anyone did, then hurried toward the cavalry, standing restlessly on her right. No one had given them the order to engage, and now she was glad of it.

Branches whipping against her face had opened her cheek, and the wound stung as sweat rolled into it. She wiped at it, blood smearing her glove. "We must return to the road," she said to a cavalry captain who'd come forward, his eyes wide and worried. "The battle is lost, and we have to get out of here."

"How? Where? Are you sure?"

Elektra didn't like being questioned, especially right now. Her heart thumped madly, and she could hardly breathe. Was it possible to die of fear? Losing the battle and dying that way wasn't as bad as Braeden catching her; she mustn't give him a chance to do it. "We're leaving." She gasped it out between panicked breaths. "We get onto the road south, turn east at the crossroads, and make for Arcius." She pulled her horse around, and headed for the road, hoping the others would follow. If they were smart, they would. It was obvious by now that things weren't going their way.

By the time she reached the road, dragoons pounded down it, trying to get away from the outflanking enemy troops.

"Are they following you?" she asked an officer as she drew level with him.

"Doesn't look like it, thank the gods," the officer said, though he looked over his shoulder as he rode. "They did their best to push us toward their camp and I wasn't having it."

"Good man," Elektra said, hoping more of her troops showed such sense. She slowed down a little and looked back, relieved that most of her cavalry had joined her. Then she urged her horse on, and it bounded eagerly down the smoother road. The moon shed little light, but she was glad of it, since that would make her a less clear target. She remembered Braeden's charger Kazmir, and shuddered. She doubted her horse could outrun him.

Everything depended on her head start, so she let her horse gallop for a time, but as the panic subsided, she pulled back. Arcius was still a long way off, and she needed to spare him.

Several officers she barely knew now flanked her, probably waiting for orders. She'd only become friendly with the infantry officers, and a sob caught in her throat as she wondered if she'd see any of them again. She cantered until they reached the crossroads, then pulled to a stop and faced the officers. "We'll turn east here, but won't rest until we reach Kersenstadt."

"What if they pursue us there?" someone asked.

Elektra licked her dry lips. "If their commander is who I think, they won't come within ten leagues of that place."

LENNART

"Ensden can't put you off forever," Alona Brynner said. "Kaltental is large, but it can't possibly support an army of his size through the winter. And now you hold this end of the river, he can't get more supplies that way."

"Maladena can send them by sea," Tavio Sora said. His large, mournful dark eyes nearly swallowed his face. By now Lennart realized that Sora would never see the bright side of things, but that viewpoint could sometimes be more useful than an optimistic one.

"Surely Norovaea won't let them pass the straits." Geffrey Manier frowned as he looked at the map spread out on the table. Lennart had reclaimed Birkenfels as his headquarters for the time being. Once his allies were gathered, it would be an easy matter to march up both sides of the river to Kaltental.

"Norovaea must let them pass," Sora said. "King Arryk's treaty dictates that he must not interfere with any imperial activities. As long as Queen Beatryz supports Teodora in this war, Maladena is considered an imperial ally."

'You're correct," Lennart said. "And I won't blame Arryk for keeping his nose clean. He must do what's best for his country."

"Maladena will send many ships," Sora said. "Great warships to accompany those carrying supplies. Your fleet cannot hold them."

"Perhaps not." Lennart stared at the map. The strait separating Norovaea from Kronland was narrow. He wondered if his few ships might at least harry the Maladenes, and then he thought of something better. "That's it," he said. "A blockade. My twenty ships will be more than enough, and we needn't put Arryk in an awkward position."

"Do you have any idea when Maladena might send those ships?" Manier asked Sora.

"I'm sure they've already sailed. They will try to get in and out of Kaltental, and be clear of the Anglana straits before the weather turns."

317

"We can't let them get through," Lennart said, wishing he had a bigger navy. It had been enough to deal with Sanova, but the Maladene navy was larger, and one of the finest in the world. "I'll write to my admiral, and tell him to prepare for blockade. And I'll tell Meldahl to see the ships are well-supplied with armaments. I'll leave the details to General Lofbrok."

Lennart stared at the map, his elbows propped on the table while the others were silent, waiting for his orders. He had enough to march on Ensden now, even before Braeden and Trystan returned with reinforcements. Kendryk had already written that Mattila wouldn't cooperate, though Lennart had half expected that.

Lennart slid his index finger up the map, tracing the river north. "My scouts tell me there are three enemy regiments here," he said. "They'll join Ensden soon, though they're likely living off the land right now. We could march on them, and maybe draw Ensden out before he gets settled in even further."

"He won't come out," Brynner said. "He'll sacrifice those three regiments instead. Knowing him, he'd sacrifice five or more."

"Then we should let him make that sacrifice," Lennart said, standing. "We'll go now. We'll take out these regiments, then keep moving north, show Ensden we mean business. Any other allies can catch up to us later." Securing southern Terragand had been strategically useful, but Lennart was getting the uncomfortable impression that Ensden might think he was shying away from a fight. Lennart planned to disabuse him of that notion.

GWYNNETH

Gwynneth awoke with a start as the coach came to an abrupt stop. She heard loud voices, and peered out the window. It seemed they were near the top of the mountain, with the border straight ahead. Perhaps someone was meeting them.

Gwynneth sat back in her seat, patting her hair. That was more an impulse than anything; she doubted she'd need to impress a border official as long as she had the king's seal. The door opened with a brief knock, and a tall man climbed in, pulling off his hat as he entered.

"Good afternoon, Your Grace," he said in Galladian.

Gwynneth stared at him as he sat on the bench across from her, Catrin scrambling to make way.

"And you are?" Gwynneth asked.

"Count Peryn LaFontant." He fixed a hard, dark-eyed gaze on Gwynneth. "In personal service to His Majesty, King Gauvain Brevard."

Gwynneth's breath caught, her first thought for her children. "What's happened?" she whispered.

The count reached inside his doublet, and pulled out a letter. Gwynneth recognized the king's seal, and broke it with trembling hands.

"*I am very sorry, Gwynneth,*" he wrote. "*But you must come back at once. Natalya has discovered our mission. If you don't return with Count LaFontant, I will never see my daughter again.*"

"Oh gods," Gwynneth leaned back, the letter fluttering to the floor. "Of course I'll go back. Poor Gauvain." She'd worried about her own children, but never expected Natalya to use Joslyn in this way. She looked at the count. "Can you tell me if my children are all right? Surely the Maxima hasn't ..." she trailed off, unable to say any more.

"The king brought your children to the palace as soon as the Maxima uncovered his plan. Unfortunately, she had already removed the Lady Joslyn from your home."

Gwynneth was relieved that her children were all right, but full of fear for little Joslyn. Natalya had become so strange and ruthless of late, and had shown such little affection for her daughter. "I'll return." She was disappointed that she'd been stopped so near her destination, but hoped she might salvage the situation in Allaux. She'd speak to Natalya as soon as she returned.

"Very well." The count's eyes narrowed, and Gwynneth wondered if he blamed her for Gauvain's troubles. "I'll leave you with a small escort and return to Allaux straight away. The king will want to see you as soon as you return, but it's best if I can put his mind at rest sooner. And perhaps if the Maxima is assured of your return, she can be persuaded to see reason."

Gwynneth nodded, and before she said another word, the count was gone.

"Oh gods," Catrin said, once the door had shut behind him. "Whatever will you do?"

"Go back," Gwynneth said. "I have no choice. I won't be responsible for any harm coming to Joslyn."

"Do you suppose the Maxima will be terribly angry with you?" Catrin asked, her eyes wide.

"I'm sure she will," Gwynneth said. "Perhaps we should think about where we can go, since I fear we will no longer be welcome in Allaux."

"The king will want you to stay, won't he?"

"He will; he's so kind and would never throw us out. But I don't want to increase the problems between him and Natalya. Oh, I wish I had my own money." Gwynneth pounded the coach's shabby seat cushions in frustration. "It's hard to go anywhere without it."

She tried hard to think, as the coach turned around. If it weren't for her children, she wouldn't even return to Allaux, but she needed to be certain they were safe. Besides, not facing Natalya could be considered cowardly, and likely wouldn't help Gauvain's cause at all. Gwynneth would go, and take the consequences. Then she would have to find somewhere to stay until she could return to Terragand. Norovaea might be safe, but Gwynneth feared once there, Arryk would never let her leave again. Since she knew matters there were in such disarray, she'd be tempted to stay and sort things out for him.

Kendryk had written that he'd gone to Brandana to negotiate with Brynhild Mattila, but Gwynneth couldn't picture spending any time near that woman, let alone throwing herself on her hospitality. He was headed for Ummarvik next, but that seemed unstable as well. None of the other Kronland rulers were good prospects either, except perhaps Kendryk's aunt in Helvundala.

Gwynneth would write to her and make sure the letter had gone before she reached Allaux. She needed a backup plan.

BRAEDEN

By midmorning, Braeden had checked all the dead and wounded, and inspected the few prisoners. Elektra wasn't among them.

"If we give chase, we can still catch her," Trisa said.

Braeden didn't know what to do next. His mission had succeeded, and he'd scattered the enemy. He doubted they'd threaten Lantura again anytime soon. But one prisoner said that Elektra had escaped with a few hundred cavalry. Her being so close, and relatively undefended was a mighty temptation. Braeden wondered how much Prince Benda would mind if he took a small force in pursuit. "Do we know which way they've gone?"

"Likely toward Arcius," a young officer spoke up. "Kersenstadt isn't far, and they can get there fast on the main road."

That decided it for Braeden. He wouldn't go anywhere near that place. "No point in pursuing then." He hoped he didn't sound a coward. "They will have reached the city by now, and from there it's no great distance to the Arcius border. They'll be safe, but they won't be able to threaten us from there."

Trisa and the other young officers seemed disappointed, but the general agreed with Braeden. "Our job is to defend Lantura," he said, "not chase Inferrara spawn all over the land. She's learned her lesson, and won't try our borders again with the small numbers she has. Likely she'll return to her mother, her tail between her legs."

Considering how Elektra felt about Teodora, Braeden figured that was unlikely. But whatever she did, he'd have to be satisfied that he'd thwarted her for the time being, and hope he'd get another chance at her.

Prince Benda was delighted at Braeden's success, and offered him his little army straight away. "You can take them with you," he said. "Might impress Princess Kasbirk into helping you sooner. Less talking for you."

Braeden liked that idea. He wasn't much suited to sitting around in palaces negotiating. And now it was so near winter, he worried Lennart might undertake a big action without him.

With the year wearing on, there was little time to lose. Braeden led his little army north into Isenwald, stopping in Oltena to pick up the force Princess Galena had promised to put at his disposal. To his relief, she had commissioned no further songs.

By the time Braeden reached Kronfels, Isenwald's capital city, he led an army of nearly eight thousand. Princess Kasbirk was eager to have him move on, so he took little time to persuade her to offer a few thousand additional troops. Braeden remembered Kronfels well, as Teodora's bodyguard during Edric's heresy trial. He had to believe his circumstances were better now, though he'd give it all up to have his family, and his place in the Sanova Hussars back. He left the city after only a fortnight spent gathering up the new troops, and waiting for Princess Kasbirk to sign an agreement with Lennart.

In the meantime, he'd received a message from Trystan that Podoska's army was ready to go, so rather then head straight north, Braeden went east first, hoping to intercept Trystan, and march into Terragand together. He met up with the Podoskan force just shy of the Terragand border. From a distance, Braeden saw that Karolyna Martinek was in command, though Trystan rode at her side, his face like a thundercloud.

"I hope you're right about Lennart giving me a command," he told Braeden as soon as they were out of his sister's earshot. "It's bad enough I couldn't convince Mother to let me be in charge, but Karolyna refuses to give me a command of my own. As her little brother, I should serve under her while I learn how to be an officer." Trystan said that last in such an excellent imitation of his sister that Braeden had to laugh.

"She's in for a surprise then," Braeden said. "I wish we could've convinced your family you have far more experience fighting than the rest of them put together, but I've got something for you."

"Did you bring me a pretty souvenir from Lantura?" Trystan asked, leering at Trisa, riding at Braeden's side. She stared back at him, narrowing her eyes. Braeden wondered that Trystan didn't recognize her, though she'd grown up a great deal recently.

"Something better," Braeden said, with a wink for Trisa. He led Trystan to where the officers of the Isenwald and Oltena forces had gathered. "I'm putting you in charge of this lot, General Martinek. I'd give you Lantura's too, except I promised their prince I'd command personally."

"Are you certain?" Trystan looked both surprised and pleased. His combined command would outnumber his sister's by several thousand. "I doubt Lennart will agree."

"He already has," Braeden said, enjoying the quick change in Trystan's demeanor. The sullen, angry boy riding at his sister's side had turned into a brisk, confident young man. "I wrote to him and asked, once I saw how things were going with your family. It didn't seem right."

Trystan swallowed hard, then turned to Braeden, his eyes shining. "I thank you," he said. "I swear you won't be sorry."

"I know I won't be," Braeden said.

TEODORA

"I know how you can help me," Teodora told Daciana. She saw her friend was restless, and much as she liked having her near, knew she'd have to find something for her to do. Teodora had wanted to be certain Daciana was well in both mind and body, and after the ritual she had recovered in no time at all. The same hadn't been true for Teodora, who was still weak and exhausted. She wondered if this was how it would be for the rest of her life.

"Are you finally going to let me kill Princess Gwynneth?" Daciana asked, grinning so her fangs showed. She and Teodora were having tea in the library on a chilly afternoon, the windows shut tight against an icy wind. Teodora had confided her plans for Gwynneth awhile ago, but hadn't come up with a good way of carrying them out.

"Yes." Teodora leaned back in her chair. She tired so easily. Everyone at court tiptoed around her as if she were an old lady, which she had to admit was what she looked like now. She'd explained the sudden change as the aftermath of a terrible illness, which also helped account for her absence. Teodora doubted anyone believed her, though she didn't much care. "I've found a way to get you to Galladium without arousing suspicion, since you are far too recognizable." While relations with Galladium were tense, it was not an enemy country, so she couldn't send Daciana at the head of a marauding band like she normally would.

"I can work in the shadows well enough," Daciana said.

"I hope so, since you're not known for your understatement or discretion," Teodora said with a fond smile.

It had taken time to figure out how to get to Princess Gwynneth. She lived near the Maxima's palace, her house heavily guarded, while neither she nor her children went anywhere unaccompanied.

"This mission will require you to behave somewhat differently from what you're used to," Teodora said. "But I've found out that Princess Gwynneth and King Gauvain are close. He visits her daily."

"Weren't he and the Maxima ...?" Daciana began.

"He and the Maxima had been involved, but she ended it some time ago, and he's been consoling himself with the princess ever since." Teodora had to admit the knowledge that Kendryk's wife seemed unable to stay faithful to him gave her some joy.

"Are you sure the king is as unattractive as you think? From what I've heard, both the Maxima and Princess Gwynneth are beautiful women."

"Oh, they are." Teodora waved her hand. "And I'm sure they'd never pay him the least bit of attention if it weren't for his position. But the fact is, the king being close to Gwynneth will make it easier to reach her."

"How so? Are you suggesting I try to seduce the king? Get in line as it were?" Daciana smirked.

"Not quite," Teodora said. Though it was true Daciana's looks were unconventional, she was rather striking, and Teodora had no doubts she could win over anyone she chose. "But I've hit upon a way to spend time with him, and by extension, Princess Gwynneth. It's time for Zofya to go to Galladium and get married. You will go along as one of her companions."

Daciana laughed loud and long. "You want me to pass myself off as a court lady?"

"Why not? You can play the role well enough if you wish, and no one will ever expect to find you in a courtier's dress."

"*I* never expected to find myself in one." Daciana frowned. "I'm not sure I can pull it off."

"You can. It will take a little practice, but you might enjoy it."

"Will Zofya know about any of this?"

Teodora shook her head. "No, as far as she's concerned you're a distant cousin assigned to her as lady-in-waiting."

"She'll hate that." Daciana still didn't seem to see the merits of the idea. "She'll prefer to have her friends along."

"She'll have a friend or two, but she'll also understand that she must bring companions with political or diplomatic value."

Daciana grimaced. "So am I understanding you correctly? You wish me to travel to Allaux with your daughter, befriend the king, then get close to Princess Gwynneth so I can kill her?"

"Kill her and her children," Teodora said. "I realize it might take time, especially as the Galladian court might view Zofya and her attendants with suspicion at first. But I will instruct her as to her behavior, and with any luck, she'll win the king over before too much time passes."

"I won't deny that it sounds interesting, though very different from what I'm used to. I rarely operate with stealth. How do you want me to kill them?"

"I don't much care, except to be certain that no Bernotas child remains alive. I'd also prefer it if you didn't get caught."

"It'll be a challenge, I'm sure of it," Daciana said, though she already looked more cheerful. No doubt she was looking forward to being free of the palace and its confines.

"It won't be easy, though I have every faith you will manage it. I'll have Zofya get ready, and send you my dressmaker in the meantime, since you'll need a suitable wardrobe."

"How awful." Daciana was the only woman Teodora knew who viewed the prospect of a new dress with dismay. "Though I suppose I must blend in."

"As much as it's possible for you to do so, though I believe you will create a stir at the Galladian court. No one will ever have seen anyone quite like you."

"That is the truth," Daciana said with a broad smile.

ELEKTRA

"I apologize, Your Grace," Princess Zelenka said, "But I'm afraid I must ask you to return to Atlona straight away. Your mother has ordered it."

"I can't do that." Elektra smiled sweetly at the old woman, then took a slow drink of wine as she tried to think. She'd hoped Arcius would offer a refuge while she regrouped, but it seemed it was not to be. Elektra now had to worry that the princess might try to return her by force. "I have orders to join General Ensden in Terragand, and for now, the needs of war outweigh my mother's wishes."

"Your mother's wishes take precedence over everything." Alarys Zelenka's voice was shrill. With beady eyes tucked into folds of fat in a reddened face, she was even less pleasant to look at.

"Not in this case." Elektra drained her glass, put it on the table with a bang, then stood. "Thank you for the refreshments, but I must go now."

She didn't make it to the door before the princess spoke. "I'm afraid I can't let you do that. I hate to use force, my dear, but I will if I have to."

Elektra turned to face her, struggling to keep her voice steady. "That would be most unwise, Princess. Rumor has it I will be empress before long, and you can be certain I will remember such an action." She'd heard no more about her mother since leaving the capital, but if she was weakened, perhaps the princess had received word of it.

The princess smiled unpleasantly. "Oh that. Your mother was ill for a time, but she's well now, and stronger than ever." Something about the way she said that last part made Elektra doubt it, though she was glad of the information.

Elektra shrugged. "Still, she's not getting any younger. You'd be wise not to antagonize me."

"Perhaps." The princess had stood, though she made no move toward Elektra. "But the fact remains that your mother still rules the empire, and you do not. I hope you don't take this personally."

"I will, unfortunately for you." Elektra fixed the princess with a hard glare, even as she had to force herself to keep from shaking. She couldn't go back now, especially after such a humiliating defeat. She had to redeem herself, and not return to Atlona until she rode at the head of a triumphant army, was empress, or both. "Goodbye, for now."

Elektra turned on her heel, and went out into the corridor, letting the door slam behind her. She had to move quickly now, but not give the princess's guards any sign that they were anything other than the best of friends. She forced herself to dawdle until she reached the stable yard. Most of her remaining officers were in the area, seeing their horses groomed and checking their equipment.

"We must go at once," Elektra said to the first one she saw. "Right now." She beckoned to a few others standing nearby to come closer. "It's possible they'll try to stop us, but we must get away."

"But we haven't had time to resupply," a cavalry captain said, frowning.

"No, we haven't," Elektra said, while she tried to come up with a plan. They wouldn't last long without food and munitions, but they wouldn't get them here. She wished for Major Linser, but would have to manage without him, since it seemed none of her infantry officers had survived the ambush. "We must get them elsewhere. It turns out the princess is not our friend." She couldn't say more, since no one was likely to understand why she didn't want to return to her mother.

The captain's frown turned angry. "Are you saying she is an agent of the enemy? If so, we should take the princess captive, and make the kingdom secure for the empire."

That was a complication Elektra didn't need, and she doubted it could be done. "I'm not certain if she's an enemy agent," she said. "But I believe she might betray us anyway." He didn't need to know to whom. "We don't have the numbers to act against her, so we should leave before she can stop us and get reinforcements elsewhere."

The captain chewed the end of his mustache. "I'm sure you're right, Your Grace, though it's a bad time of year to be out there without food for us and fodder for our horses."

"I agree," Elektra said, putting force into her voice. She might be young, and a head shorter than this captain, but he would obey her. "Our orders are to join Count Ensden in Terragand. The princess wishes to stop us from doing so. And since we aren't strong enough to stand up to her, we must go. We'll head for Sanova. My uncle is the queen's consort, so I'm certain I can get help from him." Elektra had never met her uncle, but she knew no one else in Sanova who might help. And besides, her mother had often ranted about her brother trying to cause problems, so perhaps he and Elektra would find common ground.

"Very well." The hope of high-level help seemed to convince the captain, and that was all it took.

In less than an hour, Elektra's small force was riding for the gate of Princess Zelenka's palace. By the time they reached it, twenty guards blocked their path.

"What will we do, Your Grace?" the captain, now riding at her side, muttered.

"We ride straight through. They are not enough to stop us." Elektra raised her pistol, and spurred her horse. "Follow me, and don't stop until we've reached the other side of the gate."

LENNART

The weather turned suddenly, with nothing left of the golden autumn. Still, it felt good to be on campaign again. The fog muffled the sounds of marching feet behind Lennart; even the jangle of his horse's harness seemed muted. He had to move cautiously. With visibility so poor, he risked stumbling upon the enemy before he was ready.

Lennart had sent scouts ahead on both sides of the river, even though he was certain the enemy had camped on the right bank. The dense fog blocked all sight of the river to his left, so he pulled out Raysa's most recent letter to pass the time. Creased and dirty, he'd already read it at least a dozen times, since it was the first long one she'd sent after little Kataryna's birth.

The naming service at the temple had gone well. Lennart had been worried because he needed his heir to be named and dedicated under the Quadrene creed. He could hardly lead an army against the old faith while his only child was blessed under its tenets. He and Raysa had agreed to a compromise, since he realized her own faith's blessing was important to her: she would take the baby for a public blessing in the Tharvik main temple, then conduct a small, private ceremony at the palace while her priestess did the honors. But that hadn't been necessary.

"The Maximus was so kind," Raysa wrote. *"He called on me and Mother Kassya, explained the ceremony, and the reasons behind everything he said and did. I was so pleased to find he'd use the words directly from the Holy Scrolls, since I'd worried your Edric Maximus had conceived of new rituals. Even Mother Kassya couldn't find fault with words given us by the gods, and decided she'd bless Kataryna right beside the Maximus. It was very touching, and the people in the temple were so excited to see the baby. I nearly cried through the whole ceremony."*

Lennart smiled, imagining the pretty picture his wife and daughter must have made. If his people hadn't loved Raysa so far, surely they would now. He wished he had been there, but was glad it was done. Ludvik Meldahl had already drawn up new documents for the succession, appointing himself and Raysa as joint regents until Kataryna turned seventeen, should anything happen to the king. Lennart offered a quick prayer that he'd still be alive to celebrate that birthday alongside his daughter, with no need for her to take on responsibilities prematurely.

He'd also written to Princess Rheda in Helvundala as soon as he knew he had a girl, asking her to consider a future marriage between Kataryna and Toland Falk, Helvundala's young ruler. He hadn't received a reply yet, but didn't expect any objection. It was soon to be making such plans, but Lennart liked the boy, and a marriage with Helvundala would be a painless way to extend Estenor's influence into that kingdom.

He folded up the letter and stuffed it in his pocket, whistling a cheery tune under his breath.

"Your Highness, please," a young officer riding at his side said. "We do not know how near the enemy is. Any noise ..."

"Oh, right," Lennart said, finding it hard to be quiet when he felt so happy. So he contented himself with daydreaming just a little. After a quick victory over the enemy here, he'd head straight for Kaltental. Tora Isenberg stood by to set sail as soon as Lennart arrived, and even sent word that Prince Kendryk had persuaded Prince Dahlby to offer troops from Ummarvik. They wouldn't be many, but with the troops Braeden and Trystan brought would represent half of the Kronland kingdoms. Lennart was sure that the remaining rulers—except for Arcius—wouldn't be far behind, especially if he soon delivered a victory over Ensden.

That done, he would bring his wife and daughter over, just for a short visit. He missed Raysa terribly and couldn't wait to meet the little one.

"Your Highness, the enemy lies ahead." A scout appeared out of the fog, his face muffled in a large scarf.

"How far?" Lennart asked.

"Not two leagues to their pickets."

"Hold up," Lennart whispered the order, and the marching behind him came to a halt. Then he listened carefully as the scout explained the enemy disposition. "It's not ideal," Lennart told his officers, "but we'll have to make it work. We still have surprise on our side, but getting our numbers into that narrow valley will be difficult."

The scout's best guess was that there were under three thousand of the enemy, a mix of infantry and cavalry, camped in a valley along the river, with artillery placed on the high ground. As long as the fog held, Lennart decided not to worry about those guns just yet.

Geffrey Manier objected when Lennart insisted on leading the attack. "It's too risky, Your Highness. We cannot have anything happening to you, especially in such a minor engagement."

"Nothing will happen." Lennart grinned, while a servant strapped on his cuirass. "I doubt they'll even see me."

"Oh, they'll see you." Manier eyed Lennart's burly frame. "Even in this fog. And they'll be expecting you. All it will take is one lucky shot—"

"That's enough now," Lennart said, his tone friendly, but making it clear there'd be no further argument. "I'm leading, and that's final. You can ride beside me. It's only right to have Kronland represented like this."

That mollified Manier, who swung into his saddle after strapping on his armor. "You're right." He glanced over his shoulder and lowered his voice. "And I know you're a trusting sort, but if I were you, I'd keep an eye on Tavio Sora and Alona Brynner. There's no telling what they'll do if things turn against us, even for a moment."

"I only look like a trusting sort." Lennart said. "I've been keeping an eye on those two since the beginning. Let's do this before the fog lifts."

TEODORA

"But I'll die!" Zofya wailed when Teodora informed her she was going to Galladium.

"No one ever died of a bad marriage." Teodora had expected trouble from Zofya, but it didn't matter. Now she had a plan for Daciana's mission in place, there was no time to waste.

"But it's the middle of winter; surely I'll die of cold, going all that way, over those mountains." Zofya's eyes were wide, as if she expected to run into snow monsters.

Teodora shook her head. "People travel back and forth all year round, and you'll have a warm carriage. I'm also having a lovely fur cloak made for you."

"You are? Might I see it?"

"It was to be a surprise, so not yet. But don't worry; it's fit for a queen." Teodora was relieved, though not altogether surprised, that Zofya hadn't mentioned Aksel Roussay. Perhaps her guess was right, and Zofya had forgotten about him after all this time apart.

Zofya slid back into her chair, worry in her eyes. "I was sure I wouldn't go until I was at least sixteen. I'm not sure I'm ready to be married, especially not to some old king."

"I'd wanted to wait, but your progress at school has been so good, it seems you're ready now. And the sooner you are established in Allaux, the better." Teodora would say nothing about the assassination plan. "Galladium has been a very unsatisfactory ally, and I'm counting on you to change that."

"I'm not sure I can, all by myself."

Teodora almost couldn't bear to look at her daughter; she seemed so small and vulnerable huddled in the big chair. She wondered if the ritual had made her go soft. But neither of them had a choice. Teodora had received worrisome reports that Gauvain was looking to Maladena for a marriage, and Teodora could not allow that to happen. She wouldn't feel secure until one daughter sat on the Galladian throne, and another on the Norovaean.

She'd received word of Elektra's mishap in Lantura from Princess Zelenka, so it was only a matter of time before the girl came crawling back. Elektra had been full of herself, but only because she'd had everything handed to her. It was quite another matter to lead a small army through hostile territory in the winter. This time she'd have no money, no allies, no chance of success.

For the moment, all her hopes rested on this daughter, so she forced herself to smile at Zofya. "You've been taught everything you need, and you are an excellent student. Everything depends on your relationship with the king, and I'm certain you will win him over. He has a weakness for pretty women, and you, my dear, are very pretty."

"Am I? You're not just saying that because you're my mother?" Zofya flushed with pleasure, which made her even prettier. She'd inherited Teodora's dark hair, even features and pale skin, but she was altogether softer and daintier.

"I would never coddle you or give you false compliments; you know that about me by now. You've turned out well, and I'm pleased. It will make your job much easier. All you have to do is make your husband fall in love with you, and that ought to be easy enough. Once he sees you, and realizes how clever and sweet you are, it won't take long." Teodora drummed her fingers on the table, wondering how much information she ought to give Zofya. She decided a little was better than none. "You've probably heard rumors of the king's other relationships. The one with Natalya seems to be over, but he's now involved with Princess Gwynneth."

"But she's so beautiful," Zofya said. "And clever too. I can't compete."

"Gwynneth won't be around much longer. I'm sure the king will be sorry to see her go, but you can offer him comfort."

"I see." Zofya still looked uncertain, but she seemed to catch on quickly enough.

"And it's critical you have a child as soon as possible. Once you've given the king an heir, your position will be certain, and you will wield considerable power, whether or not the Galladians like it."

"Yes, I understand all about that." Zofya was looking more self-assured already. "I've learned a great deal about politics and the Galladian court, and I know having a baby is most important. I hope I will like the king well enough that it's not too hard."

"You liked him well enough when I first told you it might not work out. Quite the tantrum you threw, as I recall." Teodora remembered that with amusement.

"Yes, I remember. But that was before I met ..." Zofya trailed off, then closed her eyes. "Oh Mother, I've tried so hard to stop thinking of Aksel. I know I'll never see him again, but I worry I'll always be in love with him, and that my husband won't compare." A tear rolled down one cheek when she reopened her eyes.

So she hadn't forgotten.

Teodora was a little sympathetic, remembering her own engagement to a man she'd just met, and already disliked. She hadn't been in love with anyone else, but could think of a half dozen other young men she would have preferred. "You can't look at it that way. A husband is a husband, and love has little to do with your relationship. It's better if you can be friends, but it's not required. And once you've had a child or two, you can amuse yourself with a man more to your liking."

"That seems very far away," Zofya said. "And I can't picture liking anyone in Galladium. They'll all be odd and foreign."

"They will, at first. But in time, you'll become accustomed to them, and I'm sure you'll even meet people you like. I'll send a few of your friends and cousins with you to keep you company. But no matter how long you live there, or how many children of yours are Galladian royalty, never forget who you are and where you belong. You are an Inferrara, a daughter of Olvisya, and your first loyalty will always be to the empire. Is that understood?"

Zofya lifted her head, her eyes shining. "I understand."

GWYNNETH

Gwynneth had worried about a confrontation with Natalya when she reached Allaux, but nothing happened right away.

Gauvain came to her upon her return, her children in tow.

"Thank you for keeping them safe," Gwynneth said, after the excitement of their reunion had died down and they'd gone to the nursery. "I'm so sorry about Joslyn."

"Natalya won't return her." The king sat across from Gwynneth, looking weary, and as if he'd aged ten years while she'd been away. "I don't even know where she's keeping her. I suppose since using her as hostage for my good behavior worked once, she'll keep using her that way."

"I wish there were a way for me to help you somehow." Gwynneth felt a pang of helpless despair. "But I'm sure she'll never listen to me again. Was she furious?" Gwynneth whispered, casting a glance at the closed study door. At this point she trusted none of her servants, and hoped no one had a way of listening at the door. Upon her return, she'd had the room's furniture moved all the way to the windows, claiming she needed the light, especially now autumn was turning to winter.

"Oh yes." The king looked at the door too, and slid his chair a little closer to Gwynneth's. "She was very angry, though she remained calm. It was frightening, to be honest."

"I expected her to appear right away to shout at me," Gwynneth said. "I almost wish she would. I do feel terrible."

"You shouldn't," the king said. "This was my decision, and my mistake. You were only being a loyal friend."

"Not to Natalya," Gwynneth said.

She didn't have to wait long, though long enough that her nerves were tightly wound by the time Natalya appeared.

Gwynneth looked at her carefully, trying to gauge her mood. Natalya's eyes were hard, but that had been usual lately. When Gwynneth began with an apology, she raised her hand.

"There's no need for any of that," Natalya said. "It's in the past, and frankly, I don't wish to hear any excuse you've concocted."

Gwynneth's cheeks burned, but she bit her tongue. She probably deserved whatever was coming.

Natalya took a seat, warming her hands at the fire. She stared into the flames for a moment, then said, "We must look to the future, don't you agree?"

"I do," Gwynneth said. "I've given it a great deal of thought, and it's best that I leave, the sooner the better."

"Where would you go?" Natalya said. "I don't dislike being rid of you, but it seems hardhearted to put you and your children out just as winter is coming, especially since you have no home."

It was hard to keep from bursting into tears. Natalya no longer spoke to her as a friend, even an annoying one. It seemed Gwynneth had killed her oldest friendship. "I'll find a place," Gwynneth choked out.

"No." Natalya turned to face her. "I think it's best you stay here for a time. It seems you owe me a favor or two; don't you agree?"

Gwynneth nodded miserably, realizing she was unlikely to enjoy any task Natalya found for her.

"Good." Natalya settled back into her chair. "Once Terragand is safe, I won't keep you from joining your husband, but for now, you can make yourself useful here."

"All right," Gwynneth said, unsure if she should be relieved that at least Natalya wouldn't keep her from Kendryk. She prayed Lennart would hurry up and win.

"Let's start with the king," Natalya said.

"I understand if you don't want me to see him anymore. And since Joslyn is staying with you now, he has no reason to visit." It seemed best not to comment on that situation.

"He doesn't have that reason." Natalya smiled coldly. "But he'll still want to see you from time to time. He's become rather accustomed to complaining about me to you, and I hate to deny him that comfort. But when he sees you, things will be different."

Gwynneth couldn't speak, suspecting what was coming next.

Natalya leaned forward just a little. "From now on, you will report everything to me. Every detail of your conversation, no matter how irrelevant it seems."

"The king doesn't confide in me about policy."

"That's all right, though I'll be happier if you lead him in that direction."

Gwynneth nodded, realizing she'd find a way to leave Galladium as quickly as possible, no matter the weather.

"And I will know if you don't tell me the truth, or don't tell me everything."

Gwynneth wasn't sure how that could be true, but decided she didn't want to test it. "All right," she said, her mouth dry. "I'll tell you everything, no matter how trivial."

Natalya stood. "That's a good start." She turned toward Gwynneth. "I understand you don't like this, but don't plan on leaving right now. You will remain my guest here in this house and all your needs will be seen to. But I'm afraid I'm unable to come up with any pocket money for you, and can no longer keep up the expense of your own carriage. Naturally, you can use one of mine any time you want."

In other words, Gwynneth had no way to leave. And after the failure of her mission, she couldn't rely on the king to help her either. She would have to do as Natalya wanted, and wait for a chance to get away.

ANTON

Susanna poked Anton's ribs. "Time to get up, sleepyhead."

"Too cold," Anton muttered, snuggling closer to a warm, soft Susanna. He didn't need to look outside to see it would be another foggy day, impossible to stay warm no matter how hard they drilled. And they weren't drilling too hard right now, since no one expected a big battle before spring.

Susanna poked him again. "I'll get up too. That way you have no reason to stay." She flung the blankets off both of them, and jumped out of bed, scrambling into her clothes before Anton could move. No matter how motivated, he had never been able to get dressed that fast, even though his clothes were less complicated. Still, it was cold enough he got dressed quickly.

"Stay here," he told Susanna. "I'll see if someone has coffee." He grabbed a blanket from the bed and wrapped it around her shoulders, since her teeth already chattered. "I'll be right back." He kissed her on the nose, then grabbed his cloak and two tin cups before leaving the tent. It had probably been light for some time, although everyone slept late because of the gloom. But someone had built a fire, and Anton smelled the coffee. The quartermaster didn't let on where he'd found it, but Anton suspected the fellow of rooting around in a merchant's cellar in one of the towns along their way.

After another soldier filled Anton's cups, he made his way back to the tent, holding them carefully, making sure he didn't trip over anything. He'd just put both cups on the table in front of Susanna, when a nearby bugle sounded the alarm.

"Probably just a drill," Susanna said. Anton never heard it sounded for any real reason. As far as he knew, the enemy was at Birkenfels, some fifty leagues away, and unlikely to leave this time of year.

"I should go anyway." Anton reached for his pistols, but left his armor. It might help warm him, but it would be cold at first. "The sergeant has been counting us these last few times. Go back to bed if you want, and I'll join you later." He kissed Susanna again, then left the tent, falling in next to a few of his comrades passing by. One of them was still struggling into his clothes.

"Blasted awful time for a drill," one fellow said.

"They wouldn't do it at a good time," Anton said. "What's the fun in that?" He loaded his pistols as they walked. The last time he didn't bother, and the sergeant clubbed him across the ears for it. That seemed unfair, since few of the pikemen carried pistols, but Anton wasn't about to argue when the sergeant was in a mood.

They made their way to the little parade ground in the center of camp, and by the time they reached it, nearly the whole regiment was assembled. "What's going on?" Anton asked as he fell in next to Stasny.

"Drill, I expect." Stasny shrugged. "Can't see anything."

They stood around for a while, the damp chill seeping through Anton's cloak. "Wish they'd hurry, whatever they're doing."

Soon there was a commotion, as Count Michalek and several officers thundered onto the parade ground on horseback. "Form up," the count shouted, his face redder than usual. "We're under attack."

That seemed odd, since it was quiet all around. Maybe the enemy hadn't arrived yet. Anton waited for the sergeant to hurry over with orders. "Who's attacking us?" he asked.

"Lennart," the sergeant gasped. "The king of Estenor himself."

"The king is attacking us?" Anton found that hard to believe. "Personally?"

"That's what it looks like," the sergeant said. "The pike wagons will be here in a minute, but we'll start marching now. He's attacked the southern end of the valley and our cavalry is holding him off, but we must back them up."

Anton still hadn't quite grasped what was happening. This wasn't like any battle he'd ever been in, with it so quiet and no one seeming very upset. He tried to focus on what the sergeant was saying.

"We're outnumbered pretty bad if he's brought everyone. But if we're smart about it, we might keep them from getting into the valley."

Anton realized what the sergeant meant. They needed to stop the enemy long enough for everyone else to get away. He thought of Susanna, wondering if anyone had told her what was happening. She needed to gather the necessities and head north. "I need to let Susanna know," he said under his breath to Stasny.

"Someone will, I'm sure. They'll have time to get away."

"Gods, I hope so," Anton said, dancing on first one foot, then the other. It was all he could do to keep from breaking ranks, and running back to camp. "She'll need help."

"Steady man," Stasny said, looking sympathetic. "She'll get it. And likely she's been through this before."

"What if we lose?" Anton whispered, fear surging back. He was unlikely to be shot at by any big guns, but he thought of the numbers Lennart had. "If he's brought his whole army, there's no way we'll win."

"We don't know if he's brought his whole army," Stasny said. "Not yet at least."

ELEKTRA

Until the ambush, Elektra had never paid much attention to her small cavalry, but it impressed her with its performance now. Not only did it hold firm when she challenged Princess Zelenka's guards, but her rearguard fought an efficient action against their pursuers after they broke through. Elektra was in such a state she forgot to give the order, but her officers acted anyway. She hoped they would be as resourceful in the next weeks.

They might have escaped Princess Zelenka, but their prospects looked grim. Winter was coming on fast, and they'd abandoned all of their supplies during the ambush. At least Elektra and her officers carried a fair amount of coin so they could buy the necessities for a short time. They traveled through the eastern part of Arcius, so far untouched by war, so they found markets selling food, and barns full of hay.

But it wasn't safe to stay in Arcius, and Elektra didn't know what to expect in Sanova. She planned to contact her uncle in Novuk, but that was so far away, it would take weeks for him to respond, if he responded at all. He might not be at all inclined to help Teodora's daughter, no matter how much she told him she hated her mother. So she did her best to stock up on supplies while hurrying for the Sanova border.

Princess Zelenka, it seemed, decided not to pursue her, but Elektra was certain she'd sent word to Atlona. By now Teodora might have dispatched her own forces after her. Once she reached Sanova, it would be a little more difficult for them to apprehend her, legally at least.

Elektra shivered, pulling her cloak close around her. The land flattened out as they neared the border, and stretched out ahead, gray and featureless. The clouds hung so low, the horizon blurred into a hazy mass. Towns and farms were few, the long grass withered and gray.

Though her officers had been enthusiastic about their escape from the Zelenka palace, reality demoralized them as the days wore on. With such small numbers, they stood little chance, should they run into any of Lennart's allies.

Elektra hated having to go so far around Lantura and Podoska to reach Terragand, but she didn't dare risk staying in Kronland. She must get through Sanova somehow without starving; it was her responsibility and no one else's.

No one stopped them at the border. Sanova was at peace now, and likely didn't care about what went on in Kronland. The land was poor, the population sparse, and Elektra tried not to worry about where she'd next find food. They quickly ran out of hay, though the horses reluctantly ate the grayish grass. At least they wouldn't starve. But people couldn't eat that grass and Elektra saw nothing else for leagues around.

She rationed the little food they had, but though all of them were hungry all the time, they'd still run out in a few days. As they drew level with Podoska, Elektra considered raiding into it before her troops became too weak to do so. Farmers living near the border said that its army had gone to join Lennart, so the rural areas and borderlands might be poorly guarded.

Elektra didn't send out scouts, since Sanova wasn't hostile, and scouting took energy no one had. So she was surprised when she came upon a large cavalry camp at a crossroads one evening.

The sight of the Sanovan flag caused a cramp of anxiety, until Elektra remembered that Braeden Terris was no longer a Sanova Hussar. The hussars still fought for her mother, after being lured away from Mattila with everyone else..

Before riding into camp, Elektra washed her face and re-braided her hair. She looked a sight, since she hadn't changed clothes in several weeks after losing all of her things in the ambush. She ordered a page to polish up her rusty cuirass and her weapons. She doubted she'd appear belligerent, but wanted to look prepared for anything. She would need to beg for food, and hoped she would pull it off gracefully.

Once she was ready, she rode to the camp perimeter, flanked by her senior officers. "I'm the Archduchess Elektra," she said, remembering to sound haughty. "Take me to your commander."

The guard, a stout young man with a dull-looking face, nodded, his mouth wide open, then ran off. Elektra followed him, looking around the camp, wondering who commanded here. This was a Sanovan cavalry unit, but perhaps not Novitny's famed hussars. Still, it looked in good condition, and Elektra wondered if it was joining Ensden.

An officer came to greet her. "The commander will see you right away, Your Grace. Please follow me."

Elektra dismounted, and entered a large tent in the middle of camp. She bit back a squeak of dismay when she saw the officer in charge, a lanky red-headed young woman standing behind a map-strewn table. Even in the gloom of the tent, there was no question who it was.

Elektra lifted her chin, and hoped to keep her voice from shaking. "I believe we've met before, Captain Dura." She swept into a chair before being offered.

Dura looked down at her, then said, "I want to speak to the Archduchess alone." She waved to a servant, who led Elektra's officers back out.

Elektra's hand went to her dagger under her cloak, though she doubted she could do anything if this woman attacked her. But then she remembered that the captain, and not she, was in the wrong. She went on the offensive. "How is it you're in charge of the Sanova Hussars? It seems odd, after what happened in Brandana."

"What are you talking about?" Captain Dura sat down, glaring at Elektra. "We're reorganizing after being assigned back to Ensden. My superior retired, and I've been recruiting here, since Ensden's put me in charge. So you can refer to me as Colonel Dura, Your Grace." She said it with a frightening amount of venom, "And since I have the strong impression you will need my help, I suggest you make no unfounded accusations. Is that understood?"

KENDRYK

"It seems we're going overland," Tora Isenberg said, leaning across the table to hand Kendryk Lennart's latest dispatch. "The king wants us at Kaltental within the month, but all of his ships are busy blockading it."

"It says here he'll send them for us, if we want," Kendryk said after reading the message. He and Isenberg had returned to Prince Ossian's palace to coordinate with his army.

"It's unnecessary," Isenberg said. "The most important thing right now, is keeping Maladene supplies out of Kaltental. Besides, it's not far. If we leave soon, we'll get there well before Lennart arrives. I would rather keep those ships in place, and make things easier for us in the long run."

"Then I agree," Kendryk said. In the past few months he'd nearly made friends with the business-like Isenberg. It had taken some time to make her stop treating him like an incompetent youngster, but everything changed when he persuaded Prince Ossian to supply several thousand troops.

Kendryk had just about given up hope, even though the prince's cousin, the friendly Duke Arvus backed him consistently. But Kendryk received a letter from Braeden, sending greetings from his aunt in Oltena, and explaining that he and Trystan between them had brought four Kronland kingdoms into the alliance. Kendryk passed the news on to Prince Ossian rather casually, but the duke took it from there.

"It's humiliating," Duke Arvus shouted, stomping all over Ossian's chilly hall, his voice echoing from the rafters. "Everyone is doing their share, and here we sit, practically next door, too scared to move."

"I'm not scared," Prince Ossian said, "just cautious."

"That's wise of you," Kendryk said, shooting the duke a look, hoping he'd hold his tongue for a moment. "But think of how terrible your position will be when Lennart wins. Mattila is sure to throw herself to his side and then you'll be isolated. Terragand will always be your friend, but I'll have little influence at first." Kendryk hoped humility might do the trick. "I would hate it if Lennart caused you problems, but I won't be able to stop him."

"It's always best to choose the winning side," the duke added.

"I've chosen wrong before," Prince Ossian grumbled. "Arryk looked promising when he first arrived."

"Lennart is not Arryk," Kendryk said. "My brother-in-law is a fine man, but he came here without the backing he needed. Lennart hasn't made a significant move in all these months because he wants Kronland behind him. And now he has much of it. Unlike Arryk, he's an excellent general. Your troops won't be wasted."

It took most of the night and a great deal of wine, but between the two of them, Kendryk and the duke finally wore Prince Ossian down, and he agreed to send an army of five thousand to Terragand under Kendryk's and the duke's joint command.

Kendryk was pleased that he would arrive in Terragand at the head of a force that Lennart had no part in raising. Though Lennart's letters remained friendly, Kendryk worried he preferred to keep him out of the action as long as possible. If Lennart won Terragand without Kendryk's presence, it would be clear to everyone that Kendryk was nothing more than a puppet. He would have far more credibility if he contributed to a victory.

Before departing for Terragand, Kendryk wrote to Gwynneth, hoping the news that Lennart planned to engage soon would cheer her up. Her recent letters had been lacking in animation, very unlike her. She said little about what was happening, but Kendryk suspected it was because she was unable to. Every letter he received from her had been opened before being resealed, and he supposed his would be treated the same way. He wished he understood what Natalya was doing, and why it affected Gwynneth so terribly, but received no answers. Even Gauvain's letters were pleasant, boring, and devoid of any useful information. It seemed everyone was afraid of Natalya, and Kendryk couldn't wait to get his family away from her.

The morning of the army's departure dawned gray and cold.

"I'd never thought to do this in midwinter," Kendryk said to Isenberg as they rode along the beach. They would follow it for a time before the road turned inland, heading toward Terragand.

"Neither does Ensden, with any luck," Isenberg said. "We all learned to fight in the winter during the war against Sanova. The key is to set up solid supply lines so you don't have to live off the land. We don't use huge hordes of cavalry either, so we have fewer horses to feed than most armies."

Kendryk noticed that the general made meticulous preparations with her quartermasters, buying up vast amounts of supplies all over Ummarvik and renting warehouses in key towns. A steady stream of wagons would follow them all the way to Kaltental.

The icy wind blew sleet into Kendryk's face, but he smiled into it. If all went well, he was returning to Terragand for good..

LENNART

Lennart wasn't used to fighting on this kind of terrain, but this was a good place to practice. Little was at stake, but if he figured out a way to dislodge this small army, he would feel more at home in Kronland.

An imperial cavalry unit held the mouth of the valley, and Lennart knew his muskets would break it in no time. Pike were useless here. In fact, Lennart saw little need for them at all. His muskets were more accurate than any in the empire, his musketeers better-drilled and faster at reloading than any others. He kept his small cavalry in reserve, though even without Braeden in command, they were eager to be part of the action. "You'll have plenty to do once we get through this lot," he told a cavalry captain who had ridden over to receive his orders.

The captain frowned. "It sounds hot in there." He nodded toward the road running alongside the river, steep hills rising on the other side. Great billows of smoke came from it as the fog slowly blew away under a gray sky. The gunfire was muffled but steady.

"A bit warm." Lennart was twitchy. He wanted to get moving, since he would be leading the main force once the way cleared. "Won't be long now," he told the captain. "You can get your unit ready to go."

An adjutant came galloping up the road. "Our muskets have broken through, Your Highness," he said. "There's pike behind their cavalry, covering nearly all the flat ground, from what I can tell."

"They won't be there long." Lennart looked up at the steep hilltops. If the enemy commander had any sense, he would have placed his artillery up there. But with the valley so narrow, they would only be effective on a short stretch of road. Best to get down it before the fog cleared altogether and they could aim. He turned to Geffrey Manier. "Give the order," he said. "We're going in."

Another battalion of muskets marched forward, ready for Lennart to lead them. He liked what he saw up ahead. The enemy had a few thousand pike, but weren't able to deploy properly in the cramped space. The road crested a small hill, and Lennart noticed the enemy camp behind them, already in disarray. Everyone was getting out while they could. The only way to go was north, which suited Lennart just fine. He would likely kill a good number here, take even more prisoner, and let the rest run to Ensden, telling him what had happened.

It had been some time since he'd been in a proper battle, and the joy built up in Lennart , a wild feeling hard to hold back. He took his place at the head of the musketeers, and looked back at them. "Slow and steady now," he said. "Until they break." He paused for their laughter. "Then you can chase 'em all the way to Kaltental if you like."

A cheer went up behind him and Lennart urged his horse forward, the Estenorian standard fluttering above his head. He knew he made a nice, big target, but he didn't worry. The gods were with him in this, he felt it now. The light wind cleared the fog ahead of him, making it easy for the enemy to see what came toward them.

To their credit, the first ranks of the pike held firm much too long for their own good. Lennart hated seeing such stout fellows fall like that, but before long, his muskets mowed down the enemy with some regularity. Lennart kept a steady pace going forward, shouting encouragement, getting off shots with his pistols when he got a chance.

The first big block of pike broke and fled, causing confusion as they ran into the ranks behind them. Someone smart led there, as the block broke apart in orderly fashion, let those fleeing run through, and closed up again. Lennart spotted sleeves of musketeers at the edges of the pike, but that was the wrong place for them. If the muskets had been in front, it might have been a fairer fight.

The pike held firm, but only for a little while and by then, Lennart had ordered the cavalry forward. The remaining soldiers were already so demoralized, just the sight of mounted troops made them break and run. Lennart waded in with his saber, cutting down those who couldn't get away. It seemed plenty in the reserve ranks made for the Kaltental road without looking back. Lennart concentrated on those he could reach, and made prisoners of all who surrendered.

Before noon, he'd destroyed two regiments, killed one commander, and taken another prisoner. It seemed only one had gotten away, but with so few troops he was unlikely to make a stand anywhere near here.

Lennart looked around at the carnage, pleased. "That'll send Ensden a message. He can hide behind Kaltental's walls for now, but I'm coming for him."

BRAEDEN

"Lennart's made good progress." Braeden looked up from the message left for him at Birkenfels, handing it to Trystan.

"Why didn't he wait for us?" Trystan asked, giving the paper back to Braeden rather than passing it on to his sister, who clearly wanted to know what was going on. "I would have enjoyed a good fight."

"I doubt he needed us." Braeden noticed he wasn't as unhappy about missing out on a battle as he used to be. "He can manage more easily if we're not all in the same place until he's ready to fight Ensden."

Trystan paced the floor of the tiny library. "What if we don't reach him in time? What if Ensden engages him too soon?"

Braeden moved closer to the fire, warming his frozen hands. They were aching in a way that worried him. He hated the idea of turning into an arthritic old man before he was done here. "We'll be lucky if Ensden engages him at all, though likely Lennart will try to starve him out."

"Will someone tell me what's going on?" Karolyna Martinek snapped, grabbing the message from the table.

Braeden didn't care for the duchess. She was a lot like Trystan in demeanor, and even a little bit in looks, with that reddish hair and odd yellow eyes. But while Trystan tempered his belligerence with humor and an admirable amount of loyalty, Karolyna possessed no such virtues. All she cared about was victory in battle.

"To be fair, she doesn't have much choice," Trystan had told Braeden once. "Being the heir to Podoska means nothing if she can't hold the throne by force. I can think of at least two brothers and a sister who'd be happy to grab it from her if they could."

"Doesn't she worry they'll take it while she's gone, if something happens to your mother?"

Trystan shrugged. "Even if someone tries it, Karolyna's got the army, and no doubt she'll get Lennart's backing if she needs it."

"So why didn't she come out to fight when you did several years ago?"

"She was pregnant. Left to her own devices she would have gone anyway, but her husband and Mother forced her to stay. She's never forgiven me for that."

"Karolyna has children?" Braeden couldn't picture a less maternal person, except for perhaps, Teodora.

"Three at least," Trystan said, shaking his head. "Might be more by now. I stay far away from that lot, since she has the most awful brats."

"Worse than the rest of you?" Braeden hoped Trystan realized he was joking.

"Probably not worse." Trystan grinned and shook his head. "You make a good point."

After that, Braeden tried to see Karolyna differently, although he had to admit his knowledge didn't make her any more pleasant or friendly. Mostly, Karolyna seemed to think Braeden was so far beneath her he didn't exist, and she only addressed him if he stood directly in her way.

Karolyna read the message, crumpled it into a ball, and threw it on the floor. "Wonderful." She stomped around the room while Trystan joined Braeden at the fire, rolling his eyes. "This is dated nearly a month ago. Lennart is probably at the gates of Kaltental by now."

"Probably," Trystan said. "We'd better join him as soon as we can then."

Braeden was silent, thinking. Something bothered him about the whole plan.

He was silent long enough that Trystan noticed. "What's wrong?"

"I'm not sure," Braeden said. "Just a hunch. I understand Lennart needs us at Kaltental, but I'm worried."

"There's no one else to worry about," Karolyna said with a snort.

"Elektra's out there," Braeden said.

"With a few hundred troops," Trystan said.

Braeden still couldn't shake the feeling. "It's probably not her, but it might be someone else. Or maybe it's nothing."

Trystan frowned. "Your instincts are better than anyone's. We shouldn't disregard them."

"Well, I will," Karolyna said loudly. "This is ridiculous. Lennart needs our numbers at Kaltental and has ordered us to go, so we're leaving now."

Braeden was inclined to agree, but still didn't feel good about it. He went ahead with his preparations, but Trystan was far too perceptive. "You won't rest until you're certain the archduchess is no longer a threat."

"I doubt it's her," Braeden shook his head. "I worry that Terragand is vulnerable, with all of Lennart's forces concentrated so far north. It's the perfect time for Teodora to make a grab."

"If she can. All of her resources are tied up with Ensden, and Lennart will trap him."

"As far as we know. That's the part that bothers me." Braeden appreciated Trystan's trust, but wished he had something more concrete than a hunch to offer him. "And there's something else. I'm sure the Sanova hussars serve Ensden now, but it makes little sense he'd keep them up there, trapped inside the city. He'd make better use of them sending them around to outflank us."

Trystan's eyes lit up. "That makes a great deal of sense. They'll wait until we all head north, then block us up in the Velta valley, just like Lennart is doing to the enemy right now. Fall on our rear while we're busy with Ensden." He paused for a moment then said. "I agree with you and think we should make provision for it. Lennart will understand and no doubt approve."

"Will he? His orders were exacting."

"They are, but I'm sure he hasn't considered this. Why don't we do this: you'll take most of the cavalry and patrol this area. We still hold the Garsten Gap, so no one will get through there. But if anyone else tries the route we took, you'll find out and be able to meet them. Even if you aren't enough to stop them, you can slow them down and let the rest of us know what's coming."

"Are you sure?" Braeden asked. "Your sister won't like it."

"This isn't her decision," Trystan said, a gleam in his eye. "You needn't take any of Podoska's troops, but you can have the Lantura cavalry and I'll offer all of mine. That'll give you nearly a thousand. It's not enough to stop a big force, but will be more than enough for a smaller one. What do you say?"

"I say that sounds like a good plan.".

TEODORA

"I don't understand what's taking so long." Teodora regarded Livilla sharply. "You promised Aksel would be converted soon, but it's been months and nothing has happened. Perhaps I need to use more forceful methods."

"He's difficult to persuade," Livilla said. "I haven't talked to Father Marcus in some time, so I will see how things are going, and if we must, make adjustments. But there's no rush, since Elektra isn't here and likely won't be for awhile."

Teodora ground her teeth. After escaping Princess Zelenka's ineffective clutches, Elektra crossed the Sanovan border and disappeared. Teodora's angry letters to her brother and his wife, Queen Ottilya, went unanswered, as usual. That they might harbor Elektra filled her with unease. On her own, Elektra wasn't much of a threat. But what if she persuaded her uncle and the queen to back her against Teodora? With Sanova no longer at war, they might put considerable resources behind her. "I'll get that girl back here, one way or another."

After Livilla had gone, Teodora decided she didn't want to wait any longer. She left her study and went straight to the family wing of the palace. She paused outside the old nursery, hearing a hissing noise and lively chatter through the door. Teodora opened it and swept in.

Aksel and a dark-haired young man stood at a table, staring intently at a yellowish liquid which smoked, bubbled, and made a dreadful noise in a beaker. Aksel looked up as Teodora entered. "Your Highness?" The question in his voice was no doubt because of her deteriorated appearance. Teodora had forgotten that he hadn't seen her in some months.

"Don't mind me," she said, then nearly choked on a foul smell rising from the beaker.

"We'd better stop," Aksel said. "Can you put it away?" he asked the young man as he came toward Teodora. "What is it, Your Highness? Is it the archduchess?"

It took an instant for Teodora to realize he was asking about Elektra. It was possible he knew nothing about what had happened to her in the past several months. "Oh, she's fine. With the army, somewhere in... well, I'm not exactly sure where she is right now."

"I was worried," Aksel said. "She never said goodbye or wrote. I wondered if I'd offended her."

"Oh, she just had to leave in a hurry. Come, let's take a little walk." Teodora took Aksel by the arm and steered him into the corridor. She was about to choke on the terrible fumes clogging the room.

"All right. Be sure you seal that bottle, Marcus," Aksel called over his shoulder. "And open a window."

"So you're finding Father Marcus a help to you?" Teodora asked as they walked down the long corridor. It wasn't the ideal place for a chat, but at least she didn't need to worry about eavesdroppers.

"Oh yes," Aksel said, eyes all aglow. "He's a marvelous scientist, but so knowledgeable about many other things. Our conversations are fascinating."

"Do you discuss religion?" Teodora looked at Aksel out of the corner of her eye.

To her surprise, Aksel flushed. "Well, as it turns out, religion is an area where I know more than he does."

Teodora laughed. "That's impossible, since Father Marcus was trained by the League of Aeternos. Surely no one would be better versed in religion."

"The League training is excellent; I agree." Aksel stopped in the middle of the corridor and turned to face Teodora, hands clasped behind his back. She wondered if he always stood that way when he was about to embark on a tedious lecture. "But it's still lacking. Those of us following the Quadrene Creed have had a few years' head start in studying the Scrolls. I'd like to think Marcus has perhaps learned more from me than I have from him."

Teodora stared at him. "Surely you're not saying Marcus believes your views are even a tiny bit correct."

"That's exactly what I'm saying. In fact, of late he's been reading the sermons of Edric Maximus and has found them very enlightening." Aksel's blue eyes behind the spectacles were so guileless, it occurred to Teodora he didn't realize what he'd just admitted.

Perhaps she could lead him further. "Is that so?" she asked, trying to sound innocent. "It sounds like you've nearly turned Father Marcus into a Quadrene."

"I don't know about that." Aksel flushed modestly. "But I like to think I've at least persuaded him to understand why I believe the way I do. If he comes to the true faith, it will be through the guidance of the gods, not because of my efforts."

Teodora was dumbfounded. It sounded like Aksel had nearly succeeded in a conversion when it was supposed to be the other way around. Teodora would need to get rid of Marcus before he turned heretic himself. "That's very, hm ... interesting," she managed. "You ought to be congratulated." She rounded on him then, and Aksel's eyes grew wide. "You've led a League cleric into heresy. Few do that and live to tell about it. Of course, Father Marcus will not."

It seemed what he had done had finally dawned on Aksel. "Your Highness, please. Don't punish Marcus for this. We've only been talking; I'm sure his faith remains as firm as ever." There was no question of the panic in his eyes.

"We'll see about that." Teodora folded her arms and looked up at Aksel, smiling. "I'm afraid he must explain himself to the temple interrogators."

"Oh please, no." Aksel's voice trembled. "Please. This is all my fault. Please punish me instead."

It seemed the idiot really cared about his friend. Teodora wondered how she could put that to use. She needed leverage over her daughter and she needed it soon. "I have the perfect solution," she said, her smile sweet. "First, we will meet with Livilla Maxima and you will dedicate yourself to the true faith."

Aksel made a choking noise. "I can't—"

"I'm sure the gods will understand you're doing it to spare your friend's life."

"Surely, Your Highness, there must be—" Aksel's face was the picture of anguish.

"There is no other way," Teodora said, enjoying her victory. "You will convert now, or Father Marcus will die. Die horribly, I might add."

"My brother was right—you are a monster. I'm sure you realize the gods will condemn you for this, along with your other atrocities."

"You needn't worry about my relationship with the gods. Now come, let's go to the temple and when we're done there, I'll help you write Elektra a letter, telling her about your newfound faith."

"I'm afraid I don't understand." Aksel was flushed, still trembling with anger.

"Come along now." Teodora took Aksel's arm and dragged him down the corridor while he cast anxious glances toward the nursery. Naturally his friend would be gone by the time he came back. "Elektra will be pleased to learn you're no longer a heretic."

ANTON

During the attack, they abandoned everything except for Susanna's cart.

"As long as we keep it, we can start over," she insisted, when Anton suggested leaving it behind so they could escape more quickly. Kaltental was still far away, the cart was heavy, and the roads terrible.

Once it became clear that Lennart was unstoppable, Count Michalek himself ordered his regiment's retreat. As a result, he was the only commander who survived the attack, along with most of his soldiers.

They didn't get far before realizing that the greater danger came not from the enemy, but from the elements. The shortest day of the year passed, and with it came a blizzard that never seemed to end. With no tent and no blankets, Anton didn't know how he'd keep the two of them alive.

"We'll need these things later," Susanna said, tears in her eyes, when Anton suggested trading their goods for warmer clothes, maybe even shelter somewhere.

"We won't need them at all if we're dead," Anton said, worried at Susanna's blue lips. "People are desperate for food and liquor; I'll drive a hard bargain."

She finally agreed and Anton crawled out of their little burrow, dug into a hillside, facing away from the wind. If they stayed huddled together, they might not freeze to death. It was daylight, but still dark as the wind drove snow sideways. Anton tucked a cheese and a bottle under one arm, and pulled his cloak tighter with the other. He knew where to start.

He struggled through deep snow and what passed for a camp. Almost everyone used what little equipment they'd salvaged to dig little caves like Anton and Susanna's. The highest-ranking officers had the good fortune to live in the huts of an abandoned village nearby. Anton saw smoke coming from a chimney, so he tried that door first.

He pounded on the door and heard "Go away," from inside.

Anton grinned, recognizing the count's voice. "I've got liquor," he shouted.

After some grumbling and rustling the door opened. Count Michalek looked a sight, his hair disheveled, his eyes blood-shot, a dirty blanket wrapped around his shoulders. "Oh, it's you," he said. "Don't remember your name, but I do remember that you've usually got liquor. And a pretty wife, if I'm not mistaken."

"Yes to both," Anton said, brushing the snow off his cloak before stepping inside. The one-room hut was crowded, with at least four other officers and two dogs lounging against the walls. A pot bubbled over the fire and the air was steamy. "I've got excellent Sanova brandy," Anton said, "and I can get more, but I'll want something in return."

"Cheeky, aren't you?" the count grumbled. "Though it's true I ran out of liquor two days ago and I'm not feeling so great. What do you want?"

"Shelter," Anton said, "And a few blankets."

"You won't fit in here," the count said, looking around the crowded room.

"I don't want to stay in here," Anton said, thinking he didn't want Susanna surrounded by officers who might be inclined to take liberties. "Where are your horses?"

"There's a little stable a few doors down," the count said, "though there's a couple servants already in there."

"Is there a hayloft?"

"Don't know." The count shrugged. "But you're welcome to work things out with those already there."

"And blankets," Anton said "At least two, nice thick ones."

"And what are you offering in return?" Anton handed over the bottle, and the count held it, staring at it longingly.

"That brandy," Anton said. "And this cheese. It'll go well with that stew over there." Whatever bubbled on the hearth didn't smell very good, but Anton's stomach growled anyway.

"I don't care about the cheese," the count grumbled. "But I'll need more liquor soon. I'll take all you've got."

Anton didn't want to give him everything, especially if the weather cleared and they were able to move on in a few days. "I'll give you as much as I can," he said, hoping to keep something to trade by the time they reached Kaltental. They might still have fancy clothes and food, but nothing sold like alcohol.

"All right," the count said. "Bring it now and you'll get a place in the stable, and we'll find a blanket or two for you. Oh, and I'll want a look at that pretty wife of yours too."

Anton kept from rolling his eyes. Frozen and pregnant, Susanna wasn't looking her best, and was unlikely to be her usual cheerful, flirtatious self. "All right," he said. "I'll bring more brandy and a young lady."

He hurried out into the blizzard, hoping he made it back before the count got too drunk and forgot their deal. Anton tucked his head down against the wind and made his way back to their burrow. It was hard to remember where it was, with everything covered in white and no noticeable landmarks.

But then he heard Susanna's shriek, cut off on the wind. Anton broke into a run in that direction. Before long, he saw a few shadowy figures ahead and heard Susanna's voice. "Let go of me, thief, or I'll kill you."

Anton drew his pistol, hoping his powder had stayed dry.

GWYNNETH

"It seems Zofya Inferrara is on her way here," Gwynneth said to Natalya. She was visiting the Maxima's palace, offering her weekly account of what she and the king had discussed in the previous few days. "Gauvain received a letter from Teodora saying it's time to finalize the marriage."

"Good." Natalya leaned back, looking satisfied. "It's past time to get this done. Perhaps having a young, pretty wife will help Gauvain to stop sulking."

"A teenage daughter of Teodora's," Gwynneth said. "I can't imagine her being much fun. Though I'm sorry for the poor thing. She's only fifteen."

"She'll be all right," Natalya said. "I met Zofya in Atlona, and even at twelve, she was very self-possessed. And there's another thing you can do to help me."

"What's that?" Gwynneth's heart sank. Informing on the king wasn't so bad. She'd let him know in so many words she was no longer a safe confidante, so he gave her more of the same: complaints about Natalya's stubbornness, musings on policy, and this last bit of information. Gwynneth wondered that Natalya didn't know about it already.

"You can make friends with her," Natalya said. "I doubt she'll want much to do with me, but you're another matter altogether."

"I can't imagine why she would like me at all, let alone want to be my friend."

"You have Maryna. She's young, but so serious, I'm sure she would be a good companion to a girl a few years older. And just think of the hope for the future, if Kendryk's and Teodora's children become friends. And secondly," Natalya leaned forward, an amused smile on her lips, "I learned something interesting about Zofya. It seems she fell in love with your little brother."

"With Aksel?" Such a thing had never occurred to Gwynneth, but it wasn't too surprising. Aksel was appealing in his way, and young girls especially might find him attractive. "Oh dear. No hope for that romance." She hoped it hadn't been too upsetting for Aksel, or worse, brought Teodora's anger down on him.

"No chance at all, the poor children." Something like sympathy passed Natalya's eyes. Sometimes Gwynneth wondered if she was softening up just a little. "But the fact is, as Aksel's sister, you might appeal to her. It doesn't hurt to try."

Gwynneth shrugged. "All right, I'll do my best."

"I know you will." Natalya smiled, then kissed Gwynneth on both cheeks as she took her leave.

Sometimes, it felt like nothing had changed between them.

A convoy of elaborate carriages bearing the Archduchess Zofya and her twenty attendants entered Allaux just a few weeks later. Gwynneth and Maryna received an invitation to the palace for the ceremony to welcome her.

"I'm very sorry for her," Maryna said as Catrin dressed her hair in a more adult style for the occasion. "She's so far from her family, has to marry a man she's never met, and now she must walk through the king's throne room with hundreds of strangers staring at her."

"I feel sorry for her, too," Gwynneth said. "Natalya thought you might make friends with her."

Maryna frowned. "I don't think so—has she forgotten Zofya is an Inferrara? I can't be friends with the daughter of the woman who treated Papa so dreadfully."

Gwynneth smiled at that. Maryna was nice to everyone, but also fiercely loyal, treating her friends' enemies with icy politeness. "I understand," she said. "But the archduchess was good friends with your Uncle Aksel, so perhaps she's all right."

"Perhaps." Maryna looked in the mirror as Catrin stepped back, and shook her head, curls bobbing on her shoulders. She sighed. "If Natalya wishes it, I will try. Though I'm sure she's brought friends of her own."

Gwynneth looked at Maryna in the mirror. With the more sophisticated hairstyle, she looked at least fifteen herself. She was turning into a pretty girl, though it seemed she might lack Gwynneth's startling beauty. Her hair had darkened to a light brown, her eyes were neither as wide nor as bright as Gwynneth's, and she had a hint of a snub nose. Gwynneth prayed it wouldn't get any worse. She smiled at Maryna. "None of her friends will be as nice as you. But don't worry, you needn't do anything today. It will take the archduchess time to settle in, and then there'll be a big wedding."

Maryna stood and faced Gwynneth. "Mama, will I have to marry a king someday?"

"Only if you want to." Gwynneth took her by the hand. "You'll have to marry someone suitable. It would be best if he can help you increase the power of Terragand. But when the time comes, I'm sure several men will meet those requirements, and you can choose the one you like best."

"I hope so." Maryna frowned as they made their way to the throne room, and Gwynneth decided not to mention she already had someone in mind. Kendryk wrote to her that Lennart had been impressed by young Toland Falk. Only a year younger than Maryna, he was not too closely related, and a marriage with Helvundala would be ideal. Still, it was too early to bring any of that up.

Gwynneth had to admit that Zofya conducted herself well. There was no question that Gauvain's throne room was intimidatingly grand, and the Galladian aristocracy were unabashedly curious about their new queen, not hesitating to remark about her loudly.

The girl was small and dark-haired, with a slight resemblance to Teodora. She carried herself well, and aside from flushed cheeks, did not appear to be nervous or worried at meeting her soon-to-be-husband. A long ermine cloak fell from her shoulders over a dark red, richly embroidered gown while a bevy of beautifully dressed women followed her.

When she reached the king, Zofya sank into a curtsy, but kept her dark eyes lowered for only a moment, and was ready to meet the king's when he came down the stairs to take her hand. "Welcome, Your Grace," he said, giving her a warm smile, the one he did best.

Gwynneth thought the archduchess's answering smile appeared quite genuine. Gauvain had worried she'd find him old and unattractive, but Gwynneth had reassured him that his charm and kindness more than made up for any shortcomings. Besides, when it came to husbands, looks weren't all that important. Gwynneth was certain she'd still love Kendryk even if he weren't handsome.

Gauvain murmured something into Zofya's ear and she nearly laughed, though she stopped herself. Her smile remained, showing a rather sweet dimple in her right cheek. By the time Gauvain led her into the banquet hall, they were both smiling, their heads together like old friends.

As Gwynneth followed, she offered up a prayer that the king would find happiness with this girl and that Natalya's influence would wane as a result.

ELEKTRA

"But I must get to Kaltental before there's a battle," Elektra said, aware that she always sounded whiny in front of Franca Dura.

"Why?" Franca shook her head "My orders are to attack Terragand from the east. This is the best kind of work for cavalry; Ensden won't need you near the city."

Elektra wanted to argue that her infantry would be needed, then remembered for the thousandth time she didn't have one. Even though she'd become accustomed to leading cavalry and had gotten to know her officers, it wasn't the same. She needed to get another infantry regiment, and the only way to do that was to show Count Ensden what an effective leader she was. "I'm not much good at this," she admitted. Franca was hard to deal with, but Elektra found that honesty went over well, especially if she made herself look bad.

"You're not," Franca said. They rode side-by-side along a quiet Sanovan road, heading north until they could turn west into Terragand. "But you might still learn."

"I never paid much attention to cavalry tactics," Elektra said. "The only things I ever learned, Braeden taught—" She didn't catch herself in time, and peered fearfully at Franca. They never mentioned him, and it seemed better that way.

Franca turned toward her. "So let me get this straight. Braeden kidnapped you, but because he's a kind man, he didn't kill you and even taught you some useful things."

So they would have it out now. Elektra nodded, deciding there wasn't much point in arguing that Braeden only spared her hoping to harm Teodora even more.

"So, he didn't kill you, and he helped get you back to Mattila, while you surely promised you wouldn't betray him. Which you did the moment you walked into camp." Franca threw her a contemptuous glance, then turned away, muttering a curse under her breath.

"I had to do it," Elektra whispered.

Franca rounded on her. "Oh really? No, you didn't. You could have let him deliver you to Mattila, and let him escape."

"He escaped anyway, thanks to you." Elektra wished she didn't sound so defensive. After all, it was Franca who'd practically committed treason.

"Barely," Franca said. "And who knows if he survived. If I find out he's dead, I'll kill you."

Elektra didn't know what to say to that, and pulled her horse a little farther away from Franca.

Franca was practically snarling now. "Maybe I'll kill you anyway." She looked back at the officers following them, and Elektra followed her gaze. She wondered if any of them would defend her if Franca tried anything.

"That would be unwise," Elektra tried hard to keep her voice steady. "It's bad enough you deceived Mattila, but killing me would make you a traitor and rebel for sure."

"Huh," Franca said. Her eyes were still narrowed, but she seemed to calm down a little.

Elektra prayed it would be enough, and resolved to double her own guard, especially when she slept.

There was not much love lost between the two forces. Franca's cavalry didn't possess the reputation and quality of the Sanova Hussars, and Elektra's officers saw them as barbaric mercenaries.

Elektra had always found the wings and lances of the hussars rather romantic, but Franca did away with those. "I recruited quickly," she explained to Elektra, "and didn't have time to train lancers. So this lot will just have to do with pistols."

Elektra thought she ought to work on training her own forces better, but Franca left no time for that. "My orders are to harass Lennart's rearguard and that's what I plan to do. If you want to head north and join Ensden, be my guest. Of course, you'll receive no further help from me."

And that was the problem. Elektra still had no food of her own, and her money was gone. Snow covered the ground, and the horses ate only because Franca sent a constant stream of outriders to gather hay from the few farms in the area. There was a slight chance she could get to Novuk and her uncle before they starved, but she had no idea how he'd receive her. And even if he welcomed her, she doubted she would then be able to reach Kaltental before a battle. Especially since Lennart was already on the move.

"We heard Lennart left Birkenfels with most of his force a few weeks ago," Franca said. "The rest of the Kronland armies will most likely join him, since he will need every last soldier if he's to be a match for Ensden. That ought to make Terragand easy pickings for us."

Elektra didn't know what to do. She prayed to Vica for guidance as earnestly as ever, but received no sign. She wondered if Franca herself was the sign, unpleasant as the thought was. She'd have to decide soon, before Franca turned toward Terragand. Perhaps something would happen to change their path and Franca would help her get to Ensden after all. And in the meantime, Elektra would do her best to make sure she did nothing further that might make Franca want to kill her.

KENDRYK

Kendryk was dismayed to approach Kaltental in terrible weather with no sign of Lennart.

Isenberg didn't seem bothered. "I'm sure the weather's slowed him down," she said. "He'll be here soon. And with so many of the enemy scattered about, I'm sure we can keep ourselves occupied."

Kendryk wasn't sure what that meant, but Isenberg soon made it clear. Most of Ensden's force was inside the city, but he'd sent smaller ones to garrison the surrounding towns.

"Might as well clear them out while we wait for Lennart," Isenberg said. "Who knows, if we make them suffer enough, it might draw Ensden out?"

"But we don't want him to come out yet," Kendryk protested, horrified at the thought of being attacked before Lennart arrived.

"Ah yes, timing is always a problem," Isenberg said, apparently unbothered at the prospect of total disaster. "But we're not alone. Duke Orland is operating to our south, and Generals Kalstrom and Lofbrok are just across the sound from us, on the other side of the city. They won't let us face Ensden alone."

"Well, you know best." Kendryk attempted a smile, though his mouth felt rather dry. He wondered when he'd become so fearful. He couldn't remember being this frightened even as Teodora marched on him with all of her armies. Of course back then, he was unbearably depressed by the combination of Gwynneth's betrayal and destroying his own country to thwart Teodora. Now he had relatively little responsibility, and leisure to worry about his own skin. Back then, he'd hoped for death, while now he wanted nothing more than life. He missed his family terribly, and more than once considered how he might make his excuses to Isenberg and return to Allaux until Lennart won.

"It'll be all right," Count Faris told Kendryk as they rode toward their own part of camp. "Tora Isenberg knows what she's doing. Letting Ensden defeat her the way he did turned out to be smart."

"You mean she did it on purpose?" Kendryk found that hard to believe.

"Maybe not exactly, but she made an easy escape, and did a good job drawing Ensden's troops into her guns. Considering how outnumbered she was, she gave them a good pounding and escaped with few casualties. And no enemy soldier who faced those guns will soon forget them." Faris chuckled. "Those were just a small sample of what's to come. If Lennart can choose the right place to fight, he'll annihilate Ensden."

"You seem confident," Kendryk said with a grin. "And your assessment of Isenberg is extremely favorable. Are you sure you aren't interested in more than a professional relationship with her?"

That made Faris laugh. "She's a fine woman, but I'm sure I'm much too old for her. That doesn't mean I can't enjoy working with her."

"She seems to like working with you too." Kendryk would be pleased if the loyal Faris found happiness, even if it was late in life. He'd been widowed before Kendryk was born, and Kendryk often wondered why he never remarried.

Faris laughed again and shook his head, though he didn't seem at all bothered by the idea.

If Isenberg's operation was any sign of the competence of the rest of Lennart's army, Kendryk had to admit he was impressed and optimistic. Without the least bit of concern for the cold weather, Isenberg set about taking over every town on the west side of Kaltental. Her little, highly mobile guns weren't heavy, but she used them to great effect, concentrating their fire on the weak spots of every fortification.

The gates usually broke down within hours, then columns of disciplined musketeers rushed in and finished off the garrisons, most often with few casualties themselves. Only one town had a wall and gate strong enough to hold, so after blasting away at it for a few days, Isenberg shrugged and gave the order to move on. "They can rot for now," she said. "They'll run out of food soon enough."

Kendryk hoped that was also true of Kaltental. Several great storms came through, so Lennart's fleet scattered to various harbors with only a few ships near the city itself. He worried that Maladena's supply ships would take advantage of the situation, but no one had seen them.

"If those Maladene captains are smart, they're staying cozy in Arenberg," Isenberg said. "When the weather improves, our ships can get back to Kaltental a lot faster than theirs can."

Kendryk hoped that things inside the city were getting desperate. He didn't wish for the citizens to suffer, but wanted them to lose patience with Ensden's army, and encourage him to come out. After seeing how easily Isenberg took down one town after another, he began to hope for an easy victory.

ANTON

Anton rushed toward the shadowy figures outside his burrow.

"Hey!" he shouted, holding up a pistol. "Stop right now or I'll shoot."

One man heard him, and stumbled aside in the snow, though the other hung onto Susanna's arm. "We'll take that cart of yours and leave you be."

"No." Anton advanced on him. "Let go of her and leave now."

"Don't think I will."

The man snatched Susanna around the waist and pulled her close. A knife's blade flashed, and Susanna whimpered as he pressed it to her cheek.

At this range, Anton was a good enough shot he could hit the man without hurting Susanna. He aimed carefully and pulled the trigger. Nothing. He'd been right to worry about keeping his powder dry in this weather. "All right," he said, lowering it, wondering what to do next. Whatever it was, would have to be fast.

"Jorge," the man said to the one who'd been inching away. "Grab that cart. And since the little boy can't stop us, we'll take the girl too."

"That wasn't part of the plan," Jorge said, though he moved toward the cart parked next to the burrow, a snow-covered canvas across the top of it.

"Plans change." The other man leered into Susanna's face, and she shuddered while his free hand ran down her front. "Oh hey." His hand stopped on her belly. "Looks like she's got one in the oven."

"Let her go," Anton said. "Or I'll kill you." He'd do it too, even though he didn't yet know how. He tried to catch Susanna's eye, because he'd need her to help somehow.

"Oh, I don't mind," the man said. "I'm not picky that way. Not at all."

Anton kept his eyes trained on Susanna, so he caught it as she tensed up and shot her elbow into the man's groin. Sometimes, being so short was an advantage. The man yelped and backed away a step, though he still held the knife.

371

"Move!" Anton shouted at Susanna as he barreled toward the man, switching his pistol to the other hand. It would work well enough as a club. Susanna yanked herself out of the man's grasp, falling sideways into the snow, and Anton hoped she wasn't hurt. He'd have to worry about that later, and charged toward the man, who was a bit shorter, but a lot sturdier than Anton.

Anton raised the pistol and caught the man's arm with the butt. The man yelped while the knife tumbled into the snow and disappeared. Out of the corner of his eye, Anton saw Susanna scrambling for it. He swung at the man again, catching him on the ear hard enough to make him go down. Anton jumped on top of him, their combined weight pushing them deep into the snow.

Anton pressed down on the man's throat with the pistol barrel and pulled out his dagger with his free hand. His head heated up, the way it did in battle. His ears rang, and a pink mist rose in front of his eyes. His face felt wet, and he realized the pink mist was blood, spraying into his eyes. He tried to get off the man, but fell back onto his thrashing legs. The man was gasping, holding his throat and making a horrid gurgling sound. Anton still held his pistol in one hand, a bloody dagger in the other. He stared at it; he couldn't remember using it. Susanna pulled on his shoulders.

"Anton." She was breathing hard. "We've got to get out of here. I tried to go after the other fellow with the knife, but he got away."

Anton staggered to his feet, struggling to balance in the snow. "We can go to the count. He'll give us shelter."

"We can't." Susanna clung to his arm, tears streaming from her eyes, though her voice was firm. "He yelled at me that he was going straight to the count to tell him you'd murdered a man over a girl."

"What'll we do?" Anton wiped blood from his face. Even in his confusion, Anton was proud of Susanna's self-possession. He looked down at the body, rapidly being concealed by snow.

"We'll cover it up," Susanna said, "and we'll leave."

"Leave? Right now?" Suddenly exhausted, Anton wasn't able to think. "We'll die out there."

"Maybe." Susanna wiped her tears and climbed through the snow to her cart. "But it's better than having you hang. I couldn't bear that." She sniffled as she rummaged in the cart. "Get into the cave," she said to Anton over her shoulder. "Take off that bloody shirt and doublet, and I'll find you something else. We'll put on all the clothes I have in here and dump everything we can't eat. And we'll go right now, since everyone will be stuck here until the storm is over."

"All right." Anton crawled into the burrow and pulled his shirt off, shoving it out into the snow. Without the two of them in here, it was freezing, and he shivered until Susanna handed him another one. Made of fine, embroidered silk, it wouldn't be very warm, but Susanna gave him two more, and a linen one to put over that. A velvet doublet completed the look, though the sleeves were too short, and it was rather tight over all of the shirts.

Out in the snow, Susanna pulled on two pairs of breeches and shed her skirt. Once they'd put on as many clothes as they could, they shoved the rest into the burrow, along with nearly a dozen bottles of brandy.

"We'll keep a few bottles for ourselves," Susanna said.

Anton was starting to realize that he'd just murdered a man, and even though he'd had good reason, he was frightened and sad at the same time. His teeth chattered, but not from the cold.

"You need a drink right now." Susanna handed him an open bottle. "It'll warm you up. Hurry."

While he took a few swigs, she pulled out all the food in the cart along with two bottles, then wrapped it all in the canvas cover. "The cart will slow us down," she said. "We can take turns carrying this." She shoved the bundle into Anton's arms while she pushed more snow over the corpse.

Anton was no longer accustomed to alcohol and it went straight to his head, though it felt deliciously warm. He hoped he'd be able to walk, then remembered to pray. He usually didn't, but realized they'd need help outside the ordinary if they were to survive out there.

LENNART

"There's no point in carrying on in this weather." Tavio Sora was as negative as ever.

"I suppose you're right." Lennart looked out the window at the whirling snow and stopped himself from pounding the table in frustration. He prided himself on being able to move his army in any weather, but it seemed this blizzard would thwart him. "At least the enemy won't be able to move either." As the weather worsened, Lennart had halted his march in a small town at a bend in the river.

Most of the citizens had fled as the remnants of the enemy army marched through a few days before, but they returned quickly, as soon as the army was gone. This was no time of year to hide in the woods. Lennart sent messengers ahead to reassure the townspeople they needn't leave on his account. He'd quartered his troops on them, but they knew to behave or they'd answer to him. He'd sweetened the deal by bringing a small, heavy chest of coin to the burgomaster's house, which resulted in a friendly invitation. The house was comfortable, and the man had a pretty daughter, a young widow whose husband had died in battle a few years ago.

Lennart loved Raysa dearly, and wrote to her every day he wasn't on the road, but he still enjoyed a pretty face and a bit of flirtation every now and then. Still, being cooped up indoors while the storm raged made him restless. He decided to brave it for a moment to go to the stables. He was likely to find a few officers there, exchange a few jokes and perhaps smoke a pipe. Lennart had taken up the habit after Alona Brynner introduced him to some excellent tobacco, imported from the Maladene colonies overseas. He hoped he didn't run out before the battle, because he doubted he'd find any more before Kaltental.

He'd just made himself comfortable on a barrel in the barn, when a snow-covered messenger burst through the door. "Been looking all over for you, Your Highness," he said.

Lennart jumped down. "Is it the enemy?"

"No, it's Trystan Martinek, marching into town with a large force."

"I'll go meet him," Lennart said, forgetting about the storm. "No, wait, bring him and his officers to the house." He turned to one of his own officers. "Get to the quartermaster, see about accommodations and something to eat right away. I'm sure they'll be cold and hungry." He shook his head and muttered, "Showing up in this weather, the rascal," before hurrying back to the house, a smile on his face.

"Sweetheart," he said, poking his head into the little parlor where the pretty widow sat with her knitting. "Could you cook up a big mess of something? Seems we're having a few generals over for dinner. Oh, and bring up more of that wonderful wine you have."

"Certainly, Your Highness." The woman had already dropped her knitting and offered Lennart a dazzling smile. "I'll make a big pot of my potato soup. It's quite famous here in town."

"I'll bet it is." Lennart chuckled, then went back to the front hall and paced until the door opened, blowing in Trystan Martinek on the swirling snow. A woman came in behind him, along with a few other officers.

"Have you lost your mind?" Lennart clapped Trystan on the shoulder, knocking great clumps of snow to the slate floor. "Marching around in this weather?"

"We didn't want to delay." Trystan shed his hat and cloak, wiping away snow that had collected in a scraggly beard. It did nothing to make him look older. "And it wasn't too bad until a few leagues from here. Then we decided we might as well head for real shelter."

"Good man." Lennart couldn't stop grinning. He looked over Trystan's shoulder. "And this must be the young lady." He winked at Karolyna Martinek, and was met by a scowl, though she covered it with a quick bow and a brusque "Your Highness." No flirting with this one then. Not that he wanted to. Lennart decided the duchess wasn't bad-looking, but her demeanor was rather unpleasant. Not his type at all. He was glad Braeden had convinced him to let Trystan have command of the Oltena and Isenwald forces. "Come in," he said, leading the way to the dining room. "The lady of the house is preparing something warm for you right now. You can tell me the news while you eat."

He'd already noticed Braeden's absence. "I hope Terris is all right," he said as they sat down. The widow bustled in with bread, cheese and the promised wine.

"He's fine," Trystan said, "but he's stayed behind with most of the cavalry. I hope you don't mind."

"I assume he had good reason," Lennart said, though judging by Karolyna's scowl, she didn't agree. He took a long drink of wine. "Why don't you tell me what's happened."

TEODORA

"There's nothing for you to worry about." Teodora gave Aksel her nicest smile. The poor boy had been so miserable lately. "I'm sure the archduchess will write back soon. She likes you very much."

They sat in Teodora's study where Aksel had just finished writing Elektra a second letter, after the first had met with no response. Teodora had sent a copy to Sanova and one to Kaltental, just in case Elektra really had joined Ensden. The weather had been terrible everywhere, slowing everything down, including the mail.

"There's nothing she can do to help me." Aksel's eyes were red-rimmed, and nothing remained of his usual liveliness. Teodora's spies reported he hadn't set foot in his laboratory ever since Father Marcus's arrest.

"She can keep you out of the Arnfels." Teodora offered a broad grin, then laughed to herself at Aksel's shudder. She was certain he considered her evil personified.

"I don't care if you send me to the Arnfels again," Aksel said, his voice dull.

"Oh, you will. I'll be sure to make it worse than the last time. And I'm sure the archduchess will care."

"I'd rather go there than spend any more time with you." Aksel looked up, a spark of rebellion in his eyes.

"No need to be rude." Teodora enjoyed it when Aksel showed spirit. Normally he was rather bland, compared to his siblings. "I'm only doing what's best for the empire, and ultimately that will benefit you as well."

"I don't see how." Aksel glared at her. "You've taken me away from my home, imprisoned or killed my best friend, forced me to convert to a religion I detest, and write lies about it to your daughter. And don't even get me started on your daughters." Aksel brought a fist down on the table, and Teodora jumped, though she was enjoying herself. "I don't know what you've done with Elektra, but it's clear you have no idea where she is or what she's doing."

Teodora rolled her eyes. "Aren't you clever."

"You've obviously done something to drive her away, and I'll be very surprised if she responds to any of your letters."

"They're *your* letters, remember?"

"She'll know you're behind them. I would say none of those things to her the way you wanted me to say them. She knows me better than that and won't be fooled for an instant. But I doubt very much that anything you've done to Elektra is as bad as what you've done to Zofya." Now his face was turning red. "What kind of horrible mother sends her fifteen-year-old daughter to marry a stranger twice her age? I can't imagine what she's going through right now." Aksel's lip trembled.

Teodora wondered if he really had cared for Zofya more than he let on. He was more than upset enough on her behalf. "Zofya will be fine," she said. "She will be Queen of Galladium if she isn't already."

"Has it ever occurred to you that perhaps she doesn't care about that?"

"No, it hasn't." Teodora leaned forward, smirking as Aksel shrank back. "What she cares about or wants is irrelevant. I'm surprised you don't realize it already, being a king's son. Though it appears you had a rather lax upbringing."

"You're hardly one to criticize my parents." Aksel was as angry as she'd ever seen him. "And you'd better believe you'll be sorry about this before long."

Teodora laughed out loud. "Are you threatening me?"

"As if I could." Now Aksel's eyes bored into hers, and Teodora found it hard not to shrink back herself. "No, I'm just telling you what will happen. You started something you can't control and now you have too many enemies. When even your children hate you, it's a bad sign, in case you didn't realize it. Your own lover trying to kill you should have made you understand you're beyond help."

That was going too far. Teodora slammed a fist down on the table. "Shut up, you insignificant little—"

Aksel stood suddenly, then glared at her. "All your deeds will come back to you a hundredfold." He leaned down, propping his fists on the table, his face now uncomfortably close to hers. "And since everything you've done is bad, you're doomed." He straightened up. "Look at your face; it's started already. All of your evil deeds have taken your youth and health, and I'm sure it won't be long before the gods reward you with death. I'm not a vengeful person, but I'll celebrate the day you die."

Teodora stood up too. "Get out," she said, pointing to the door. "I don't have to listen to this from you, you little worm."

As he left, the door slamming behind him, Teodora sat back down and breathed in deeply. She knew his words meant nothing. An ignorant boy, shouting at her in anger. But she shivered, and wondered how little life she had left, and if there was any way to undo the damage.

She was uneasy all day, and finally talked to Livilla about it. "Do you really think the gods will punish me for the things I've done in service to the empire?"

"Of course not," Livilla said, her voice turning soft in a way that never failed to comfort Teodora. "But I worry about those deeds that came about because of anger, rather than calculation."

"Like what?" Teodora felt Livilla and her other advisers usually prevented her from doing anything too dire.

"Like Larisa Karsten." Livilla's voice was grave.

"I'd forgotten about her." Teodora shuddered. She'd known at the time it was wrong and had done it anyway. "I suppose no brother of Arryk's will ever forgive me for that."

"It's unlikely," Livilla said. "But the gods might. They frown upon taking life when it's not warranted, but perhaps you can atone."

Teodora felt weak and tired. She wanted to give up, but Aksel's words still rang in her ears. "What must I do?"

Livilla stared at the wall. "Father Marcus still lives. Perhaps you can pardon him."

"I can't," Teodora said. "He's a heretic and falls under your jurisdiction."

"I'm willing to offer a pardon," Livilla said, "if he'll agree to recant. But you can be the one to tell Aksel."

"But if his friend is free, how will I keep leverage over Aksel?" Teodora wasn't willing to give that up.

"You won't," Livilla said. "But you'll have shown kindness and perhaps someday that will bear fruit. Besides, the prince has already done what you wanted him to do. You don't need him for anything else right now."

"I doubt he'll appreciate it," Teodora grumbled.

"Maybe not, but that isn't the point. The gods will approve of you showing mercy, even if Aksel does not."

"Will showing mercy help me live longer?"

Livilla sighed. "Likely not. But it might slow the decay."

"It's worth trying I suppose." Teodora hoped that Livilla didn't see how desperate she was.

BRAEDEN

Rather than wait around at Birkenfels for information to come to him, Braeden rode out with scouting patrols. He hoped he wasn't wrong about this. He'd feel a real fool if it turned out that no one was coming and he'd missed out on a big battle up north. But he was familiar with how the Sanova Hussars operated, remembering how they'd tried to attack Kendryk's base before the first battle. Even with Novitny no longer in charge, his replacement would work the same way.

Braeden didn't like to think about facing his friends in a fight. If he hadn't had a price on his head, he would have already returned to them. He and Kazmir ambled along a quiet country road, snow swirling around their heads. At least the worst of the blizzard had passed and it was possible to patrol again. Braeden had been stuck in a peasant cottage for the better part of the week. Now he was certain he smelled of cabbage soup, maybe permanently.

Braeden's mind wandered. Perhaps when he'd fulfilled his obligation to Lennart, he would rejoin Novitny in Sanova. Trisa said they were operating on the Briansk border; there was always action to be found there. Braeden shook his head. They likely weren't here and with any luck he'd stumble on Elektra instead, still trying to work her way to Ensden. He'd already decided that if he didn't kill her in battle, he'd put her in the Birkenfels dungeon. Kendryk's cousin Balduin still rotted there; maybe they would be friends.

"Horsemen ahead," Trisa muttered at his side. Visibility was so poor in the snow, they'd come upon them rather quickly.

"Assume they're hostile," Braeden said, knowing of no other patrols in the area. "Give the order." Best to charge up on them before they realized what was happening. It was unlikely they'd be expecting opposition here.

A small group ahead came into view, and Braeden heard the click of wheellock pistols and the clang of sabers being drawn. From their silhouettes, they didn't look like hussars, but they didn't have to be. After all, Elektra had escaped with her own small cavalry.

"I'll want a prisoner," Braeden said. He doubted this was any kind of main force and he'd like to know what lay ahead.

"Charge!" he shouted, drawing both pistols and spurring Kazmir forward. As they drew closer, the others turned, trying to get away. Braeden shot at one of them, his pistol ball bouncing off of armor. He cursed under his breath; not close enough to go through. With the other pistol, he aimed for a leg and got it. The trooper yelped, then slid sideways off his horse, which kept running. Braeden had his prisoner. He let his troops chase the rest as far as they could, while he dealt with this fellow. He jumped from Kazmir's back and knelt in the snow next to him.

"My leg." The young man's teeth were chattering while he tried to stop the bleeding with one hand.

"Here, let me look." Braeden pulled off his glove and pushed the man's hand aside. Not so bad. "It's bleeding quite a bit and hurting too, most like," he said, happy that this one would live, and talk too. "But it looks like a flesh wound. We'll get it tied up and you'll be fine."

By the time he'd had a page bring a bandage and hoisted the prisoner onto a spare horse's back, Trisa had returned with the rest of the patrol. "It was a scouting party," she said. "Only twelve. We got eight or so, but I'm afraid a few got away, so they'll know we're here."

"We won't stay here long," Braeden said. "Let's get back to that town a few leagues back. We'll doctor this fellow up, and then I'm sure he'll be happy to answer our questions, won't you?" He grinned up at the man before mounting Kazmir.

They found an inn before they reached the town and took over the dining room.

"Food and ale," Braeden called to the innkeep. "We won't stay long." He could already see the fellow scowling at the snow they'd tracked in, melting all over his nicely scrubbed wooden floor.

Once the prisoner's wound was cleaned with brandy and bandaged, Braeden patted him on the shoulder. "You won't be part of this fight," he said, "but it's best if you tell us what we can expect." He handed him a mug of ale and let him take a long drink.

The man downed most of it, then looked at Braeden. "You're not supposed to be here. We were told that Lennart's forces went north, leaving only small garrisons at Birkenfels and a few of the larger towns."

"You had good information," Braeden said. "But I had a hunch your lot would be out there. Who's in command?"

"Franca Dura," the man said.

Braeden swore under his breath. He might have known.

"Ensden made her colonel straight away and sent her to Sanova to recruit," The man went on. "That's where she picked me up. I've been with her cuirassiers for two months now."

"So that's what she's calling them, eh? No more wings, no lances." Braeden had to make an effort to cover his shock. He shouldn't be surprised at Franca's quick rise—there was no one more capable—but she couldn't be over twenty-six. He would have expected Ensden to choose someone far more senior.

"No," the fellow offered a pale grin. "It's pistols and heavy plate for us. Me and the rest couldn't get the hang of the lances in the few months we had to prepare. Besides, they're not needed for this kind of work."

"Probably right," Braeden said, then took a long drink of ale while he thought about what Franca was likely to do next. "I'll let you tell me all about that work in a minute. But first I have another question. Have any of you seen the Archduchess Elektra while you traveled through Sanova?"

"We saw her all right." The man almost laughed, then grimaced. "She and her scraggly little cavalry and three dozen dragoons have been with us since the Podoska marches. Colonel Dura doesn't like it, but she can't seem to get rid of her."

Braeden grinned widely. "I might be able to help her with that."

ELEKTRA

Franca stomped and cursed, using words Elektra had never heard before. A few survivors of a scouting party had appeared, telling of an attack by an enemy patrol. "No one was supposed to be there," Franca shouted.

Elektra backed away from the table. She supposed she ought to appreciate that Franca included her in her councils, but it was often an unpleasant experience. "Do we have any idea who it might be?" Elektra asked, while Franca breathed hard, eyes flashing fire while trying to calm down. "Did the scouts see anything?"

Franca shook her head. "No, they didn't. Not that it matters. The problem is, the enemy is expecting us now."

"Do they know where we're headed?"

Franca sat back down. "I don't know. It depends on if they got a prisoner. This lot hurried away too fast, and because of the snow, they didn't see much."

Elektra wanted to carry out their plan so badly, she could taste it. Franca had hit on it, and for the first time, Elektra agreed with her, enthusiastically even. If they could pull it off, the rebels would be forced to surrender, the war would end, and Elektra would get much of the credit. If she succeeded, she wouldn't even mind sharing the glory with Franca, who in spite of her unpleasant personality, excelled at her job. "I think we should go ahead anyway," Elektra said.

"You would." Franca snorted. "I should have known you'd be more excited about stopping heresy than any military operation."

"This is both, isn't it?" Elektra kept her chin up. Her confidence had returned and she wouldn't let Franca bully her.

"I suppose so." Franca leaned her elbows on the table, cupping her chin in her palm. "I want to go ahead too. The enemy won't have a big force here, and if we move fast, we might still pull it off, even if they figure out what we're up to."

"I agree," Elektra said, then stood. "Let's go right now."

It was a tricky plan, especially since Heidenhof was one of the most strongly garrisoned cities in Terragand. Lennart clearly wanted to keep the heretical Maximus safe. But since no one expected the enemy to be near, the gates of most cities remained open during the day so trade could continue.

At first, Franca didn't want Elektra to be involved. "It's dangerous, and you can't lose your nerve."

"I won't," Elektra said, wondering why she felt so confident. Or perhaps her desperation had turned to something else. She'd have to play a vital part in this mission, or die in the attempt. And if she pulled this off, she'd gain not only Franca's respect, but everyone else's. It would be hard for her mother to bully the hero who'd single-handedly brought down the Quadrene heresy.

Dressed as a farm woman, bundled up against the cold, Elektra rode through the gates of Heidenhof on the seat of a wagon. Most of the bundles and barrels in the wagon were empty, but when the guard asked what they carried, Elektra unwound the scarf over her face enough to smile at him and say, "Ale, and a little flour. But mostly ale."

"We don't mind seeing more of that." The guard grinned and winked at her. "Welcome to Heidenhof."

Elektra smiled once more before covering her face again. It wasn't as though she needed a disguise; no one here would expect her or recognize her, but it was still cold. The wagon trundled over the cobbles toward the market square. Bundled-up people ran about and the market itself was busy. It seemed everyone was coming back out, now that the blizzard had passed.

The stall was already set up by the time Elektra arrived. It sat on the outer edges of the square, in an area that got little traffic. Most of the activity was behind the stall, where nearly fifty imperial troops, disguised as farmers and merchants, gathered within an hour of Elektra's arrival. One young woman manned the stall, selling an occasional barrel of ale to the few customers. They had just enough goods piled up in front to seem plausible.

Elektra strolled off with only one guard at her side to inspect the temple. She was surprised to find it as impressive as many in Atlona, though it was true this was the religious seat for all of Terragand.

"I think I'll go inside," she said to her guard, a little more loudly than necessary. "I'd like to pray."

Maybe she'd get lucky and spot the Maximus. Getting to him here would be so much easier.

It was chilly and dim inside the temple, with only a few candles burning at the altar. Elektra gasped when she realized that the walls had been stripped bare of hangings and no icons hung over the altar. She wondered how the heretics expected to worship with nothing to pray to. Well, that nonsense would end soon, and Elektra would restore the art along with the proper worship.

She wandered around the aisles, but there was nothing to look at, and the plainness depressed her. The Maximus never appeared either, so she returned to the marketplace. They'd have to go ahead as planned.

GWYNNETH

"The queen wishes to pay a call on you," Gauvain said with a smile. He didn't visit as often, now he'd married, and seemed happier than he had in a long time.

"She does?" Gwynneth had been wondering how to insinuate herself into the queen's circle, and was on the verge of hinting to Gauvain that she'd like an invitation. "Why?"

"She was good friends with your brother in Atlona. When she heard you were here, she wanted to meet you."

"Perhaps she has news of Aksel. I would love to talk to her about him."

Gauvain sighed. "I think she might have had a crush, which makes me feel even worse about the whole thing."

"Maybe she did, but you have no reason to feel bad. Zofya might be young, but she seems sure of herself, and she looked so happy at the wedding."

"I hope she was. I hope she is. I've tried to be as kind as possible, letting her take the lead in everything. Natalya is anxious the marriage be consummated at once, but I will not do that until Zofya is ready."

"That's wise." Gwynneth smiled at him. "And kind, as expected. Yet, you and the queen spend a great deal of time together."

"We do." Gauvain's face lit up. "She's so clever and I enjoy talking to her. I worried a girl her age might be silly and superficial, but she is far from that. I'm hoping we can become good friends, at least."

"You will. Natalya can cool her heels. In the long run it's more important you and the queen have a good relationship." Gwynneth didn't mention that she hoped Gauvain's kindness would soon draw Zofya entirely away from her mother's influence. Teodora likely wished to be the power behind the Galladian throne through her daughter, but Gwynneth doubted it would be as easy as she expected. "I'd be happy to receive the queen at any time that's convenient for her."

With Gauvain gone, Gwynneth sent a message to Natalya, telling her that she was doing as instructed. Then she sent for Maryna.

"The queen will visit us soon," she said. "I realize you don't like the empress, but please try to be kind to her daughter. Remember she's far from home and if she makes new friends here, well, she might find she likes her mother less."

"How can she like her mother at all?" Maryna asked with a huff.

"I'm not sure. But can you imagine how angry Teodora will be when she finds out we've become her daughter's new friends?"

Maryna giggled at that. "You're right, Mama. That would make her very angry. I will of course be kind to the queen."

Queen Zofya came the next day, accompanied by only four ladies-in-waiting. Gwynneth received them in her drawing room, which became crowded by the time Gwynneth included her own ladies and Maryna's governess.

"I'm so honored, Your Highness." Gwynneth curtsied deeply, pleased that Maryna did the same without hesitation.

"Please." The queen stretched out tiny hands and took one of Gwynneth's, pulling her closer. "The honor is mine. Prince Aksel told me so much about you, it's like I know you already."

"I'm so glad you got to know him," Gwynneth said, leading the queen to the best chair in the room and waiting for everyone else to settle around her. "I hope he's well."

Zofya frowned. "I hope he is, though I'm afraid I haven't seen him in months. Mother didn't approve of our friendship."

"Oh dear," Gwynneth said then paused, seeing the queen wanted to say more on the matter. She let her talk, and a long list of complaints about Teodora followed. Gwynneth tried to keep from agreeing loudly, but was happy. Getting this girl away from her mother's influence would be easy, it seemed.

Natalya would be pleased. Gwynneth just needed the Maxima to thaw enough so she could ask her if she might go to Terragand. Kendryk had written that he had arrived there, and that Birkenfels remained safe. By the time she reached it, she hoped Lennart would have won a significant victory.

Gwynneth let the queen talk, smiling and nodding, and offering refreshments as they arrived. She looked Zofya's ladies over discreetly. One was young and probably a friend brought from Atlona. Two looked old, with gray hair and worn faces—likely distant relatives. The fourth was the hardest to categorize. Though she dressed correctly and didn't say a word, something about her didn't fit. She had a pale, sweet face with dark ringlets falling around it, and it was hard to say how old she was. Her eyes were most unsettling. Although large and beautiful, their dark brown was almost black, and looking into them was like staring into a pit with no bottom.

Gwynneth had to keep from shivering, and tried to convince herself it was just a trick of the light. Once the queen stopped complaining about Teodora, Gwynneth introduced Maryna, who had the presence of mind to ask about the scientific work Zofya had done with Aksel. That was the right subject, and the queen chattered happily for another hour.

When she finally left, she kissed first Maryna, then Gwyneth on both cheeks. "I haven't had such a nice time since I first arrived here. I hope you don't mind if I invite you to the palace."

"I would like that very much," Gwynneth said, and was pleased that Maryna seemed to feel the same.

ANTON

Anton couldn't believe they were seeing the walls of Kaltental.

"That must be it," Susanna said, sitting down on a low wall that ran alongside the road with a sigh. "We've made it."

Anton sat down next to her and put an arm around her shoulders. "I owe it all to you. I would never have figured out what to do."

She smiled up at him. "We did it together. Us and baby here." She put a hand on her belly, and Anton laid his over it.

"He's just along for the ride," Anton said. "You're feeling all right?" Even though Susanna hadn't complained, it had been a long, hard journey and he worried that it was too much for a pregnant woman.

"Tired and hungry, but fine." She stood and took Anton by the hand. "The city can't be over two leagues off. Let's go before they close the gates."

They'd had a stroke of luck after leaving the camp. After struggling through deep snow on the road alongside the river and barely surviving a cold night huddled in an abandoned shed, the weather cleared. It was still cold, but the wind died down and the snow melted a little bit each day. They took advantage of one sunny day to lay out their layers to dry on rocks along the river, and once they were no longer wet all the time, Anton began to believe they'd make it.

Though they had to ration it carefully, they had enough food, and the many layers of clothes kept them from freezing to death. Now all that remained was getting inside the city and explaining himself to the nearest recruiting officer. With any luck, Michalek's regiment was at least two days behind; Anton was certain it hadn't been able to move as fast as he and Susanna had, covering twenty leagues a day. By the time it reached Kaltental, he'd hoped to disappear into the ranks of another unit and never see any of the others again. He was sad about friends like Stasny, but survival was more important, especially since he'd have a family to worry about.

Anton knew it would be hard, since they'd lost all their money with the quartermaster, who'd disappeared after the battle with Lennart, and they no longer had any goods to sell. Their layers of finery had turned to rags, the food had been eaten, the brandy drunk long ago. Anton hoped to get in with a somewhat solvent commander, and at least get a loan if he wasn't paid right away.

Now he worried even more as they finally approached Kaltental after crossing the river on a long bridge. The gate was shut, though a line of people and wagons stopped before it.

"Will they let us in?" Anton asked the man standing in front of them. He led a donkey, laden with bundles.

"Most likely," the man said. "They're just being careful. They've got Estenorians camped to the north and west and don't want them walking in."

"Are you bringing supplies to the city?" Anton asked the man.

"Yes, though I have little to sell. But prices are high, since Lennart has cut off shipping from the river and blockaded the port on the other side. The only food and supplies that get in come from the surrounding countryside. I bring herbs my wife and I grow in the garden and dry for the winter. This is the last bunch." He patted one of the bundles on the donkey. "But we've made enough money to keep us for a while."

Anton hoped he wasn't leading them into a worse situation if food inside the city was scarce. Perhaps he should have looked for Lennart's forces and offered his services. But it was too late for that. Susanna leaned against him exhausted, and he needed to find a safe place for her. Tramping across the countryside, looking for the Estenorians didn't seem a good idea right now.

"They open the gate twice a day and let us in and those inside, out." The man went on. "All you have to do is prove you're not an Estenorian."

Anton wasn't sure how he'd prove that, but decided not to worry about it. After a while, the massive gate swung open and the line moved. A stream of people, horses and carts came from the other side.

When they reached the gate, the guard looked Anton and Susanna over with amusement. "You two escaped from a mummer's troupe?" he asked, to laughter from the other guards.

Anton lifted his chin. "I'm sure you already heard the news of Lennart's victory further down the river. My regiment survived, but my wife and I were separated from them in a blizzard. I'd be happy to reenlist inside the city if I'm needed."

The guard looked him over carefully and Anton stared straight back. Nothing he'd said was a lie.

"What about the girl?" the guard nodded at Susanna. "Can't have her lazing around, a useless mouth."

"I'll work," Susanna spoke up before Anton said anything. "I'm a good cook. I'll look for a position right away."

The guard looked at them long, then finally nodded. "All right," he said. "The two of you are in luck. The army has been losing soldiers to disease and desertion. We try to stop 'em from leaving, but too many sneak out anyway. Ask your way to the Granter Pike; they'll probably take you on. Likely they can use a cook too."

"Thank you," Anton said, relief and gratitude washing over him. "Thank you."

Then he and Susanna hurried inside the gates before the guard could change his mind.

ELEKTRA

It took forever for evening to come and the market stalls to empty, their owners breaking them down and packing them up in wagons. Elektra's bunch went through the motions, but as the square emptied, they slipped away in ones and twos. With the city so busy, they wouldn't attract attention. Some headed toward the Maximus's palace, while others made for the gates. Because of the cold weather, no one looked suspicious wearing layers of clothing concealing all kinds of weapons.

Elektra was calm through the afternoon, but now her mouth dried out and her heart pounded. She still had hours to go before they acted, and she hoped she could survive the suspense. She and a few of her guards went to an inn where they ate a dreadful, greasy stew, which unsettled Elektra's stomach. Now she felt nauseous on top of everything else.

By the time the temple bell tolled seven, it was completely dark, the streets quiet. Elektra made her way to the Maximus's palace and hoped her troops at the gate would succeed. It was one thing to nab the Maximus in his own home, and quite another to get him out of a well-fortified city. She and Franca considered trying to take it over, but decided it would be too hard to overcome the whole garrison. They just needed to get the Maximus out, disappear into the night, then secure him in a small castle Franca took over a week before.

Now that it was time, Elektra wondered if the whole scheme wasn't wildly fantastical. She was surprised Franca was going along with it. Then she wondered *why* Franca was going along with it, and if she perhaps had another motive—to be rid of Elektra, for instance. Elektra thought she might be sick.

She stood at a corner of the palace, watching the guards milling around at the main entrance, well-lit by four torches in sconces on the wall. It was the only spot that appeared well-guarded, although most of the other entrances were protected by a great wall that encircled the rest of the property. Elektra had eyed the wall, but it was tall and very smooth. Even with the right

393

equipment, she doubted she could get enough troops over it before being discovered.

No, her plan would work well enough. Now she waited for the distraction. It came soon, with an angry shout and a woman's piercing scream. Elektra smiled. That young dragoon volunteered because she claimed to scream better and louder than anyone. It seemed she was right. The guards looked at each other, then about half of them went toward the commotion.

"Now," Elektra whispered, though everyone knew what to do. She'd already pulled out a pistol and drawn her sword. In such close quarters, she'd be lucky to get off one shot.

She managed one as she ran up the stairs to the great door, and a guard crumpled to the ground, rolling down several stairs before stopping himself, groaning. Elektra ignored him and ran past, her sword ready. She was sure the door was barred, but that was part of the plan too. Many of the guards had fallen, or were locked in combat with her own troops, who'd materialized out of the shadows in overwhelming numbers.

She headed straight for the door, dodging a guard who lunged at her, but he was quickly engaged by someone behind her. Now only one stood before her, a young man, wide-eyed and trembling, close to Elektra's age. He'd do perfectly. He held out his sword, but his hand shook, and she knocked it to the ground before he could use it. Some guard. At least the others put up a better fight in spite of the hopeless situation.

Before the young man did anything else, Elektra grabbed him by the arm and pulled him close to her. She held the point of her sword to his throat. This hadn't been part of the scheme, since everyone thought Elektra too small to grab anyone and hold them. But since this fearful guard presented himself—a gift from Vica, she thought to herself, grinning—she might as well do the honors.

"Stop it," she shouted. "Lay down your arms or he dies."

She turned the young man around and pushed the sword a little harder against his throat until he squeaked. He must have been related to someone to get this job while so incompetent. She smiled as swords and pistols clattered to the stone stairs and the cobblestones of the square.

"Open the door," she shouted.

"I c-c-can't," the young man quavered.

"Not you, stupid," she nudged him in the ribs. "Someone inside."

Another guard appeared. "You'll never get away with this."

"Tell them to unbar it or he dies." Elektra dug the point in and drew just enough blood to make the other guard turn pale.

"All right," he said, opening a small door at eye level.

Franca and her cavalry should be here anytime now. The gate was too far to hear sounds of fighting, but Elektra had no reason to believe her people hadn't been able to overcome the guards there. "Now tell them to hurry up and open that door."

The man said something to the person on the other side and after an eternity, the great door swung open. Elektra nodded at her troops.

"Find the Maximus," she said. "Once we have him in custody, I'll let you go, all right?" she said in the young man's ear, feeling rather sorry for him since he trembled so. He nodded and seemed to shake a little less.

Now there was a commotion in the street leading to the square, the sound of hooves on cobbles and the clank of armor. Elektra sighed, relief flooding her body. Franca had made it. She turned to look at the door. The Maximus stood there. He wore his hair short and a plain black suit like any ordinary person. He didn't even look like a priest, let alone a false Maximus, but Elektra knew it was he in an instant. Even though his arms were held by two of Elektra's stoutest soldiers, he seemed completely calm and his pale eyes bored into her with considerable intensity.

"Let the boy go, young lady," he said, and Elektra realized with a start he didn't know who she was. "I'm coming with you."

She shoved the young man away, and he scurried down the stairs and into the arms of an older woman, also a guard.

"Let's go," Elektra said. "I'm sure our escort is already here."

"Are you sure that's your escort?" the Maximus asked, a hint of amusement in his voice.

Elektra turned back to the square, now flooded with torchlight, where a cavalry troop had assembled, Braeden Terris at their head.

"Good evening, Your Grace," he said, a nasty smile on his lips.

Elektra's heart launched itself into her throat and she froze, knowing she needed to escape somehow, even while realizing it was impossible. She tried running into the palace, but stumbled on a stair and fell. A pain shot through her knee, but she struggled to her feet. They wouldn't stay under her, and an unbearable tightness gathered in her forehead. Her ears roared, and the last thing she felt was the Maximus catching her as she fell.

GWYNNETH

After that first visit, Gwynneth saw the young queen often. She came to Gwynneth's house at least once a week, and invited Gwynneth and Maryna to the palace even more frequently. Gwynneth had to admit she was enjoying herself. After her falling out with Natalya, she'd become rather reclusive and missed being in society. Even though she had no money for new dresses, Catrin helped freshen up the ones she had with small alterations, and resized a few older ones to fit Maryna, who'd grown a great deal in the past months.

Maryna and Zofya had become good friends. Not only did they share an interest in academic pursuits, their heads often bent over a scholarly text, but they enjoyed discussing politics. At first, Gwynneth worried that would lead to a fight, since Maryna had firm opinions about the Inferraras and their policies. To her surprise, Zofya seemed to agree.

"My mother has made such a mess of things," she said with authority, her voice echoing around the room, while several of her ladies gasped rather predictably.

It was a sunny afternoon, with just a hint of spring in the air. Zofya and Maryna occupied a window seat in the queen's sitting room, while Gwynneth tried to engage at least a few of the ladies in waiting. Most were terribly dull, but a few could make reasonable conversation.

"I don't think there was any reason for war," Zofya went on.

"Oh, I agree," Maryna said. "If only the empress had been less stubborn. Papa was willing to come to an agreement with her, but she treated him abominably."

"She does that to everyone," Zofya said, a little too loudly. "That's why she doesn't have a friend in the world. Well, except for Livilla Maxima, who is lovely, though I'm sure she's able to intimidate my mother well enough."

At the mention of Livilla, the dark-haired lady Gwynneth had noticed at the first visit started visibly. Gwynneth turned to her with a smile. "Do you know the Maxima?" she asked in Olvisyan. She'd noticed this woman never took part when Galladian was spoken.

"A little." The woman had a strange voice. It was thin and raspy, but she spoke so softly it wasn't unpleasant. "She nursed me back to health once when I was ill."

"They say she's a famous healer," Gwynneth said, glad she could finally talk to this woman. She'd wondered about her since the beginning.

"I swear she performed a miracle on me. I was so near death."

Gwynneth saw that when the woman smiled, she kept her lips firmly pressed together. Perhaps she had crooked or rotten teeth.

"It seems you have recovered well, if you could make the long journey." Gwynneth still found it hard to meet the strange, bottomless eyes.

"I have." The woman looked around, and seeing everyone else engaged in conversation elsewhere, scooted her chair closer to Gwynneth's. "It was important that I came with Queen Zofya since I have a particular mission concerning you."

Gwynneth raised her eyebrows. It would explain why she was so unlike the other ladies, but she wondered why she was confiding in Gwynneth, of all people. "Concerning me?" she asked, now on high alert. "And who's sent you on this mission?"

"I can't say much here, since my employer is at odds with the empress. Your Grace, I must speak with you alone, and soon," the woman said, her voice so low Gwynneth had to lean forward to hear her at all.

"With me? I'm afraid I don't understand."

"My employer knows of your troubles with Natalya Maxima and wishes to help you."

Gwynneth drew her breath in sharply. "How in the world does he know?"

"She. It doesn't matter. What matters is that we have good reason to get you and your children away from Natalya Maxima as soon as possible."

Gwynneth wasn't sure what to say to that, and just stared, wide-eyed.

The woman looked around. Even though no one seemed to pay them any attention, she dropped her voice to a whisper. "I work for Brynhild Mattila, and she has learned things about Natalya that should cause you great concern."

"Mattila?" None of this made sense to Gwynneth, and she shot a glance at the queen, still chattering away with Maryna. "Why in the world would she want to help me?"

"She hates Teodora," the woman said. "Any enemy of the empress is a friend to her."

"I'm not at all sure I want to be friends with her," Gwynneth said, her voice tight. This conversation made her distinctly uncomfortable. This woman might very well be an agent of Natalya's.

"She understands that, and will offer you proof of her esteem. And should you wish to accept her help, I can get you out of Allaux so you can return to Terragand where you belong."

"Why in the name of Vica would I trust you?" Gwynneth whispered furiously, shoving her chair back, so she wasn't so close anymore.

"I understand why you don't." The woman's eyes laughed at her. "It's hard to trust anyone in this den of wolves."

"Too true," Gwynneth said, then stood. "I must get the duchess and take my leave. I'm sure the queen has other obligations."

The woman stood at the same time and Gwynneth noticed she was tall, with an almost feline fluidity to her movements. "I don't expect you to trust me. But should you ever need help, understand Mattila has good reason to get you away from here. If you need me, send an invitation to the queen, but address it to Fernanda Vastic."

Gwynneth took a step back. "Thank you, but I'm sure that won't be necessary, Miss Vastic." She nodded by way of farewell, and hurried to take Maryna home.

LENNART

"We can starve Ensden out, but that's not good enough," Lennart said. He'd finally reached the outskirts of Kaltental and gathered his generals. "Now that the winter storms have passed, we can expect pressure from the Maladene fleet, and I don't want to risk him getting resupplied. We need to draw him out now."

"I understand the urgency," General Kalstrom said. "But how do you propose to do it? We have him nearly surrounded and it would be no great matter to close off the one gate on the eastern side. Once their supplies stop coming in altogether, they'll come to an agreement soon enough."

Lennart's patience was thin. Did no one understand that an agreement wasn't what he needed? "I must fight him and defeat him," he said. "I've been here a year now, and while I've secured most of Terragand, it doesn't mean much until I've defeated the empress's best general in battle."

"We can take the city by storm," Trystan Martinek said.

Lennart noticed a few of the older generals rolling their eyes and exchanging knowing glances. It angered him that they didn't see Trystan's worth, though he supposed they'd had no example of it yet. Shouldn't his trust be enough? "That's better," Lennart said, nodding at Trystan. "We should at least discuss the possibility."

"Excuse me," Kendryk said, clearly ill at ease in a military council. "I have an idea. I'm not opposed to taking the city by storm, but that might prove costly and as far as we know, we're still somewhat outnumbered. What if we make Ensden believe he can escape without engaging us?"

"It'll never work," Karolyna Martinek said impatiently. "He knows we surround him."

"But what if we don't?" Kendryk asked, looking down his nose at Duchess Martinek.

Lennart stifled a chuckle. The woman could cut it high and mighty, but nothing beat Prince Kendryk for haughtiness when he felt like it.

"I don't understand," Karolyna said.

"I'm not surprised," Lennart said, with a look that indicated she should keep her opinions to herself. He turned toward Kendryk. "I see where you're going with this. Ensden would rather starve than engage us. But what if he thinks there's a way out?"

"Exactly," Kendryk said, sounding more excited now. "What if he thinks he can march out toward the western beaches, the ones you escaped from." He nodded in Isenberg's direction. "And if he can break out of the city and get to a beach, the Maladene navy will pick him up."

"I like that," Lennart said. He enjoyed puzzling things out like this, especially with another mind just as good at it. What a shame Kendryk had never had serious military training. He might have made quite a clever general. "What if for instance, we gave Ensden reason to believe that we were planning to attack from the east?" He continued. "It makes sense, with Kalstrom's and Lofbrok's armies still in place on that side. Then he receives word from Maladena that they'll launch a rescue by sea."

"Maladena won't help us by sending such a letter." Karolyna couldn't keep her mouth shut.

"They won't." Kendryk shook his head. Perhaps he was amazed at her dullness even more than Lennart was. "But we might make them believe it."

"Forge a letter, for instance," Trystan put in.

"Now we're getting ideas," Lennart said, his excitement rising. The idea of a big victory wasn't as satisfying as it could be. It had to be a famous victory too, one that would make a good story. "Perhaps it's time we let one or two Maladene ships through the blockade. Or at least, ships that look like they're Maladene." He turned to Tavio Sora. "Do you reckon you can compose a letter that would sound suitably official?" When Sora shrugged, then nodded, Lennart turned to the rest of the table. "Does anyone know if Ensden reads Maladene? I should probably ask before we write something fancy."

Alona Brynner said, "He does. He speaks and reads well enough since he was a junior officer under Montanez in Cesiano years ago."

"Excellent," Lennart said. "Let's do this. Sora, you'll stay here and we'll work on a letter. The rest of you move the whole army to the west side of the river. We'll do it quiet and use that bridge about fifteen leagues downstream."

"That'll take days," Isenberg said.

"It will, but it'll take longer than that to figure out how to get this message to Ensden. I want Lofbrok and Kalstrom to pull out quietly from the beaches leaving a skeleton garrison—let Ensden think you're still there. We'll set up far enough to the south to be out of sight, but close enough we can catch Ensden before he reaches the beach. And let's back away from the city altogether."

"I doubt Ensden will believe it," someone said.

"He won't." Lennart pondered for a moment. "We'll include something about that in the letter. We'll tell him a force is attacking us from the south; maybe say Teodora has raised another army and we've marched off to stop it, while he's stuck inside the city. We'll work on it while getting everyone into place." Lennart stood, and there was a great clatter as chairs pushed away from the table. "Those of you who don't have troops to move far, get them drilled and in shape for battle. It won't be more than a few weeks now."

BRAEDEN

"So you're saying this is the Archduchess Elektra?" Edric Maximus looked at the girl, still unconscious and lying on a bench. "Teodora's daughter?"

"Her heir as well," Braeden said. "And more trouble than anyone I've ever known. I don't want to imagine what would have happened to you if I hadn't stumbled onto her scouts."

"I would expect Teodora's daughter to be trouble," Edric said with a grin. He seemed unbothered by the fact that he'd nearly been kidnapped and possibly murdered. Franca had said it was all she could do to persuade Elektra not to kill the Maximus on the spot.

"Now what do we do with her?" Braeden asked. He was having a bite to eat in the Maximus's palace, mostly to kill time so Franca could get away. "I hoped to put her in the Arnfels and see if we can extract concessions from Teodora in exchange for her eventual freedom."

"That seems the reasonable thing to do," Edric said, still staring at Elektra. "But I'm not sure. Perhaps there is another, greater advantage to be gained."

"I don't understand," Braeden said. "What other advantage is there except for concessions from Teodora?" He figured it was best not to mention he'd prefer to see Elektra dead. At this point he was more than willing to do the deed without hesitation.

"When Teodora dies, Elektra will be empress, is that correct?" Edric asked.

"Yes."

"How old is the girl?"

"Sixteen," Braeden said.

"So when she comes to the throne, there will be a regency."

"Yes, but only until she turns seventeen." Braeden hoped she wouldn't live that long.

"Interesting." Edric stared at the wall, while Braeden polished off the rest of his meat and boiled potatoes. For a Maximus, Edric kept a simple table.

"What do you have in mind?" Braeden asked, pushing away his empty plate.

"I'd like to talk to her at least, when she wakes up. But first I'd like to know why she fainted from the shock of seeing you. Clearly, the two of you have a troubled history."

"That's one way of putting it," Braeden growled.

"Let's go into the other room and you can tell me," Edric said. "I'd rather you not be here when she wakes up, since I don't want her to faint again."

"She's more likely to try to kill me," Braeden said, grumpy now he was realizing Edric wanted to deprive him of his prize.

"All the more reason to keep you separated then." Edric showed Braeden into a small room off the larger receiving hall where Elektra still slept. "Now tell me everything."

That took the better part of an hour, by which time a servant stuck his head in the door to tell them the young lady was awake.

"Let me go to her alone," Edric said. "It isn't wise for the two of you to be in the same building together, let alone the same room."

"Do you want to tell me what you have in mind? I'm not sure how I will explain to Lennart that I had her in my clutches and let her go."

"You needn't worry about that. I'll write to him in the morning. Will you join him now, or are Dura's Cuirassiers still a threat?"

"They're not a threat," Braeden said vaguely. Franca had said only that she was leaving the area and would trouble the Maximus no more. Braeden suspected she might make for Kaltental, not wanting to miss out on the fun. "But I'm not leaving you here unprotected."

"I have my guards." Edric smiled.

"You've got to be joking," Braeden said. "If I hadn't shown up when I did, there's no telling where you'd be right now. I'll stay in the area and make sure no other mystery force appears."

"Do whatever you think is best. I'm very appreciative of your help today. Though I'm curious how you overcame the Sanovan force so quickly."

"They took off once it was clear we outnumbered them and had the archduchess trapped in the city." Braeden hoped Edric would let him leave it at that. The reality had been rather different.

"I'd love to nab that Maximus," Franca had said. "Elektra is right for once; it would end the war quickly. Isn't that what you want?" She scowled at Braeden when he appeared to cut her off on her way to Heidenhof.

"I do," Braeden said. "But even more, I want Elektra dead."

"I don't blame you," Franca said. "She's got a rather high opinion of herself for someone who can't pull off the simplest operation. And all she cares about is looking good in front of the empress."

"Teodora is a hard woman to impress," Braeden said, grinning.

"I don't care," Franca said, then sighed. "If you don't want me to capture the Maximus and stop the war, I won't fight you about it."

"Good," Braeden said. "I'd hate to fight you."

"I hate it that you're with the enemy," Franca burst out. "It feels wrong."

"It does," Braeden said, then told her what he might do once he'd finished with Lennart.

"You should go now," Franca said. "Novitny would be thrilled. And no one will notice if you're not here."

"I'll notice," Braeden said, "You understand. But Lennart will win soon, and then I can go."

"I hope you're wrong about that," Franca said. "If your lot wins, then what'll become of me?"

"You'll join us in Sanova," Braeden said, wishing that could happen right now.

"I'd like that," Franca said. "But in the meantime, I'll get out of your way if you won't let me take the Maximus. Do what you want with Elektra. I'll probably head north."

"I won't chase you." Braeden turned Kazmir toward Heidenhof. "And Franca," he said. "I hope the next time I see you, we'll be on the same side."

It was hard to shake off the heaviness that came over him, both at letting Franca ride into danger and at seeing Anton's horse. One of the first things he'd asked upon meeting Franca was, "Where did you get that charger? A Norovaean, isn't he?" He was identical to Skandar, though Braeden reckoned that breed all looked much alike.

"He is," Franca patted his neck. "Bregir's a good fellow, though on the spirited side."

"Where did you get him?" Braeden found his mouth was dry.

"Bought him from Mattila, of all people. Back when Livilla Maxima paid us off, I had coin and the general didn't."

"Where did she get him?" Braeden looked at the horse more closely. "I knew a Norovaean once, named Skandar."

The horse nickered and Franca gave him another pat. "That would be a good name for him. Don't know where Mattila got him, though she acquired a few fine chargers after defeating Arian Orland. Are you all right, sir?"

Braeden had made a choking noise. He hung on tight to Kazmir and let a wave of nausea pass. "I suppose that's it then," he said softly, then told Franca about Anton. "I've been hoping all this time he was still alive, but if Mattila got his horse, it seems unlikely."

"I'm so sorry, sir. Now I feel awful about it."

"Don't," Braeden said quickly. "I'd rather you had him than anyone else in the world."

Franca took a deep breath. "Maybe you shouldn't give up hope. Mattila took a few dozen prisoners when she defeated Orland. She forced them to enlist in her army. If your stepson was the lucky little scrap you say he was, well then he might be a soldier in Ensden's army right now."

Braeden had to chuckle. "He'd hate that."

Still, once he'd left the Maximus and Elektra behind, and made his way back to Birkenfels, he couldn't help but feel a new wave of sadness, knowing he'd never see Anton again.

GWYNNETH

Deep down, Gwynneth realized that having anything further to do with Fernanda Vastic would be unwise, but Natalya was proving to be difficult. At her next visit, Gwynneth brought up leaving for Terragand, but she counseled delay.

"You ought to wait until Lennart has defeated Ensden decisively," Natalya said, her eyes hard. "There's no point in going all that way and finding out Terragand isn't secure."

"But it *is* secure," Gwynneth insisted. "Lennart holds nearly all of it now except for that northern bit. If I go to Birkenfels, I'll be perfectly safe."

"I'd rather not risk it," Natalya said. "I'd never forgive myself if anything happened to you or the children."

Gwynneth tried not to react to that with disbelief, but she didn't quite succeed.

Natalya's eyes softened. "Things between us are difficult," she said, "but you're still my friend and I feel responsible for your well-being. And I am so fond of the children."

That at least was true. Maryna and Devyn had continued their lessons at Natalya's school and Maryna especially was the Maxima's favorite student, excelling in every subject and hanging on her every word. "I know." Gwynneth attempted a smile. "I'm just terribly anxious, so far away from the action. And I miss Kendryk so much it hurts. It seems so unfair we've had to be apart for so long."

"Many things are unfair," Natalya said gravely. "But we must endure them anyway. Now, we must discuss how best to influence the queen. You've done well turning her away from Teodora."

"That was easy enough," Gwynneth said. "She was already resentful of her mother when she got here. I let her talk about it and the more she talks, the angrier she gets."

406

Natalya offered a rare smile. "Now it's time to change her attitude toward the king. I'm afraid at this point she sees him as a beloved older brother. That won't do, since Gauvain needs an heir and he needs one soon."

"She's still so young."

"I understand." There was perhaps a glimmer of sympathy in Natalya's eyes. "But it can't be helped. It's important for the future of the kingdom. I'm sure you'll be discreet. But I want you to impress upon her the importance of her role. I believe she likes Gauvain well enough, but he will wait for her to act first, so she must."

Gwynneth sighed. "I'll do what I can. Oh, and before I go, I wanted to ask what you know about one of the queen's ladies-in-waiting."

"A ridiculous, silly bunch." Natalya shook her head.

"Most of them are, but I'm curious about a Fernanda Vastic. She seems so different from the others."

"Oh yes, the one with the strange eyes and annoying voice." Natalya chewed her lip. "I might have to consult my notes, but if I recall, she's a distant cousin of the empress's. No doubt she wanted to get her out of the country. Relatives have a way of causing trouble when they don't have enough to do."

"She rather seems like someone who might do that," Gwynneth said, hoping Natalya would take the hint if she'd heard anything interesting.

"Probably, though as far as I can tell, she's caused no trouble here." Natalya drew her brows together. "She hasn't done or said anything untoward, has she?"

"Oh no." Gwynneth shook her head. "No, she just looks rather odd, and I wondered if there was a story behind it. It seems not."

"Some people just look interesting when they're not," Natalya said with a smile as Gwynneth got ready to leave. "Now, don't forget what I said about the queen."

"Of course not," Gwynneth said, even as she wished with more intensity she could be gone from here tomorrow.

It was a shock to return to her house and find Fernanda Vastic waiting for her in the drawing room. "I'm very sorry, Your Grace," she said. "But I have urgent news for you."

"Really?" Gwynneth found that hard to believe. "It's funny," she said as they both sat down. "I was just asking the Maxima about you."

Fernanda smiled. "I don't suppose she told you anything interesting."

"She did not, though she might be lying."

"Possibly, but I have no reason to believe she knows anything about me."

"I'm sure the Maxima checked the background of everyone accompanying the queen."

"Oh, I'm sure she did." Fernanda smiled again, that odd, tight-lipped expression. "But Mattila would make certain she found nothing of interest."

"I suppose she would," Gwynneth said, waving for Linette to order tea. Lately, Natalya never offered her anything when she went to visit. "So, what do you have for me?"

Fernanda reached into her bodice and pulled out a tightly folded note. "A message from your husband."

"You're joking," Gwynneth said, though she had to steady her hand as she took the note.

"I'm not." Fernanda settled back into her chair with a rather smug look on her face.

Gwynneth shot her an angry glance before she unfolded the paper. Then she gasped. The note was in Kendryk's hand, using one of their personal ciphers. "How?" she gasped, dropping it into her lap while she caught her breath. "How did you get this?"

"It's a rather long story," Fernanda said.

"I don't care," Gwynneth said, refusing to read the note until she knew more about this. "You must tell me how you got this." She glanced down at it. "The cipher is one we haven't used in some time. That's odd."

"It seemed safer, considering the Maxima has long had the key to the one you normally use."

Gwynneth stared at Fernanda. She'd expected as much from Natalya, but was amazed to hear it confirmed, especially by this person. "All right." She took a long drink of tea, waving Linette away after she'd poured for both of them. "Linette and Avaron, please leave us for a few moments." Whatever was happening here, she wanted no one else finding out about it.

ANTON

"It's not too awful for you, is it?" Anton asked Susanna, as he did several times a day. He knew she got impatient with his hovering, but he couldn't help himself. The way things were going, he was likely to fight a big battle around the time she was ready to have the baby. Anton wished he'd been able to avoid re-enlisting.

"I'm fine." She leaned back against the flat pillows on the little bed. They lived in a damp, drafty attic on the fourth floor of a very tall, skinny house. "I'm tired, but that's to be expected."

"You can stop working now," Anton said. "I'm making enough money."

That was true, but not the whole story. Colonel Granter, who led Anton's new regiment, paid his troops plenty. But there was hardly anything to buy in the city and the little available, was terribly expensive. Anton and Susanna spent a month's pay on a week's food. They couldn't go on like this much longer.

Susanna smiled at him and took his hand, pulling him down next to her. "I don't want to stop working. It's not that bad and it's a good way to get extra food." She'd been hired on by the regiment as a cook's assistant. Anton worried the work was much too hard for someone as small as Susanna, pregnant or not, with the huge iron pots she needed to lift and carry. But she sometimes got extra scraps of food at the end of the day, since the cook—a rotund, grandfatherly fellow—took a liking to the two of them. "I'll work until the baby comes and then I'll try to take some time off."

"By then we'll have won the battle." Anton tried to sound cheerful, but he doubted they'd win. All the troops inside the city were optimistic and eager to fight, but none of them had faced Lennart. Only a few days after Anton arrived, word came that Lennart caught up to Count Michalek's fleeing regiment and finished it off. That Anton and Susanna left so quickly saved their lives, at least for now. But Anton didn't want to take his chances against Lennart again.

"I'm sure you'll win." Susanna smiled before drifting off to sleep.

Anton tried to stretch out beside her on the hard straw mattress. The blankets smelled of mildew and the bed frame was too short for him. He had to huddle up like a baby to keep his feet from hanging over the end. He worried over the terrible possibilities. They were stuck inside this city, food becoming more and more scarce as Lennart's troops spread across the countryside. If Ensden stayed inside, they'd all starve to death sooner or later. Colonel Granter said the Maladene navy would break Lennart's blockade, but Anton didn't believe that either.

The other alternative was to fight. And Ensden still had greater numbers than Lennart, though that wouldn't last if they died of plague and starvation in here. If they fought, they might win. But Anton remembered Isenberg's deadly little guns and Lennart's disciplined ranks of musketeers. Granter's regiment had nothing like the discipline of the Michalek pike, all of them now dead. Anton didn't see how his new comrades would stand up to Lennart's combined forces.

He turned onto his other side. He'd also heard a rumor that Prince Kendryk commanded an army out there with King Lennart. Anton wondered how he might get to him. It would mean desertion, but he'd be willing to risk it if it meant saving his and Susanna's lives. But for now, he was trapped inside the city. No one could leave. He'd have to wait for battle and make a run for it, though he didn't know how that would work.

He worried that Susanna would have their baby right in the middle of all this. If it was hard for them to survive right now, Anton didn't see how a tiny baby would. He swallowed down the lump growing in his throat, screwing his eyes shut against the tears.

He hated this helplessness. It was as though nothing had changed since he was a little boy, standing by while terrible things happened first to his father, then his sister, and then his mother. He almost didn't feel like the same person who'd saved King Arryk at Birkenfels, or fought pirates with the count, or helped rescue Prince Kendryk.

Eyes still shut, he prayed to Ercos, promising that if the gods saved Susanna and the baby from what was coming, he'd read the Holy Scrolls again, but pay attention this time. He'd become religious like Prince Kendryk and follow every rule, no matter how difficult. When he opened his eyes again, they were wet, but he felt a little bit better. So far, he'd always survived. He knew he could do it again.

BRAEDEN

Rather than wait around to find out what Edric did with Elektra, Braeden returned to Birkenfels. Just thinking about the archduchess made him angry, and he didn't want to waste any more time on her. He made sure the area around Heidenhof was heavily patrolled, though he doubted there was any further threat. No one on the imperial side except Franca knew where Elektra was, and he trusted her not to tell anyone.

Braeden reached Birkenfels late in the evening and drank a tankard of ale, alone in the kitchen. He couldn't decide what to do about Franca. She'd head north and likely threaten Lennart's forces from the rear. She'd promised not to devastate Terragand as she went, though she'd likely need to plunder supplies. If Braeden didn't tell Lennart what was coming, he'd feel like a traitor. But if he told Lennart, his army would be waiting for Franca, putting her in terrible danger. There was no good solution.

Braeden sighed, staring into his nearly empty mug. It was time for bed. He'd come up with something in the morning. He left the kitchen and started up the stairs to the room he used when he was here. A light still burned in the library, so he poked his head in.

"You're back already," said the old man sitting at a table, hunched over a book. Baron Persyn was the senior officer when Braeden wasn't here, and a veteran of the Zastwar wars, though he'd long ago become an arthritic bookworm. Still, he kept things going at Birkenfels well enough.

"Some interesting events at Heidenhof," Braeden said. "Though things turned out all right."

"You must tell me in the morning," Persyn said. "You look like you're ready to fall asleep on your feet."

"I am." Braeden grinned. "I'll see you at breakfast."

"Oh, wait," Persyn said, rummaging among papers on the table. "This came for you yesterday. It isn't marked as urgent, though it's from Prince Kendryk."

"Thanks," Braeden grabbed the letter, deciding to read it once he'd crawled into bed. It was still far too cold to be standing on a stone floor, surrounded by stone walls unless you were belly up to a roaring fire. And with only a small garrison at the castle, fires were scarce.

In bed, an extra blanket wrapped around his shoulders, Braeden opened the letter. He hoped Kendryk would tell him of Lennart's reaction to Braeden's decision to stay here, though he was almost too tired to care.

Kendryk mentioned that Lennart had every faith that Braeden had made the right decision and to expect a letter from him soon.

"He ought to have time to write while we figure out a way to lure Ensden out of the city. I hope you will find nothing dangerous near Birkenfels, though I appreciate you defending the area. But if all seems secure there, perhaps you can leave a trusted lieutenant in charge and undertake a mission for me.

I am concerned about Princess Gwynneth and my children. Something in Allaux has gone wrong, and it seems she is unable to leave the city. I had hoped to have my family join me after Lennart's victory, but I'd rather not wait any longer. Birkenfels is secure, and it's safe to travel through the rest of Kronland right now. I am not ordering you to do this; rather, I'm asking as a friend, if you will go to Allaux and bring Gwynneth back with you."

Braeden put the letter down and rubbed his eyes, though he was awake now. He did not relish the idea of tangling with Natalya, for that could be the only person preventing Gwynneth from leaving. But for Kendryk, he'd try. He continued reading.

"I'm sure that Gwynneth and Natalya have fallen out somehow. I don't get the sense that Gwynneth is a prisoner, but she isn't free to do whatever she wants. I hoped if you were able to get me out of the Arnfels, you might remove my family from Allaux without too much trouble."

Braeden snorted at that. He'd had considerable high-level help with the Arnfels, but he'd have none here. It would help to understand what exactly was going on before he planned a daring rescue.

The next morning, Braeden wrote a quick letter to Kendryk, handed it off to a messenger, then made plans to travel to Allaux with a small escort. He'd leave most of the cavalry Trystan had given him here, and under Baron Persyn's direction, knew it would be deployed effectively. "I'm going to pay the Princess Gwynneth a visit," he told Persyn. "Seems she's ready to return here and needs a friendly escort."

The baron raised his eyebrows. "Can't King Gauvain provide one?"

"It's what Prince Kendryk wants," Braeden said. "He'd feel better about having a friend in charge than some Galladian popinjay."

"Now that I can understand." The old soldier's face broke into a smile.

GWYNNETH

Gwynneth waited for the door to close behind her ladies, then leaned forward. "I want you to explain exactly how this letter got into your hands and when."

"Don't you want to read it first?" Fernanda's eyes had a dangerous sparkle.

"No, I want to know why my husband would entrust Brynhild Mattila with a letter to me." It was true she was dying to read it, but preferred to do so in private, not under the stare of this impertinent, possibly dangerous woman.

"It's complicated," Fernanda said, taking a long drink of tea, clearly enjoying herself.

"I'll probably manage to understand," Gwynneth said.

Fernanda took a bite of pastry, chewed it deliberately, and brushed an imaginary crumb from her lip. Gwynneth tried not to scream with impatience.

"As you know..." Fernanda took another sip of tea. "Your husband paid a visit to General Mattila a few months ago."

"Yes. That was hardly a secret."

"His visit was not. What he discussed with her, however, was not what everyone thought."

"Are you saying he went for a reason other than trying to win her over to Lennart's side?"

"He did." Fernanda took another pastry.

Gwynneth wished she hadn't ordered any food. She hoped the tea was running low. "So what was the reason?"

"Your husband had concerns about Natalya. Not only because of your letters, but because he learned that she and Lennart are conspiring to divide up the kingdoms of Kronland between Estenor and Galladium. They'll even let Teodora have a piece as long as she doesn't stand in their way."

"That's a lie," Gwynneth whispered, all while admitting to herself it was also her worst nightmare.

"If you say so. Your husband, of course, is not in favor of this plan, because Terragand would become an Estenorian territory, with no need of a prince to rule it."

Gwynneth considered Lennart a friend, but in the back of her mind she had always wondered what his true ambitions were.

"All right." Gwynneth did her best to stay calm. She still didn't see the whole picture. "How in the world is Brynhild Mattila involved in this?"

"General Mattila has ambitions that run counter to this scheme. She is close to becoming the ruler of Brandana. She would lose it all once Galladium takes it as part of its portion."

"I'm willing to assume that, for the sake of argument at least." Gwynneth shook her head. "But why does she want to help me?"

Fernanda smiled. "In this situation, your husband is Mattila's natural ally, and she wishes for a strong, independent Terragand to stand with Brandana. She'd like to put him back on the throne in return for his support against this conspiracy. It's clear to her you are of invaluable support to your husband, and we question his ability to assert himself without you. But most of all, you would owe the general a favor."

"We're done here." Gwynneth stood. "There is nothing I can do for her." Much as she wanted to hope that someone might help her, she could not bring herself to trust someone as treacherous and ambitious as Mattila. Besides, she had not ruled out the possibility that Natalya was testing her loyalty with this woman's tempting proposal.

Fernanda stayed in her chair, relaxed, looking up at Gwynneth with laughter in her awful eyes. "Don't you want to hear what the favor is first?"

"Not really. Please go now." Gwynneth headed for the door.

"You will back Mattila's claim to the throne of Brandana," Fernanda said to her back. "And then it will be possible for her to help you restore Terragand to its former glory. You must realize she's immensely rich."

Gwynneth stopped short. "Mattila doesn't care about Terragand at all." She turned around slowly. "She's a ruthless, ambitious opportunist."

Fernanda smiled more widely now, showing a hint of white teeth. So they weren't rotten. "She is. She's still happy to help you if it's in her best interest."

"I doubt that very much, and I have little interest in helping subvert the rightful ruler of Brandana," Gwynneth snapped, certain now that this woman was in Natalya's employ. "It's time for you to go." She pointed at the door.

"Oh come, Your Grace, surely you can see the sense in my proposal. I can see how anxious you are to get out of Natalya's clutches."

"I don't know what you're talking about." Gwynneth turned back to the door. Before she could reach it, Fernanda stood in front of her. "How?" Gwynneth gasped. The woman had moved impossibly quickly.

"Special training." Fernanda shrugged. "Now please, Your Grace, go sit. We need to talk some more."

"No," Gwynneth said, making a half-hearted attempt to dodge around Fernanda, even though she worried it wouldn't work.

"Yes." Fernanda took Gwynneth's elbow with an iron grip and steered her back to her chair.

Gwynneth fell into it, her knees weak. "Who are you?" she whispered.

"Exactly who I told you. An employee of Mattila's on a special mission. That mission is to help you escape Allaux and return you to your husband."

Gwynneth took a deep breath, trying to calm herself. "All right," she said. "Suppose I agree and we go to Terragand. Mattila helps us get rid of all foreign interference. Under what conditions will Kendryk rule after that?"

"The same as he did before," Fernanda said.

"I doubt that."

"The only difference will be a special alliance with Brandana. Kendryk will be asked to support her claim to its throne. "

"She has no claim. I'm certain Kendryk won't support her."

"Are you sure of that?" Fernanda had a gleam in her eye. "Wouldn't you prefer to discuss it with him in person."

More than anything in the world, Gwynneth thought, hoping her face didn't show it.

"Then let me help you do that." Fernanda's voice turned gentle, and even her strange eyes seemed softer.

Gwynneth sat silently. Finally she said, "You've given me much to consider. I'm still not sure if I believe any of it. I must read Kendryk's letter and make sure it's not a forgery."

"I can assure you it's not. I watched him write it."

"While he was with Mattila?"

Fernanda nodded.

"And then he gave it to you?"

"Yes. And he will explain under what conditions you can consider it safe to trust me."

Gwynneth still didn't think she ever would, but she would have to read Kendryk's letter first, and then decide.

LENNART

It was hard for Lennart to wait, but everything was going according to plan. It took a long time to get all of his troops into place, then wait for the fake Maladene ships to create a feigned engagement so the false letter made its way into Ensden's hands. Lennart had picked his spot; now he only had to herd Ensden into it when the time came.

Ensden had had the letter for at least a week and would certainly move soon. The letter had emphasized the need for rapid action. Though winter was nearly over, the storms in the northern sea were especially unpredictable, and any ships near the shore might not wait there for more than a few days. Once the weather cleared, Ensden would have to leave Kaltental.

The weather stayed dreary, with endless wind and rain while Lennart tried very hard to be patient. But one morning, he awoke to silence. No rain drummed on the slate roof of the house he slept in. No wind rattled the window panes. When he sat up, he saw weak sunlight slanting onto the floor. He jumped out of bed, grabbing his dressing gown and calling for a servant. He planned to be in the field before mid-morning.

By the time he reached the stable yard, stuffing a crust of bread into his mouth and washing it down with vile-tasting tea, others were preparing as well.

Prince Kendryk was mounted and waiting for him. "Do you think he'll come out?" Kendryk asked as they rode out on the streets of the town and headed for the gates.

"He'd better," Lennart said, raising his hand in greeting as a column of soldiers marched past double-time. "Who knows how long the weather will hold. He won't want to be stranded on the beach when the ships can't reach it." His anticipation rose as they passed through the open city gate. They stayed in a town ten leagues south of Kaltental, but only five leagues from the battlefield where he hoped to intercept Ensden.

"I realize it was partly my idea," Kendryk said, his face grave. "But I feel a little bad, using subterfuge like that. It doesn't seem honorable."

Lennart offered a sympathetic nod. "Honorable doesn't win battles. We must win here and soon."

"I know," Kendryk said. "I can't wait for it to be over."

"I can't wait for it to start." Lennart urged his horse to a canter and Kendryk followed. By the time they reached the battlefield, most of Lennart's troops and guns were in place.

"Ensden ought to be on his way by now," Lennart said. He was anxious, though he knew it would take time to get a large force like that out of the city and onto the road. They might need all day to get here. Perhaps they wouldn't engage until the following day.

The morning wore on and it was noon. The commanders had a bite to eat at tables set up on the field, while the soldiers ate standing up and at the ready. Lennart had sent scouts to watch the road all the way to Kaltental, and they reported in every hour. By mid-afternoon, he'd still received no sign from the city.

"Perhaps they're still getting ready," Kendryk said, clearly trying to sound reassuring. "They wouldn't be nearly as prepared as we are and will have troops quartered all over town. They might need a whole day at least to muster."

Lennart looked up at the sky. Fluffy white clouds scudded across it, and though a brisk wind blew, a storm seemed unlikely. "Maybe he'll come out tomorrow. It's his only chance."

"I'm sure he will," Kendryk said.

They slept on the field that night, and Lennart had pickets put on high alert. Ensden was a canny old fellow, and Lennart wouldn't be surprised if he waited until after dark to march out and slip past. Lennart slept poorly, every sound making him wake and look around, wondering if the noise he heard was the tramp of thousands of distant feet.

Everyone rose at dawn and got ready again. Through Lennart's fatigue, his nerves jangled and he felt fidgety. He dismounted, and paced up and down the field, pretending to inspect first one unit and then another. That at least helped pass the time. Noon came and went with no movement from the city. No one would say the words, but Lennart saw from their faces they believed Ensden wasn't coming. He was beginning to believe it himself.

The weather was fair when he went to sleep, but he awoke in the middle of the night to the drumming of rain on his tent and the rush of a rising wind. A storm was on its way. By morning, scouts coming from the beach had confirmed it. Even the ships on Lennart's blockade had sailed into harbor. Ensden wouldn't come out now.

"He didn't fall for it," Lennart said to Kendryk as they rode back to the town and its comforts.

"Maybe he did," Kendryk said. "But he decided not to risk it anyway. Perhaps he's waiting for reinforcements."

"Who would send reinforcements?"

"I don't know," Kendryk said, his voice grave, his eyes tired. "But one thing I've learned about Teodora is that she often has the best luck at the worst moments."

ELEKTRA

Of all the ways Elektra had been imprisoned, this one was the nicest by far. Still, it was annoying that it had to be at the hands of the biggest enemy of the faith, Edric Landrus. Elektra always dined with him and his guests, and slept in a beautiful bedchamber inside the palace. She went anywhere she wanted on the first two floors of the palace and spent all the time she wanted in the garden—that garden with its massive walls.

For all of the respectful treatment, guards stood at every entrance and stayed at her bedchamber door while she slept. But no one made any move to confine her further or threaten her in any way. Elektra was beginning to hope she might survive this experience, though she wondered why she was being held here.

Once she got over the shock of seeing Braeden and realizing Franca had betrayed her, she felt it her duty to argue with the heretic Maximus. Surely Vica had put her here to bring about his conversion. On occasions they were alone at dinner, Elektra tried to persuade him back to the true faith.

But it was hard to start an argument with Edric. "I understand why you believe what you do, Your Grace." Unlike Braeden, he always said those words with the proper gravity and respect. His pale eyes, though unnerving, were kind, and his deep voice always softened when he spoke with her. "I used to believe the same as you. I was well-educated in the faith and thought I understood the ways of the gods. But I needed to read the Holy Scrolls to realize my errors. It was difficult to accept at first." He paused and waved over a servant. "Would you like more wine?"

Elektra thought she should refuse because too much wine made it hard to argue well. But Edric served the most marvelous wine, even though the food accompanying it was on the plain side. "Thank you," she said, deciding it would be the last glass of the evening. She took a few small sips then said, "But I have read the Holy Scrolls and I disagree with you about everything."

"Have you read all of them, from beginning to end?"

"Well no, that's unnecessary. Livilla says many parts are too boring or irrelevant to our time, so only the good bits are needed."

Edric chuckled. "And who decides what the good bits are?"

"Why Livilla does. Only a Maxima can do that."

"I'm a Maximus." Edric took a long drink, then grinned as he put the glass back on the table.

"Not a real one." Elektra took a few more sips. "I don't mean to offend you since you're very kind. But you were not ordained by the Imperata, and instead, chosen by a heretic prince. I'm afraid you don't have the same authority someone like Livilla does."

"You make a good point." Edric didn't seem the least bit offended. "I don't have the same authority as Livilla. My authority comes directly from the gods, rather than from the Imperata."

"I'm very sorry." Elektra realized her voice was too loud, but couldn't restrain her indignation. "That is terrible heresy. I cannot accept it." She banged her now empty glass down a little bit hard.

Edric looked amused, which made it all harder to bear. "What if I told you that you have the same authority? That the gods speak to you as directly as they do to any Imperata or temple official?"

Elektra stared. How did he know? For he looked at her as if he understood that Vica had spoken to her. Finally she said, "Holy Vica has spoken to me a few times. Not in words, but when I called on her in a moment of need, she guided my words and helped me know what to do."

"That's precisely what I mean," Edric said. "And you are very fortunate, that you've had that experience already. Many people go their whole lives never having that communion with the gods. You've been blessed."

"I agree," Elektra whispered. Then she looked up at him. "Are you saying the gods spoke to you in similar ways?"

Edric nodded. "A few times, yes. Always in moments of dire need, when I had exhausted all of my own resources and was certain the end was near."

Elektra remembered her terror when Braeden wanted to kill her. "That's exactly when I received help. I was so frightened, so certain I would die. Then I felt a curious strength, and when I spoke, I said the right things to save myself."

"Then there is nothing a Maxima can teach you," Edric said. He sighed and stared straight ahead for a moment. "You can rely upon yourself and your communication with the gods. If you remain humble, ask them to show you the way and read the scrolls every day, you will become wiser than the Imperata herself."

"That's wrong," Elektra whispered, though she desperately wanted to trust his words. More than anything, she wanted to stay in that state where she was convinced she did the will of the gods and they lent her strength. No doubt, no confusion.

She swallowed and forced herself to look Edric in the eye. It was almost harder to do when his eyes were soft and kind than when they bore a more distant chill. "Why am I here?" she whispered. "Why didn't you let Braeden kill me?"

A smile spread across Edric's face. "Because you have an important part to play. Braeden doesn't see it. He's blinded by his hatred of your mother. But I see it, and the gods sent you to me so we could find the way together."

GWYNNETH

After leaving Fernanda in the drawing room, swearing on the gods she'd return soon, then telling the guards to keep a close eye on her guest, Gwynneth hurried to her bedchamber. She laid Kendryk's letter on a small table and went to a bureau, where she pulled out a large bundle of letters, tied with a blue ribbon. These were all of Kendryk's messages to her, since the beginning of the war. She took them back to the table and shuffled through them until she found the ones she needed.

They had used one cipher until just before the battle at Birkenfels, then agreed to switch to another. They hadn't had a chance to use it until after Kendryk's escape. Now Gwynneth needed a good example of the old one. She huffed impatiently at the poor light, then pulled her chair over to the window, still holding the recent message and an old letter side-by-side. Once she took a closer look, the handwriting appeared to match perfectly and she saw no mistakes in the code.

She breathed a little more slowly now and scrutinized the recent letter some more. It was dated the previous summer, when Kendryk had written to her from Brandana several times. Gwynneth went back to the table and rummaged until she found one of those letters. They were written on the same paper, with what appeared to be the same ink. The way the letters occasionally faded out even made her wonder if he'd used the same quill.

Reasonably certain that Kendryk had written this, Gwynneth settled in to read it, surprised she remembered the old cipher perfectly.

"I am worried you will not trust this unexpected messenger," Kendryk wrote. *"But even worse would be placing our trust in Lennart or Natalya. If they get their way, nothing will be left of my kingdom. They must be stopped and the only person able to do it is Mattila. She alone can raise an army and lead it to victory against Lennart. Once she's crushed him, she will deal with Teodora. I doubt Natalya will continue with this plan once her allies are destroyed.*

"You must let Fernanda help you, since I will not have the strength to do what I must without you, especially if you are Natalya's hostage. You and the children must leave Allaux. Fernanda will make all of the arrangements and bring you safely to Zeelund. I wish to keep you in neutral territory until I can be sure Terragand is secure. It is almost completely under Lennart's control and he won't hesitate to take you prisoner if doing so will help him control me."

Gwynneth's eyes filled with tears. This was all her fault, for trusting Natalya and making it possible for Lennart to come here. There was only a paragraph left, so she wiped her eyes and read on.

"I know you will not trust Fernanda as she's a creature of Mattila's. But she has proven herself already in a way I will explain to you when we see each other again. For now, be assured she acts with my blessing. To prove it to you, she will carry a token of mine. You will know it well. Once you are certain of her, do not delay. I will meet you in Zeelund soon."

It made a great deal of sense, though relying on Mattila for help was a lot to bear. Gwynneth put the old letters away, folded up the one Fernanda had given her and tucked it into her bodice. She returned to the drawing room where Fernanda had fallen asleep in a chair.

Afraid to touch her, Gwynneth cleared her throat loudly and Fernanda woke with a start. "Took you long enough," she grumbled, yawning widely, though she was at least polite enough to cover her mouth.

"Kendryk says you have something of his," Gwynneth said, looking down at Fernanda.

"I do." She slid a hand into a well-concealed pocket in her skirt and pulled something out.

Gwynneth gasped. It was Kendryk's signet ring. She'd never known him to take it off. She snatched it from Fernanda's hand and inspected it closely. There was a tiny flaw in the gold, right between two of the small diamonds set into a circle around the engraved crest. Gwynneth turned the ring over. The score continued into the back of the ring. It had been damaged years ago by Kendryk's father during a tournament.

"Well?" Fernanda asked, her raspy voice louder now.

Gwynneth realized she'd been turning the ring over in her hand for at least a minute. "It's his." A terrible thought struck her. "You didn't kill him to get this from him, did you?"

Fernanda scoffed. "You've received many recent letters from him I'm sure. If I'd killed him months ago, you would have heard by now." She shook her head. "Still so suspicious."

"Can you blame me?" Gwynneth's knees wobbled so she sat down, still clutching the ring in her fist. "I've checked everything and it all fits, though I still don't like it."

"That makes sense. Mattila has been your opponent for a long time." Fernanda regarded her with that black gaze.

Gwynneth shuddered. "Even though it doesn't feel good, staying here for months while Natalya does gods-knows-what seems even worse." She forced herself to look Fernanda in the eye. "I'll come with you."

TEODORA

The letter from Daciana came while Teodora was closeted with her advisers, but she didn't dare open it. No one but Livilla knew anything about Daciana's mission, and Teodora wanted to keep it that way. When Gwynneth and her children turned up dead, it was best if it looked accidental, with no connection to Teodora.

"That'll be enough for today," Teodora said, standing up.

Countess Biaram looked at her, surprised. It was still light outside and they seldom left Teodora's study before midnight.

"I've decided you deserve an evening off," Teodora said, smiling.

The countess looked even more surprised, and Solteszy shook his head as he gathered up papers. "I hope Your Highness has planned a relaxing evening. You've been working very hard."

"It's true I have," Teodora said. "But we're close to having a plan for Norovaea in place. We can finish with the details tomorrow." She hoped that the message from Daciana would tell her what she needed to go forward. If Gwynneth was already dead, Teodora would order her agents in Norovaea to act sooner.

After hurrying to her bedchamber and sending the servants away, Teodora opened the letter. Her hands trembled, either from excitement or premature old age. She read it quickly then slumped back into her chair, finally relaxed.

It had taken Daciana a great deal of effort to gain Princess Gwynneth's trust. *"I used all the tricks we came up with. You were wise to plan so thoroughly because she asked every question we anticipated and some we hadn't. By the time you receive this, we ought to be on our way and it's possible she and the children are already dead. If you hear nothing further from me, I was killed or captured in carrying out this mission."*

"Gods forbid," Teodora muttered to herself. Daciana refused to tell her exactly how she'd carry out the plan, but Teodora made her swear she wouldn't choose anything suicidal. "I gave everything to bring you back to health," she'd said. "I can't do it again."

"It won't be needed," Daciana said. "You will not regret your sacrifice. I hope you realize I'm very grateful." Her black eyes had softened in a way no one but Teodora ever saw.

"I don't regret it anyway," Teodora said. "Words can't describe how happy I am you are doing this for me. I'm sure you will succeed."

After reading the letter over two more times to make sure she had missed nothing, Teodora folded it up and walked over to the window. The sun was going down, golden rays slanting across the garden in full spring bloom. What a fitting time to cut down Gwynneth and her children. It was almost poetic.

It might have already happened, since the letter was dated nearly two weeks before. Either way, it was time to put the Norovaean part of her plan in motion. Arryk should be out of the way soon, and with Gwynneth dead, Aksel would be the new king. Releasing Aksel's friend under Livilla's strict supervision had at least made Aksel somewhat cooperative, and Teodora hoped he'd be a tractable puppet. It was a shame she wasn't able to locate Elektra, but she could be sent to Norovaea whenever she turned up.

That left only Kendryk. It didn't really matter precisely when Gwynneth and the children had died, or how. What mattered was Kendryk hearing about it as soon as possible from Teodora herself. She didn't think the news would stop Lennart in his tracks, but if Kendryk suddenly became a devastated, demoralized, useless ally, Terragand's future might become less certain.

Kendryk would take the news hard and with any luck, withdraw from public life. And without his enthusiastic backing, Lennart might struggle to retain the support of other Kronland rulers. Teodora was aware that at least several of those who provided him troops had been rather reluctant. It would take little to pressure them into neutrality.

Teodora worried about Ensden, still trapped in Kaltental after all this time. She'd hoped the Maladene navy might get him out, but so far they had failed. Ensden's armies still outnumbered Lennart's, but after what she'd been told of Lennart's methods, she was uncertain of Ensden providing a decisive victory. She hoped he'd be patient enough to stay put until she thought of a way to help him. Perhaps removing Kendryk from the opposition would do the job.

It was time to write him a letter.

ANTON

Susanna's time was close, and Anton worried he'd be called away to fight, now that spring had come.

"I don't need you here the moment the baby comes," she said, smiling at him as they had a late supper in the kitchen. "The midwife knows her business and you'll be back after the battle. Though I doubt it'll all happen at the same time."

"That would be just my luck," Anton grumbled into his stew. No one seemed to know what was going on. His sergeant told him that Ensden was waiting for something or someone, and there would be no battle until that thing had happened. When Anton wasn't drilling, he roamed the streets of Kaltental, hoping to learn something useful.

He found out that Lennart's armies had disappeared. Anton suspected a trap, but the sergeant thought there might be another explanation.

"What if the empress sent another force from the south and he's busy fighting them right now?" The end of the sergeant's pipe disappeared under a drooping mustache.

"Wouldn't we have heard something about that?" Anton asked. "Wouldn't they want Ensden to come out and help?"

The sergeant shrugged and Anton left, figuring it made more sense for him to get information on his own.

And one day, something happened. Anton had walked into the street after stopping in at his usual tavern for a bite to eat when a boy ran past.

"They've opened the eastern gate!" he shouted and kept running.

Anton wasn't too far from there, so he turned down the next street and headed east. Only a few people had heard the news, but they went in that direction too. Anton hoped it wasn't the enemy, though he doubted there'd be so little commotion if it were. Near the gate, people lined the streets, staring curiously, though Anton saw nothing.

"Who's come?" he asked a man standing against the wall of a building.

"Word is that reinforcements from the empress have arrived," the man said.

"Lennart didn't stop them?"

"Seems not." The man shrugged. "It's a good-sized cavalry, from Sanova they say."

"The Sanova Hussars?" Anton's mouth dried up as he spoke.

"Not sure. It's said they're led by a fierce red-haired woman."

Anton's breath caught in his throat. He'd been looking for a red-headed Sanova Hussar since Skandar had been sold. Now he stared down the street as eagerly as the rest.

She wore no helmet, so he spotted her from a distance, though Anton never even noticed her face. Even from a hundred paces, he was certain she rode Skandar.

"Oh gods," he said a little too loudly, so folk around him stared. "Excuse me," he said, pushing through the crowd. By the time he reached the street, Skandar had passed him. Anton broke free of the crowd and ran. "Skandar!" he shouted. "Skandar!"

He didn't watch where he was going. He needed to get up the street to where Skandar had turned a corner, out of sight.

"Hey!" He gasped as something stung his face. "Mind where you're going."

Anton stumbled to a halt, and stared into the grim face of a boy no older than he was. He sat high on a charger much too big for him, brandishing a riding crop. He must have flicked it into Anton's face when he ran into his horse. He was already riding on, but Anton caught up and walked alongside. "Can you tell me who your commander is?"

"Why do you care?" the boy asked scowling, though he put the crop away.

"I might know her," Anton said.

The boy shook his head. "Then you would know Franca Dura commands Dura's Cuirassiers. She's famous."

"Franca Dura," Anton said, "That's what I thought. Thanks." He slowed down and the boy pulled ahead. He remembered something else and ran to catch up. "Hey," he said.

"What do you want?" The boy looked impatient at this point.

"Where are you lot staying?"

"We're not," he said. "Colonel Dura must meet with the general and learn his plans, but I expect there'll be a battle in the next day or two."

Anton let him go, but followed at a distance. He couldn't lose track of Skandar now, though he hadn't figured out how to get to him. Colonel Dura looked like someone you shouldn't tangle with. Still, he'd come up with something.

Once he followed the cuirassiers to the large house where General Ensden stayed, he knew how he could find out more. In the crush of soldiers and horses, he slipped into the courtyard and headed for the stables. He didn't see Skandar, but he saw Franca Dura, going into the house. So he must already be inside. Anton sauntered into the stable as if he belonged there, then peeked into each stall, looking for Skandar.

He found him near the end of the first row. He stared at Skandar, who stared back. Anton was sure he remembered him. "Hello Skandar," he said softly.

"What are you doing here?" a liveried groom came around his side.

"I, er, work here," Anton said, staring desperately at his horse. He looked well-fed, his coat glossy. He might have even grown a little.

The groom looked Anton over. "No you don't. No one wearing rags works at the general's house. Off with you now." He threw a brush in Anton's direction and Anton retreated. He'd have to think of something else.

He returned to the courtyard and looked around. Troopers milled in the courtyard, most of them getting their horses put away. Anton didn't notice the boy he'd spoken to. He needed to find out where they were going next, so he found a dark corner, sat down on the cold ground and waited.

ELEKTRA

"How is it going?" Edric poked his head inside the door of Elektra's study. He'd set up a little room for her to work in. It reminded her of school, though she didn't mind too much.

Elektra looked up from her reading. "Quite well. It turns out Livilla was right and the boring bits of the Scrolls really are boring."

Edric smiled, then came in and sat down near her table. Obviously he was trying very hard to convert her to his heresy. "That's true, though at the pace you're reading, you're about to get to an interesting part."

"Why can't I skip to it?" For now, Elektra saw no harm in cooperating. She had set up a makeshift altar to Vica in her room, and prayed diligently that the goddess would help keep her on the right path. Besides, she was flattered at being treated like a fellow scholar. Before his fall into terrible error, Edric had been one of the temple's most promising young priests. Elektra was sure she might learn a great deal from him without trusting everything he said.

"The context is important," Edric said. "The interesting parts make more sense when you understand when and why they were written."

"All right." Elektra shrugged. "It's not like I have anything better to do."

"There's no better way to pass the time. I suppose it's too soon to ask if you've had any change of heart. Doesn't all of this reading make you want to learn more?"

"It does, but Livilla always said that reading the Scrolls wasn't enough. Interpretation was the key thing, and only a cleric authorized by the Imperata might do that."

"That's very convenient, isn't it?" Edric's tone was still mild, but his eyes flashed. "The Imperata can make sure everything is explained to her advantage."

"That's hardly fair," Elektra said, seeing a chance to perhaps score a few points. "The gods speak to her directly. She'll understand more than the rest of us."

"The gods speak to you directly as well," Edric said.

"Goddess." Elektra marked her page, then closed the book. "Only Vica has ever spoken to me."

"How do you know it was Vica, and not one of the other gods?"

"Because I prayed to her and she answered almost immediately."

"I was meaning to ask you about that," Edric said. "Would you mind telling me what happened? I am truly interested."

"I'm sure you are." Elektra hesitated. Since some of the story involved her betrayal of Braeden, she wondered how Edric would react. She chewed her lower lip. "You might not want to hear it, since it starts with your friend Braeden doing something awful."

Edric chuckled. "I wouldn't really call Braeden a friend. He's a useful ally, though we understand each other well enough. And I'm sure he's done things in his life I might not approve of. It's not my place to judge, since the gods will hold him accountable."

"I'm not sure about that. It seems he's gotten away with what he did to me." Elektra felt her anger rise, looked at Edric's sympathetic face, and the story poured out, right through the part where she prayed at Vica's altar for twelve hours straight, hoping to receive forgiveness for breaking her vow.

Edric listened silently to the end, his expression unchanging, though he made an encouraging noise from time to time if Elektra paused. When she had finished, there was a long silence.

"Your Grace," he finally said, "You did not need to spend all of that time in penance. As far as I can tell, you acted correctly, though perhaps not heroically."

"I wasn't wrong to turn Braeden in?"

Edric shook his head. "Under the circumstances, I can't blame you," he said. "I can understand why you felt you were doing the right thing."

"Even though it wasn't the right thing."

"Is that what you believe now?" he asked, with that kind smile on his face. Elektra wondered how many people he'd disarmed with that expression.

"It's made me so many enemies," she whispered. "Braeden will hate me forever, and so will anyone who's his friend."

"Likely true, but it's a valuable lesson. Don't you agree, Your Grace?"

Elektra had to smile at that. "I suppose it is. In the moment, I was so angry and wanted revenge, and yet if I'd let him escape, I might be in a very different position right now."

"Indeed. But I can't say I'm unhappy that you're here. It's something I wouldn't have predicted, though it's surely the will of the gods."

"What are you saying?" Intense unease washed over Elektra. "Why would the gods want me here?"

"I'm not sure yet." The crease between Edric's brows grew even deeper. "But I'm certain there is a reason. Few people in the empire are as important as you. And to have you delivered here, at a moment where I might keep you safe from those who would harm you makes me certain it was no accident."

Elektra shivered. She didn't mind talk of destiny, as long as it involved her doing something glorious. But this was different. "What do the gods want from me? Surely not to become a heretic. That would be the end of everything."

Edric raised an eyebrow. "Would it? Or would it be the beginning of something better? Just imagine how quickly you might help end the war."

"I'd always hoped to end the war by conquering your heresy." Elektra couldn't help but smile at that. If that was the will of the gods they were going about it in a strange way. "But suppose I join you—which I, of course, will not. How will that improve anything? My mother will continue on her path and I'm powerless to stop her."

"Are you?" Edric asked. "Truly? No one is better placed to bring Teodora's ambitions to an end."

"Don't say those things." His matter-of-fact tone made her nervous. "I told Braeden I wanted to kill my mother, and I do hate her. But doing the deed would be a terrible crime."

"I'm not certain you're right," Edric said. "But don't worry about it for now. Keep studying, and I'm sure the gods will show us the right path."

Elektra wondered when she and the false Maximus had become "us," but she couldn't deny she was terribly curious about the future.

GWYNNETH

"Mama, please don't let us go with that woman." Maryna was near tears.

Gwynneth smiled at her in what she hoped was a comforting fashion. Her own doubts were barely beneath the surface. "We must leave Allaux," she explained again. "Papa will meet us in Zeelund."

"Why?" Maryna shook her head. "It makes no sense. And something is wrong with that Fernanda Vastic—even Zofya doesn't like her."

"We don't have to like her," Gwynneth said, "but she will help us get away from here."

"Natalya won't want you to go." Maryna's tears spilled over.

"No, she won't." Gwynneth looked around her bedchamber. Her trunks were packed and now the maids were getting the children's things together. They couldn't take everything, just enough for the few weeks it might take to get to Zeelund. Fernanda had assured her she had plenty of money for everything they needed, and had even handed Gwynneth a purse so she could get whatever she wanted for the journey. Gwynneth hadn't had actual coin in so long she was terrified of spending it, so she hid the purse under her skirts. She sat down on the bed, pulling Maryna down next to her. "It's too complicated to explain but we cannot trust Natalya."

"How can you say that?" Maryna dashed her tears away. "She's the *only* person we can trust. Just because you've had a fight with her doesn't mean she's not your friend. She will always be your friend."

"I know that." Gwynneth tried to smile but couldn't quite manage it. "But what Natalya is doing right now is not what's best for our family or for Terragand. That's why we must go away."

"I don't agree." Maryna's tone was stern in spite of the tears. She might be her father's daughter, but she was considerably stronger-willed. "I don't believe I'll come along."

"You must," Gwynneth said. "I'm your mother and you must do as I say. Natalya will agree with that, I'm sure."

"She would not agree with us going."

"No and that's why we can't tell her." Gwynneth put her arm around Maryna's shoulders and pulled her close. "You must trust me, all right? I will always do what's best for you, and you must believe that even if you don't understand."

"All right." Maryna wiped her eyes. "I will trust you, Mama."

"That's a good girl." Gwynneth kissed her cheek, wondering how much longer she'd be able to get Maryna to do what she wanted. Her strong will would help make her a good ruler, but she would have to learn to listen to counsel, even when she didn't agree with it.

The carriage came to Gwynneth's back door well after dark. It was a plain black one, though the interior was comfortable enough.

"You'll be crowded in here," Fernanda said, handing up the children after Gwynneth. "I hope you can manage without servants."

"I suppose I can." Gwynneth pulled baby Renata close. She wished for Catrin, but there was no room, and more than one carriage would attract attention. "Are you coming with us?"

"Oh yes." Fernanda wore plain black breeches and a black leather coat. "I'll be driving the carriage."

"Can I drive it with you?" Devyn was already climbing out of his corner.

"Maybe tomorrow." Fernanda frowned at him. "It's better to learn when it's light."

"I don't want him being a bother," Gwynneth said, shaking her head at Devyn.

"It's no bother." Fernanda slammed the door shut, then looked in the open window. "But first, I want to get far away from here. Close the window now, fasten the door from the inside and don't open it for anyone but me. I don't expect trouble, but if any comes, I'll handle it."

"All right." Gwynneth tried smiling, but she was so nervous she worried she might be sick. It would be too awful to be caught by Natalya again.

The carriage rolled through the dark streets, stopping only at the northern gate. Gwynneth heard a guard, then Fernanda's voice, and laughter. A moment later, the gate creaked and the carriage continued through it. Gwynneth allowed herself to breathe. By now all of the children but Maryna had fallen asleep, and even though it was dark, Gwynneth felt her daughter's accusing eyes on her.

She held the baby close, and to her surprise, the rocking of the comfortable carriage lulled her into a deep slumber. When she woke up, it was morning, and they appeared to be deep in an unfamiliar forest.

Before the sun rose above the tree tops, the carriage drew to a halt in front of a small wooden house with a thatched roof. Fernanda opened the door while the children yawned and rubbed sleepy eyes.

"We'll stay here for the day," she said. "If we are pursued, they will look for us on all the roads. We'll rest here, and I'll hide the horses and carriage in that shed over there."

Gwynneth climbed out and looked at the little building, nearly hidden in the trees. "You've thought of everything, haven't you?" She ventured a smile at Fernanda.

"I told you I had." Fernanda picked up Stella, who started screaming, so she put her back down again.

"Will you come in with us?"

Fernanda shook her head. "I'll take care of the horses and sleep for a bit, then patrol the area until we leave tonight. Get something to eat—there's food inside, so you won't need to cook. There are enough beds upstairs for all of you, since I'm afraid there's not much to do but sleep. Please don't go outside. We can't risk anyone catching sight of any of you."

Gwynneth shifted Renata onto her other hip. "Thank you for taking such good care of us."

"I do what I can." Fernanda grinned widely for the first time, and Gwynneth glimpsed oddly pointed teeth. That must be why she didn't like showing them.

The children were already running into the cottage, so Gwynneth followed them. When she turned to close the door, Fernanda still stood near the carriage, watching her.

ANTON

Anton didn't have to wait long, sitting in his corner of the courtyard of General Ensden's house. He was glad, because it was chilly in the shade. In less than an hour, Franca Dura burst out of a side door.

"Get my horse," she shouted and a groom ran off.

Anton sprang to his feet. If she left now, it would be hard to follow without a horse of his own.

While she waited for Skandar, Franca gathered her officers. "That fool Ensden wants to sit here while Lennart starves him out. I won't let him."

"What'll we do?" someone asked.

Anton inched closer. So far no one had noticed him.

"We'll find Lennart." Franca pulled on her riding gloves.

"But he's got a huge army," another voice protested. "We can't take him on ourselves."

"No one has seen that huge army of his in weeks." Now a groom brought Skandar and Franca sprang onto his back. Anton stared at him desperately. "We can at least go take a look. I told Ensden I'd report back to him, but he can't stop us if we want to cause Lennart a little trouble."

"That's more like it." A huge captain swung onto another charger that had come out with Skandar. "Does Ensden worry he'll lose?"

"He thinks he can win," Franca said, "since he's certain Lennart has lost most of his army through the winter. And there's little food this time of year. In another month, he hopes what's left of Lennart's army will be starving."

"How boring—not to mention cowardly," the captain said as the officers— all of them now mounted—headed for the courtyard gate. Anton wondered if he might steal a horse somehow, but there were too many people around here. He wouldn't be able to follow on foot for long, but he'd go as far as he could.

The officers clattered down the street until they reached a big square where the rest of the troopers waited for them. "We're leaving," Franca called out. "We'll go out the western gate, find Lennart and cause him some trouble." A cheer went up, and they rode off.

Anton ran after them for as long as he could, but he was out of breath by the time they reached the gate. He stopped there, watching as it closed behind them, refusing to believe he'd never see Skandar again.

Two days later, Anton's regiment was mustered. "Is Lennart out there?" he asked the sergeant when he got a chance. The sergeant had been appreciative when Anton shared what he'd learned about Dura's Cuirassiers and was friendlier than usual. He wasn't even mad when Anton was a few minutes late to roll call because he'd been saying goodbye to Susanna.

"Sounds like it," the sergeant said. "He's been waiting for us a while now, about five leagues off. But now Dura's got herself surrounded and sent a message to Ensden, asking for help. He can't say no; she's got the best and biggest cavalry, so he's got to do what he can to save her."

Anton felt overwhelmed with all the things he had to worry about. First was Susanna. If the battle wasn't over in a day or two, she'd probably have the baby before he got back. He didn't even want to think of what might happen to her if they were defeated. Then he worried about Skandar, out there in a dangerous place, ridden by one of the most reckless officers Anton had ever heard of. He might have approved of Colonel Dura far more if she were putting some other horse in danger. He also worried about himself. He'd lost all of his armor long ago and didn't have enough money to buy much shot and powder, so his pistols wouldn't be good for long.

But no one cared if he was scared, so when the order to move out echoed through the ranks, Anton had to march along with everyone else.

KENDRYK

"I hoped Ensden had an officer of some spirit. I'm glad this Franca Dura finally showed up." Lennart had seemed depressed for weeks after his ruse failed, but he was a changed man once he heard Dura's Cuirassiers were looking for him.

"*Spirit?*" Kendryk asked. "She sounds insane. Dura can't have more than a few thousand cavalry and she's trying to draw you into pitched battle."

"No." Lennart chuckled as a page strapped on his cuirass. "She's trying to draw Ensden into a pitched battle. I'd hoped some of his subordinates didn't approve of his mutual starvation plan, but until now, none of them had the guts to do the deed."

They weren't starving yet, but in another month, finding enough food for Lennart's combined forces would become challenging. This part of Terragand had been picked over so many times, nothing remained. Kendryk thought he'd become hardened to the plight of his people, but his heart still contracted with every burned village and every dead body he saw. "*My fault, my fault,*" was all he could think.

He was also certain he'd made a mistake leaving Gwynneth in Allaux. Braeden's note came a week before, and Kendryk hoped he had reached Galladium by now. He'd feel a little better if he had his wife and children close by.

All depended on Lennart now. If Ensden came out to fight, he would still be likely to have greater numbers with many veterans among them. Anything but a decisive victory for Lennart would give the other Kronlanders excuses to stay neutral.

Kendryk sighed while putting on his armor. Lennart was brave, or maybe reckless enough, to wear nothing more than a simple breastplate, but Kendryk didn't see the point in taking unnecessary risks. Teodora had taken the beautiful armor he'd worn at the first battle, but he'd replaced it with something plain, though it was thick and serviceable.

He'd agreed to combine his forces with Tora Isenberg's, and Lennart said he'd put them on the left flank. The action would be heavier in the middle, but Ensden's only escape route was to the northwest and the road to Ummarvik. It would be Kendryk's and Isenberg's job to cut off any retreat.

Karolyna Martinek held the middle. She, Trystan and Lennart had had a big argument, and even though Trystan's numbers were larger, Karolyna insisted on taking the place of honor. "Podoska was your first ally," she told Lennart, though that wasn't true. Helvundala had been first, though Geffrey Manier would never put himself forward like that.

To everyone's surprise, Lennart gave in, though the forces of Estenor and the other Kronlanders surrounded the smaller Podoskan army. Trystan remained angry about it, and Kendryk worried he'd take unnecessary risks to distinguish himself. Karil still served as one of Trystan's officers, and Kendryk didn't want him put in any more jeopardy either. But battle was dangerous, and many people Kendryk cared about might be hurt or killed. That paralyzed him more than his own fear, so he did his best to put it out of his mind.

Kendryk and Trystan rode together, past the center and to Trystan's position, just to the right of Kendryk's. Lennart commanded from the far right, on Karolyna's other side. "Will it work?" Kendryk eyed the strange formations. Rather than put his forces in the typical blocks of pike supported by muskets with cavalry on the wings, Lennart kept his few pike in reserve, then set up alternating smaller blocks of musketeers and cavalry. Artillery sat behind and between them, but could be moved quickly. Kendryk understood the logic, but the fact remained, no one had ever fought a pitched battle this way before.

"I'm certain it'll work." Now that the battle neared, Trystan seemed to have put his indignation aside, and excitement colored his cheeks. "Lennart is a genius to do it this way and Ensden won't know how to react. Even if part of our line doesn't hold, we can maneuver so quickly it'll be easy to fill in any gaps."

"It sounds good in theory," Kendryk said, hoping the others were right. They had reached Trystan's position, at the top of a small rise overlooking the Osental, a broad valley between the Velta and the mountains to its west. Lennart's artillery ranged below them, and Trystan's forces had already moved into battle formation on the plain.

Trystan turned to Kendryk. "You needn't worry on your end. Tora Isenberg knows what she's doing."

"I know." Kendryk managed a small smile. "Take care, General Martinek, and I'll see you after the battle."

He rode along the ridge, Count Faris and a few officers behind him. It had rained the previous night and a heavy fog lay over the valley, though it was breaking up. Kendryk paused and looked into the distance through a glass. Great dark blocks crawled toward him, red banners fluttering above them. The enemy, at last.

He hurried on until he reached Tora Isenberg, waiting with her suite at the farthest end of the ridge. "Ready?" Kendryk asked.

"More than." Isenberg pulled off her glove to gnaw on a fingernail, though she didn't seem frightened. "All that time waiting, I worried I'd lose my mind. Thank the gods for that crazy cavalry commander."

"I'm glad all of you are so confident."

Isenberg turned to him with a grin. "We haven't tried this before, but it'll work."

"I hope so," Kendryk said.

"Do you reckon they're in range?" Isenberg peered through her glass.

"From those little guns?" Kendryk didn't mean to disparage Lennart's artillery, but they weren't as impressive in size as what he was used to.

"Ha," Isenberg said. "Just wait."

He didn't have to wait long. The enemy came near now, marching at a brisk pace. From where Kendryk stood, they looked endless, waves of soldiers, horses and weapons stretching into the distance. His mouth was dry and he wished he'd brought water.

"It's time," Isenberg said quietly, and the orders went down the line to everyone, including Kendryk's officers. He felt rather useless, but decided that was better than trying to get involved and making an awful mistake. His horse started as the guns below him boomed, then the troops below them moved forward in orderly fashion.

"Looks like Franca Dura got the middle," Isenberg said, looking to the right.

Kendryk gasped. An enormous mass of cavalry came straight down on the Podoskans, and he hoped Karolyna Martinek was as tough as she acted. Even from a distance, the clash of the two forces made a tremendous noise and Kendryk shuddered at the sounds of the aftermath. The two armies broke apart and the cavalry charged again. Then he gasped in horror. Just two assaults by Dura's cavalry had broken the Podoskan line. "Oh gods," he said.

Isenberg was looking too. "It's all right," she said. "Lennart and Trystan will handle it."

BRAEDEN

When Braeden reached Allaux, he went straight to Princess Gwynneth's house. "I'm afraid she's not in," one of her ladies-in-waiting said. They stood just inside the front door, and it was clear she would not ask him in to wait.

"When will she be back? I'll come see her then." If Natalya wasn't allowing visitors, he'd find another way.

"I'm not certain." The lady's eyes darted off to the side. "She's gone out of town on a visit."

"What?" This wasn't good—maybe Natalya had taken her somewhere, since Kendryk was sure Gwynneth couldn't leave on her own. "Is the Duchess Maryna in? I'll talk to her if she is." The girl was old enough to give him information at least.

"The children left with Princess Gwynneth," the lady said.

"Who have they gone to visit?"

"I'm afraid I can't say." The lady looked uncomfortable, and clearly wasn't telling the truth. He could hardly force it out of her, at least not yet.

Braeden sighed, then mounted Kazmir and headed for the Maxima's palace. He didn't relish tangling with Natalya, but who else would know where Gwynneth was? To his surprise, he received similar information about Natalya. She had departed Allaux just yesterday, but no one would tell him where she had gone.

Braeden swore with frustration. He was almost certain that Gwynneth and Natalya had gone away together, but couldn't for the life of him think why, and more importantly, where. Only one other person might be able to help him, but he doubted his chances of seeing the king were very good. He'd try anyway.

Before showing up at court, he found a good inn with a stable for Kazmir and ordered a bath. He'd been on the road for nearly a month and looked it. And he knew how they were at the Galladian court. If your looks weren't up to snuff, no one would say a word to you. Braeden's hair and beard had grown long once again, but he decided he was more likely to be recognized that way, so he left them alone. He had no fancy clothes, but changed into something clean. Hopefully that would work.

It was mid-afternoon by the time he reached the royal palace, and the majordomo on duty looked as snobby as Braeden had expected.

"What is your business?" He looked Braeden up and down, clearly finding him wanting.

"I must speak to the king. It's urgent."

The majordomo snickered. "And who might you be?"

"Braeden Terris. The king knows me."

The man snickered some more. "If you say so. What is this about?"

"Princess Gwynneth. I have an urgent message for her and can't find her."

"What the princess does is hardly the king's concern," the majordomo sniffed.

"Well, you'd be wrong." Braeden tried to keep his anger down. He was tired and hungry and didn't have time to spar with this overdressed flunky. He was certain the fellow had his eyebrows penciled on. "The king will want to be told she's left town."

"You can see him tomorrow." The man shrugged. "He and the queen are seeing the last petitioner of the day. In fact, Her Majesty is returning to her quarters right now."

"I don't need to see the queen," Braeden said. "And this is urgent. Please at least tell the king I'm here. Prince Kendryk will be very displeased if he finds I've failed to locate Princess Gwynneth and the children."

"Princess Gwynneth?" A girlish voice rang out behind Braeden and he wheeled around.

He suppressed a gasp at the sight of a miniature Teodora.

"Do you know something about Princess Gwynneth?" the girl demanded.

"I have an urgent message for her, Your Highness," Braeden said, realizing this must be Zofya Inferrara.

"Then we must talk right away." She waved a tiny hand at the majordomo. "Gresson, tell the king to join me in my chambers when he's done. Tell him I ... what is your name?" she peered up at Braeden. He doubted Teodora had ever been so pretty, or had such a sweet voice.

"Braeden Terris," he said. "I'm a friend of—"

"I know exactly who you are." Her face lit up and she extended her hand.

Braeden bowed over it. When he looked up, her dark eyes stared back at him, rather wide. He hoped he didn't look too frightening.

The queen grabbed Braeden by the hand and turned to the majordomo. "Tell the king I've gone to my quarters with Braeden Terris." She smiled up at Braeden, a dimple in her cheek. "That ought to make him come quickly. Follow me, Commander Terris. We have a great deal to discuss.".

ANTON

It took hours to march out to the battlefield, and Anton hoped that the whole thing would be over by the time he got there. Judging by how high the sun stood in the sky, it was nearly noon by the time the boom of the guns drew near and they had arrived right in the thick of it. Now Anton realized he missed his old comrades from the Michalek regiment; all dead now. Today, he stood next to strangers he'd drilled with only a few times. Because they'd been quartered in different houses in town, he hadn't gotten to know them the way he would have in camp.

He kept facing forward as they came in range of the artillery. On the bright side, he didn't much care when those around him died. Because they did. It was every bit as awful as Anton had feared. Worse than the time he'd faced Tora Isenberg alone. She was somewhere out there, but only one of many generals Lennart had with him.

To distract himself from the increasing horror as cannonballs fell into the crowded ranks, Anton recited the names in his head: first the strange foreign names of Isenberg, Kalstrom, Lofbrok, then the Kronlanders—two Martineks, Dahlby, Manier, Bernotas. The sergeant had told him all of those by way of passing the time as they marched. *Bernotas*. Kendryk was out there somewhere and Anton squinted into the smoke, wishing he would appear and get him away from here.

Another Bernotas fought here too, on Anton's side. The old duke Evard needed to help Ensden win today if he wanted to keep ruling Terragand. Anton remembered capturing Duke Evard with the count years ago. That had been a lot more fun than this kind of fighting. And now he was stuck on the duke's side, fighting against Kendryk. It was all wrong.

They kept marching until they got out of range of the artillery. Anton took a deep breath, hoping he'd survived the worst. They stopped and the sergeant shouted, "left face." Anton executed the maneuver as smoothly as the fellows around him, most of them hardened veterans. He'd never done this in battle, and wondered if they were finally going to do some real fighting.

As they marched to the left, the sounds of battle grew louder. Anton glimpsed cavalry, and farther ahead, infantry troops running away. Were they winning already? He thought of Franca Dura on Skandar and decided he wouldn't be shocked if she'd already beaten the enemy into submission. He hoped Skandar was all right.

"Forward!" the sergeant barked and they moved into a large open space. The enemy had been here moments before. Anton couldn't believe it. Maybe he was on the winning side. He felt bad for Kendryk, but happy for himself, because he needed to win if he wanted to keep Susanna and the baby safe. He felt a little bit of the joy that always came to him in battle, back when he fought at the count's side.

"Hold!" came the order and Anton hoisted his pike onto his shoulder, the tip facing forward. He didn't see what was coming; cavalry perhaps. The two ranks in front of him held their pike lower, braced against their feet. Anyone facing them would be staring at stacks of bristling spear-tips.

Then he heard the pop of muskets and fellows around him started falling. Lennart would have musketeers, just as he had on the Velta. Pike didn't do much good against those. Anton wanted to drop his pike and draw his pistols. He might stand a chance with those.

The sergeant ordered, "Push!" right before a musket ball dropped him. Anton looked away, not knowing what to push against. Much of the first rank had fallen, and Anton took a few steps forward. Now he was that much closer to the enemy, with no good way to fight them. He wondered about Dura and her cavalry. They might be able to run down the musketeers.

A commotion rose on Anton's right, and he saw enemy cavalry attacking the right flank of his block. He stood near the middle, and there was nothing to do anyway, except watch his comrades fall. "*Hate this hate this hate this,*" he muttered to himself, holding the pike in position because he didn't know what else to do. Any joy at possibly winning had fled some time ago.

A woman with a leathery face took the sergeant's place and shouted the order to fall back. The gap cleared by the cavalry rapidly filled up with enemy troops. Anton wondered what the rest of Ensden's army was doing. His rank peeled off in a somewhat orderly retreat, though soldiers kept falling. The enemy's muskets fired fast now, and their cavalry picked away at the edges. Anton needed to get away before there was nothing left.

"We're drawing them into range of our guns," someone said and Anton hoped that was true. Might that be part of the plan? As they marched away from the front line, the fighting increased and it was hard to tell what was happening. Shouldn't there be less action back here? Anton's hand itched to draw at least one pistol, but he needed both hands to hold the pike.

Now shots flew from all directions, and Anton wondered how he'd keep from getting hit by his own side. Were the officers confused too? The smoke blew in thick drifts and he occasionally glimpsed a standard, not always one he recognized. He wished he could do something. It was the worst, standing here, part of a huge block, unable to move.

Suddenly, shouts came from his right, then soldiers ran toward him. Anton squinted. Imperial troops. He took far too long to register that they were fleeing, and in a strange direction too. It would make more sense to head back toward the city. In fact, Anton planned to do so at the first opportunity.

"Where are you going?" he asked a man limping past, a little slower than the rest.

"Away," the man said. "And if you're smart, you'll go too. Lennart's turned our own guns on us."

"What?" That made no sense. The only way Lennart's troops might have gotten to Ensden's guns would be by overrunning the imperial positions. Which meant they'd lost the battle. How had things changed so quickly? Or maybe hours had gone by and he hadn't noticed. Anton stood there, still confused, while men around him started dropping their pikes and running off to the left.

Anton looked for officers, saw none, then dropped his pike as well. They'd have to execute the whole regiment for abandoning their weapons. He pulled out his pistol, hoping his powder remained dry. He didn't plan to run in the same direction as everyone else. He wanted to head for the city and Susanna.

Anton battled against the flow of running soldiers, now a huge stream. In the distance, guns boomed, but they seemed far away and no danger at all. Anton did his best to dodge fleeing soldiers, find the direction toward Kaltental, and hope he didn't run into the enemy.

He finally reached what seemed to be the right road. It was muddy, the surface churned up by at least one army using it that day, so he walked along the side, holding his pistol, smoke still swirling around him. He walked for a long time, thinking he must be getting closer to the city, but then a commotion behind him made him pause. Enemy troops ran down the road, laughing and shouting, with no one to stop them. They must be heading for the city. The city and Susanna.

Without thinking, Anton drew his other pistol and stepped into the road. There were at least several hundred soldiers coming his way and he couldn't possibly shoot all of them.

"Stop!" he shouted. "You can't go that way."

Now they stood in front of him. "Yes we can." A musketeer with a smoke-blackened face grinned at him. "The king himself said we're allowed to plunder the city until nightfall."

"No!" Anton raised both pistols, but before he fired, a huge stick rushed at his head, and he heard a loud crack, followed by blinding pain and distant laughter as he fell face-first into the mud.

TEODORA

"Go away, Your Highness. I don't want to talk to you." Aksel Roussay was back in his laboratory, but he was still sullen and difficult.

"That doesn't matter." Teodora took a seat at the table Aksel was working at. "What are you doing?"

Aksel opened his mouth, but before he could speak she said, "Oh never mind. I forgot—I don't care."

Aksel shook his head, then sat down. "What do you want?"

"I want you to get ready to go to Norovaea. You will become king soon."

"You're joking. My brother is the king and if something happens to him, my sister will succeed, and her children after her."

"Your brother won't be king much longer. As we speak, he's likely being overthrown by his own nobility."

Aksel looked at her, disbelieving, then said, "I'm sure they'll want Gwynneth to be queen, if they pull this off, which I doubt."

"Perhaps they do," Teodora said, relishing the moment. "The problem is, Gwynneth is dead, and so are her children."

Aksel turned pale. "That's a lie. They're safe in Allaux, and even you can't get past Natalya."

"I've found a way." Teodora smiled. "Your sister and her children are dead, and you will be king of Norovaea."

"I'll kill you," Aksel shouted, and launched himself across the table at Teodora.

She jumped out of the way, and Aksel tumbled to the floor.

He pulled himself up using the edge of the table. "You won't get away with this," he snarled, wiping blood from his lip.

"You'd better not try that again." It hadn't occurred to Teodora to bring protection, since Aksel was usually not aggressive. She had a better way to control him. "Don't forget your friend Marcus still lives under Livilla's protection, but that will change if you cause me any trouble."

"I hate you," Aksel said, though he made no move toward her.

"Join the crowd." Teodora walked around to the other side of the table. Best to keep it between them. "How you feel about me makes no difference. You will pack your things and get ready to go to Norovaea. Elektra will join you as soon as she returns and will marry you in Arenberg."

"No." Aksel shook his head, a stubborn set to his jaw. "You will not force her into marriage like you did Zofya. I won't be party to that."

Teodora laughed. "Elektra won't mind marrying you, I'm sure. It's a very different situation."

"I don't mind marrying her either, but I do mind having you as a mother-in-law."

"Oh, I'll be far away. I doubt you'll see me often."

"But you'll still expect the two of us to do everything you want us to."

"Of course. But you needn't worry about that now. Pack your things and get ready to leave for Norovaea in the morning. You'll sail from Capo since I can't risk losing you somewhere overland." With Teodora's luck, Aksel was likely to disappear just like Elektra had.

"I won't go." Aksel stood up straight now, a dangerous gleam in his eye.

"You will. Don't be stupid."

"If I'm to be king, I'll do my duty. But I won't go until I've received confirmation of my brother's overthrow."

"That's a certainty, and only a matter of time."

"Then I'll hear about it when it's happened. And I'll want to speak to a Norovaean diplomat in person, since I won't take your word for any of this." He swallowed hard, but still stared at her intently. "And I'll want the same confirmation of my sister's death and of her children's. I can't believe anything you say, and I will not act until I have independent proof."

"Your friend—" Teodora began. At least she still had that leverage.

"Marcus is doomed already." Aksel's voice shook a little, but he steadied it. "If the fate of Norovaea is at stake, I'm afraid I must sacrifice him for the good of my country. I won't let you manipulate me that way. I'll do what I have to, but I'll do it on my terms. I'm not king yet, and I hope I never will be. And I hope you're lying about Arryk and Gwynneth." Aksel's eyes were as hard as she'd ever seen them. Perhaps she'd created a monster. "I hope for your sake that you're lying. Because if it turns out you've had a hand in my brother's overthrow and my sister's death, I won't rest until you're dead."

"Some threat." Teodora smirked. "You're still my prisoner and so is your little friend. You can wait if you like." She got up to leave, but turned back at the door. "But you might as well pack. I'm sure the news you're waiting for will be here any day now." She swept out and left him standing there.

BRAEDEN

Queen Zofya led Braeden down several long, magnificent corridors, through a maze of rooms, one more fabulous than the last, until they stopped in a small sitting room. She sent all of her ladies outside to wait for the king, with instructions to show him in when he arrived.

Braeden could hardly believe he was alone here with another daughter of Teodora's, though Zofya was much friendlier than Elektra. It appeared she had been on very good terms with both Gwynneth and the Duchess Maryna.

Once the door had closed behind the others, Zofya moved her chair close to Braeden's and bent her head to his. "I'm afraid Princess Gwynneth and the children are in terrible danger," she whispered. "Natalya Maxima has gone after them to try to save them, but I fear she'll be too late."

"I don't understand. Didn't she go with Natalya?"

Zofya shook her head. "Natalya didn't want her to leave, but I learned that Princess Gwynneth was tricked into going by an agent of my mother's, a Fernanda Vastic. I'm certain she plans to kill her."

An icy chill washed over Braeden. "Why does your mother want to kill Gwynneth?"

"No one knows, and I'm sure that's why Natalya has gone. She hopes to capture Vastic and find out."

"How did you learn all of this?"

"Natalya spoke with the king before she left. In case she didn't succeed, she wanted him to know what was going on."

"I still don't understand," Braeden said. "How did Vastic get close to Princess Gwynneth?"

"That's my fault." Zofya sniffled a little. "My mother sent her along as one of my attendants. I was told she was a distant cousin. She seemed odd, but I suspected nothing too terrible. I should have known better."

"I don't see how." Braeden patted the queen's hand, still lying on his arm. "At least, you found out in time."

"I didn't find out anything." Zofya sighed. "It was all Natalya. The king told me, even though I can't do anything to help my friends. But now you're here." Her eyes lit up. "I'm sure we can come up with something."

"Maybe." Braeden had no idea where Vastic had taken Gwynneth, and he'd brought only a small escort. "I'll do what I can."

Then the door burst open and the king rushed in. Braeden had never met him before, though he'd seen him from a distance a time or two. He jumped to his feet and tried to bow, but the king came straight toward him, grabbed his hands and kissed Braeden on both cheeks.

Unprepared for such a warm reception, Braeden blushed and stammered, unsure of what to say next.

The king quickly noticed his discomfort. "I'm afraid I rather fell all over you, Commander Terris, though I've rarely been so glad to see anyone. The queen and I have been so anxious, and all we could do was pray that the gods would send someone to help. I'm relieved they've answered our prayers."

Braeden sat back down after the king and queen were seated, then said, "I hope I can help, but no one can tell me where Princess Gwynneth has gone."

"That's a problem," the king said. Braeden noticed that he and the queen sat close together, their hands clasped on the king's lap. A happy marriage then, in spite of the odds. "Natalya rushed off saying she wasn't sure exactly where they'd gone either, though she hoped to pick up their trail. I offered to send help, but she didn't want to make a big fuss yet."

Braeden made an indignant noise. "If Princess Gwynneth is in danger, how can we not make a fuss?"

"Exactly," the queen said. "I really don't understand the Maxima sometimes."

Braeden wanted to say that no one did, but decided it wouldn't be politic. He took a deep breath and tried to sort out his thoughts. "I'll try to find them. Did Natalya leave any information at all? Any direction they might have gone?"

"Princess Gwynneth was told they were going to Zeelund," the king said. "Natalya learned at least that much. There are one or two main roads that would send them in that direction."

"I need a map," Braeden said, a plan forming in his mind. "I need every detail of those roads for the first fifty leagues from Allaux. They will need to stop at some point, get food, and rest or change their horses. Someone will have seen something."

The king's face collapsed into a relieved smile. "Of course." He turned to Zofya. "See? He knows what to do. The gods have answered our prayers."

"Maybe they have," Braeden said. "I'll get ready to go while you find me someone who's traveled those roads often to guide me. I'll do the rest. But I'd keep praying if I were you."

GWYNNETH

After dozing in the carriage for so long, Gwynneth didn't feel like sleeping. So she prepared a simple meal for herself and the children with bread and sausage she found in a basket in the kitchen. She paused as she laid it out, wondering if she ought to trust any food provided by Fernanda. Even though she'd brought them this far safely, Gwynneth still felt uneasy. If anything, her anxiety was worse now than before.

Something about the way Fernanda had looked at her as they went into the house; something didn't feel right. And those awful teeth—like fangs. Gwynneth shivered, and took a bite of sausage. She'd wait a few more minutes before letting the children have anything. Likely a ridiculous precaution. The strain of the past few months had no doubt caught up with her and now she feared everything.

After a good twenty minutes, she didn't get sick, and the little ones complained of hunger. She fed them and played games with them for the next few hours. The day wore on, and no one was poisoned. Gwynneth shook her head at her baseless fears, and herded everyone upstairs for a nap. Two small connected rooms, each with their own door, faced the little landing. She put the four older children into the two beds in one of them, and laid baby Renata on the single bed in the other. She went downstairs one more time.

Gwynneth unbarred the front door and stood in the doorway, looking around. The day was sunny, though it was cool here in the shadow of the trees. She saw the little shed in the distance, and all seemed quiet there too. Gwynneth closed the door and slid the iron bar, then went to the few windows to check their latches.

Upstairs, she went into the children's room. All slept except for Maryna.

"You should sleep," Gwynneth whispered. "It's quiet outside, and it'll be a few more hours before we can leave."

"I can't sleep," Maryna murmured. "I won't stop worrying until we are in Zeelund and see Papa."

Gwynneth smiled and kissed the top of her head. "I won't stop worrying until then either. But it's better to rest when we can. We still have a long, hard journey ahead."

Maryna nodded, hugged Gwynneth around the waist, and lay back down next to Andres. Devyn and Stella slept in the other bed, the covers kicked off and tangled, Stella lying crosswise over Devyn's legs. Gwynneth smiled down at them, and checked that their door was latched from the inside, before going into the adjoining room. She latched that door as well, then lay down next to Renata, also sleeping soundly. After the noise of constant traffic outside their windows in Allaux, it was blissfully quiet here.

Gwynneth slept long and deep, and didn't wake until she was choking and bathed in sweat. She heard crying in the distance without understanding that it was one of her children for at least a minute. She shook her head to clear the fog, but that made it worse. She squinted. The sun was almost down and the light dim, but there was something else, like fog. No, it was smoke.

Suddenly wide awake, Gwynneth jumped out of the bed and snatched Renata who whimpered and rubbed her eyes. She ran into the next room.

Maryna stood in the middle of it. "The house is on fire, Mama." Her tone was surprisingly calm. "The doors are locked and we can't get out."

"Fire?" Gwynneth looked around wildly. She saw only smoke, smelled it too. "If we hurry, we can go downstairs and out the front door." The thatched roofs of houses like these often caught fire first.

"No." Maryna was struggling not to cry. "We can't get out."

"What do you mean?" Gwynneth shifted Renata onto one hip and ran to the door. She drew the latch back and pushed on the door. It didn't budge. She pulled, though that didn't help either. Panicked now, she ran into the other room. That door was locked too. Someone had barred it from the outside. She didn't want to think about who had done it, though she knew very well. "Oh gods," she sobbed, watching the smoke rise through the cracks in the floorboards. Even if the doors had opened, the fire burned below them.

"We must go out the window," Maryna said. She struggled with the latch; it didn't open either. It was big enough for them to climb through, but its small panes of heavy leaded glass rested in sturdy frames.

"How will we—" Gwynneth began, then shrieked as the glass shattered.

Devyn had thrown a chair at the window. She stared at him, astonished. When had he grown so strong? He picked it up and threw it again, breaking a bigger hole. "You go first, Mama," he said. Gwynneth stared at him. He picked up a pistol that had been laying on a table.

Maryna had already thrown a blanket over the jagged edges of glass and wood on the windowsill. "Hurry," she said. The smoke was thick now, the heat intense.

Gwynneth hoped the floor wouldn't break before they all got out. "No," she said. "All of you first." She ran to the window and looked down. Two floors up, but the house wasn't tall. A few bushes against the wall might cushion their fall. Even if they broke a few limbs, they'd survive. But then Gwynneth saw her.

Fernanda stood below the window, flames from the fire below lighting her face. She smiled up at Gwynneth, her pointed teeth looking eerily like wolf's fangs, her eyes glowing a strange yellow in the fiery light.

"Can you catch the children?" Gwynneth called down to her.

Fernanda threw her head back and laughed, a high-pitched shrieking cackle, while she drew a long curved blade from her belt. "This will catch them well enough."

Gwynneth shook all over. How could she have made such a terrible mistake? Trusting such a person? And now she'd pay for it with her own death and the deaths of her children. Her knees buckled, but she hung onto the windowsill.

"Move, Mama." Maryna snapped at her.

"I can't," Gwynneth murmured, but someone shoved her out of the way the same instant the report of a pistol crashed in her ear. Gwynneth shrieked. Was Fernanda shooting at them?

"I missed." Maryna sounded very far away to Gwynneth's ringing ears. "Devyn, you try."

Another crash and a whoop from Devyn. "I got her!" then more quietly, "I think."

Gwynneth staggered to the windowsill, while behind her Maryna and Devyn discussed how hard reloading in the dark was. She couldn't think of where they'd gotten pistols or learned how to use them. When she looked down, Fernanda still stood there, but now one hand held a bloody arm while the long blade lay on the ground. Gwynneth would jump, do her best to overcome Fernanda, then catch her children.

"Give me that pistol, Devyn," she said, stretching out her hand toward him.

"But I haven't reloaded." He handed it to her anyway.

"I'll use it as a club. She's not any bigger than I am, and she's hurt." Even as she said it, Gwynneth knew she didn't stand a chance. She climbed onto the windowsill and looked at Maryna. "I'm so sorry," she said. "You were right. I made a terrible mistake. I'll distract Fernanda and you must jump first. Devyn will throw the baby down, then the other little ones."

The flames roared now; they licked through the floorboards and out the first-floor windows. Sweat ran down her face. She stared down into Fernanda's yellow eyes and jumped.

LENNART

Geffrey Manier was talking, but Lennart couldn't hear him. His ears rang, and guns fired in the background, though the battle must be over by now. Sweat ran down Lennart's face and he wiped it with the back of his gloved hand. He didn't think the day had been that warm.

If it was over, then he'd won; he was certain of that. But he still wasn't sure how it happened. He stood in the middle of the battlefield, near what had once been Ensden's front line and asked, "Ensden? Did we get him?"

Manier shook his head. "We don't know yet. But Evard Bernotas is dead." Manier still sounded very far away, though Lennart understood if he listened carefully and watched his lips move.

"Just as well. Kendryk's claim is stronger with him out of the way." Lennart walked across the battlefield. At some point he'd dismounted, or fallen off. He didn't remember, so he looked himself over. Dirty, but not muddy, like he'd fallen. "What else?" he asked Manier, who'd dismounted and now walked beside him.

"We carried the day decisively," Manier said. "Only the Podoskan center took heavy casualties. Karolyna Martinek is badly wounded and it's uncertain if she'll survive."

"Dura's charge was something else." Lennart grinned, remembering, and wondered if Franca Dura had survived. If she lived, he hoped he might persuade her to fight for the winning side the next time.

"Indeed. I confess I was worried for a little while."

"Me too." It wasn't so hard to admit now that everything had turned out so well. The decisive moment was when the Podoskan center broke. No one expected him to move his front lines quickly enough to outflank Ensden on both sides. Lennart knew it was possible, but hadn't done it before; no one had. Once it actually happened—Leyf Lofbrok and Trystan Martinek trapping a huge swath of Ensden's army between them—Lennart realized he'd been muttering prayers under his breath while everything unfolded before his eyes.

Ensden's unwieldy pike squares maneuvered too slowly, and it didn't take long to crush them between waves of muskets and light cavalry. It worked exactly as Lennart had hoped. The enemy fought hard, as he'd expected, but when they finally retreated, they ran into steady artillery fire. Overrunning Ensden's gun positions and turning those onto their own soldiers was an unexpected gift and made the victory complete.

Manier kept talking. "Karolyna Martinek took the heaviest losses, though we took at least a few thousand more. I'll have better numbers soon. We have another problem."

"What's that?" Lennart's ears still rang, even as his vision cleared. It was as if a film covered his eyes and now broke away. The colors became vivid—blood and mud and torn flesh. He looked away and stared at the sky, now overcast, even though the smoke of battle had cleared.

"Looting," Manier said. "The enemy turned and ran for Kaltental and our fellows went after them. They captured thousands and killed a good many more. But then ours kept right on going, and now they're inside the city, making a mess of things."

Lennart sighed. "We'll have to stop them, I suppose." He was suddenly exhausted, but he never allowed looting. He didn't need the people of Terragand seeing his army as the aggressor.

"I'll give the order." Manier mounted his horse. "There's still plenty of troops about who didn't join in." He rode off toward the city.

Lennart kept walking. Several of his suite followed him, but he didn't want to talk to them. He came across a field hospital, offered a few words of encouragement to the wounded and kept going. The battlefield was vast, but most of the bodies strewn across it belonged to the enemy.

In the distance, he saw Prince Kendryk approach, flanked by Count Faris and Tora Isenberg. "Your Highness." Kendryk looked rather pale, likely from the sight of so much carnage. "I congratulate you." Upon reaching Lennart, he dismounted and pressed Lennart's hand.

"Terragand is yours." Lennart smiled, pleased he could do this for him.

"I can't believe it." Kendryk's eyes were damp. "I still expect an enemy to suddenly appear. Or maybe I'm dreaming."

"The enemy is gone." Lennart clapped Kendryk on the shoulder. "Though I'm told we captured a good number. Many of them might be Kronlanders, and you might persuade them to join us. Why don't you come with me and we'll look them over."

ANTON

Anton still lay in the mud when he woke up, but at least he wasn't dead. Pain shot through his jaw if he tried to move it, and a loose tooth wiggled under his tongue. He raised himself up on one elbow and looked around. A number of imperial troops sat or lay on the ground around him, and beyond them he saw the halberds and helmets of guards. So he was a prisoner. This time, he'd at least been captured by the right side, though he didn't see what good it did him.

He sat up all the way and tried to think, remembered why he was here, and staggered to his feet. He had to get to the city and find Susanna. He made his way to the friendliest-looking of the guards.

"What do you want?" The guard looked Anton up and down, scowling.

He'd planned on using his smile on her but decided against it. Instead he did his best to seem sad, which wasn't hard. "I need to get to the city. My wife is having a baby, probably right now. I give my word I'll return as soon as I know she's all right."

"Ha! Do you think I'm stupid or something?" The guard lowered her halberd menacingly. "You're not going anywhere."

"But I have to."

"What you have to do is stay right here." The guard took a step closer to him, her weapon's point a little too near his chin.

Anton stepped back. He'd have to think of something else. The guard looked away toward a commotion on the road and Anton wondered if he might sneak past. But there were so many other guards, he doubted he would make it, especially while he was still wobbly.

Another guard turned toward the prisoners. "Up!" he shouted. "On your feet, you lazy buggers. King Lennart himself wants to inspect you."

Anton made his way toward the road. He'd always been curious about Lennart, though he didn't care much about him right now. Still, he might never get another chance to see the man in the flesh.

461

Guards lined the road and Anton stood as close behind them as he dared, a crush of bodies pressing him from behind. It seemed he wasn't the only one who was curious. A mounted group came into view, a tall bare-headed man wearing a battered leather coat in front. The guards cheered and Anton stared. He'd never seen a king so un-kingly in his dress and yet so kingly in his bearing. And then he gasped as the man on the king's right came into view. It was Prince Kendryk.

Anton almost shouted, but held back. He needed to wait until Kendryk was close enough to hear him, since he doubted he'd get more than one chance. When the king drew almost level, Anton shouted. "Prince Kendryk! It's me, Anton. Prince—" before a guard shoved an elbow into his stomach.

Anton bent over, gasping, hoping Kendryk had heard. Now several guards had moved in front of him, blocking his view. Likely he'd failed and he'd never see Kendryk again. But the guards moved aside, and a familiar voice said, "Anton? Anton Kronek?"

Anton straightened up, and couldn't keep from grinning. Kendryk had dismounted and now stood right in front of him as the guards gawked.

"Thank the gods," Kendryk said. "We were certain you'd been killed along with Arian Orland."

Anton shook his head. He didn't know what to say.

Kendryk was beaming. "You'll come with me, if that's what you want."

Anton nodded. His voice caught in his throat. Maybe it was relief at seeing a friendly face on a day like today.

Then Kendryk had him by the arm and the guards moved aside.

"You'll meet the king first," Kendryk said, "and then we'll talk."

Anton nodded again, still unable to speak, and let Kendryk guide him to where the king still sat his horse, an amused smile on his face.

"Found an old friend, did you?" he asked Kendryk.

"Your Highness, this is Anton Kronek." Kendryk gave Anton a gentle shove in the king's direction, and Anton executed a hasty bow. "He helped rescue me and killed Daciana Tomescu himself."

The king jumped off his horse to face Anton. "A true hero. How did you find yourself in this position, young man?" He nodded toward the crowd of prisoners.

Anton finally found his voice. "I was captured when Arian Orland was killed and they made me fight for them, even though I didn't want to."

The king clapped him on the shoulder, and Anton staggered a little. "It's happened to more than a few good soldiers, but you're lucky I dragged Prince Kendryk along to look you lot over."

"Very lucky." The shock was wearing off, and Anton remembered Susanna. He licked his dry lips. "Your Highness, I don't wish to be a bother, but I must get to the city as quickly as possible. My wife is having a baby and I must find her."

The king's eyebrows shot up and he frowned, while Anton hoped he hadn't been impertinent. "Big day you're having, young man. I'm afraid my troops are already in the city. I've sent someone to stop them looting, but who knows how bad it got."

Anton bit his tongue hard. He didn't want to think about enemy soldiers finding Susanna.

Kendryk stood next to him, a hand on his elbow. "Your Highness," he said. "Might I take Master Kronek to the city to search for his wife? I doubt I'm needed here."

The king beckoned over a few mounted guards. "Accompany Prince Kendryk and this young man into the city and keep them safe."

"Thank you, Your Highness," Anton choked out.

Someone brought him a horse and helped him onto it. It had been a long time since he'd been on horseback, but it felt good and familiar. Kendryk rode next to him, a few guards at their backs. Once they had left the king behind, Kendryk said, "A great deal has happened to you since we last met. But surely Anton, you're too young to be married."

"We're not married officially," Anton said, "but she's having my baby. Her time was close when I had to leave the city." He'd never really felt too young before, but now with Prince Kendryk acting fatherly, he wondered if he'd been an idiot, putting Susanna in such a position when he wasn't able to take care of her. "It's a long story, but I'll tell you all of it later."

"I don't wish to pry." Kendryk shook his head. "And I'm glad to find you alive. I'm just surprised you were so easily ensnared by a young woman."

Anton had to laugh at that. "That's not how it was; not at all. But I love her, and I'm terribly worried about her."

"Of course," Kendryk said. "We'll find her, and then we'll figure out what to do next."

GWYNNETH

In the gathering gloom it was hard to see where she would land, but when sticks and leaves crunched under her, Gwynneth knew she'd fallen into a bush. She lost track of Fernanda for a moment while she fumbled for the pistol, which she'd dropped on the way down. She had to get away from the wall to give the children room to jump.

Gwynneth staggered to her feet, her skirt tangling around her ankles, and ran straight into Fernanda, who hadn't moved. Gwynneth put her head down, like a bull, and pushed Fernanda onto the ground. Behind her, she heard a small crash and a squeal; hopefully that was Maryna. She couldn't worry about the children right now until she got rid of this creature.

Fernanda lay under her for a second, and then Gwynneth found herself on her back, with the pistol flying out of her hand again. Fernanda wasn't heavy, but she was strong. She sat on Gwynneth's legs, pinning them down, her good arm pushed against Gwynneth's throat.

Gwynneth struggled and gasped, her arms flailing at her sides, knowing she had moments left to live before Fernanda started on her children. All she could do was draw it out as long as possible. She bucked her hips up, throwing Fernanda off balance and releasing the pressure on her throat for an instant. She made a fist and swung one arm around, hitting Fernanda on the ear. Fernanda slid to one side, and Gwynneth remembered her injured arm. She brought her other fist around and connected with the bloody spot. Fernanda shrieked and rolled off Gwynneth, lunging for the sword still on the ground. Gwynneth scrambled for it. If Fernanda got hold of it, she would finish them in seconds.

The flickering light of the fire glinted off the blade and Gwynneth pushed her palm down on it while sticking out her elbow, hoping to push Fernanda away. But the blade sliced along Gwynneth's palm and disappeared. Blood poured from her hand, though it didn't hurt. Gwynneth pushed her hand against her thigh and tried to see where Fernanda and the sword had gone.

When she looked up, Devyn held it. He was tall for his age, but still too short for the long curved blade, and swung it clumsily at Fernanda as she barreled toward him, running him down. Devyn disappeared under Fernanda, and the sword fell back to the ground. Gwynneth scrambled to her feet and threw herself on it as Fernanda reached for it. Blows fell against her ribs, first from Fernanda's fists, then heavier blows that must have been kicks. Gwynneth gritted her teeth, refusing to cry out. She wouldn't let the children think she was beaten.

The kicks stopped and Gwynneth rolled onto her back, breathing hard. Devyn had his arms around Fernanda's waist, trying to pull her to the ground. Gwynneth found the sword and curled her fingers tight around the hilt. Maryna screamed somewhere in the distance. Had Fernanda brought an accomplice? Gwynneth prayed now, harder than she had in some time. She and the children might overcome Fernanda on their own, but they'd need divine help if anyone else had come.

Gwynneth struggled to her knees in spite of the sharp pain in her middle and the blood pouring from her hand. She had to hold the sword in her left hand, but she would still kill Fernanda with it if it was the last thing she did, which seemed likely. She tried to stand, but fell, and then someone grabbed her from behind.

"No!" Gwynneth shrieked and struggled.

"Shh," a familiar voice crooned in her ear. "It's all right. You need to stay down."

Maryna, sounding close by now said, "Mama, you must sit still. Natalya is here, and everything is all right."

"Natalya?" Gwynneth felt so weak she did nothing but lean into those arms, still holding her tight.

"Who else?" Natalya's voice was soft.

Gwynneth broke down at last. It really was Natalya, and now all of her children stood around her, safe. Maryna held Renata, and Devyn had Andres and Stella by the hand.

"I don't ... I don't ..."

Now she cried in great gulping sobs that came so hard she could scarcely breathe. Natalya settled back onto the ground, still holding her, rubbing her shoulder and shouting at someone.

A man came and pressed on her hand, which made her cry harder. It hurt now, but then he put a salve on it, and it became numb while he wrapped bandages around it.

Gwynneth finally slowed her breathing, though the tears wouldn't stop flowing. "Fernanda..." She gasped. "Did you get her?"

"She ran into the woods. I've sent people after her. I doubt she'll get far in the state she's in. I'm very sorry we didn't get here quickly enough. I thought she wouldn't try anything until after dark, and I didn't want to risk being seen."

Gwynneth rolled over and slid to the ground, her head in Natalya's lap. "I don't understand. How is it you are here at all, let alone just in time?"

"It was Maryna." Natalya stroked the mad tangle of Gwynneth's hair away from her face. "She came to me before you left Allaux. Please don't be angry with her. She was so worried, and right to be."

"I'm an idiot." The tears stopped, but now Gwynneth felt guiltier than she ever had in her life. "An idiot and a terrible mother."

"Not at all." Natalya kept stroking her hair. "You did what you thought was best. And you were well-deceived." She put an arm under Gwynneth's shoulders and pulled her into a sitting position. "I am certain Fernanda is Teodora's agent, since no one else would try anything so atrocious. The letters and the ring you carry must be forgeries."

"Of course they are." Gwynneth shook her head. "It seems they knew exactly what was needed to convince me."

"The operation was carefully planned." Natalya said. "What remains unclear is its purpose. There's no question she acted under Teodora's instructions, but I'd like to know what was behind them. Until I catch Vastic and interrogate her, I want to keep this quiet."

Gwynneth nodded, certain she'd never argue with Natalya again.

BRAEDEN

Braeden learned from the last inn he'd stopped at that a large armed party had passed not an hour before. It had to be Natalya. He'd rather it were Gwynneth, but he'd be happy to find her at all, even if he had to tangle with Natalya first. The light was fading quickly, the forest road narrow and rutted, unsafe after dark.

Braeden urged Kazmir on and his escort kept pace. They rode in silence until Trisa said, "Smoke up ahead."

Braeden squinted at a brown cloud billowing up through the trees, perhaps a league distant. "Let's hurry," he said, urging Kazmir to a canter. "Sure to be trouble up there." It was the wrong time of year for a bonfire, and the smoke was the color of a thatched roof burning. Even if Princess Gwynneth wasn't in danger, someone else might be.

As they drew nearer, he could see the flames and spurred Kazmir until he galloped, even though the road was hardly visible now. Before long, a clearing appeared, full of soldiers standing around. A house burned in the middle, though no one seemed to be trying to put the fire out. Braeden pulled Kazmir to a halt, and his men stopped behind him. He didn't want anyone getting the wrong impression, so he dismounted and walked toward a cluster of people near the burning house, making sure his pistols were loaded.

He laughed out loud with relief when he spotted Maryna and Devyn, the smaller children clustered around them. A soldier heard him and whirled around, ready to stop him, but Braeden shook his head and kept going.

"Braeden!" Devyn shouted and ran toward him. "Mama, it's Commander Terris."

"Hello Your Grace," Braeden said as Devyn ran up to him, flushed and dirty. "Are all of you safe?"

"We are." Devyn positively bounced as he walked alongside Braeden, toward the fire. "That Fernanda tried to kill us, but Mama and I fought her, and then Natalya came."

"Who's Fernanda?" Braeden asked Devyn, then offered a small bow as he came up to Maryna and the other children. "Who tried to kill you and why?" He looked beyond Maryna, and in the flicker of the fire, saw Princess Gwynneth, tattered, dirty and bloody, leaning on Natalya as they came his way.

"Commander Terris!" Gwynneth smiled weakly, and Natalya raised an eyebrow. "I didn't expect you here."

"Your husband sent me." Braeden didn't want to say why with Natalya right there, since she was the reason.

"Please tell me he's all right." Gwynneth looked ready to cry. Judging by the streaks on her face, she'd done some of that already.

"Last I heard he was fine; joined up with Lennart, getting ready for a big battle up north. With any luck, it's already happened. I'm sure the king will keep him out of harm's way," Braeden added hastily when Gwynneth's eyes widened.

"Yes, I'm sure." Natalya added, her arm around Gwynneth's waist. "You can tell me why you're here later on, Terris. But first I have a job for you."

"With all respect Your Holiness, my job is to escort the princess and her children back to her husband."

"And they will be returned to him before too long." Natalya smiled, the flames reflecting in her eyes. "But I am certain this Fernanda acted on Teodora's orders. I wish to flush out Teodora's purpose, but need to keep Gwynneth and the children hidden for a little while. I'd like her to think she's succeeded and learn what she plans to do next."

Braeden didn't like it, but wasn't sure what to do about it. He and his escort were outnumbered at least five to one. "Might I at least send Prince Kendryk a message telling him they're safe? He'll worry."

"I will send him one with the next messenger, and let him know you're on a mission for me. I want you to pursue Fernanda Vastic and return her to me."

Braeden raised his eyebrows. "Why me?"

"You're good at this sort of thing. Can you tell the commander what you saw, Gwynneth?"

"It's possible it was a trick of the light," Princess Gwynneth began. Braeden had never seen her so frightened and uncertain. After he offered an encouraging nod, she went on. "She stood right there below the window looking up at us, and I was certain her eyes had turned yellow when they'd been black before."

This had to be a mistake. "It might have been a trick of the light, but I knew someone with eyes like that. Fortunately, she's dead. What does this Fernanda look like otherwise?"

"About my height," Gwynneth continued. "Slender, but very strong. I thought she would squeeze the life out of me. Curly dark hair, about chin-length, and pale skin. Oh, and some of her teeth were very pointed. She'd be pretty if she didn't look so odd."

Braeden listened with a rising sense of dread. Daciana Tomescu was dead—several of his friends had seen it happen. Yet it was hard to believe there could be someone else alive who looked and behaved so similarly working for Teodora. He wondered if Natalya had an inkling, but her face remained blank. Then he told himself it was possible Gwynneth had imagined some of this in her terror. Everyone knew about Tomescu's strange eyes and teeth, so perhaps this Fernanda looked a little like her and the princess had filled in the gaps. Now he was more than anxious to get a closer look at this woman.

"All right," Braeden said. "I'll find this Fernanda and bring her back to Allaux. But promise me you'll write to Prince Kendryk first thing."

"Certainly." Natalya smiled. "And thank you. Take your people, and as many of mine as you want. She went that way." She turned and pointed toward the woods in a northerly direction.

Braeden shouted for Kazmir and for Trisa to gather the rest of his escort. He didn't care to have any of Natalya's troops along.

"Oh, and Terris?"

Braeden turned back toward Natalya, impatient now. "What?"

"Please, not a word to anyone that Gwynneth and the children are alive. Until I've learned what Teodora is trying to do, it's better she believe her agent succeeded."

"If you like." Now Kazmir was here and Braeden swung into the saddle. He looked down at Natalya. "Don't worry, Your Holiness. I'll find this Fernanda Vastic and bring her to you. I'd like to sort this out as much as you do."

"I knew I was right to ask you to do this. Now off with you before she gets a longer start."

Natalya swatted Kazmir on the rump and Braeden headed for the forest. Once he rode into the trees, darkness closed in around him.

ANTON

It must have taken an hour for Anton and Kendryk to reach the city, and by then it was nearly evening. Anton was so worried it was hard sitting still in the saddle. That made his horse nervous, and he had to work to keep it moving forward. At least that gave him something to do.

Kendryk kept up light conversation, bringing him up to date on everything that had happened on their side. In spite of his worry about Susanna, Anton was relieved that Maryna, Devyn and the others still lived in Galladium, well out of harm's way. It seemed Kendryk didn't like the way Natalya was running things, but Anton was certain she would take good care of his family.

By the time they entered the city, order had mostly been restored. It seemed there had been looting and a bit of violence, but the city remained intact. Anton breathed a little easier. He directed Kendryk to the house he lived in, conscious for the first time of the ugliness and filth of the neighborhood.

"I'll tell you the whole story later," Anton said, "but by the time we got here, we had no money, so this was all we could manage." He was ashamed, wishing he had taken better care of Susanna.

Kendryk looked the tall, rickety house up and down, seemingly unable to keep from wrinkling his nose. Or maybe it was the smell of the area, since everyone here emptied their chamber pots straight into the open gutters. "I'm sure you did your best." He smiled at Anton as they dismounted and handed their horses over to a guard. "But things will be better for you now. You, your young lady, and your baby will have everything you need."

"Thank you." Anton turned away because Kendryk's eyes were so soft and sympathetic. He hardly dared to hope that their lives would improve soon. He led Kendryk around to the back, to the staircase he always used to get to the attic. The landlord would be excited to see a live prince in his own house, but Anton didn't have time for that. He took the stairs as quickly as he could without leaving Kendryk behind. Pale dusky light came through the few windows, just enough to see where he was going.

The whole house stood quiet. Everyone was likely staying put until things had settled down and the soldiers were gone. Anton's own door was shut tight, but surely Susanna had stayed in after he had gone. He knocked, since the door only latched from the inside. No reply. "She might be sleeping," Anton said, mostly by way of reassuring himself. He knocked again but was still met by silence.

Finally, he pushed on the door. It hadn't been latched, and swung open. The room was dark. Anton hurried to the table and lit a lamp with trembling hands. Light flooded the tiny, clearly empty room.

Kendryk stepped inside. "It's all right Anton. We'll find her. Perhaps she's gone to stay with friends?"

"I hope so," Anton said. They went down a few streets to the regimental kitchen, but it was dark and silent. The cooks and their helpers had gone with the army. "The midwife," Anton said. "I don't know why she'd go there instead of sending for her, but I can't come up with anything else."

The midwife lived a few streets in the other direction, and only opened the door after Anton pounded and shouted for several minutes.

"Oh, it's you," she said, opening the door and letting the two of them in, though her eyes grew wide at the sight of Kendryk.

"Please tell me Susanna is here," Anton said, looking wildly around the room.

"She is, but ..." The midwife sighed heavily. "My dear boy, I'm so sorry."

"Sorry for what?" Anton wanted to shake her. Anything was better than the dread rising inside him. "Where is she?"

He sensed rather than saw the midwife exchange a look with Prince Kendryk, who nodded slightly.

"Come along," she said, leading them into an adjoining room.

It was so quiet, and he knew what was coming, but didn't want to believe it. The midwife carried a lamp to the side of a bed. Someone lay on it, a sheet over their head. Anton stumbled, and Kendryk's steadying hand caught his elbow.

"You don't need to see," Kendryk murmured in his ear.

"Yes, I do." Anton didn't want to, but this was his only chance to say goodbye.

When the midwife pulled the sheet back, Susanna looked the same as always, though paler than usual, with dark circles under her eyes. Anton touched her cheek. It was ice cold. "How long?" he whispered, not trusting his voice.

"This morning." The midwife's voice came from somewhere behind him. "The lot of you had marched out only an hour before. The pains came on quick and she ran over here, before things in the city got even more confused."

"W—what ..." Anton found he couldn't speak. He sank to his knees at the side of the bed.

"What happened?" Anton heard Kendryk's voice and felt his hand on his shoulder.

"It went wrong, like it sometimes does. Nothing to be done."

Kendryk took a breath, as if to ask further questions, but Anton shook his head and said, "No. Please." He didn't want to hear any more. Then he realized he'd forgotten. "What about the baby?" He whispered it.

"I'm sorry. The little boy didn't make it either."

At that, Anton thought he would cry, and bit his tongue until it bled so he wouldn't. He didn't care what the midwife thought, and knew Kendryk would understand, but he couldn't let a single tear fall. If he broke down now, he might never recover. He had to take this loss just like he'd taken all the others.

He knelt at the bedside a while longer, halfway listening to a murmured conversation between Kendryk and the midwife. Something about a burial. Anton wanted to say he'd pay for it, but remembered he didn't have a single copper to his name. He'd have to think of something, so he dragged himself to his feet, feeling a hundred years old.

He turned around in time to glimpse silver passing from Kendryk's hand to the midwife's. "Have the Maximus say the words, and put them both in the temple crypt."

Anton drew in his breath. Temple crypts were only for the wealthy. But the midwife nodded, still staring at the coins in her hand.

Kendryk looked at Anton and said, "Come. You can visit them soon, then every day for as long as we stay here."

Anton nodded, still biting his tongue, turned around to look at Susanna once more, then followed Kendryk out the door.

KENDRYK

Kendryk felt terrible for Anton but didn't know how to help him. He ordered a room prepared for him at the house he stayed in, and made sure he didn't have to worry about anything. Kendryk would listen if Anton wanted to talk, but he hardly spoke a word in the first few days after they'd found the girl.

When Kendryk received word that she and the baby had been interred below the temple, he took Anton to the catacombs so he'd know where they were. He and Anton stood in silence, staring at the plaque in the wall. Made of pink marble, it said simply, "Susanna Stengel and infant."

"I wish I had given her my name," Anton said, and turned to Kendryk. "Thank you for this place. I could only have afforded a mass grave."

"I could do nothing less at such an awful time." Kendryk's voice wobbled, and went quiet, since Anton didn't betray the least bit of emotion. Kendryk wanted to tell him it was all right to grieve, that no one would hold him in lower regard for showing understandable pain. But Anton remained tight-lipped, his eyes devoid of their usual sparkle. Kendryk hoped it would return someday.

While Kendryk made plans for an offensive against Teodora with Lennart, Anton spent his days in various Kaltental taverns. He was always in his room when Kendryk came back to the house in the evenings and Kendryk suspected he was drunk, though he hardly wanted to press the issue. Even sending for Karil didn't help. Anton seemed happy to see his old friend, but promptly dragged him off to a tavern, and they got drunk together. Kendryk wondered what he'd do once his own children had troubles in their love lives. Hopefully none would do anything as dramatic as impregnate and lose a camp follower.

Kendryk didn't mean to be snobbish, but he felt Anton was meant for better things. He was brave, clever and—most of all—good, if he managed to keep the drinking under control. He'd also outgrown the gangly, awkward phase he'd been in when Kendryk had last seen him, and had become quite good-looking: tall and well-built, shoulders broad from dragging a pike, with a lean, expressive face enhanced rather than marred by a scarred cheek, and brown eyes slanted just enough to look exotic. It was no wonder that the girl had laid claim as quickly as possible, but now Kendryk worried losing her would destroy a promising young man.

"He needs a change of scene," Lennart said, when Kendryk confided his worries to him. They walked in circles in the small garden of the Kaltental burgomaster's house, after spending the morning hunched over a map-strewn table. "He needs to get away from where it all happened."

"I agree," Kendryk said. "But I had hoped Braeden would bring Gwynneth and the children soon. Anton was such great friends with Maryna and Devyn. Surely seeing them would lift his spirits. And they're still too young for him to take out drinking."

Lennart snickered at that, then asked, "How old is your daughter again?"

"Almost thirteen." Kendryk wondered how much she'd grown. He'd been gone so long.

Lennart sighed. "You might want to reconsider that friendship. She's just at the right age to see a fellow like Anton and fall in love."

"Really?" Kendryk couldn't picture his little girl being anything but sensible. "She knows she must marry a prince, or a duke at the very least."

Lennart laughed. "What she knows she has to do will have no bearing on it. No, trust me on this. You're setting up a dangerous situation. I'm not saying they can't be friendly if they come across each other every now and then, but don't throw them together. You'll have nothing but grief."

"You're probably right." Kendryk was amused, and a little annoyed that Lennart was likely correct. Now he thought about it, Maryna was old enough for an undesirable crush to be a worry. "Perhaps I'll take him to Heidenhof when I go, though I'd hoped to wait for Gwynneth." Truth be told, he worried that he'd received no word from her or from Braeden.

"Give it a few more days. Maybe you'll hear something soon," Lennart said as they turned at the garden wall and started back toward the house.

They were halfway back when a servant came running. "Urgent message for you, Your Grace," he said, putting a rather dirty letter into Kendryk's hand.

"Perhaps it's from Gwynneth," Kendryk said as he opened it, though the hand on it looked unfamiliar. Lennart stood by as he read it. No doubt he was anxious to know that Gwynneth was all right.

Kendryk had to read it three times before it sunk in. His knees buckled and he fell to the garden walk.

"Gods, man; what's happened?" Lennart grabbed him under the arms and pulled him up to sit on a low wall. Then he picked up the letter from where Kendryk had let it fall and read it. He sat down next to Kendryk and patted him on the knee. "It's from Teodora, so probably a lie."

Kendryk hoped that was true, but Teodora's tone had been so convincing, in that sharp, decisive script that had never failed to deliver bad news in the past. He couldn't speak, but shook his head, hoping Lennart would understand.

The realization that they were gone, all of them, was too much to bear. Gwynneth most of all, whom he loved more than was reasonable. Maryna; friend as much as daughter—more than once he'd worried she was too good for this world. Devyn; so fierce but always full of laughter; sweet, quiet Andres; boisterous Stella, and little Renata, a baby he'd never even seen.

He must have made a noise of distress because Lennart put an arm around his shoulder. "See here," he said, pointing at the letter, though Kendryk saw only a blur. "She says Daciana Tomescu did it, so it's a lie. Tomescu is dead."

Kendryk nodded again. He'd been there when it happened, though he hadn't seen it. Still, everyone was sure she'd been killed.

Lennart went on. "Think about it. Why would she send something like this? To upset you, that's why. She must have known Ensden was doomed, and had to come up with another way to get under our skins."

"But where are they then?" Kendryk found his voice, though it trembled terribly. "Why haven't I received word from them in so long? Why haven't I heard from Braeden? I told him to write as soon as he found them."

"Letters get lost." Lennart's tone was annoyingly soothing.

Kendryk wanted to hit him. "All of them?"

"There's a war on." Lennart sounded like he was trying to reason with a child. "Letters are delayed or lost all the time. If they went by ship, they might have been intercepted by the Maladene navy. Or perhaps they put the letter on a Maladene ship which got hung up on our blockade. There are a lot of reasons."

Kendryk nodded, though he didn't understand. "Why would Teodora send me this if it's not true?"

"Because she's evil." Lennart stood up and stomped around. "You ought to understand that better than anyone. Because if she can't destroy you by force, she'll find another way. Don't let her do it."

"All right," Kendryk said, though he still didn't know what to believe. But he let Lennart lead him back into the house and sat there without moving for a long time. His thoughts always turned to that awful letter and what it meant. If he was to go on, he didn't dare think about it. But if it was true, he didn't think he wanted to survive.

ELEKTRA

One night before dinner, Edric said, "Your Grace, I must speak to you alone."

His voice was so serious Elektra worried it was bad news. Had her mother discovered her location and was demanding her return? She hoped Edric wouldn't give in to such a request. Elektra waited for him in his study and he came soon after, shutting the door behind him.

He sat behind his desk then said, "I've received news that's sure to be discussed by our dinner guests, and I wanted you to find out first."

Elektra nodded, her heart beating a little faster.

"King Lennart has defeated Count Ensden at Kaltental. The battle was decisive and the count is dead."

Elektra made a small noise. She hadn't known Ensden well, but he'd been a fixture at court for most of her life.

Edric looked sympathetic. "It's excellent news for my cause, but a disaster for yours. Your mother will have few options now."

"I don't understand. I thought Lennart was here to reconquer Terragand on Kendryk's behalf, and it seems he's done that. Won't he go home soon?"

Edric shook his head. "I'm afraid not. Lennart is determined to spread the Quadrene Creed through all the empire and will not rest until your mother is defeated."

"Oh gods." Elektra worried she might be sick. Much as she hated her mother, she didn't want to see her birthright overrun by a foreigner before she ever had a chance to be empress. "And now, there's no one to stop him."

"Not yet, though the empress is resourceful. She's come back from other difficult situations. As optimistic as my allies are, I'm not keen on underestimating Teodora. Doing so has cost us too much already."

"What's to become of me then?" Elektra asked in a small voice. "I suppose Lennart will want me for his prisoner."

"Perhaps." Edric's tone was far too casual. "But you needn't worry—he's no monster."

"That's easy for you to say." Elektra's hands shook, so she buried them in her lap. "You won't be his prisoner."

"You have a choice in this." Edric looked at her as if she should understand his meaning.

"I don't understand."

"If you should convert and publicly support Lennart, I'm sure he will be happy to install you as empress when he overthrows your mother."

Elektra realized she was staring, her mouth open in an unbecoming way.

"It's quite a good opportunity for you," Edric went on as if what he had proposed wasn't shocking, heretical and treasonous, all in one sentence.

Elektra shut her mouth. "I don't—" she croaked, then cleared her throat and tried again. "I—are you saying that if I convert to the Quadrene Creed and support Lennart, he will make me empress?"

"I can't speak on his behalf. But he knows you're here and is praying—as am I— that you find the truth. If you do, I'm sure he'll be pleased. He'll be here in a few weeks, so you'll have time to consider it."

Elektra knew she should refuse emphatically and indignantly, but the words wouldn't come. She feared choosing the wrong path and angering the gods, but just as much, she feared never getting her chance to rule. "I—I will have to pray about it," she stammered at last.

"That's what I suggest," Edric said. "But keep in mind, when Lennart comes, and you show yourself an adherent of the true faith, and a staunch opponent to your mother, he will see you as a natural ally. I will support you in every way I can, should you choose this path."

Elektra nodded. "Is it all right if I don't join you for dinner?" she asked. Being casual and conversational right now seemed impossible. "I just—"

"I understand. I'll have something sent up for you." Edric still looked at her, his eyes brilliant. "I can see you were surprised at the idea, which surprises me in turn. I'd thought you rather ambitious, and was certain you'd already considered the possibility of throwing in with Lennart if he prevailed."

Elektra had to laugh at that. "Apparently I'm not ambitious enough, since it never occurred to me." She sobered. "What if I'm unable to convert? Will you let Lennart make me his prisoner?"

"No," Edric said it so quickly and decisively Elektra knew he meant it. "I would have your conversion come from the heart, not because of fear. If you cannot make a change by the time Lennart comes, I'll find a way to keep you here for the time being. I realize it's not ideal for you, but it's likely better than the alternative."

"It is." Elektra stood up, ready to go to her room now and think all of this through. "And thank you for that. I've had enough of imprisonment, but being here is not so bad."

"I'm glad of that." Edric stood as well. "And I will pray that the gods show you the way that is right for you."

Elektra hoped they would, and quickly.

LENNART

Now that the allied armies were giddy with success, Lennart took advantage of the moment to press his cause. "Terragand is secure for the time being," he told a gathering of the Kronland generals. "But if I leave now, it won't stay safe for long. After that, it's only a matter of time before Teodora brings the other kingdoms to heel."

"Sounds like we need to take the fight to Teodora," Arvus Dahlby said. "And soon, before she and Mattila kiss and make up."

"That's exactly what I was thinking." Lennart was sure Trystan would back him on this, and he hoped Manier would as well. "She has no army right now, and I don't see why we can't take Atlona before winter." It was now full-blown, glorious spring, and Lennart intended to take full advantage of the weather to get as far south as possible. "We'll meet no opposition before Arcius, and I expect to make peace with Princess Zelenka once she understands what she's up against. We'll cross the mountains by mid-summer and be at the gates of Atlona before autumn. His Grace can spend the winter in the Palais Arden."

He smiled at Kendryk, who hadn't said a word. Lennart had hoped the prospect of action against Teodora might perk him up, but he stared at the wall above Lennart's head, his face expressionless. Teodora's letter had put him in an awful funk, but it had to be a lie. Lennart had to hand it to the woman—she knew how to get under a fellow's skin.

Once plans to march south were completed, Lennart dismissed everyone except Kendryk. "What do you think? About time we took on Teodora herself. Ought to be fun."

Kendryk looked at Lennart, his eyes glassy. "I suppose. But first I need to look for my family. At the least, I need to speak with Natalya so she can tell me what really happened." He looked down at the table.

"I'm sure Braeden's taking care of matters well enough. It was smart of you to send him, and he can do far more than you can. I'm sure you'll hear something soon. In the meantime, I need you to come with me, to talk the other Kronlanders into giving me more troops and supplies."

"I'm not sure I can do that," Kendryk whispered. Lennart worried he might cry on the spot. He felt awful for him, but needed him to hold it together, for everyone's sake.

"You can." Lennart raised his voice, hoping he sounded bracing, rather than bossy. "You need a little time. Why don't you head for Heidenhof ahead of me? I'm sure Edric Maximus will be happy to see you. When you're feeling better, you can set yourself up at Birkenfels and rebuild your army. That way you can come with me while making sure you leave Terragand well-defended."

"I'd like to see Edric," Kendryk's eyes had lit up just a little at the suggestion, though his voice remained dull. "But I can't imagine how I'll afford an army."

"I'll make you a loan," Lennart said. "It's no problem. It'll give you something to do until I can join you, since I have plenty to do here." It would take him at least a month to get things organized here in Kaltental. Karolyna Martinek had survived, but it would be a long time before she would lead an army again. She was in such a pathetic state, Lennart didn't have the heart to give command of her troops to Trystan, though he had more than earned it. It wasn't like there was much left to give anyway, so he had Geffrey Manier absorb the few under-size battalions into his army.

The larger matter was handling the thousands of prisoners they'd taken after the battle. Lennart was happy to have any willing soldier join him, but it took time to assign everyone to the right unit, get them equipped and then trained to his standards. He had a larger force than anything Teodora might raise, but he wasn't taking any chances. Even though he'd sent another messenger to Brynhild Mattila, he'd received no response.

"I have an even better idea." Lennart leaned back in his chair. "Why don't you take young Anton with you? He likely could use a change of scene, and will give you company on the journey."

"That's a good idea." Kendryk brightened just a little. "I'm worried he'll drink himself to death in the Kaltental taverns. If he's in Heidenhof, Edric will make sure he behaves himself."

"No one can stand up to Edric," Lennart said with a grin. "Not even me. That settles it then," he added, before Kendryk thought of any more objections. "Tell Anton to get packed, and the two of you can join me for dinner tonight. We'll send you off in style."

TEODORA

"What am I going to do now?" Teodora was too upset to scream at anyone. That alone was worrisome. She'd gathered Solteszy, Countess Biaram and Livilla in her study late, after she'd already sent them to bed an hour earlier. The message telling of Ensden's defeat and death had just arrived by the fastest courier. Her army was gone: killed, captured and scattered.

"Perhaps nothing," the countess suggested. "Wait to see what Lennart does. Likely he will install Kendryk as ruler of Terragand and go home. Once he's gone, you can deal with Kendryk."

"I've already dealt with Kendryk." Teodora offered a mysterious smile. Until she received independent confirmation of Gwynneth's death, she'd say nothing, but could at least amuse herself with cryptic hints. "But I find it hard to believe that's all Lennart wants. At the least he will make demands on behalf of Kronland, demands I can't agree to. And then what? Will he march on Olvisya?"

"It's hard to say," Solteszy said. "If he does, we are in a very weak position. I don't see how we can build up our forces in time if he comes this way."

"I doubt I can get more help from Maladena," Teodora said. "They're about to go to war with Galladium, and Beatryz already complained mightily last time I asked for money and help from her navy. She won't give me anything else."

"You should ask anyway," Livilla said. "She won't be pleased about Lennart either."

"I suppose I will." Teodora slumped in her chair, exhausted and defeated.

"There is one other possibility," Livilla said, looking uncharacteristically cautious.

Teodora groaned, knowing what was coming next. "It's impossible," she said. "Even if I were willing to do it, Brynhild Mattila won't, I'm sure of it."

"You must at least ask her," Livilla said.

"I can't imagine under what circumstances she'd agree to it. Between the two of us, we humiliated her terribly. Can you imagine what she'll demand if I ask her to return to the fold?"

"She'll ask a great deal, it's true." Livilla was looking rather tired herself. "But what if Lennart gets to her first? She sent Kendryk packing last year, but things have changed. What if Lennart offers her Brandana with no conditions except opposing you?"

"He can't do that," Teodora whispered.

"He can make the offer," Livilla said. "How he plans to pull it off is another matter, but at least he's presenting her with the possibility."

"I can't bear it," Teodora said. "Of all people, why is she always the one who has what I need at the worst times? How can the gods be so cruel?"

"They are not cruel, Your Highness, but they are mysterious. I understand Mattila is a great trial to you and always has been. But she can either be of great help to you, or of great help to your enemies."

"But she *is* my enemy," Teodora wailed. She hated sounding like this in front of the others, but she was so tired.

"Not in the same way that Lennart is," Livilla went on. "Nothing is certain, but I think he will not leave Kronland until he has established the Quadrene Creed in every kingdom, perhaps even in the empire."

"He wouldn't dare." Teodora exploded, the blood churning in her veins in a way she hadn't felt before. "What right does he have, this foreigner, to come here and tell my subjects what to believe?" Now the blood rushed to her head and a terrible pain pierced her whole body to the tips of her fingers. She must be ill.

Teodora blinked away the black and red dots in front of her eyes and said, "The gods will help us combat these heretics. I will write to Beatryz, but I'll make no overtures toward Mattila—" she gasped for breath as the pain returned, sharper this time.

From very far away she heard someone ask, "Your Highness, are you—?" just before the pressure exploded into shards of agony, like a great temple window breaking onto her head. She tried to speak, but her mouth wouldn't move. Nothing would move. She refused to close her eyes, but a black curtain drew over them as she slid out of her chair and under the table.

ANTON

Even though he was only fifteen, Anton reckoned he'd been through a lot. He'd lost his whole family when the war started, then lost Lora, lost the count, lost Skandar, and now he'd lost Susanna and their baby as well. He was plenty miserable, but that was like nothing when he looked at Prince Kendryk.

And that was what he did all day, as the carriage bounced down the road that ran alongside the Velta. Anton felt Lennart had packed them off a little quickly—he wanted to stay in Kaltental a while longer. He didn't go see them every day, but it was nice that Susanna and the baby were close by, even in a gloomy temple crypt. And if Princess Gwynneth and Maryna and Devyn were alive, as the king seemed convinced they were, Anton wanted to be there when they returned. He wouldn't mind seeing Braeden again either.

But Lennart seemed sure they were both wallowing in misery there in the city. Kendryk had even started drinking in taverns with Anton, so maybe he was right. Lennart didn't seem to be the type to put up with much wallowing, though Anton wondered if he'd ever had much to be sad about. But when the king told you it was time to visit the Maximus, you went. And he provided a nice, comfortable carriage with the best accommodations along the way, when you could find them.

Still, whenever Anton looked at the road, he remembered the last time he'd traveled it, struggling through snowdrifts with Susanna, worried they'd freeze or starve to death, and realized how much happier he'd been then. He groaned and leaned his head against the wall.

"It'll get better," Kendryk said, his voice dull.

"You don't believe that," Anton said.

"I have to, or I can't go on. You must pray to the gods and trust they will comfort you."

"You don't believe that either," Anton said, even though he realized he sounded rude. He didn't much care, and neither did Kendryk, it seemed.

"Perhaps not, though I try. Edric Maximus will help us."

"Is he anything like Natalya? Except for the beautiful woman part; you know what I mean."

That at least brought a smile from Kendryk. "Nothing like her at all, but you'll like him." He took a deep breath. "It's hard, Anton, but you have to consider the future. Do you know what you want to do? Whatever it is, I'll try to make it possible."

Anton suddenly realized that if Kendryk's children were dead, he'd likely look at Anton as if he were a son. He already acted like a father, the way he fussed when Anton drank too much. He leaned his head back against the cushions. "I used to want to be a soldier more than anything. And I loved being Count Orland's page, but then I hated serving in the infantry." He decided not to say anything about the fear that overcame him in battle the past few times.

"That's understandable," Kendryk said. "You were fighting on the wrong side and I imagine being in one of those huge blocks of infantry is rather different from being on horseback. Would you be interested in serving in the cavalry again?"

That made Anton's heart beat faster, and he felt a twinge of joy when he imagined being on horseback again. "I might," he said. "But I'm not sure how I can. I have no horse, no weapons, no equipment and no money." Lennart had gifted him with a small purse, but Anton had already spent half of that on liquor for the journey.

"I'd take care of that," Kendryk said. "Now I'm ruler of Terragand again, I have money, even if I have to borrow it from Lennart." He smiled wryly. "I need to build up an army again, because Lennart won't be here forever, and I'm sure Teodora will pounce as soon as he leaves."

"If she survives," Anton said.

"She always survives." Kendryk shook his head. "She'll be a threat until I see her dead body, and I don't expect to do that for some time."

"Lennart reckons he'll be in Atlona before winter," Anton said, hoping it would happen.

"That would be nice, but I've learned not to expect too much." Kendryk's eyes clouded over, and he was silent for a moment. Then he said, "But Teodora or not, I will need my own army, with its own cavalry. I'll put one of my experienced officers in charge—someone like Merton. But I'd like to give you a horse, equipment and a commission."

Anton stared. "As in an officer commission?"

"Yes," Kendryk said, a faint smile on his lips.

"But I was only ever a page." Anton didn't want to argue, but he still couldn't believe it.

"An excellent one. Arian told me how brave and resourceful you were. You showed that ten times over when you helped me escape. I've always wanted to reward you for that, and couldn't until now. Please let me do this for you, if you want it."

"I want it," Anton said, a lump growing in his throat. He doubted he'd ever see Skandar again, but now he'd get a new horse; something that had been only a dream for so long. "Thank you," he said, looking Kendryk in the eye. "I won't disappoint you—I promise."

LENNART

"You'll wear a groove in the dock, Your Highness," Tora Isenberg said with a smile.

Lennart smiled back, but didn't stop pacing. He'd spotted the sail on the horizon, but with the seaward wind so stiff, it might take the better part of an hour for the ship to claw its way into the harbor.

Isenberg kept up with him all the same, and soon Leyf Lofbrok joined them. Lennart remembered a joke he was sure Lofbrok didn't know, and Isenberg knew a more ribald version of it. They passed the time with laughter, though Lennart's face was stiff with cold by the time the ship drew near.

He stopped pacing and stood at the end of the gangplank impatiently, forced to acknowledge a long string of functionaries disembarking, come from Tharvik to pay their respects. He didn't need them here, but since he'd been gone for so long, no doubt the more insecure wanted to be sure of the king's favor. "Damn nuisance," Lennart muttered to himself as an elegant aristocrat bowed low before him, but remembered to offer a polite smile before the idiot left him alone.

At last it was time. From somewhere behind him, Lofbrok shouted orders, and he heard the muffled clatter of hundreds of troops drawing themselves to attention. A trumpet sounded, and there she was finally, making her way down the gangplank, clutching a fur cloak close against the wind. A strand of hair, the color of light honey, came loose and whipped across her face.

Lennart couldn't wait any longer, and bounded up the gangplank, pulling Raysa into his arms, even as cheers went up behind him. He pulled back a little, then kissed her all over her cold face until her tears wet his lips. "Is everything all right?" He looked down at her.

"It's perfect," she whispered. "I've missed you so terribly." She wiped her eyes with the back of a gloved hand, and smiled. "Do you want to see your daughter?"

Lennart wondered if his face might split from grinning. He'd stopped the queen's entourage in the middle of the swaying gangplank, but he wasn't about to move until he held his little girl in his arms.

Silvya Meldahl stepped out from behind Raysa, holding a fur-wrapped bundle. "The Princess Kataryna," she said with her solemn air, placing the bundle into Lennart's arms. He pushed fur out of the way until he saw a large blue eye peering up at him, then pushed some more until he saw the other eye, a tiny nose, and a mouth like a rosebud. A surge of emotion caught him off guard, and he had to look away and blink for a moment.

Raysa tugged at his arm. "We must get her out of the wind."

"Of course." Lennart held the baby tight in one arm, offered the other to Raysa, and they stepped onto the dock, into a pandemonium of cheering, the late afternoon sunlight catching the glitter of armor, the breeze waving green banners lining the way back to their carriage.

"You didn't have to make such a fuss," Raysa said, once the door shut behind them and the carriage lurched forward.

"How could I not? This is a big moment for me, but it's also important for Estenor. And all of these troops here—they haven't been home in a long time, and you're their queen. Some of these fellows are nearly as excited as I am."

The baby struggled in Lennart's arms, then made a few pitiful squeaking noises. He peered into her face anxiously as she screwed it up into a scowl. "What's wrong with her?"

Raysa laughed. "She doesn't like being wrapped up so tightly. She especially hates anything on her head, much like her father." She took Kataryna onto her lap and pulled the fur hood back.

When Lennart looked again, the blue eyes were wide, the toothless mouth open. "Do you reckon she's afraid of me?"

"Like you, she isn't afraid of anyone, though I'm sure she's curious."

Lennart hadn't known what to expect, having never spent time with babies, and was delighted by her chubby beauty. "She looks just like you," he said. "If you were fatter."

"You should have seen me right before my time. I *was* fat."

Lennart put an arm around his wife. "I'm sure you looked beautiful." Though it was true when he squeezed her shoulder, it didn't feel as fragile as before. "Seems motherhood agrees with you." He squeezed again, a little lower this time.

Raysa snuggled into his side. "It does. I always worried a little, that I wouldn't know what to do. But of course she has several nurses who take care of everything, and all I have to do is play with her."

"That sounds like fun," Lennart said, as the carriage pulled into the courtyard of the burgomaster's house.

"What a charming little house." Raysa handed the baby back to Silvya, who'd appeared out of nowhere.

"It's smaller than what you're used to, but we won't be here long." Lennart tucked her hand under his arm as they walked through the door. "As soon as you've recovered from the journey, we'll head south."

Raysa stopped and frowned. "To war?"

"Yes," Lennart said. "To war."

EPILOGUE

MARYNA

"Maryna, is that you?" King Arryk sprang off his chair and ran to meet her, sweeping her into his arms. He didn't seem to care that dozens of people stood around staring, so Maryna decided she didn't mind either.

She threw her arms around her uncle's neck, burying her face in his shoulder. She hoped she'd been able to hide her surprise at how much he'd changed. "It's good to see you, Your Highness." She pulled back to smile at him as he put her down. Though she'd grown almost as tall as her mother, Uncle Arryk had still scooped her up as if she were a little girl.

He grinned down at her, and kept an arm around her shoulders as he turned to face Natalya. That smile was the same too, though the rest of his face was worn, his eyes blank and sad. He had become old in the few years since Maryna had last seen him. "What brings you to Arenberg, Your Holiness?" He frowned. "It's not a good time for a visit. The situation is unstable and dangerous."

"That's why I'm here." Natalya offered a graceful curtsy. For this visit, she'd changed back into her old Maxima's robes, which made her look dignified and radiant. Maryna expected her uncle to fall in love with her at once, although Natalya explained they didn't like each other very much. They had been children together in Arenberg and had never gotten on. Maryna hoped that might change now they were both grownups. Arryk needed someone to make him happy, and Maryna knew Natalya was lonely now that King Gauvain had Zofya.

"I don't understand," Arryk said, showing the two of them into a small antechamber, shutting out the curious stares of the courtiers in the throne room. "But come, I'll send for refreshments and you can tell me everything."

Maryna was still half-frozen from coming off the ship, and sipped happily at a large mug of chocolate, while eying a platter piled with small, buttery biscuits. Natalya had already explained everything to her on the long voyage here, but Maryna didn't understand completely. She was thrilled that Natalya insisted on bringing her along over her mother's objections, but hoped she was smart enough to help.

"Teodora has made a surprising move." Natalya told Arryk about Fernanda's terrifying attack in the forest. "Please tell me you've heard from Aksel recently," she said when she'd finished.

The king still looked stunned at hearing how close his sister and her family had come to a horrible end, but nodded and said, "I received a letter a few weeks ago. He seems well enough, though unhappy. Teodora released him from the Arnfels some time ago, but keeps him close by in her palace and seems to enjoy tormenting him. She even forced him to convert to the old faith by threatening a friend of his. She also wants to marry him to her eldest daughter, though that hasn't happened yet."

"Poor Uncle Aksel," Maryna burst out, though she'd never met him. Her mother always told her he was the nicest of the three Roussay siblings, and Maryna pictured him as tall and handsome like Uncle Arryk, though more scholarly. She liked daydreaming about helping him with his scientific work someday.

"Indeed." Natalya smiled at Maryna. "That's the piece I was missing. Now I know Aksel is alive and in danger only of becoming an Inferrara in-law, I think I understand what Teodora is up to."

"What?" Maryna and Arryk chorused.

"She's making a play for your throne." Natalya looked pleased with herself. "You've been having trouble with the nobility here, have you not?"

"Yes." Arryk sighed and looked sad. "I've had the most wonderful ideas for reform and they resist me at every turn. They don't seem to understand I want to do what's best for all the people of Norovaea."

"No, they wouldn't understand that," Natalya said, nibbling on a biscuit. "They care only about losing their power and privileges. But that's a discussion for another day. The immediate problem is this: I believe Teodora has sent agents here to foment rebellion and I wish to flush them out."

"She has? Who are they? *Where* are they?" Arryk looked around as if he expected Olvisyan spies to step out from behind the draperies.

"I'm not sure, though I can guess at the who. It seems Teodora wants to overthrow you, and replace you with Aksel, whom she thinks she can manipulate. That's why she tried to kill Gwynneth and the children. Just Gwynneth wouldn't be enough, because Maryna would succeed her."

Maryna drew in her breath. She'd never thought about the fact that she was in line for the Norovaean throne, and she didn't want it. All she cared about was ruling Terragand someday.

"With you dead or deposed, and Gwynneth and her children dead, Aksel would be next in line. If he married Elektra, she'd be queen and likely to do her mother's bidding."

Arryk's fist came down on the table with such force that Maryna nearly spilled her chocolate. "We had a treaty. I sent her my brother in good faith and shiploads of money I can't afford. I even sent the first installment early, though that wasn't part of the agreement. That woman has no honor at all."

"No, she does not." Natalya seemed unruffled at Arryk's outburst. "But we have already thwarted her by preventing the murder of Gwynneth and the children. And it sounds like I've arrived in time to help you thwart her here."

"Good." Arryk looked more than ready to put everything into Natalya's competent hands. "But might I ask why you've brought my niece into such a dangerous situation?"

"It's simple." Natalya smiled at Maryna, deep dimples appearing in her cheeks. "Maryna will be the decoy that exposes Teodora's agents."

Thank you for reading Hammer of the Gods!

Please don't forget to give this book a quick review on Amazon. Even just a two-word, "Liked it" or even better, "Loved it" review helps so much. Positive or negative, I am grateful for all feedback from my readers.

.

The story continues in Book Four of The Desolate Empire series:

Winter of the Wolf
COMING LATE 2016

Sign up to be notified at christinaochs.com

Cast of Characters

Karil Andarosz, a former prisoner of Teodora's, now Braeden's traveling companion

Teodora Inferrara, Empress of Olvisya, Queen of Moralta and Marjatya
Her children: **Elektra, Zofya** and Rudofo
Mother Luca, Elektra's personal priestess
Livilla Maxima, religious leader in Olvisya
Daciana Tomescu, guerilla commander and friend of Teodora
Ahbert Solteszy , Head of the Imperial Council and Teodora's closest political adviser
Meryl Biaram, an adviser to Teodora
Elyse Rastell, lady-in-waiting to Teodora
Sibyla, Teodora's personal doctor
Mother Hela, an instructor at Livilla's school
Mother Dava, an army priestess

Niklas van Ensden, Teodora's primary military commander
Brynhild Mattila, a general working for Teodora
Beatryz Inferrara, Queen of Maladena, cousin to Teodora
Alona Brynner, an infantry colonel under Ensden
Quintin Linser, an infantry major
Count Michalek, commander of an infantry regiment
Tavio Sora, a Maladene colonel serving under Ensden
Stasny, an infantryman
Susanna Stengel, a sutler in Mattila's army

Galladium

Gauvain Brevard, King of Galladium and childhood friend of Kendryk
Natalya Maxima, religious leader in Galladium
Joslyn, their daughter
Garin Dorais, captain of Kendryk's guard
Peryn LaFontant, Gauvain's messenger

Estenor

Lennart Ostberg, King of Estenor
Raysa Sikora-Ostberg, Queen of Estenor

Ludvik Meldahl, his chief adviser
Silvya Meldahl, his daughter and lady-in-waiting to Queen Raysa
Kelsi Brun, captain of the *Drekir*
Tora Isenberg, a general
Dolf Kalstrom, a general
Leyf Lofbrok, a general

Norovaea

Arryk Roussay, King of Norovaea
Aksel Roussay, Arryk's and Gwynneth's youngest brother, Teodora's hostage

The Faith

Teodora the Holy, ancient founder of The Faith
Quadrenes, followers of the reforms of Edric Maximus
League of Aeternos, a group of clerics specially trained to counter the Quadrenes
Vica, the sister goddess
Ercos, the son god

ABOUT THE AUTHOR

Christina Ochs is the author of historical fantasy novels Rise of the Storm, Valley of the Shadow, and Hammer of the Gods. Her first series, The Desolate Empire, is based upon the events of the Protestant Reformation and the Thirty Years War (1618-48). Many of her characters are also based on historical figures.

With a bachelor's degree in History and an MBA, Christina uses her writing to indulge her passion for reading and research. Publishing as an indie author provides an outlet for her entrepreneurial side and she is an avid supporter of fellow authors, both independent and traditionally published.

Christina lives in a semi truck full time, traveling the United States with her truck driver husband and two cats, Phoenix and Nashville.

You can learn more about her at her blog: http://christinaochs.com or follow her on twitter @therollinwriter